# THE KIND MOSAIC: I
# CONVERGENT LINES

*To: Stephen*
*Welcome to the Kind!*
*Michelle Cori*

# THE KIND MOSAIC: I
# CONVERGENT LINES

## MICHELLE CORI

**Kind Mosaic: 1, Convergent Lines**
Copyright © 2017 Michelle Corsillo

All rights reserved. No part of this book may be reproduced or transmitted in any form or by any electronic or mechanical means, including photocopying, recording or by any information storage and retrieval system, without the express written permission of the copyright holder, except where permitted by law. This novel is a work of fiction. Names, characters, places and incidents are either the product of the author's imagination, or, if real, used fictitiously.

Cover designed by Michelle Cori

Cover artwork images by Deposit Photos

Interior illustrations by Michelle Cori

Book design by Michelle Cori

Edited by Mia Kleve

Trade Paperback Edition September 2017
Printed in the USA

# DEDICATION

For Fin.
Thank you for coming along and being my anchor,
I would have never known the possibilities without you.

# ACKNOWLEDGMENTS

Life is funny, you never know where it will lead you. Such is the case with me and writing. When I was young I loved it, and I've always been an avid reader. Elementary school put an end to those thoughts. Instead I turned to music and art, which is where my life took me for many years.

In December of 2002 I found myself burnt out, pregnant, and looking for something more. An interview with J.K. Rowling and Jim Butcher caused me to consider writing. Years passed and life got in the way for a while. I wrote when I could and read more. I returned to shopping at my first comic book shop, where I reconnected with Mimi and Alan. That was the first step in this staircase I've been climbing. Through them I met Frank Beddor, David Mack, Anina Bennett and Paul Guiuan. I took classes from Anina and Paul, learned more, while finding direction.

The next step came in December of 2009 as I visited my favorite author's page. There I discovered Sherrilyn Kenyon was coming to teach a seminar in my area with several other authors. It was December 23rd and I had just finished Christmas shopping, I spent the last five hundred dollars in my savings to attend. That, as they say, is history. It was my first Superstars Writing Seminar and it changed my life completely. I haven't missed a Superstars Writing Seminar since. That step turned into several flights of stairs. The seminar introduced me to authors who turned to mentors. They're Eric Flint, Dan Wells, Brandon Sanderson, Kevin J. Anderson, Rebecca Moesta, Tracy Hickman, Dave Farland, Lisa Mangum, James Artimus Owens, Sherrilyn Kenyon, Jim Butcher, Todd McCaffrey, and Jody Lynn Nye.

Through Superstars I have received so much; what I didn't expect to find was a job. But I found that too, with Kevin and Rebecca. The last couple of years working for WordFire Press have been amazing. I love being surrounded by the best: Mia Kleve, Quincy Allen, Tara Henderson, Alexi Vandenberg, Erika Kuta Marler, James Sams, and Dave Butler.

My family is always there for me, especially as I travel or disappear to write. Thanks: Finley, Mom, Dad, Jamie, Seth, Dillon, Del, Ali and the Wife's family. My beta readers, Jamie Young, David Shogren, Alexi Vandenberg, Ali Young, and Erika Kuta Marler. To Pat Olver for the much needed input and proofing. Karmin Ovard, I appreciate the help with the dialect. Mia Kleve my editor, thanks for making the experience a pleasant one and *Convergent Lines* a better book.

I reached my first big goal with this book. It only happened because of the people who I was lucky enough to have come into my life and push me to be better. Now on to the next one.

-Michelle Cori

# THE KIND

**Kind**: (kahynd) - noun
1- A class of individuals who share a mixture of fae and human blood.
2- A title used to describe an ethnic group derived from thousands of years of mixing human and fae blood. Much like the fae, who prefer the title Gentle Folk, the title for their offspring with humans is Kind.

# PROLOGUE

Life is filled with many days. Most run into one another and become indistinguishable, but sometimes, you're lucky enough to have a day that will never end. That day lives on in your memory, playing over and over, at the back of your mind, in a daydream or when the Sandman sprinkles his dust. Such as June 8, 1988, a day which I never stopped living. The day that changed my young life, a day for which I remember details, but don't know if they happened or if I filled them in …

*Grayson James Penrose*

# CHAPTER ONE

### Wednesday, June 8, 1988, Santa Cruz, California

My name is Grayson Penrose; later that summer I'd turn fifteen. Boarding school had finally gotten out for the summer, and my parents had taken us to our beach house in Santa Cruz. Guy, my older brother, didn't want to come down to the boardwalk with me. Instead, he'd locked himself in his room where he stayed on the phone with his secret girlfriend. If my parents found out, they'd kill him. He's the first-born Penrose male. This meant he would have an arranged marriage, even if our parents hadn't arranged it yet.

Mom and dad had allowed him the summer here with us before he joined the KIC, or Kind Inquisition and Council, the Kind's form of military, police, government and college. There he'd spend the next decade of his life in servitude and celibacy. I left him to sulk and went down to the Santa Cruz Boardwalk alone.

As I walked on the boardwalk, a hot wind blew my hair in my eyes. Perhaps I should cut my hair? The length drove my mother crazy and at the time I hoped I might get it to look like Michael Hutchence's hair, the lead singer of INXS. But I only succeeded in looking like Robert Plant. I'd hit the weird period in my growth, tall and awkward. I didn't know what to do with my limbs. Today I wore a white Cult T-shirt, long black shorts and baby blue Ray-Ban Wayfarer sunglasses. To skate I wore my Vans.

I stepped on the beach and regretted it immediately as sand filled my shoes. On the boardwalk I found a bench; I sat and emptied my shoes of sand. Disgusted with myself I pulled off my backpack and got my sketchpad and pencil out.

I started drawing young as something to do, what I didn't expect to find was a talent for realistic sketches. My drawings seemed so real, one day I reached into the image and grabbed a pair of sunglasses I'd drawn. Now I worked on a pair of flip-flops that I'd left in my room. This skill was also useful for creating money. I use the term "creating" loosely; even with magic the object must come from somewhere. Due to this, I limit my use of the skill.

Done, I looked around to see if anyone happened to be nearby. Nobody. I reached into the pad and pulled out the flip-flops. The page now appeared blank.

As young as I was, I shouldn't have been able to do anything but the simplest of magic. It was a secret I kept from everyone, especially my family. Better for everyone to think of my brother as the gifted one.

I put my shoes and skateboard into my backpack, then I headed down to test the water. As I did, I noticed the pier to my right. My attention caught on a girl sitting atop one of the pilings. *How did she get up there?* The piling rose more than six feet above the boardwalk. She looked out at the ocean, the wind blowing her hair. Curious, I moved closer until I could lean on the piling opposite her. No one in the crowded boardwalk seemed to notice her.

She wore cutoff jean shorts, and a blue tank top, with matching Keds. Squinting, I tried to see her face, but her hair obscured my view. There was an arcade with its doors wide open a few feet away, with a jukebox, which started a new song. A melodic song, one I didn't remember hearing until that moment. Later I'd find out the name of the song; at the time, the strange music fit the moment. As if the song caught her attention, she turned to look at the arcade. Her bright blue eyes stopped on me. I froze. I didn't dare to breathe as she stared at me. She cocked her head to the side, and her dark brows drew together as if in confusion. At first, I thought maybe she thought I was ugly, a freak, or some weirdo staring at her. I turned away.

Her features were elf-like, with wide-set eyes, a button nose, and small, almost pointed, ears. Suddenly shy, I hoped she didn't find me lacking. I looked back at her, but she was gone. Confused, I pulled my sunglasses off and looked around. I rubbed my eyes, wondering if I'd imagined the whole thing.

"You should be more attentive to your surroundings." I turned and saw the girl looking at the jukebox. The song, which had just finished playing, started again.

"Did you do that?"

She laughed. "Yes, I did. It's my favorite song," she said in a thick, familiar accent. I moved to stand closer to her. She was maybe five feet tall, and so beautiful it made my toes curl with a rush of emotions I'd never felt before. For most humans, I've heard the description of love at first sight as being stars, violins, and magic. I experienced all of those things and more: energy, in hues of blue, flowing around her.

"You must be a Kind. You could see me."

Swallowing hard, I struggled to find my voice, "Yes, I am of the Kind."

*Kind* is a word we use in our world to describe ourselves, so not to draw attention. She smiled, and my stomach dropped like I'd hit a dip on a roller coaster.

"I'm Lydia. What's your name?"

"I'm Grayson or Gray. Do you live around here?"

"I like it. I've never known a Gray." When her song ended she picked another. "No, I'm spending the summer ... I came here." She turned from the jukebox. "I want to go to the amusement park. Would you go with me? I haven't been before."

I grinned at her. "I'd love to."

My heart sped up, excited that she wanted to spend time with me. She jumped up and down, clapping her hands together.

"Come on, I've got some quarters, let's play some games first," she said as she turned and disappeared into the crowded arcade. Tons of kids gathered around the machines, watching those with money play. I made my way through the crowd, following Lydia. When I reached the back corner I realized I had lost her. The back appeared to be a graveyard of ancient machines, and was empty of any people. An old fortune teller machine caught my eye: Balthazar the Great.

The fortune teller looked like the typical one you would expect to see in an arcade. The wooden box was ornately carved, and looked to be from the turn of the twentieth century. This close, he looked more human than robotic. Balthazar's "body" was from the waist up. He wore a gold vest with a black suit jacket. He had long black hair with a matching goatee, but his head was bare, no turban like the Zoltar fortune tellers. The biggest difference, though, was that instead of a crystal ball a silver, ornate pocket watch dangled from his left hand and a book lay open near his right hand, almost as if he could turn the pages and read from it.

I took a couple of steps closer. When I got close enough the machine lit up. I shivered; I could feel magic coming from the machine. I wasn't surprised when I looked down and saw the old, frayed plug, loose on the ground. I looked back up at Balthazar; his bright, golden eyes were open, staring at me. He looked at me, then down. I swallowed. He wanted me to put a coin in his machine.

I fumbled in my pocket for a quarter, knowing better than to ignore an encounter with a magical being, even if it was an arcade fortune teller. I inserted the quarter into the brass slot and stood back.

Balthazar's pocket watch began to swing back and forth as he flipped the pages of the book. His eyes were focused on the book, but I found it hard not to look at the pocket watch; it was hypnotic. After about a minute the watch stopped swinging and his attention returned to me. His mouth opened and smoke that smelled of pipe tobacco started pouring out.

# CONVERGENT LINES

As the smoke cleared a card was spit out into a tray below Balthazar. I reached in and grabbed it. When I look back at Balthazar the lights had turned off, returning it to an old, broken machine. I looked at the card.

The side facing me had an image of Balthazar with "Your Lucky Numbers: 8, 16, 27, 28, 42." I flipped the card over. It read:

**Balthazar's Life Rules & Guidelines**

**Rule #3**
NEVER BE REACTIVE. You will lose whenever you are.

**Balthazar's Fortune for Grayson:**

Today is the start of a very long journey, one with adventure and joy. The road is long and winding with hardships aplenty. In time you shall find your map, until then go forth and explore. In the darkest of times do not despair, for many are with you.

Unfortunately, you have been dealt the blow of the Chinese's ancient curse: You shall live an interesting life.

I scratched my head, not sure what to make of Balthazar's fortune. My name on the card dispelled any doubts about it being magical.

I looked up at Balthazar and said, "I shall heed your advice." It's always best not to piss off anything magical, and as thanking acknowledges a debt, I was careful not to say "thank you." No one wants to be indebted for something simple.

Putting the card in my back pocket, my thoughts immediately returned to Lydia. As soon as I went down another row of arcade games, I forgot all about Balthazar.

I finally found Lydia in front of *Super Mario Bros*; she'd already put the quarters in for two players. From the corner of her eye she looked at me as I came up to my joystick.

"I thought I'd lost you."

"Not that easily. I just got distracted for a minute." I didn't want to tell her about my strange encounter.

She hit play. Three times in a row she beat me. With hurt pride and something to prove, I came back and won the next two games. We moved on to Skee-ball and pinball, then some *Ms. Pac Man*. My self-esteem recovered when I came back to even the score.

To end our arcade challenge we played a game of air hockey. How can something so little hit the puck so hard? She got my left hand twice. My left is my dominant hand, but didn't feel much like it now as it tingled with numbness.

"You play like a girl," she said.

"Really? It isn't a bad thing. I'm two ahead, and my next one wins it," I tossed back at her.

"The puck is still in play. I could still win."

"Anything is possible, I suppose." I lifted my hands as I said it and she took advantage of my lack of defense to score another point.

"Now you're only one up," she said as she stuck her tongue out at me.

"You must have a couple of brothers or sisters, probably both?"

"Nope, it's just me. My parents are dead. I've always lived with relatives, until I started school, then I usually stayed at the school during summer break. This is my first summer vacation, like, ever." It was strange to hear a girl with a Cornish accent try to talk like a California Valley Girl. I found everything about her charming. Taking advantage of my infatuation she won the game.

"Let me buy you lunch," I offered.

"It's the least you can do, you lost. I accept. But only if it consists of boardwalk food. I haven't ever had a corn dog, cotton candy, or funnel cake, and I've only had a Coke once."

"You've been deprived of the delicacies of America. A wrong I intend to set right. Come with me and I'll educate you on the finer points of American junk food." I reached for her hand, and she let me take it.

I discovered many things about Lydia; she was fast, freakishly strong, and could eat me under the table. Her exuberance was intoxicating, but sometimes I got a little peek behind her defenses and saw someone just as lonely as me. We were two of a kind, and my fate was sealed.

"I don't know about this yellow stuff. What did you call it again?" she asked.

"It's mustard."

"I haven't seen mustard such a bright yellow. It should be brown."

"Not American mustard. Just try the hot dog with both the ketchup and mustard. It's awesome. If you can get away tomorrow, I'll treat you to McDonald's."

She perked up, "I've not been to McDonald's."

"I figured. Just try the hot dog, you'll love it."

She sat on the edge of the pier as she eyed the hot dog with suspicion. Her legs dangled over the side, swinging back and forth. I sat firmly behind her with everything safely on the pier. Memories of the previous summer and Guy, my brother, pushing me off the pier haunted me. Lydia bit into the hot dog. The ketchup and mustard splattered all over her face and shirt. She chewed her dog as I used my magic to make the mess disappear.

She eyed me. "That's pretty good." She took another bite, careful not to get any more on her. "You're young to have those powers, if I'm not mistaken. Don't boys come into their magic later?"

"Are you good at keeping secrets?"

"Your secrets are mine. That's what best friends are for, right?"

"Best friends? You don't know me very well; what makes you say we're best friends?"

"Because, you know we are. We're of a Kind and kindred. I know you're a boy, but I'd think you could see it as plainly as I."

I laughed at her, "How is it I feel as if we've known each other forever?"

"Like I said, kindred. Tell me your secret and I'll share one of mine. Then we'll be even."

"We can't ever be even, Lydia. You came along and saved my summer. You're letting me share all this cool stuff. My secret is this: I have a lot of powers already. I'm afraid to share my abilities with my family. Especially since I'm the youngest."

She tilted her head in that way of hers before responding, "I don't know what it's like to have the pressures of a family. I only have faint memories before I started boarding school at five. I'm thirteen now; it's why they let me out on vacation. You know how much importance they put on the number thirteen."

"I'd say I envy you, but I have a feeling we have a similar existence," I said.

"I know you've been dying to ask, so I'll tell you. My family is the Rosdews. I'm adopted, not from the original line, and I know you probably wouldn't be allowed to associate with me if your family became aware of my bloodline. It's been a regular problem for me at school."

The Rosdews and Penroses are like north and south, polar opposites. The Rosdews wallow in the darker side of magic, with an affinity for spirit magic. The Penroses usually fall in the middle, with strong ties to the light court of the fae. Her concerns were valid; I've never known our families to mix.

A raven circled us and landed close to Lydia. The bird proceeded to hop over to her. She broke apart the leftover hot dog bun. The bird sprang up on her leg as if it were her pet. She fed it the bread and she patted its head.

"My family doesn't care what I do. *Should* it come up, I'd just say you're a Rosdew. They don't have any problem with them, and have no cause to investigate if you are adopted."

She smiled half-heartedly, "It will come up. It always does. For now, I'll take your company anytime I can get it." The bird nuzzled against her stomach.

"This is weird. Is that your bird?"

She laughed. "Yes, he's my familiar, Rowan, and has been as long as I can remember. Unlike you, I'm not very good at magic, except for communicating with him and sometimes stealing some of his abilities."

"Is that how you got up on the piling, and the speed?" She smiled and nodded her head. "Where did you get all the quarters then? I assumed you conjured them."

"Ravens are accomplished thieves. I simply managed to grab

several handfuls of quarters. All the money went right back into the machines; I kind of borrowed it."

I laughed. "I'm not judging you, Lydia. Come on, let's ride the rides. It's getting late, and the lines will be long."

We rode every ride and played all the games until the park closed. As we walked out of the park, she grabbed my hand and asked me if I'd walk her home. I did and discovered she lived only about a half mile from my parents' beach house.

"Are you sure you won't be in trouble for being late?"

"I'm sure. My Grandmother left this afternoon to go to an important meeting. Her staff is supposed to look after me, but I've already had it out with Mr. Bossypants. He threatened me, saying if I caused him any trouble he'd make sure my Grandmother didn't allow me to come back next summer. We came to an understanding."

"If you're sure. Do you want me to meet you here tomorrow?"

"Yes. How about around eleven? I want to sleep in for like the first time in my life." I laughed at how happy the idea made her.

"Okay, can I teach you to skateboard tomorrow?" She jumped up, wrapped her arms around my neck, and kissed my cheek. Startled, I wrapped my arms around her, afraid she'd fall. "Gray, you simply are the best guy ever! I can't wait." She kissed my cheek again and I blushed, thankful for the dark.

"Rowan is going to follow you home, so don't freak out. If he knows where you live, we'll be able to communicate back and forth through him."

"Okay," I said, as I looked at the raven sitting in a nearby tree.

"Goodnight Gray, and you should probably stop blushing." Of course, I blushed harder and she laughed again as she disappeared. Not wanting the day to be over or to be parted from her, I waited. A moment later a light on the second floor turned on and the window opened.

"Don't tell me you're a Peeping Tom?" she said with a smile.

I stammered, "Ah, no." Rowan cawed in a way which sounded as if he might be laughing at me. She looked over at the bird and laughed. "I know, Rowan."

"Are you having a conversation with the raven?"

"Don't be mean or you'll hurt Rowan's feelings. He likes you at this point, don't change his opinion. If you should need to talk to me, just whisper Rowan's name three times and he will come. You can give him a message; I'll get it. Now, I need sleep. You wore me out. I'll need rest if I'm to learn to skateboard tomorrow."

"Good night, my Lydia," I said, bowing formally to her. I reverted to my training at school; everything in our society is formal. Lydia's eyes widened. "What?"

"You just called me your Lydia."

"I did?"

She nodded her head and I thought back. I had. It seemed right. I looked back up at her. "Because you are. Sleep well," I said, and I ducked around the corner with Rowan cawing overhead.

# CHAPTER TWO

**September 20, Little Cornwall, Connecticut**

Everything was packed. All I had left to do was wait for my ride. I didn't want to go. The holiday ahead should be a burden lifted off my shoulders. Instead, the weight felt heavier than ever. Sitting on the bottom stair of my family's home, I stared at the door. Why should I feel like this? After all, it wasn't my wedding taking place in less than forty-eight hours. The approach of Guy's wedding had caused the floodgates of my past to break open. Haunted by my past, I found myself looking back, examining every little detail. Maybe this time I could figure out what happened.

Everyone else had been in Cornwall, England for a couple of weeks. I'd stayed behind because my company, PenTech, needed my attention. Any excuse to work was a good excuse. It kept my mind from wandering to places best left alone.

I should have taken comfort in the fact my brother liked Kensa Marrak, his fiancée. Once Guy was married, I would be expected to marry soon after, and it wouldn't be because I wanted to. Chances were good I'd be forced to marry someone I didn't know, and my bride would be much younger than me due to the length of my brother's betrothal. Then we'd be pressed to have children and sucked into Kind politics; my freedoms would wane. At least I didn't carry my brother's burdens.

With what little energy I could pull together, I rose, grabbed my bags, and headed out the door to the waiting Audi. Our chauffeur, Henson, was leaning against the car. He greeted me and opened my door, then took my bags. He's worked for my family as long as I can remember. Henson, the only trusted human in our service and an honorary member of our family. He has big ears, which stick out at strange angles, gray stubble on his head, and the darkest eyes I've ever seen. His job description would be more manservant than chauffeur, as he helped wherever he felt needed. His family had been servants to the Penroses for more than a century. Henson didn't have any children. Instead his two young great-grand-nephews are being groomed to replace him, for my father and my brother.

"Good afternoon, Grayson. Are you ready?"

"Hello, Henson. Yes, I'm ready."

He reached into his pocket and withdrew an envelope. "Would you do me the favor of delivering this to your brother and his bride? It's only a letter and a couple of photos, not much."

"I will. Bet it will be his favorite gift."

He smiled with his large, pearly white teeth. "Thanks, I hope you're right. Your mother promised me a video of the ceremony."

I cocked an eyebrow. "She did?"

"Be easy on your mother, you don't know the burden she's carried. With what I've heard of her family, I'd say we're lucky she turned out the way she did."

"Henson, you're too kind."

"I'd better get you there. Are others joining you on the flight?"

"Yes, a couple other KIC members are coming. They won't leave without me, though."

He shut the door, and without another word we drove to the airport. All the way I stared out the window at the countryside, losing myself in thought. The last twenty years of my life had been hard and lonely. Somehow the light at the end of the tunnel seemed farther away now.

The benefit of marrying in the Kind world meant you were, at long last, an adult and able to make your own decisions. You were free from your family's rule, but at the cost of a bride. You usually didn't get to meet your spouse until right before the wedding, and you'd count yourself lucky if you could stand to be in the same room with one another. I'd checked into seeing if my parents had been trying to arrange something for me, and the answer I kept arriving at said no.

Life after school had turned out okay, for the most part. My parents had little to do with me. So as long as I did what everyone expected, I found myself left to my own devices. It helped that I had started my tech company, PenTech, which specialized in creating shielded electronics able to function around Kind magic. My British cousin Lowen Penrose was the head of the Penrose family as well as my partner. He ran our offices in England. Once I figured out how to work with computers and electronics, my family and many in the Kind invested in my company. It had allowed me to stay out of the KIC and focus on my work in the U.S. Honestly, I couldn't ask for a better professional life. It did much in helping me forget about other parts of my life.

Henson drove me to our family's jet, which would fly me to Cornwall for the first time. Every time I thought of Cornwall, memories of *her* came back, of her sitting in the fading light as if she were a bird, of warm summer days skateboarding and swimming.

My thoughts wandered; I lost time, as I tended to do often these days. Soon, Henson delivered me to our hangar in what seemed to me like no time at all. He opened my door and grabbed my bags.

"Thank you, Henson. I'll see you soon, and I will deliver your letter." I held up the card and then slipped it in my pack. I reached over and gave him a hug.

"Goodbye, Gray. Give my love, and hurry back."

"Will do, Henson." I grabbed my bags and boarded the plane.

Sitting across from one another mid-way down the aisle were a KIC member and a member of the Elder Council. Eva

Arundel sat to my right. "Arundel" has come to mean aristocrat in the Kind. And she embodied the very meaning. Eva is everything I'd expect of an Arundel female. She has white blonde hair and skin so pale you could see the blue blood flowing in her veins, and sharp features, her chin, her nose, even her eyes. I knew she had to be at least twice my age, but in appearance, we could have been contemporaries. I'd never found her very attractive, probably more to do with her personality than her appearance. She held the highest rank in the KIC as a healer, or doctor, and provided oversight of the Nancarrows and their Doctor Frankenstein testing. She's the KIC expert in areas of medicine.

The Arundels tended to be the healers of our world; whether the ailment is a physical or mental issue, they're usually who you would seek out for help. They also come from the light court of the fae and claim the most royal bloodlines. In contrast, the Nancarrows are the opposite. They rose from the darkest side of the fae, with specialties in dark magic. The best way to describe them is to liken them to a mad scientist. They're the only family in the Kind to embrace science.

Sitting opposite her was her father-in-law, Davidson Gwyn, a member of the Elder Council. "Grayson, how good it is to see you on the eve of such a grand event," Davidson said as he stood to greet me.

"Good to see you too." I produced the biggest plastic smile I could. He wished my family well. Somehow, I just didn't care. If I became fully human tomorrow and walked away from everything, it would be okay with me. I wanted freedom.

"You know my daughter-in-law Eva?"

I bowed to her, taking her hand and kissing it. "Of course, the lovely Eva, healer of the Kind."

She batted her lashes at me, loving the attention. She'd been screwed on the arranged marriage jackpot. She drew Davy Gwyn, Davidson's son. Davy is a beanpole with stringy blond hair and a clammy look about him. The Gwyns are a family heavily tied to the light and associated with the water fae.

Davidson towered over us, with a barrel chest, massive arms, and giant mustache. At heart he's a gentle giant, but powerful. I'd never want to duel him. How he could have sired Davy was one of the Kind's greatest mysteries. Davidson reminded me of butterscotch in every way, the tone of his skin, hair, and eyes, even his clothes. If he's butterscotch, Eva is vanilla.

The pilot came in to greet us. "Excuse me, are we ready to get under way?"

I answered, "Yes, everyone's here."

"We'll be under way in ten minutes. I'll come over the intercom when we're ready to depart."

"Understood."

The pilot is human, all pilots are humans. The Kind, and other creatures of magic, have a habit of affecting mechanical devices at the most inopportune times. Magic often affects these devices like an EMP, blowing them out. I've solved this, and I make a living making technology that works for us. We design or alter computers and cars with more shielding. Though the Kind generally agree about not risking our magic while piloting a plane.

The pilot came on the intercom. "Please take your seats and fasten your seat belts. We're cleared to leave."

My plan was to get some sleep while we were in the air. The next two days would be crazy for family members. Once underway, the steward made her appearance, serving wine to my guests and bourbon for me. I downed my drink and explained my desire for sleep, which they did not begrudge me. As soon as I closed my eyes, I drifted off into oblivion.

Cornwall was much the way I thought the English countryside would be: cold, wet, drizzly, and green, with the stereotypically English cottages everywhere. A car waited for us when we arrived at the small airport. My guests were dropped off first to their accommodations at another estate, then the driver took me to the original Penrose estate "Kolon," which means heart in Cornish. The driver turned down a long country road with nothing around. We must have traveled for more than a mile before a immense manor loomed in the distance.

It's impressive. Never, even after all the descriptions, did I imagine such extravagance could be real. The driver pulled us into a circular drive with a large central fountain surrounding a group of bronze satyrs playing instruments to beautiful nymphs. The driver opened the door for me and grabbed my bags. As I started for the doors, they opened to reveal a male and female servant dressed in black and white, much like you would expect to see on an old BBC television show.

They both bowed and greeted me, asking for my name. "Ah, yes, we've been expecting you, Master Grayson," said the male servant. Come on, Master Grayson?

"I will show you to your room," said the maid. I followed her to the east wing and my room on the second floor. She opened the door and let me enter first. I hoped my eyeballs didn't pop out of my head too much. The room was large, complete with a wardrobe in which I could escape and visit Aslan, and decorated with a hunting motif, in rich brown velvets and brocades. A massive mantel in white marble with sculptures of various animals surrounded a roaring fire in the hearth. The maid walked about the room showing me features, such as the hidden big screen television, stocked bar, and remote controlled window shading.

She left me alone, with the promise of telling my brother I had arrived. Thrilled to be left in this room I headed to the bar, poured myself a glass of scotch, and sat upon the canopy bed to relax. Some time later my brother appeared. I jumped up and hugged him, happy to see him.

"What do you think? Is this place amazing or what?"

"You aren't getting me out of this room. Send in the wenches and I'll spend the rest of my life here."

He laughed and poured himself a drink.

"So tell me, honestly, how is Kensa? Did you end up getting a better deal than most?"

He gave me a toothy grin. "She's beautiful, kind, smart, and enjoyable to be around. I can't imagine she's faking, either. I'm happy with the hand fate has dealt me. I think you'll like her. I can't wait for you to meet her." He took a sip of his drink. "Oh, and get this: Mother likes her. They get along beautifully. Either Kensa is the coolest woman in the world or the best actress I've met."

I cocked my brow at him. "You're speaking of Jessamine Penrose, formally Jessamine Nancarrow, being won over? I thought only Henson capable of such."

"The one and only."

"I'm happy for you, Guy. I'll admit I've been worried. I hope this is the end of the prophecy and the start of a happy life for you."

He patted me on the back, "So do I. But you'd better get ready for dinner, you'll want to dress for it. They're rather formal here."

"Black tie?"

"Yup, hope you came prepared, 'cause I can't loan you my clothes. You're too big."

"Ha-ha." He likes to get a jab in about the fact that I took after our father, Jowan Penrose, more than he did.

"What time is dinner?"

"Six PM sharp, and don't be late; you've got forty-five minutes. Just enough time to shower and dress." I rolled my eyes at him. "I'll be back to get you in forty minutes, so I can take you to meet my Kensa."

"I'll be ready."

He nodded and left me. I opened my suitcase, which held a change of clothes, a sketchpad and art supplies, and a novel from W.L. Townsend, my favorite author. I rummaged through my art supplies looking for the baggie of dry-erase markers; they'd slipped to the bottom. With the baggie in hand, I went to the bathroom and started the shower. While it warmed, I walked over to the full length mirror lining the wall opposite the double vanity.

Marker in hand, I wrote my spell upon the mirror. *Open to my closet and remain open to me alone.* I gave the GPS coordinates of the mirror in my closet back home in Connecticut. Then wrote, *Allow me to walk through.* The spell disappeared into the mirror, which rippled as if a stone had been tossed into it. I stuck my hand through to test my spell. It felt like cold, thick water, just before it freezes. I walked through the mirror and ended up in my very own closet. Rummaging through my clothes, I chose a charcoal colored suit, a gunmetal shirt, and black tie. Happy with the selection, I grabbed a pair of shoes, socks, and returned through the mirror portal.

Twenty minutes later, I finished getting ready and poured another drink. I timed my brother in sips, and when I reached the bottom of the glass, he knocked on my door. He took us through the maze of wings and corridors to the grand dining room. The room had already filled, and my parents waited by the door. To my shock and horror, my mother ran to me, throwing her arms around my neck and planting a kiss on my check.

I wanted to say, *Who are you and what have you done with my mother?* But I refrained. I figured I must be dreaming, or someone had replaced my mother with a doppelgänger.

My parents and I made small talk as Guy brought his bride over to meet me. Kensa wasn't what I expected. She was tiny with the grace of a dancer or flames, which probably described a redhead better. With pale skin and bright green eyes, she truly was one of the most beautiful women I'd ever seen. Guy had hit the jackpot.

"Kensa, may I present my brother, Grayson, or Gray. Gray, this is my Kensa."

She held her hand out, and I kissed it. I decided she smelled of cinnamon, sweet smoke, and caramel. "It's a pleasure to meet my younger sister, finally. My brother is a lucky man," I said with a genuine smile.

"You didn't tell me how handsome he is. How is it you haven't been married off?"

"He's a confirmed bachelor, love; dedicated to his work."

"Guy is right, but I like to think I'm waiting for the perfect woman."

"You're funny, Gray. Come on, let's get seated." He showed us to the table.

Dinner passed in a blur of conversations and multiple courses, followed by cigars and scotch in the library. I turned in early, claiming jet lag, not a complete lie but not the whole truth either.

# CHAPTER THREE

### June 1988, Santa Cruz, California

I skated home from Lydia's to find my house dark. Overhead I heard a bird as I kicked my board up to go in. Guess Rowan had figured out where I lived. Inserting my key, I turned the handle on the back door to a dark kitchen. I sighed, glad I didn't have to explain where I'd been all day. Heading for the fridge, I grabbed some fruit before going to my room. On my way, I noticed Guy's door was closed and a dim light coming from under it. Guess the house wasn't empty. In my room I turned on my lamp and put my things away.

I pulled the ticket from Balthazar out of my back pocket as I grabbed my sketchpad. Just to be safe, I taped the ticket into the front cover of my pad. I figured it would be best to hold on to a fortune given to me by a magical arcade game. With it safely stored, I turned to a blank sheet of paper.

I started to draw a skateboard for Lydia: a Santa Cruz, like the town and my own board. I completed the lines of the board, wheels, and all the parts. Now for the illustration on the board; I decided upon a raven, like Rowan. The raven took longer than the board. I made several starts and stops before I was satisfied. I opened the drawer of my nightstand for my marker set. With the outlines in place, I colored in the raven in shades of black, blue, and purple. I liked the result. Next, I finished with chrome for all the metal parts, and purple wheels.

This skateboard would be a first for me. I've never drawn something I knew existed, then edited by putting my illustration on it. I looked at the page for a long minute, almost afraid to grab it. With a deep breath, I closed my eyes and reached my hand into my sketch, to feel the edge of the board and the grip tape on the top. With a tug the board became reality. It lay in my lap, bottom down. From the top the board looked just like mine. I walked over to the light switch, turned it on, and flipped the board to examine my work.

To my surprise the illustration looked even better than I imagined. I hoped Lydia would like it. The clock on my nightstand read after two in the morning. I put the board in my bag and headed to bed. I closed my eyes to relive the day for a second time.

## 10 AM, Thursday, June 9, 1988

*Tap, tap. Tap, tap,* the sound woke me. At first, I couldn't figure out what was causing the insidious tapping. A shadow on the curtains of the window caught my eyes. I pulled aside the curtain to see Rowan. He clicked his beak against the window over and over. Impatient bird. Stubborn, he continued to hammer the window as I tried to figure out how to open the lock. It took several attempts before I finally got the window open. When I did, Rowan hopped through without invitation. He took up a spot on my bed, dropped something, and cawed at me.

I wondered how he'd figured out the location of my room. Rowan was a smart bird, so I went to see what he had. Sitting down on the bed seemed to pacify him some. He stopped squawking and started to push the thing he'd dropped toward me with his beak. I picked up a piece of paper. Ah, a note from Lydia.

*Gray,*

*I can't meet up with you today. My grandmother is making me go with her to a party. She wants to start my introduction into society. Her words not mine. Wish I could get out of it but it might be for the better. It looks like it's going to rain today. It also sounds like she has a social calendar planned for me, so as soon as I can get away, I'll send Rowan with a note. Hope you aren't mad. I'm sorry. I'd rather be with you.*

*Lydia*

My heart sank as I put the note back on the bed and reached for my sketchpad. I wrote a response, telling her I looked forward to seeing her again soon. Done, I folded up the note to give it to Rowan. He eyed me like he expected me to do something. I knew one thing, there's no way I was going to stick the note in his beak. Instead, I set it down on the bed close to him. Rowan looked at me, alternating which eye he used. "What am I supposed to do, Rowan?"

He looked at me and cawed. Exasperated I asked, "What?"

Oh, he was acting as if he were waiting for a tip, and in this case a tip in the form of food. "I don't have any food."

He glared at me. I sighed. "Let's go down to the kitchen."

He cawed and hopped over to me, taking that as the invitation he'd been waiting for. Next thing I knew Rowan was sitting on my right shoulder. Now let me say, ravens are much larger than you think, and Rowan was even bigger than that. They also have claws. I swallowed hard, hoping Rowan didn't plan on hurting me. Resigned to feeding the bird, I headed for the door. I poked my head into the hall in time to see my brother walk into his room and close the door. With the path clear, I headed toward the kitchen, hoping my mother wasn't there. She hates animals.

I did my best to be quiet. So did Rowan. He seemed to understand the need for secrecy. There was no one in the kitchen. Rowan made a strange popping noise with his beak. I decided it sounded like anticipation. I chuckled and asked, "Are you hungry?"

His answering caw had the distinct sound of a yes. Come to think of it, a lot of the sounds he made were like mimics of words. Rowan eyed me from his left eye as if he knew I'd come to a conclusion. I then realized he was probably smarter than me, and the tales of Odin's ravens Huginn and Muninn were probably correct. Let me tell you, having a large, intelligent predator on your shoulder is a very scary thing; he could peck my eyes out from his perch on my shoulder or use those giant claws on me. I took a deep breath to calm myself before I developed ornithophobia. I moved slowly, careful not to make any sudden moves. I left the main kitchen light off and headed for the walk-in pantry. I took Rowan into the pantry with me and turned the light on, leaving the door open just a crack.

"Okay, Rowan, what do you eat?" Rowan shifted excitedly. "I guess I'm on the right track. How about I show you a few things and you pick what you want?"

He made his strange popping noise again. I pointed to a box of sugary cereal and Rowan squawked.

"Well, that was easier than I thought it would be. I kind of wish you could tell me what you want. Can you talk like a parrot?"

Rowan stopped his excitement and glared at me; my stomach dropped. He raised his beak up high and looked at me out of the corner of his eye, clearly insulted. I made a mental note to remember he was a sensitive bird.

"Sorry, ah, no offense meant."

A sound behind me drew my attention and the pantry door swung open to reveal my mother. I swallowed as my mind began to swim with excuses and explanations of why I was standing in the middle of the pantry with a raven on my shoulder. Did I mention my mom hates animals?

"What are you doing in the kitchen with the lights out? Who were you talking to?"

I stood there waiting for her to notice Rowan. She glared back. "Cat got your tongue? Are you hoping for a staring contest? Come on, Grayson. Answer me."

Then I realized there was a lack of claws digging into my shoulder. I don't know where Rowan got off to, but I think I liked that bird.

"I was talking to myself. I came down here to get something to eat and couldn't decide."

My mother's eyes narrowed as she glared harder at me. "I don't believe you."

A sarcastic streak, which my mother had never experienced, reared up. I do have a death wish. "Fine! I came down here to look for ingredients for a potion I've been planning. It cures hunger."

I swear I saw lasers in her eyes; a real possibility with my mom. Over her left shoulder on a high shelf, I saw Rowan shaking his head at me.

Suddenly my father called from out in the kitchen. "Jessamine. Come on. We need to go."

"We'll continue this later. You will not speak to me as you just did, ever again. Or it will be the last thing you ever say."

I reached up and rubbed my throat, knowing she *could* take my voice, with her Ursula-like powers.

"You're grounded. Do not leave the house. We shall discuss this later in greater detail."

"Yes, Mother."

"Jessamine, we need to go."

"Coming, Jowan." She left and I let out the breath I'd been holding and allowed my shoulders to slouch. Rubbing my head, I wondered how Rowan moved so quickly?

*"You know, you should pay better attention to your surroundings, especially when committing a crime."*

"Who said that?" I asked looking around the pantry.

*"Who do you think?"* said the voice again. Then I realized I wasn't hearing it with my ears, but in my head, a strange wispy male voice. I looked up at Rowan to find him staring back at me.

"You can talk?"

"*Well, of course I can, if you call telepathy speaking. I'm a descendant of Muninn. Odin gave all her descendants the ability to talk with humans.*"

I blinked several times as I tried to process what Rowan had told me. "Can you read minds, too?" I hoped not.

Rowan laughed a strange mix of laughter and squawking. When I realized I was having a telepathic conversation with a raven in my pantry, I wondered at my sanity. Rowan continued with his strange sounds of amusement as I pondered my situation.

"*Grayson,*" he said. I snapped my head and looked at him. "*I don't have to read your mind. You are easy to read.*" He chuckled some more. "*Boy, you need to hide your emotions better. What's that modern term?*" He tilted his head to the side in a manner similar to Lydia. "*It's one I like. 'Tis, poker face. You need a poker face, a bluff, and to get rid of your tells.*" He stomped his feet in excitement as he hopped up and down. "*I've got it! I shall stay with you today and help you. In return you shall feed me. Deal?*"

I'm sure my left eyelid twitched. What else did I have to do? I was sure my mom put a hex on the house in case I tried to leave. "Fine, what do you want?"

Rowan squawked and danced. "*I want cereal, the sugary stuff, cheese crackers, fruit, and a saucer of milk, too.*" I shook my head at his excitement and set out to fulfill his requests.

"*Here's your first lesson. Do not test the patience of a powerful witch, especially a Nancarrow. Learn to bite your tongue, boy, and you might keep it.*"

I stopped shaking some cereal into a bowl and looked at Rowan. This telepathy thing was going to take some getting used to. "You know she's a Nancarrow?"

This time, I hear a chuckle in my mind. "*Of course. I am a Muninn, titled and descended. My grandmother's name means memory, and I've been taught to observe the world, for I could be summoned to report back at any time. I can spot a witch a forest away, and tell their bloodline before they notice me.*"

"Then why didn't my mom sense you? With her being a

Nancarrow and their abilities?"

"Silly, silly, boy. I'm a bird. And not just any bird, but a magical one. Nancarrows have an affinity with mammals, insects, and some mammal sea creatures."

"They can't talk to birds?"

"Haven't met a Nancarrow who could, except if one of us were to decide to speak to them."

"Oh," I said and continued with preparing his food.

"You have a strained relationship with her?"

"I guess you can say that." I sighed. "I don't know what I did, but my mother has never really liked me." Rowan turned his head to the side again, as if considering this.

"Interesting. Is this why you were so worried when she entered the pantry?"

"Yeah, it's funny she's a Nancarrow, because boy, does she hate animals. I can't have a dog, cat, or even a snake."

"You have your father's approval?"

"My father and I get along well. I just rarely see him. He's high in the KIC administration and hopes to run for the Elder Council one day. I think he'll win, too. Well if my mother and her sour disposition don't sabotage him."

"She probably isn't loved; most Nancarrows aren't. They're no fun; no sense of humor. I find it fascinating, a Penrose and a Nancarrow married, light and dark."

I opened the pantry door and set the two bowls down on the counter. I grabbed a tray, Rowan's food, and started upstairs. He landed on my right shoulder again for the return trip.

In my room, I put the tray on the bed. He flew to the plate, excited. "Doesn't Lydia feed you?"

Rowan looked up at me with a beak stuffed with chocolate cereal. "When she can. Her grandmother's house is very strict. There isn't any chance of getting into the kitchen. On days she's with her grandmother, I fend for myself. When she can get away, she gets me whatever I want. No one but you knows about me."

"Makes sense. What about at school?"

"It's easy there; the school has so many animals and birds around no one notices me."

"Do you eat like this all the time? Keep it up and you'll be a fat bird."

Rowan lifted his head out of the cereal and did that thing where he lifted his head high and looked at me out of the corner of his eye. *"Teaching you to hold your tongue is going to be harder than I supposed."* I'm sure I looked sheepish. *"Get some playing cards. I'm going to teach you how to play poker."*

"But I already know how."

*"No, you don't!"*

I heard my mouth pop open. He shook his head and focused on eating again. Feeling dismissed, I turned and left Rowan to his meal. As I passed Guy's room, he opened the door. "Damn it, Gray, what did you do to mom? She's pissed, and taking it out on me."

I shrugged my shoulders and stuck my bottom lip out in a pout.

He rolled his eyes. "You aren't a girl. It won't work. Did you get lippy with mom? Are you out of your mind? You're lucky you can still speak. If I were you, I'd think of a very nice apology. Wait. Let me rephrase that, you'll do something nice, grovel or beg, whatever it takes to make her forgive you."

Here's my first chance to take Rowan's advice and bite my tongue. I responded, "I will."

"Good. She's taking it out on me. She wants me to cut my hair. I'm *not* cutting my hair, and you're not going to upset her any more and ruin my last summer of freedom. Fix it!"

Guy and his beloved hair, he wore it long in the same way California skaters and surfers did. It worked with his straight light brown hair, and the girls loved it. "I will, I promise."

"Cool," he said as he reached up and rubbed my mop of curly blond hair. At fifteen, I had already passed him by an inch. At eighteen and five foot ten, he knew he'd reached his limit, and it had bothered him something fierce. The door *clicked* behind him as he retreated into his room, and I went to search for a deck of cards.

# CHAPTER FOUR

### Morning of Mabon, September 22, Cornwall, England

My head pounded. I was hung-over; my least favorite way to wake. Usually, I don't drink much, but last night was my brother's bachelor party. It consisted of drinking old scotch and smoking cigars. After we had polished the bottle off and an equal measure of cigars, someone decided we should try to catch a glimpse of the Wild Hunt. My memory is hazy on the matter.

Sitting up gingerly, I had to hold my head. I dragged myself from the bed and headed for the bathroom with plans for a long hot shower. Bracing myself in the arched doorway, I held my breath for a minute. When I breathed back in I got a whiff of myself. Oh God, what did we do? I headed straight for the shower.

Sometimes there is nothing better than a hot shower. With a towel around my waist, I entered the big room feeling almost human, and ravenous. My suit from the night before sat in a wet, muddy mess by the fireplace, where a fire still flickered. I took one of the pokers and used the tip to pick up the clothes and throw them into the fire. Digging around in my mind I tried to figure out what we had done. My mind was a blank after we left the library. Probably best if I *didn't* remember. The wet clothes sizzled and extinguished the flames. I called a fireball to my hand and shot it, and several others, at the wet heap. The clothes incinerated to ash with the third ball and an unpleasant aroma.

 I went back to the bathroom mirror and the portal I had left open to my home. Inside my bedroom in Connecticut, I smiled, thankful to be able to use my magic to get here so easily.

 As I began to pick out my clothes, a spot somewhere near the pit of my stomach started fluttering. The sensation turned to pain, sending me to the ground. I have never experienced pain like this, but I knew what it was. A curse had lifted from me.

 I had two questions. One, why was there a curse on me? Two, who had done it and why did they remove it now? I curled into the fetal position for a while, rocking back and forth. Finally the pressure released and I could breathe again.

 I rummaged through my clothes, deciding upon tan slacks, a white shirt, and a sweater. Before leaving, I went to my bathroom and nabbed my shaving kit and something for my headache. Back in the closet, I grabbed my tux for the wedding ceremony, and back through the portal I went.

 Dressed, I headed downstairs to find food and to see if anyone else might be involved in this curse. This had to be a curse. A hex is something which affects the things around the person. A curse is much more dangerous and usually involves hurting the person or taking something from the individual. The pain combined with the pressure made me sure whoever had set the curse had died, or they were forced, unwillingly, to remove it. I wanted to understand what, who, and why. I understand from school and stories, there is also pain when the curse is placed. I mean, the point of a curse is for the victim to know they are cursed, and why. I had no idea when it could have been placed on me.

 At the base of the grand stairs, several people moved about, my father, Jowan, among them. I headed for him.

"Morning, son." He rubbed his head as if he regretted talking. In a quiet tone, I said, "Good morning, Dad. Rough night?"

"Yeah." He still held the side of his head. "Why are you so normal this morning?"

"I'm young and conditioned. Plus, I took some of mom's pain-killing potion already."

"You brought some? I didn't; neither did your mother. Oh, and I would stay away from *her* for most of the day. She isn't happy about last night."

I bit my lips as I tried not to laugh at him. My sympathy kicked in, and I swallowed my laughter. "I'll find you some. Stay here."

He nodded his head and then moaned from the pain. I turned away to hide my laughter. I sympathized with him, but how often does one observe their proud father in this type of situation? As penitence, I hurried and brought the liquid vial to him. He downed the whole thing.

I counted backward from twenty. As I hit three, he let out an audible gasp of relief.

"You're my favorite son. Well, at least right now you are."

"Thanks, Dad. I think. I won't hold you to it. I know you were in a lot of pain."

"Misery is a spiteful thing and loves company."

"Did you eat?" I asked.

"No, come on. It's best not to take your mom's potion on an empty stomach."

We walked down the hall toward the banqueting room. "Do you remember anything after we left the library? I seem to remember someone suggesting chasing the Wild Hunt?"

"We left the library?" His eyes rolled around as he thought back. "Nope got nothing, but that would explain the wet, smelly clothes. Something I don't think your mother will ever move past."

"Oh, Dad, I'm sorry. I had some waiting for me this morning, and I got a whiff myself. You're going to need to make this up big time to mom. Like a new car or new vacation home."

He hung his head. "I know."

In the banqueting room, many people were eating, including

Davidson. He waved from a table. He sat alone, if you didn't count the heaping plates of food surrounding him.

We both snagged a plate and helped ourselves. Once loaded we joined Davidson. He glanced up from a drumstick, set his food down, stood, and bowed to us. "Gentleman, please join me. My hangover is now just abating and I'm starving."

"Of course, I understand completely. Gray just gave me a potion for my head. Let me tell you, a few minutes ago, I was not doing well."

We ate and compared stories. My memory seemed to take us further into the disastrous events of the evening before, but didn't go nearly far enough to explain anything, specifically the stench.

Eventually the conversation turned to the matter of KIC, and my brother's wedding. I listened. If I mentioned a curse being upon me, I would find myself embroiled in an investigation. No way I wanted that. From listening and watching the guests, I began to surmise I had been the only one affected. If others were involved, then the rumor mills would be working full bore.

I pushed my second plate of food away, feeling much better. The conversation stalled as Davidson and my dad rubbed their bellies and nearly moaned.

"I think perhaps someone should go in search of Guy. I've not seen any trace of him and he's to marry in a few hours. While my memory is hazy, I seem to remember he downed more of the scotch than anyone else," I said.

"I'll go," Dad said. "Better make sure he's still breathing. If he misses the wedding, I think he'll be in more trouble than I am now with my wife." My dad got up and left me with Davidson.

"I meant to talk to you," Davidson said as his cell phone rang. "Hello?" He twitched his bushy mustache back and forth. Toast crumbs and the remains of scrambled egg held on for the ride. "Really?" He elongated the word. "When did this happen?" He made a bunch of sounds into the phone. "I never thought I would live to see the day. Even in death I doubt she'll find peace or stop scheming. I'll need to be there, and so will the other Elder Council members and upper KIC personnel." He hung up and slid cell into his pocket. Someone had died. Best sit back and listen; Davidson likes to gossip. "Sometimes life throws you a curve ball."

"And what would that be?"

"That Hilda Rosdew is dead."

There it was: who. But the answer made the other questions harder to answer.

Hilda was the matriarch of the Rosdew family, and very old. Damn, she must be close to three hundred years old. Davidson stroked his mustache as he considered Hilda's death, a behavior I was all too familiar with. It meant he was thinking. "Something is off, besides the hangover. Perhaps the way I smelled this morning. I wonder if we fell into a bog? A bog would explain the stench."

I laughed as my father returned with my sorry-looking brother. I had half expected him to be dead.

"Do you have any more of your mother's potion?" Dad asked.

"I might. Let me check." He nodded as he assisted my brother into a chair. "Hurry, Kensa and Guy are supposed to go before the Oracle in less than an hour."

I went again to my room and was back in a couple of minutes. Guy downed a bunch of the potion and burped.

"Better?" I asked.

My dad said, "Gray, would you grab him a plate of food? You have best man duties to fulfill."

I returned to the table with a full plate which I sat in front of Guy. A smile spread as he picked up the fork and dug in. As he ate, I sipped a very bitter cup of coffee. "Dad?"

He leaned forward so he could look past Davidson to me. "Yes?"

"Is it common to visit an Oracle before a marriage?"

"Yes. Don't worry, it's not as scary as it sounds, the Oracle almost never sees anything. It goes back to superstitions. Davidson, when was the last time the Oracle saw something?"

Davidson's lips pursed, as he considered the question. "She hasn't seen much in the last twenty to thirty years. Oh, I remember, the Teague wedding."

"Oh yes, but did she view his behavior or the future?"

"Probably both," said Davidson.

"What happened?" Guy asked.

Dad ignored Guy and asked, "Herman, or was it Henry?"

"Herman," said Davidson.

"Well, the Oracle could see he was gay and there would be no children. She couldn't allow the marriage to continue. How the couple was approved by the Council is still a mystery to me." Davidson laughed. "The look on the boy's face was priceless."

"Guy," Mother said from behind us. We all straightened, as though we had been caught doing something wrong.

"Yes, Mother," Guy answered.

"I want to help you get ready for the Oracle."

"I'm sure I can handle this on my own."

"You need to shower again, and re-dress."

Our three heads swiveled to face Guy. He sensed trouble. He put his fork down and followed her without another word.

Davidson stood bowed and excused himself, followed immediately by my father. He probably thought to run interference between Guy and mom. Left alone, I finished the coffee and decided to go for a walk round the grounds. I left the dining room through one of several doors which opened onto the gardens.

The gardens in the daylight were surreal, with flowers three times the size they should be, a labyrinth made of tall hedges, and topiaries cut to resemble animal shapes. I wandered for a bit, before the clock on my cell told me I'd better head inside for this Oracle thing.

Once back inside it became easy to figure out where I needed to go; people moved in droves toward the grand ballroom. My parents stood near the front of the room and called me over. I stood with them as the proceedings started. The crowd hushed as a man dressed in a bright red suit jacket and black pants walked to the center of the crowd. He reminded me of a circus ringmaster.

His arm shot out to his side. "Hello, all. I am Christopher Carn, the master of ceremonies for this Mabon, and the Penrose and Marrak wedding ceremony. We gather for the final reading of the couple by the Carn Oracle, Aquila."

# CONVERGENT LINES

The crowd near the door parted for the oldest woman I had ever seen. She hobbled on the arm of a big brute of a man. Aquila encompassed everything humans had come to identify as a witch. The term hag fit her perfectly: long, stringy white hair, pale skin with warts, and a hooked nose. Dressed in a drab, muddy green robe, she moved slowly to the large chair they'd prepared for her. Once she settled in, someone brought a little red velvet footstool and placed it under her feet.

Pomp and circumstance done, Christopher asked, "Are the bride and groom here?"

Guy and Kensa came forward. They met in the aisle and walked toward Aquila. Guy wore a gray suit and Kensa wore an emerald silk dress. Together, they looked great. They walked forward hand in hand. Once they reached Aquila, they bowed to her and remained standing.

"Is this them?" a squeaky voice said. Her eyes appeared cloudy, like she suffered from cataracts.

Christopher said, "Please announce yourself to Aquila."

"I am Guy Richard Penrose, first born son of Jowan Penrose and Jessamine Nancarrow."

"I am Kensa Jean Marrak, daughter of ..." is all Kensa got out before Aquila began twitching violently and making strange noises. Christopher waved at Kensa to be quiet. My parents exchanged a weird look with one another. Everyone in the room stared at Aquila as she began to stand. Someone moved the footstool out of the way, but there was no need: Aquila began to hover more than a foot above the ground. She turned her head toward Guy, opened her mouth wide, and a black mist spilled forth, enveloping her like a cloak. The room smelled of ozone, and she lifted her arm to point a finger at Guy.

"You are not who you think you are. The heir to one but not the other," Aquila said in a booming voice not her own. "You aren't the Guide I foretold."

I turned to my parents, confused. Guy looked panicked and ready to flee.

"Guy and Kensa, you are a match and shall be fruitful, but you are not the foretold male and female," she said. Audible gasps were heard all over the room. A wicked smile, a predator's smile, spread across Aquila's face. Without being told Guy took Kensa's hand and led her away.

Christopher asked Aquila. "Mistress, any further instructions for us?"

Her hair started floating around her as if charged with electricity, and gapping black holes appeared where her eyes had been. A shiver ran down my spine. Aquila sucked in air, and her head turned to view the room.

"He is here, the one who will guide us. Bring the single men before me," she said as she scanned the room. I knew something bad loomed … and somehow I was involved.

Christopher asked, "Mistress, is the female with us? Has she been born?"

Aquila stopped scanning the room and looked at Christopher like he was a fly buzzing near her. "I will try," she said. For several long moments she hovered as small bolts of lightning shot from her hair toward the ceiling. "She has been born, but when and to whom I cannot tell, nor can I tell if she still lives."

Christopher said, "Single males, even the young, form a line here, before Aquila."

A line of over twenty men and boys came forward quickly. Most would kill to be the Guide. Guy and Kensa came to stand with us as Christopher ushered each man and boy in front of Aquila. I did my best to keep a low profile behind my parents as Guy talked to them in hushed tones. He seemed worried, not angry. Kensa had tears streaming down her red cheeks.

Suddenly, panic rushed through me; it started at my toes and climbed to my throat. No one paid me any attention, so I made my way to the doors. *Screw this. I'm out of here. I don't know how or why, but the dread of the last few weeks finally makes sense. My worst nightmare is about to come true. It's me. I am the one they are looking for.* A ringing started in my ears. My freedom stood mere feet away, through the double doors.

## CONVERGENT LINES

    Outside the ballroom, I headed straight for the stairs, taking them two at a time. The haunted halls were empty; everyone was in the ballroom. I closed the doors to my room with a satisfying *click*. In answer, the flames in the hearth roared for a moment before dying down.

    I paced the floor, my thoughts running wild. Looking down at my shaving kit on the bed, I found an old set of black and white photos starring back at me. I picked up the pictures and looked down at my fifteen-year-old self and her.

    *There is someplace for me to go, some place I have not been in more than twenty years. Somewhere I might find answers to my questions.* I took out my dry-erase marker and held a destination in mind.

# CHAPTER FIVE

### June 9, 1988, Santa Cruz, California

I opened my door to something no one should ever witness. Rowan sat in the middle of the cereal bowl as if he were bathing, with his eyes closed. I shut the door with a *click*.

"What are you doing?"

Rowan jumped into the air with a squawk. He flew around the room disoriented.

"Rowan, would you calm down?" He perched on my bed with his chest heaving. "What were you doing?"

*"Sorry, fell asleep; food coma. I didn't remember where I was for a minute."* He hung his head, embarrassed.

"Okay, but why were you roosting in a bowl of Cocoa Puffs?" He turned away, and a quiet mumble sounded in my mind, which I couldn't make out. "What did you say?"

He cawed and jumped, *"I like the scent of them, thought that if I rolled around in them, I might pick up their perfume."*

"This is awkward."

Rowan glared daggers at me. *"Shuffle the cards, and we shall never speak of this again."*

"Fine with me."

Rowan leaned over to the bowl and began to eat some more. "Are you sure you want to eat that?"

Rowan seemed confused. *"I don't waste food. Shut up and deal."*

I shook my head and asked, "What are we playing and what are we playing for?" Rowan chomped on his cereal. "And for that matter how are you going to play? Not trying to be mean, but you've got claws, not opposable thumbs."

*"Three cards, you'll be the dealer, and I'll worry about my cards thank you very much."*

"Fine." I dealt us each three cards before putting the deck down.

*"Will you find a piece of paper and keep score?"*

"Yes." I tore a blank sheet from the back of my sketchpad.

Rowan hopped over and using his claws lifted the first card just a little and contorted his head so he could look at it. He put it down and hopped to the next one, repeating the process until he had seen all three cards. *"Well?"*

"I haven't checked my cards yet."

*"I noticed. Simple wagers. The point of this exercise is to keep your emotions hidden and bluff. So far you're failing."*

I lifted each of my cards a little and viewed each, as I worked to keep my face blank. Not easy considering I had a pair of Jacks and the two of diamonds.

*"I'm in. Are you in or out?"*

"In."

*"Are you sure?"*

"Yes."

*"Let's see them."*

I flipped my cards over.

*"Not bad, but I still beat you."*

What do you mean?"

"Straight."

"No way you got a straight with the first hand."

"You were the dealer, are you telling me a raven outsmarted a witch?"

I flipped his cards over. Sure enough, he had a straight.

"*I knew you had a great hand because you were excited. First game is out of the way. Impress me.*"

We played for hours.

"*You're getting better. Stop raising your left brow when you have a winning hand, and don't release an audible breath when your hand is bad. Work on that, you'll soon be there. But enough, I'm not much of a card player; do you play chess?*"

"Yes, almost every day when I'm at school. I carved the pieces to my set." I went to my drawer to retrieve it. "I made this during the school year. I hoped my father and I would start up our usual summer chess games."

"I wanted to start with cards because it's easier to see your tells. Chess, on the other hand, is a better game of strategy, everything is in the open."

I brought the board over to the bed and began setting it up.

"*Very nice.*"

"This is the first time I've used the set."

"*Are you sure you don't want to wait and play with your father first?*"

"No. I made this to be played." Then I had a thought. Picking up my sketchpad I started drawing.

"*What are you drawing?*"

"You will see." Rowan started on some of the fruit as I worked. Several minutes later I finished. I put the pad down and dragged a nightstand even with the bed as Rowan hopped over.

"Come, perch on my right shoulder."

He flew to my shoulder, excited.

"Now who isn't hiding their excitement?"

"*Quit stalling.*"

I laughed and reached into the pad. Just as I was about to grab the edge I pulled back so Rowan could see, and I explained, "It's kind of like reaching in and grabbing a rock out of a stream: always slightly off from where you expect the object to be." I reached back in, pulled out the perch I had drawn, and put it on the nightstand. Rowan looked from the page to the perch and back.

"Well, what do you think?"

He leaped off my shoulder and landed on the perch. *"Amazing, a perfect fit. You even made the diameter wide enough for my claws. You're talented. I think I shall keep you as a chess partner. After all, what else will the two of us do while she is gone?"*

"I would love to be your opponent."

*"One question before we start. Can you put the perch back, and can I reach in and pull it out or store it again?"*

"I've never tried. Let's find out."

Rowan hopped off the perch and on the bed. I picked it up knowing I would be able to put the perch back. With ease, the perch went back into the pad and became the pencil drawing again.

*"Amazing,"* Rowan said. He reached down with his beak and tapped the edge of the page. It sounded and looked solid. *"How do I grasp it?"*

I rubbed my head thinking. "Not sure; give me a moment to think this through." Rowan left me in silence as he stared at the sketchpad and walked in circles.

"Rowan, what do you know of magic?"

*"Much, but I can't do it. I rely on my speed, silence, observation, and flight to survive."*

I picked up the sketchpad and worked the spell I had come up with.

*I grant access to claw, feather, and Lydia to replace or grab as needed. May this be resistant to fire, water, wrinkles, smudges, and tears, with no one able to change the spell but me.*

I wrote it along the edge, and it disappeared once I finished the last word. "Do you want to try it?"

*"Yesss,"* he hissed.

I set the sketchpad on the bed and Rowan hopped over to it, then hesitated.

"Go ahead," I said. He tentatively put a claw on the sketchpad. It held, so he followed with a second. With both feet on the pad he slid his foot, ever so slowly, closer to the drawing. He'd edged to within an inch of the drawing when he did something unexpected, he stuck his head into the sketchpad … and it disappeared into the sketch. As he looked around, his head became a two-dimensional drawing which lined up with the headless raven on my bed.

"Rowan!"

He snapped upward and looked at me in surprise. *"What?"*

"Your head disappeared into the pad and became part of the sketch. Are you all right?"

*"I am. It was weird in there. I can't decide if it's a box around the perch or something else, but everything was white except the object"*

"Could you breathe?"

Rowan tilted his head considering my question. *"Don't know. I held my breath. Like you said, it's much like putting your head under water. I'm going to try."*

I nodded, and he stuck his head in again. The sketch of him appeared again as he moved around.

*"Strange,"* he said just before he jumped into the sketchpad to sit upon the perch. One moment he'd been a full-size raven, the next a perfect sketch of a raven sat upon a perch. Scared, I reached my hand in. For the first time, I saw a sketch of my hand in the sketchpad. In the distant I heard a caw and watched the animated pencil sketch act out. Rowan grasped the perch in his claws and took flight. I pulled my hand back as he rushed out of the pad with the perch in his claws.

Rowan landed on the nightstand as I laughed at his exuberance. "Are you all right?"

He sat on his perch doing a funny dance with his head and neck as he began to chirp, like a songbird.

"You are fantastic!"

"Glad I can do parlor tricks for you."

He stopped, cocked his head to look at me. *"That's no parlor trick. You are gifted and should keep this to yourself. Never let those of the KIC know. I wouldn't even tell your family."*

I realized the wisdom in his advice. Revealing your abilities in magic is like showing your hand at cards too soon, a losing proposition. If those around me knew what I could do they would have expectations and my freedom would diminish. I would be drawn deeper into the drama and politics. No thanks.

"I won't."

*"It is good I'm giving you bluffing lessons."*

"Yes. Tell me, what was it like in there?"

*"My guess is you somehow bend, fold, or stretch space. The most interesting part is looking out at you: it's like watching TV. You are in color with depth, but when I look around inside, everything is white and two-dimensional."*

"I'm glad you're okay, and that this worked."

Rowan bowed to me. *"No, I am honored with the gift you made and bestowed upon me. I shall treasure it."*

"A gift for a friend."

*"You call me a friend?"* he asked with a hint of something I couldn't place.

"Yes."

*"I have never had a friend before. You honor me again."*

"What about Lydia?"

*"Lydia is a friend, but different. We are the same soul, but different parts of a whole. I know where she is at any time, and if she is troubled or happy. What is between us is different, unlike anything I have experienced. If I can ever do anything for you, please ask."*

"You don't need to do anything for me, Rowan. Well, except make your move.

*"Pawn to E4, if you please."*

I moved his white pawn, then my pawn. "Is there something else you would like?"

*"What do you mean?"*

"Objects stored in the paper won't increase the weight. All I have to do is draw it. Everything but food. For some reason the food looks right, but tastes like cardboard."

Rowan eyed me. *"What do I say? No one has ever offered me such. I hunt or steal my food, and find my shelter."*

He called his next move, and I made mine as I suggested, "How about a small bag? I could make it so it fixes to your chest.

We could place the paper with your things in it. The way I worked the spell, only you, Lydia, or I could get anything out. I could add a deck of cards, a chess set, a blanket … you could store all of your things in there."

"I have nothing to give you in exchange."

"I'm not asking for anything. It costs me nothing but a few minutes of my time."

"Then please, I would love to have what you offer; everything you mentioned and some others."

"What else do you desire?"

Rowan laughed. "*A library full of books, with a fireplace, furs, and a window looking out at a mountain lake.*"

"Man, you *do* want it all. I'll draw everything mentioned on a new sheet. You shall live like a king." He called his next move and I dragged the rook to it. "But today, let me create something you can carry your things in."

"Yes."

He won the next two, but I finally beat him on the final game.

"*When Lydia is away would you like to play chess?*"

"Sure, but we'll need to find a park where we can play. My mom is too high a risk for us both."

"Yes, she is."

I picked up his perch and inserted it back into the page. "Rowan, would let me lock you in there on the perch for a couple of minutes so I can draw your pouch on you?"

He turned his head considering, as he clicked his beak. "*Will I need to be there long?*"

"No. Five minutes tops."

He hopped over next to the sheet of paper. "*I trust you; be quick.*"

"I will."

Rowan hopped into the sheet. Once he was settled, I wrote on the page: *Let me draw upon Rowan without harming him.*

I drew a square pouch affixed to his chest, with straps over and under his wings, adjustable by pulling on the strap. I gave the material the appearance of leather, then colored the bag black.

Done, I released Rowan. He flew out of the page and landed on the bed.

He rocked back and forth on his feet and tittered as he looked down at the pack on his chest.

"How does it feel?"

"*It fits. I love it, but it tickled when you drew on me.*"

I took the sheet of paper from the bed, folded it into fourths and placed it into his pack. Rowan cawed loudly with excitement. "Rowan, my brother will hear you." Rowan looked sheepish.

Then I heard Guy's door open. "Gray, did you hear that?" he said from the other side of the door. The door handle turned.

"Are you in …" His voice trailed off as he entered my room and saw me sitting on my bed. "Why didn't you answer me?"

"Sorry, a bird flew into my window and scared me, I chased it out."

Guy rubbed the back of his head. "A bird?"

"Yes, a big black one."

"A good thing mom isn't here. Why did you open your window?"

"I wanted the fresh air. Mom grounded me to my room and probably hexed the house in case I tried to leave."

## CHAPTER SIX

**Mabon, Cornwall, England**

I wrote my destination on the mirror with the marker: our family's vacation home in Santa Cruz. The words disappeared into the mirror. Before going through, I thought about the house, and figured the power would be off. I considered what I might need.

I grabbed a backpack from a shelf, a flashlight, a large pocketknife, a sketchpad, and pens. I shoved it all in the pack. With the bag on my shoulder, I walked through the mirror.

I came out into the closet of my childhood. The open door offered some daylight to work with, but not enough. I pulled the pack off, got my flashlight out, and hit the button. The closet lightened to reveal several empty hangers and one old hoodie. It smelled of dust.

Moving into my room felt like stepping through a time warp. On my desk set an old-style tube TV and record player; my old

Santa Cruz skateboard leaned against the wall next to the window. I walked over and picked up my board lovingly. I set it aside and thought about how much time I had. I figured three hours at the outside before people wondered where I'd gotten off to. Better get moving.

Downstairs things were newer. My parents still spent summers here, they must have updated some of the furniture and technology over the years. I walked out the front door into a beautiful California day. A light wind blew from the beach as the temperature hovered somewhere in the seventies. Perfect. I took a big breath, realizing how much I missed this place. I shut the door behind me and walked down the street toward Hilda Rosdew's house.

As I walked, I considered the chances of her still living there and figured they were good. A large house close to the beach? Why would anyone sell it? But would there be staff living here year-round? I thought that over; I doubted it.

From a distance I saw the large house, painted the same white and sand colors with a shingle roof. I approached from the front and checked the mailbox. On the side, it read ROSDEW. Lucky me. I went to the corner, crossed the street, and leaned against a post watching the house. No one was parked in front or on the side driveway, but I couldn't tell about the garage. Five minutes passed and everything remained quiet in the neighborhood. I walked across the street to the back of the house.

I looked around. Would the neighbors be able to witness me breaking in? The bushes on the side of the house rose high enough to block the view of the back door. What if the house had hexes? I hadn't considered that. Good thing I carried a special creation for such occasions. I took my necklace out. My mother had one of the Jernigans, the metal-touched family, make it for me. They imbue magic into metal which heats if it detects a hex. I took the necklace off, a chain with a silver charm, and held it in my hand to test the door. The metal remained cold, no hex.

I stuck my pen in the lock and whispered, "Open."

I entered an empty kitchen. It was clear Hilda had not been here for a long time. Perhaps she had had health problems towards the end and didn't travel? It would explain why I had not heard anything about her recently other than her death. The house was dark. I tried a light switch; no power. I put my backpack down, pulled out my flashlight. I began to wonder just how long it had been since someone had been here. From the condition of the house—decor, dust, and technology—the answer was a *long* time.

I put my pack back on and moved out of the kitchen with the hex-detector in my outstretched hand, being careful to stay away from the windows. The first few rooms, living room, office, water closet, were not of interest to me. Instead, I went to the second floor to find Lydia's room. I would start there, and then search through the office and Hilda's room if I had to. I found Lydia's room at the end of a hall. The door wouldn't open ... It had been closed for a long time, and swelled from weather and non-use. I figured it had to belong to her because it was the only closed door in the entire house. Using my shoulder, I forced it open.

The curtains were closed, leaving the room in darkness. *Good,* I thought, *no one will see me in here.* I found the switch on the flashlight and turned it to the lantern function. The dark room filled with light.

Her room surprised me, now that I could see it. A four-poster bed with a canopy stood by the window, white with different shades of pink lace for the bedding and curtains. I bet her grandmother had decorated the room. Lydia had always been more of an adventurous tomboy. And she loved blue; I don't remember her not wearing something blue.

To my left, I glimpsed the one thing in the room which made me think of Lydia, a large bookshelf overflowing with books and comics. This is where I would start looking. Here is where she would hide anything personal. I pulled everything down from the top shelf setting it on the ground in stacks. With five overflowing shelves, this would take some time.

I started with the first book: a copy of *Wuthering Heights*, a well-worn hardcover. Some of the pages were dog-eared, and there was nothing but an old bookmark in it. I was just about to set the book aside when I realized it was not a bookmark, but one of the many strips of black and white photos we'd collected. I set the book aside to take it with me.

Twelve books later I finished with that shelf and put them back as I had found them minus *Wuthering Heights*. I repeated the process on the next three shelves with no results. The last shelf contained comics and would take more time. Sorting through them I came to her favorite: her original copies of *Sandman*.

At the back of issue eight, I found several photos, some of us, some of just her or Rowan. I smiled as I viewed the pile of photos. Suddenly I realized I didn't own a picture of Rowan; I missed that bird. One of the last photos was a candid of Rowan and me playing chess in the park. I put them back and set the comic on the copy of *Wuthering Heights*. The rest of the comics yielded nothing. All that was left were a couple of large books, a dictionary, and an encyclopedia.

Both the dictionary and encyclopedia were hardcovers, and I almost didn't open them except, as I went to put them back, I thought they seemed light. The dictionary fell from my hand and the cover flipped open, revealing a pocket she'd created by gluing the pages together and cutting a hole in the middle. There I found the letters I'd sent her, silly little mementos like movie tickets, more photos, and one of Rowan's feathers.

I remembered she would always pick up the feathers he lost. She worried someone could use the feather against him or her. Not unrealistic; he was a magical creature and anything of theirs holds power. I collected everything and put it on the pile to go with me. Next, I opened the encyclopedia. In there it seemed she kept her valuables, a couple hundred dollars in cash, earrings, and bracelets.

Done with the bookshelf, I moved on to the dresser and nightstands. Nothing. The closet held a few clothes and shoes, but nothing else. I searched for a hidden compartment but didn't find one. I was about to give up when I thought to look under the bed. Score! A blue binder was pushed up in the far corner by the nightstand. With some crawling on the floor and sneezing from the dust I managed to grab it.

The binder was the kind with the clear pockets so you can put a cover sheet on the outside. She had used one of my drawings, of her on the pier at sunset as she stood in her favorite spot. I had drawn the picture one night as I came upon her and given it to her for Winter Solstice.

I opened the binder and found printed pages, more than a hundred in the two-inch binder. At first, I thought maybe it might be schoolwork. Then I realized what it was: one of her stories. She loved to write. For some reason, no matter how much encouragement I had given her, she had been insecure about it.

The first page read: "The Withering Heart, by Lydia Rose". She had used a pen name; I could see where she got Rose out of Rosdew, but I liked to think Penrose had something to do with her selection. It was dated September 1991. Something pinged in my head. She wouldn't let me read her books, but sometimes she would tell me stories. Well, she let me read some of her stories. For Samhain, she would send me scary short stories, and for Winter Solstice, a winter tale. I loved them. I had them bound them together into a leather volume, which I keep close. But she never let me read her longer stories.

I collected the treasures I'd found and stuffed them in my backpack. I checked my watch—set to Cornwall time. I still had another hour on the limit I had set myself. I was reluctant to leave her room because it was the first time in years I felt somewhat close to her. Once in the hall, I bit my tongue and closed the door. My next stop was Hilda's room. I pulled my charm out of my pocket. With it back in my palm, I started down the hall.

The door to Hilda's grand bedroom stood wide open. I started to cross the threshold, but the charm in my hand heated. It got so hot I nearly dropped it, but I didn't want to risk it falling into her room where I couldn't reach it. I backed out, my hand hurting. Hitting the wall of the hallway, I took a big breath and finally allowed the charm to drop. I blew on my hand to try to cool the burn. Whatever she had hidden in there, she didn't want it to be found. There was no way I could break the hex either.

I wondered if there might be anything in there I might need. Why wouldn't the hex have faded like the curse she had put on me did? Wouldn't it fade, too? I wondered. I didn't know much about black magic, but I did understand a little about hexes. Hexes were not off limits to the Kind by law, as long as they didn't use outlawed magic or hurt someone outright, they were okay. Most families used hexes like humans use locks, to keep people out.

Curses were different. Curses pulled power from the person who cast them, not just once, but continually. This made curses risky, especially powerful ones. The way around the power draw is to use a dark object. I bet she had used something of mine to make a dark object. She must have kept it on her, where it would have pulled a limited amount of power, barely noticeable. But when she had died the power source would too. I needed to get to her body as soon as possible.

I doubted what I needed would be in her room. If I was lucky, what I wanted would be in her office. Tomorrow--no, tonight--after the wedding I would go see Hilda's body. I checked my watch to find time was slipping away from me. I started down the stairs when I remembered the charm on the floor. Backtracking, I picked it up with my other hand and examined it. The silver had darkened in color.

After what happened at Hilda's room, I held the charm out over the threshold of the office before I crossed it. Nothing happened, and I sighed with relief. A massive oak desk sat on an Oriental rug to one side of the dark room. I used my flashlight to search the drawers.

In the long middle drawer, I found things one would expect: pens, clips, wax and the Rosdew's seal. The next couple of drawers didn't yield anything. A big file drawer on the left side held paperwork. I thought about taking everything with me but decided it might not be a good idea. Lucky for me Hilda had been OCD about her filing system--everything labeled and in its place.

A tab labeled "Lydia" hung toward the back. I removed the whole folder. I smoothed the others out, so when the family went through the paperwork they wouldn't know anything was missing. Most of the label were names: Angelica, Jessy, Jory, Kate and Kerensa.

I shook my head, glad not to be one of her relatives. It looked like she had taken an active interest in them. Some of the files were thick. Closing all the drawers, I did my best to make it seem like the desk had not been disturbed. As I was about to leave I reconsidered; opening the drawer I removed Jessy's file, too. I adjusted the contents again and put both folders, along with the flashlight, in my backpack. I decided I didn't need to worry about any more hexes so I put the necklace back on. With my backpack and flashlight in hand, I started to leave when my signet ring shocked me. Not a little shock either. My hand, still red from the charm, clenched tightly. I fell to my knees and dropped the flashlight.

*Damn it!* One of my parents was summoning me. They had no idea I was on the other side of the world. Another shock hit me. I had to get back, and fast. Once the summons started I couldn't take the ring off, and the longer I took, the more painful the shocks would get. If I had been in Cornwall, it would have been little more than a nuisance. I rode the waves of pain until it eased.

I left through the back door, locking the door as I did. I took off, walking fast. The street was empty and, once there, I took off running. At this point I saw no harm in anyone seeing me. I had an alibi in Cornwall. Who would ever dream I could transport myself to the other side of the world?

Back at our vacation home, I ran in the back door, locked it, and sprinted to my room and the closet's mirror.

# CHAPTER SEVEN

### June 1988, Santa Cruz, California

More than a week passed before I saw Lydia again, but Rowan came by every day at the same time. He became my alarm clock. He would tap on the window, I would wake, get ready, and skate to a park almost a mile away, near the beach. I would bring food for Rowan to eat, and we would play chess, checkers, cards, backgammon, in addition to lengthy discussions on magic, philosophy, and life. As much as I enjoyed our time, I wanted to see Lydia. I never asked about her, other than to ask what she might be doing that day. Rowan sensed my desire to see her and would tell me stories about her.

One day, we were playing a rather intense game of chess at sundown.

"Rowan, what do people see when they look at you?"

He made a popping noise, which meant he was laughing. *"I have a glamour, for a bird of my size would scare people. Funny thing* is I'm nowhere as big as my grandmother. I was bespelled so I would appear as different birds, from a finch to a starling or magpie. The glamour doesn't work on those of Kind blood."

I raised my brows at him in astonishment. "Who placed the glamour upon you?"

"I was young and don't know, but likely one of the Norse line."

I felt my brows meet my hairline. "You're telling me some of the gods have survived?"

He tilted his head and eyed me. "Yes, their descendants. Not Odin or Thor ... well, at least, I don't think so. There's a man who has the title of Odin, much like the Romans used the title of Caesar. You must understand, the binding put upon them from the Christians is quite strong. When they bound the old gods, their power was absolute."

"Has it weakened over time?"

"It's weakening, because of human's interest in what they see as old myths; the Greeks, Romans, and even Egyptians are seeing the benefit of people believing or reading their old stories. Humans have power, their thoughts and beliefs give us power."

I made my move as I considered what he'd said. "How does it work?"

"What do you mean?"

"How does being a Muninn work?"

He tilted his head up to look at the sky. "We're everywhere. I was born in the northlands and raised there. It's where I will return to mate one day. Once we're a few weeks old we go before Muninn or Huginn to be named, and their Oracle tells us where we are to go. Then we receive our grandmother's blessing and a glamour. I left the lands of my people on the anniversary of when I hatched."

"They told you that you would be a familiar to Lydia? Are there other Muninns who are familiars?"

"At first no, but I'm much older than Lydia. For years my orders sent me to watch someone or something, to be present at one event or another, then I would be called home to tell of my observations.

"When I went in front of the Oracle I received a weird reception." He started eating some cereal—still a strange thing to think he could talk and eat at the same time—and his words took on a strange crunchy sound. *"My name was picked because of the Oracle's* predictions. I was named for the magical rowan tree. In my culture, it's called 'the Salvation of Thor.' They didn't tell me my future, but in the early days, I was given tough assignments and trained harder than most. One day I was called before my grandmother. She told me I would be summoned soon and to heed the call when it came. When it did I would be relieved of the duties of a Muninn. She said they may call me again one day to hear of my journeys, but I would have an honor no Muninn had ever received."

"Really? That's impressive."

"Yes, it was. Within a month, Lydia called me to a rowan tree in the countryside of Cornwall. She was just a little thing then, about five years in age. I've been with her since."

"I'm jealous. It's nice having your company, Rowan."

"I enjoy your company too. But I have news: Lydia will come tomorrow, her grandmother has to return to the East Coast for the next week to attend to business. Lydia wants to come early, she's miserable."

I sat up so fast I smacked my leg on the stone table leg. "Ouch."

Rowan laughed. *"Somebody's excited."* He sobered and called his move to me. *"Checkmate."*

I focused back on the board and realized he was right. He'd taken advantage of my distraction. His laughter returned. I didn't think I liked the bird anymore; he played dirty.

· ෴ ·

## 8:15 am the next day

*Click, click, clack. Click, click, clack.* I sat up in bed massaging my temples, disoriented. What time was it? I glanced at the clock in time to see it turn to 8:16. *I can go back to sleep.*

*Click, click ...*

"Go away, Rowan. It's too early."

In my head, Rowan said, *"Get up lazy. Lydia is waiting for you down at the pier. You are keeping her waiting."*

"Be there in a few," I said it aloud, though Rowan had been teaching me I didn't need to. When he was near me, he kept the line open between us.

I jumped in the shower, got dressed, and grabbed my things. I had started down the stairs before I remembered to grab the bag of goodies I had packed the previous night for Rowan. After backtracking, I was nearly to the door when I heard, "Where are you going?"

I turned to see my mother. The tone of her voice told me to be careful. Swallowing hard, I put a large fake smile on my face.

"To the beach, to skate with some friends from school."

She emerged from the shadows. It was unusual to see my mother so early in the day. "Will you be gone most of the day?"

"Yes."

Her eyes narrowed. "Go and don't return early. I need some sleep, and I'll kill anybody who wakes me. I'm sending your brother out, too."

"I won't disturb you. I promise."

She started walking up the stairs. "Oh ... and we are going back home for a few days. We're leaving tomorrow."

I froze. Please, no, I didn't want to leave. I watched her, just before she reached the top, I said, "Mom?"

She stopped. My mouth felt as dry as 100-degree asphalt. "Would you consider letting Guy and me stay here? I'll be on my best behavior."

She sighed, "Your idea *is* the better solution. I will talk it over with your dad."

· ☸ ·

## Santa Cruz Pier

There she was, perched on the same post where I had first seen her; face tilted to the sun with her eyes closed and Rowan circling above her head. It's one of those moments; when I close my eyes, I can see it again, accompanied by the salty smell of the ocean and a warm breeze.

I kicked up my board and walked toward her. At the base of the piling, I stood looking up at her. She jumped down, landing next to me.

"Finally! I was getting impatient."

"Sorry, my mother wanted a word with me before I left."

*"Everything okay?"* Rowan asked.

"Yes."

*"Good, I shall leave for a while, there are things to do. Keep her safe, my friend."*

"I will."

She ran into my arms and buried her face against me. "Thank you, for being so kind to Rowan. I owe you."

"Don't tell him, but he's very entertaining and fun to hang out with."

"I'll make it up to you. You're the only one who knows anything about him, and you have treated him better than my family treats me." She released her hug.

"Well, to be honest," I said, "I don't have anyone to talk to either. I'm jealous; I want a familiar."

"Sorry, having had Rowan for so long I can't imagine life without him. Could we get you a familiar?"

"Ah, I don't know. How did you get him?"

"I was young. Let's see … I had just gotten to boarding school, and there was this rowan tree on the grounds. I felt compelled to go to the tree. I dreamed of it many times. One night I snuck out after bed and went to the tree. It was a full moon. I pulled down a branch with some berries to look at and cut my hand. The blood must have been a catalyst because he landed on my shoulder and eyed me. I lifted my cut hand to him and he took some of my blood. Shortly after that he started speaking to me in my head, and has continued ever since. No really, he never shuts up."

"He drank your blood? Gross."

"The blood was the sacrifice to the magical tree which bonded us."

"How was the time with your grandma?" I asked, changing the subject.

"Terrible and boring. I felt like I was on display. I hope she doesn't do that to me again, but I know she's going to. At least it gets me a vacation in California."

"Do you want to learn how to skate?"

"Yes, but how? Will I borrow your board?"

"No. I got you your own."

"What?"

I undid my backpack and pulled out her board and a matching helmet. She gasped as she realized what I had.

"Where did you get it? The illustration looks just like Rowan."

"I drew it to look like him."

"The board and helmet on your pad? Like what you did for Rowan?"

"Yeah. It didn't cost me anything, just time. These are yours."

Her face lit up and she hugged me again. I could get used to this. My family isn't terrible, but there has never been a lot of physical affection. Or it could be because Lydia is doing the hugging.

"I can't get over how kind you are to me. Now show me how to use this." She held the board up.

"Hope you don't mind a sore butt. Because you're going to fall on it a lot."

"No, I won't, I have exceptional balance. I'm also a quick study." She lifted her head with confidence.

She *was* a quick study, and a better skater than me. We skated most of the morning and then I took her to McDonald's for lunch.

It's interesting watching someone have their first Big Mac and fries. Lydia opened the carton and stared at the burger. With big eyes she turned to me and asked, "How am I supposed to eat that?"

My brows drew together in confusion. "With your mouth?"

She rolled her eyes. "My mouth won't fit around it."

Laughing I showed her how to squish it. Once she figured out how, she devoured the Big Mac. "This is much better than the hot dog. Also why do you call these fries?" She held one up. "They're called chips."

"In England. I'll get you some potato chips to try tomorrow."

She looked at me with narrowed eyes as if she thought I might be teasing her.

"I believe you would call them crisps. We call them chips. It's not the Queen's English here."

As I took a bite of my food, something I had never felt before hit me like a panic attack. I couldn't hide my reaction, and Lydia immediately placed her hand on my shoulder.

"What is it?"

"I don't know." The door in front of us opened, and my brother walked through. The cause of my panic was related to him in some way. I put my hand on Lydia's arm and pulled it from mine. It wouldn't do Lydia or me any good if Guy figured out I liked her.

Guy's attention turned to Lydia but didn't hold it long. "You aren't easy to locate, why is that?"

"How should I know? And why do you want me?"

A locator spell, he must have used something I valued to find me.

"So suspicious; I came here to thank you."

"Yeah, right. What did you use to find me?"

"A page out of your sketchpad, you left it on your bed. I figured it was the last thing you used. Who's the witch?"

Shit, I was linked to my sketchpad. I'd have to remember to keep it close to me. I gulped my soda trying to hide my surprise.

Now Guy focused on Lydia. "Hello. Please forgive my brother's bad manners. I'm Guy, his older brother. What's your name?"

Uh, oh, this wasn't going in a direction I liked.

"It's nice to meet you, Guy, I'm Lydia Rosdew."

He blinked as he absorbed that. Rosdew and Penrose families don't mix well, which is usually a problem. The Rosdew's affinity is spirit magic, and they tended to be necromancers. Many within our world believed the Rosdews were more connected with the Druids than the fae.

"A pleasure," he said.

"Yeah, I see you brought your charming self. Now tell me why you're here again?"

My brother's ease with people always bothered me. He made it seem so easy to make friends and be liked. Girls fell at his feet and worshiped the ground he walked on. Of course, the strong possibility he could be the male to break the binding set on the Kind by the Christians probably didn't hurt. What worried me was Lydia falling for him.

"Believe it or not, I'm here to thank you for the suggestion you made to mom. She has decided it was a good idea. They'll allow us to stay here while they return home. They'll be gone at least a week, perhaps more."

I felt my eyebrow lift. "I don't like the sound of that. It's too easy."

Guy scratched the back of his neck as he shifted his weight. "Yes, it was. But I know nothing more than you." He glanced at the order counter and must have decided he was hungry. Without another word, he walked off to order food.

Lydia watched him walk away. "Are you sure you two are related?"

"Unfortunately, yes, we are."

I watched Lydia chewing on her bottom lip. I must have been in the throes of adolescent hormones because my focus was her cherry red lips as she nibbled them.

"I guess I can see it now in the shape of your face. But you two don't look much alike."

"He takes after our mom, while I look like my dad."

Guy return with a tray of food and sat down opposite us in the booth. He opened the Styrofoam box with his Big Mac.

"So Lydia, what's a witch like you doing out here in Cali? My parents told me they picked their vacation home out here because most of the Kind don't care for the surf and sand."

She took a sip of her drink, before answering, "Don't know. It's the first time. My grandmother has a place here and asked me to spend the summer with her."

"You live in Cornwall?"

"Yes."

"Well, keep my brother out of trouble, please. It will make my life easier this summer."

She shrugged her shoulders, "What fun is staying out of trouble?"

He smiled at her.

Lydia batted her eyelashes at him. "I plan to skate, surf, eat my fill of junk food, and stay off my grandmother's radar. If Gray follows me, there shouldn't be any problems."

# CHAPTER EIGHT

### Mabon, two hours from sundown, Cornwall, England

I came through the portal with my hand burning. The pain lessened immediately. In the bathroom, I sighed with relief from being close enough for the pain to be a fraction of what it had been in California. My father probably never considered pain being proportional to distance or that I could be half way around the world when he summoned me. Honestly, I felt like a demon summoned to a pentagram.

Hurriedly, I opened my sketchpad and lowered the backpack into a page. Taking a pen, I locked it in so no one save me could get to it. I quickly checked my appearance in the mirror. My hair was windblown from the California breezes. Picking up the brush, I made my hair presentable and headed to face the wrath of my parents.

I was about to head downstairs, where I thought they would be, when I felt a slight tug from the ring. It led me down a hallway to a door near the end. By the cold emanating from the ring I knew my summoner was behind that door. I knocked.

The door opened and I found my father glaring at me, I lifted an eyebrow as if to say, *You summoned, Master?* His lowered brows said, *Not funny, get your ass in here.*

Do you ever have the feeling you're about to regret ever being born? Well, as I peered into my parent's room, I saw my brother pacing the floor and my mother looking out the window. I felt I was walking to my death.

Dad slammed the door; at least he let me get inside before he did it. My mother jumped but didn't say anything. About this time my brain registered the wrongness of this situation. First, my father never gets mad; he is the easy-going one. And my mother was quiet, almost humble, as she stared out the window. Then there was Guy, worked up to a level I'd never seen before.

"Where have you been? No one saw you leave and we couldn't figure out where you were. We've put this damnable conversation off because you weren't here. We could have used your help to answer questions and put out fires. Tell me: where were you?"

"Oh, dad, leave him alone. If I were Gray, I would disappear, too. You're just taking your anger out on him because he could do it and you couldn't."

Wow, we were in new territory here. Never in my life had I heard either of them snap like this. My mother stood quietly. Could she be the one in trouble?

"Thanks, Guy, but I should have been here for you. Aquila freaked me out." I turned to my dad. "I'm sorry. I shouldn't have left without telling you where I was going. Is there something I can do now?"

My dad's shoulders slumped.

"I guess I'll start this," said Guy. Dad nodded his head and waved his hand to continue. "Mom." She didn't look at him. "Would you care to explain what the Oracle meant?"

Her eyes slid over him briefly before turning back to the window. With tears in her eyes, she said, "Not really."

"Tell me, I deserve to know what's going on. I'm getting married in a couple of hours. If she will still have me, that is. Now explain." His tone rose on the last two words.

"You're the heir, there's nothing for you to be concerned about," she said in a low tone.

"No. She said, and I quote, 'You are not who you think you are. The heir to one but not the other.' What does that mean?"

The tears in my mother's eyes streamed down her face. "It means you're not the Penrose heir; Grayson is."

*"What?"* I yelled. There was no way I was the heir! She closed her eyes and flinched at my reaction. "Tell her she's wrong, dad."

"Jessamine, you need to explain yourself. How is Guy not the heir; our heir?"

She wiped her eyes with her sleeve. "Because, he isn't your son. I hoped and thought he was, but we just learned he isn't."

"Was it *him?*" Rage tinted the edges of his words.

"Yes, the night before he died."

My father looked stricken.

"Who?" asked Guy.

"I was betrothed before your father. He died in some magic ritual--a black magic ritual--two days before the wedding. Less than a week later I was promised to Jowan, and we married within a couple of weeks. I didn't know."

"Did you suspect it?" Guy asked.

"Yes, sometimes. But I thought Jowan was your father. I hope that doesn't change."

"Guy, you *are* my son." He walked over to my mom and put a hand on her back. "Jessamine, you should have told me."

"I didn't want you to hate me, or not want me. How could you love Guy had you known?"

He cradled her face in his hands. "I loved you the moment I met you. I never could get you to understand that. What happened to you was cruel. Your family shouldn't have pawned you off like that, and mine shouldn't have accepted, but they did and I don't regret it."

"How could you forgive me, knowing who it was?"

My father tried to smile, "I didn't know you then, and you grew up with him. We were young. There will be a scandal, so we'll want to talk to Davidson and the Marraks to minimize it. But I don't care. We'll ride this out together."

I walked over and hugged my mother.

"Thank you, Gray."

Guy stood watching us, with a distant look on his face.

"Who am I?"

Mom went to respond, but my dad stopped her. "Your father was betrothed to her before me. I didn't know either of them. She grew up here in Cornwall. Her family tried to get rid of her as fast as possible because her fiancé had been caught and killed doing black magic. She couldn't marry anyone here, because of that. My father had been a childhood friend of her dad's, and they arranged it. As quietly as possible because of the scandal it would have caused."

"Would you get to the point?"

"Yes. Your father was Alan Wayfarer."

I couldn't swallow. Guy looked as if his world had just shattered.

In a shaky voice, Guy said, "Please tell me this is a joke."

Both of my parents shook their heads.

"You raised me, the child of your worst enemy? Am I the cuckoo bird's baby? Put into your nest to raise as your own, only to find out I'm not?"

"Guy, I told you the Wayfarer and Penrose vendetta is no more. There's no hostility toward any of them. Plus, Alan was from an old distant line of Wayfarers. You can be proud of being from a strong family and loved by this one. I see no reason for this to be a problem. It happens, in our world, with the pressures of not getting to pick your mate or having to wait for years. There's no shame in anything she did. She was to marry Alan, how was she to know he'd do what he did?"

Guy stared at him with a blank look.

"I will go talk to Davidson and the Marraks, they deserve to know. This will be made public and you'll be expected to take the Wayfarer name."

"How can you handle this so calmly? Hell, you aren't even my dad."

"Watch how you speak to me. I am still your father even if your name changes. Pull yourself together. You and I are going to fix this. I raised you to take responsibility," he said as he walked over to Guy. My father stood several inches above him. He grabbed Guy into a hug until Guy relented.

"I'm sorry," Guy said.

"Don't be. It's a lot to take in. We're here for you and your new family. We'll stand together, united. Everything is going to be fine. And now you don't have to worry about breaking the curse."

"Small favors."

"Come on, let's do this. Gray, stay with your mother."

As they left I wondered if Guy had ever suspected Jowan wasn't his father? I looked down at my mother, I still had an arm around her. Is that why she was always so concerned about my brother? Not that he would be the chosen male, but that he wasn't because of his father?

Damn it! I need to stop this. It didn't matter. Now that my worst nightmare had come true, it seemed a bit anticlimactic.

"It's you I should apologize to, Gray. You lost out on having the position of heir."

"I didn't want it, still don't. I don't want to marry and I don't want more responsibility. I'm done. I'll leave and join the human world. Just don't expect me to come back."

"You can't run away; they won't let you. Only I noticed you didn't go in front of the Oracle. You're the one. Somehow, I have always known it was you. Did you witness everything, or did you duck out early?"

"I left early."

"They've created a list of every male here, married, single, widowed, child. Each shall have a personal audience with the Oracle later this evening. Your name is already on there. You can't run. You're the *Guide*. You will change everything. Maybe it won't be that bad?"

"Come with me. I don't want to do this alone."

"Do what alone?"

"If Guy can go down and face this, I think I can meet with the Oracle."

She smiled. "I would love to come with you." With this burden off her, maybe we could develop a relationship. I put my arm around her and we walked downstairs to find Christopher Carn standing at the bottom of the stairs directing people.

"Christopher," I said.

"Yes?"

"I need to see the Oracle."

"Oh, yes. Well, the line is long. Perhaps after the wedding?"

"You can send the rest of the men away. Grayson is the one you're looking for," Mom said.

Christopher stared at my mom for a long moment, then at me. "Stay here a moment. I'll be right back."

As he walked off, I released the breath I had been holding. My mother rubbed my back. "Don't worry, Gray. We'll figure this out."

"Yeah."

A door to the left of the stairs opened: Guy, Dad, Kensa, her family, and Davidson walked out. They were talking to each other, and no one seemed upset or angry. I took this to be a good sign. Dad joined us, with Guy in tow.

"The Marraks didn't care, they like Guy. We'll just have to deal with the gossip. Let's get ready for the wedding," Dad said.

"No, Jowan, we can't yet." Her attention went to me and then to Guy. "Please, will you come with us? Gray has to face Aquila."

"Why?"

"Gray is the prophesied male. He needs to go before the Oracle. No reason to make everyone else go before her." Guy and my father looked at me as the information sank in.

Christopher came back. "Aquila is ready now."

I nodded my head as my family followed. "Davidson, you'll want to be present for this. Someone from the Council should witness this," said Christopher, and Davidson came even with our group.

"What will I be witnessing?"

I spoke up, "I need to go before Aquila. She hasn't seen me yet." Davidson's eyes went wide as he realized what I was saying. He nodded and followed us.

Aquila sat in the same throne-like chair to one side of the roaring fireplace. She even had her footstool again. The door shut behind us. Christopher led us to stand in front of her.

"Aquila."

"Yes, my boy?"

"I have found him."

She smiled, showing a mouth full of missing teeth. "I knew you would. Who is it?"

"Grayson James Penrose, the first-born son of Jowan Penrose and Jessamine Nancarrow."

"Ah, yes, always figured it would be a Penrose," Aquila said.

Christopher turned back to me. "Aquila Carn is the oldest member of the Kind. As a child, she was the one who foretold of the binding and the ones who would break it. I'm her great, great grandson. Right after I was born she told me, I would know the one and would help her find you. She's almost four hundred years old. She has held on to life waiting for you."

If this were true, then I was her life's work; a strange thing to be. Mom patted my back one more time as she pushed me forward.

She cocked her head and looked up at me. Her eyes clouded over. She looked blind and I didn't know if she could see me or not.

"Come near so I can get a good look at you. I'm holding off the spirits and I am weak. We don't have long," she said in that squeaky voice of hers. I moved forward and knelt.

"You're handsome; powerful, too." She touched my check. "It's you. Don't worry, in the end, you'll have everything you want. I didn't know you would have such a good heart; hold on to it, for you have a rough journey ahead of you."

Her hand dropped and she cleverly put something in my hand without the others seeing. She fainted. I reached out and managed to catch her just before her head hit the chair. Her limp body changed, becoming stiff as the spirit possession started. I moved the footstool out of the way as the Oracle made its presence known.

Aquila's body stood before the floating began and the overwhelming smell of ozone filled the room. Her hair stood on end and an eerie dark mist billowed out of her open mouth to wind about her.

Her eyes opened, showing gaping black holes. "Grayson James Penrose, we've waited a long time for you. You shall be our Guide." The Oracle smiled a terrible smile. "Lead with your heart, do not follow."

As if a light had gone out, the spirit left Aquila. She collapsed into a heap on the chair. Christopher and I ran to help her. Christopher got there first, seeming to expect this. He cradled her head as he began to weep over her; he knew, and so did I: she was gone.

I turned to the others in the room. Guy eyed me. He understood the burden I now carried, it had been his for years. My mom cried and my dad wrapped his arms around her, consoling her. Davidson look scared. I quickly managed to put the thing she'd given me safely in my pocket.

# CHAPTER NINE

### Summer of 1988, Santa Cruz, California

The next eight days were perfect. Guy left us alone to do what we wanted. We even managed to go to Disneyland. After a couple of days of skating Lydia decided we should both learn to surf. I admit I didn't like the idea, but after the first day, I was hooked.

Lydia's grandma returned first, and her plans for Lydia started again.

During those days without Lydia and no sign of my parents returning I decided to stay home to work on Rowan's library. Good thing, too, for the weather changed. The Santa Anna winds picked up, and the smoke from wildfires made life outside miserable. Before Rowan got there, I drew the walls, fireplace, and windows looking out into a forest. When he arrived, I let him pick the details.

"I would like an oak desk, and a red velvet couch next to the fire. It will need fur rugs on the floor and soft wool blankets on the furniture. A big stereo system on one of the shelves, and several lamps."

"You have a definite idea of how you want things, don't you?"

"Yes. Don't forget a gaming table in the corner, with a comfortable armchair and a perch at just the right height. A chess set, checkers, cards, poker chips, and backgammon, too."

"You do know this is going to take a long time? And we haven't started on the books yet."

I worked for several hours on the drawing. Once Rowan approved the major pieces, I colored everything in. Once I finished, we had just enough time for a game of chess.

"You know, if you would like, you can sleep in my closet tonight?"

He looked at me. *"Are you sure?"*

"I'm sure."

*"It would be nice to sleep inside again. Lydia spoiled me with her dorm room."*

I smiled at him as I placed my piece down to a checkmate. Rowan swore.

*"You distracted me so you could win. If I were not so grateful to you, I might be upset."*

"Yeah, yeah. I like giving you a taste of your own medicine."

I got him set up in my closet, a blanket up high and a newspaper just in case, since my window was staying closed with the smoke so thick outside.

The next morning, I awoke to a downpour outside my window. No surfing, but no more fires either. I looked in on Rowan. He slept deeply in his high perch. Everything in place, I went down to find something to eat. Tired of cereal, I made scrambled eggs and toast. Guy joined me, so I shared.

"Mom called last night. They'll be back tomorrow night."

"Did they tell you what's going on?"

"No. She did say they would have news when they got back."

"I don't like this, I think mom is up to something, and that's never good," I said.

"True, but I spoke to dad last night, too. They're in this together, which never happens," Guy said.

"What are you worried about? The next ten years of your life is planned out."

"With our mother, nothing is final, everything is negotiable. Whatever it is, it has to do with me."

"Paranoid much? Last time I checked, I was mother's punching bag."

He chuckled, "I'm taking the car and doing some running around today. I probably won't be back until late. Are you staying here?"

"Yeah, I'm staying home. I want to sleep."

"Where's your little witch?"

"Doing things with her grandmother."

"Gray--" is all Guy got out in a tone meaning he was about to lecture me.

"Guy, Lydia's thirteen, I'm fifteen. We're friends, nothing more."

He picked up his wallet and keys. "I'm out. But remember this conversation. Don't let mom suspect anything about Lydia, and I promise my lips are sealed."

"See ya later."

"'Bye."

I washed the dishes and put them in the dishwasher before heading upstairs with a bowl of cereal. Rowan still sat asleep on his blanket in the closet.

"Hey, sleepy bird," I said.

He stretched and opened his eyes to look at me. *"You have breakfast?"*

I held up his cereal. "Here's your Cocoa Puffs."

*"Oh Gray, you're an angel. But would you open your window? I need to attend to a couple of things first."*

"Of course," I said. He flew out, and I went to the bed and started coloring more of his library. After hours of work, I decided I was not sure how to apply the details or books.

A dry bird landed on my bed.

"Rowan, the only way I can think to do this is for me to draw the things, especially the books you want, on another piece of paper then put it on the shelves of the library."

"Have you ever tried drawing inside one of your pieces?"

"No. I never considered going in until you shoved your head in one. I'm still surprised you can breathe in there." Rowan stared at me with a less than amused look. "Why do you ask?"

"Because, what if you took your things into the library and drew in there?"

"You want me to jump into one of my pieces and work inside?"

"Yes."

I didn't like the idea of this, but my curiosity was piqued. *What was it like inside one of my drawings? Could I draw in one?* Curiosity won. Time to jump into the page. I shut the window, grabbed my sketchpad and supplies, turned off the light to my room and went into my closet.

I sat down with the pad. I wrote my spell and waited for the words to disappear. Once gone, Rowan hopped into the paper without a care. I hoped his trust in me wasn't misplaced. Taking a deep breath, I stepped into the page …

Except nothing happened. I looked down in confusion. Why could Rowan go through but not me? My foot happened to be more than the length of the page. I pulled my foot back, then tipped my toes downward as if I were testing the water in a pool. My foot went through and met solid ground just above my knee. I wasn't going to fit. I pulled my foot back and knelt to write another spell on the page. If I formed a pocket in the page that held the created object, I should be able to expand the page to allow for my size or for large objects to go in and come out. The spell was simple, allowing the opening to expand or contract as needed for entry or exit.

The words disappear with a little *pop*. Again I tried, but this time, when I put my foot through there was plenty of room for both of my feet and then my body to enter. For the first time, I entered a drawing. I glanced around, surprised at how it appeared as if I had walked into a photograph. Rowan sat on one of the many perches I had included. Three sides of the room, the floor, and the ceiling looked as any room should, but the fourth wall didn't. It looked somewhat like the whole wall was a giant TV screen, but in the frame, all you could see were the top shelf of my closet, the ceiling and the ugly light fixture with a 100-watt bulb. After a time, I felt disoriented, the fourth wall and its view of the ceiling made me feel as though I were upside down or walking on one of the walls.

"Don't look out at your room," Rowan said. "The tangents are messing with you."

I decided I would prop the sketchbook on its side next time, that way, the wall would appear more like another wall or a door, and not induce nausea. I looked around the room. I had drawn it to resemble a cozy library from an old English manor. The room felt complete, with furs, tapestries, velvet curtains, and a fire blazing in the fireplace; a library with everything but books.

I turned to Rowan, who still watched me with interest. "Are you ready to tell me the books you want?"

"Yes."

"Let me get my supplies and we'll start." I walked over to the wall with my ceiling and stretched my hand through to my closet. If reaching in feels like putting my hand into the water, this was like reaching out of the water to grab something. Grabbing my supplies took a couple of tries before I succeeded.

An idea struck me as I set my supplies up. I took my pen and walked over to the bookcases. On the wood, I wrote the spell to return the area to paper to be drawn upon again. The words disappeared, and the wall turned into a sheet of paper with the outline of the bookcases. Rowan landed on my shoulder and looked at the bookshelf.

"You're a very talented witch. I can't imagine how powerful you'll be when you're older. I don't think I've met your match, even in a female."

"Thanks, Rowan, that's the best compliment I've ever received. Now, let's get to work. Tell me what books you want and how you want them organized." It took hours, but I finished it and then I undid the spell on the bookcase. While I was there I added a place for him to store food.

We left the sketchbook together as the sun was setting outside. The house sat quiet and empty. Funny, I figured Guy would have returned by now. I finished the drawing with one final spell on the paper: *I grant access to claw, feather, and Lydia, to have and replace as needed. May this be resistant to fire, water, wrinkle, smudge, and tear, with no one able to change it but me.*

"Here, Rowan, here's your home. Take care of it and enjoy it. You should be able to be with Lydia always now. She just needs to carry the paper with you in it."

Rowan danced around excited. *"Could I ask one more thing?"*

"Sure."

*"Would you spell it so I can hear and see everything within reach?"*

"Good idea." I unfolded the page and wrote the spell to do it. I added some food I'd grabbed for him, then I folded the paper and put it in the pouch around his chest.

*"Thank you so much. I owe you a debt which you may ask of me at any time. But if you'll forgive me, I would like to find Lydia and show her. Perhaps I'll be able to stay with her tonight."*

"Sure thing, and you're welcome, my friend. Don't forget you're welcome here anytime."

I walked over and opened the window to the deluge outside. "Are you sure you need to go outside in this? Can you even fly in weather such as this?"

*"I can. A unique ability my grandmother gave me. It's why I can travel long distances without a problem. I have an invisible bubble of protection encircling me while I fly."*

"You're full of wonders."

*"So are you. But I wish to go and see Lydia. It's been too long. The longer we're bonded, the harder it becomes to be away from her."*

"I find it difficult for me to be apart from her, too," I said, and then wished I hadn't.

*"I'm sure she feels the same,"* Rowan said from the window seal. *"Goodbye."* He hopped out my window into the rain.

I went and shut the old wooden window before everything got wet. It wasn't easy sliding it down with the amount of water streaming down. As I locked the window, I noticed blurry headlights in the driveway. Maybe Guy had finally returned?

## CONVERGENT LINES

I grabbed my favorite sweatshirt--sky blue with navy ink, the words *Ravenswood Boarding School* and the silhouette of a raven in an open book on the front. The sweatshirt had been worn in and was one of my favorite pieces of clothing. Grabbing a pair of socks, I slipped them on as the backdoor in the kitchen opened. I headed downstairs, ready to tease Guy. "Why are you out so ...." I stopped mid-sentence as I saw both of my parents standing in the kitchen.

My mom's eyes narrowed in on me. "What were you about to say?"

"Sorry mom, I thought you were Guy. He left a little while ago."

"He isn't here?"

"I don't think he is, I fell asleep and don't know."

Mom shouted, "Guy!"

No answer came, she turned on me with anger, "Where did he say he was going?"

"He didn't say."

Some wordless exchange took place between my parents. My father lifted his right hand and tapped his Penrose signet ring as he said Guy's name. I didn't know what had happened, but it was not good. Something was up, and for a change Guy seemed to be at the center.

I stood to the side of the kitchen doing my best to disappear.

"Sit in the front room and wait. We need to have a discussion," my Mom instructed.

I nodded my head and went to the front room, where I picked a chair in the far corner to minimize the attention I would receive. Ten minutes later, Guy pulled into the driveway. I heard the back door open and watched as he walked into the room, drenched.

"Your father and I just returned from Connecticut on a mission of great importance to our family and the Kind as a whole."

I swallowed hard as I realized the reason for this discussion: the burden of the Penrose males. The thing no male in my family wanted to hear, a daughter has been born to one of the three houses from the prophecy.

"Three days ago, the Marrak family gave birth to the first female in their line for hundreds of years; a first born, too. Your father and I have begun negations for Guy's engagement."

Guy paled even more.

The name Marrak meant *Knight* in Cornish. They are one of the oldest families and have a neutral political stance most of the time. Of the three families a female could have come from, this was the best possible one. The other two were the Wayfarers, who have a long, twisted history with the Penroses, and the Blyghs. I've not known very many Blyghs, their name means *Wolf* in Cornish and they are from the darkest corners of the fae.

"Of course, two other families were there, too, and it will be a fight, but Guy should be the one."

"But, I didn't think marriage arrangements could happen until she was at least eighteen years of age, not an infant?" Guy asked.

"It isn't supposed to, of course, but with the importance of this birth, we need every advantage we can get. You're very lucky, son, you might break the Kind's curse, and it could be worse, it could've been a Wayfarer or a Blygh."

"At least twenty years of celibacy ahead of me? Really? And I suppose I'll get to spend that time in service to the Kind?"

My mother went to answer, but my father put a hand on her shoulder to stop her. "Guy, this is a heavy burden. Let me be honest with you, it could be eighteen years before we can sign a betrothal agreement and ask for the Council's approval. We'll compete with multiple families for this, and eighteen years is the short end of the spectrum. It's uncommon for such a gap in age unless one is a widow. The Marraks can postpone for her up to twenty-five years."

Guy slumped against the couch as if he'd just received a prison sentence of twenty-five years.

"You'll not be the only one to wait; at least three other males are in the same situation as you. Including Grayson."

"What?" I asked. This was supposed to be Guy's burden, not mine. I could never live with such a responsibility.

Guy looked at me in sympathy as if he knew what was to come. "With stakes like this, you're now your brother's heir. If something should happen to him in the coming years, it will be your task to complete this for your family and your people. I'm sorry, boys, it is a heavy thing to bear."

"But, dad, what will happen if the Council doesn't pick our family?" I whined.

"That's not for you to worry about, your mother and I shall take care of this. We will not fail."

"Can I go to bed?" My voice sounded flat. Three sets of eyes turned towards me. A nod from my mom, and I went up to my room.

# CHAPTER TEN

### Mabon, sunset, Cornwall, England

I stood next to Guy in the garden of Kolon. We gathered under an open gazebo as the last rays of light disappeared from the twilight sky. Our guests were out in the garden, sitting. Kensa hadn't made her appearance yet, and I could sense Guy's nervousness over the delays. With the announcement, she'd gone from marrying a Penrose to a Wayfarer.

Kensa's family seemed to take it well, but the Penroses, the distant branches of the family, were on edge and angry. I stood at my brother's side. A small three-piece string group began to play as Kensa appeared arm in arm with her father. The guests rose to their feet while the bride marched our way. Guy shifted but kept eye contact with Kensa the whole time. She was ethereal, in shades of gold.

Her father reached Guy. He stopped still holding Kensa's hand.

"We are gathered here to witness the joining of Guy Richard Wayfarer with Kensa Jean Marrak. Who gives Kensa to Guy?" Christopher asked.

It was so weird to hear my brother's new name.

"I do; her father, Germin Marrak."

"Do you offer her freely?"

"Yes, I do."

Guy held his hand out to Germin. He took Guy's right hand and placed it in Kensa's left, then put both of his hands over theirs.

"Today I do not lose a daughter, but I gain a son," he said in blessing before leaving to sit. Guy and Kensa repositioned themselves, so they looked at one another.

"Do you wish to take the Kind's traditional vows?" Christopher asked.

"Yes," they said in unison.

"Guy, repeat after me." Guy nodded his head.

"My blood to your blood, my soul to your soul.

I give you my body, that we two might be one.

I give you my love, until our life shall be done.

You can't possess me for I belong to myself.

But while we both wish it, I give you that which is mine to give."

Guy smiled at her as she said her vows. My hands sweated as I grasped both rings and the binding cord.

"May I have the rings?" asked Christopher. I stepped up and handed them to him. "The ring is a symbol of eternity with its continuous form." Christopher held his palm out flat to them. Guy picked up her ring and slid it on her finger. Kensa repeated the process for Guy. "Please come forward and bind their hands."

I stepped forward and wrapped the cord around their hands in the traditional manner. Christopher continued with a blessing invoking the elements. They ended the ceremony with a kiss.

I stayed where I stood as everyone left, wishing more than anything I could escape. At the reception, I had responsibilities to my brother and I wouldn't let him down.

# CONVERGENT LINES

As people left, I watched with unease. Nothing happened. Perhaps the peace had remained due to the threat of KIC, or the protection circle drawn earlier in the day around the wedding party. Whatever the reason, I was thankful.

"It was a beautiful ceremony," said a familiar voice to my left.

"Yes, it was. I believe you played a part in keeping the peace?"

"I think the word 'enforcing' would fit the situation better."

I turned to Davidson. "Whatever the reason, I'm happy my brother had a beautiful wedding."

A smile almost reached the corners of his lips.

"Let's join everyone…"

"In a minute, we have to talk," he said in a flat tone, sounding different than he had earlier. "I've been given orders, ones I don't wish to carry out, but must. You're to stay close to me throughout the rest of the evening. Tonight, I shall seal you into your room, and in the morning, we shall fly back to Connecticut to await a full Elder Council meeting concerning your future."

My brows rose in surprise. "Are you serious?"

"Yes."

"Do my parents or Guy know?"

"No, and I'm hoping you'll help me keep it from them. I don't want to impose on their happiness, and I believe you don't either."

"Yes, I'll cooperate with you fully, if it means we can keep this quiet. With the pressures of the last few days, I do not wish to add more."

"You're a good man. I was sorry at first when I discovered this would be your burden to bear. But now … now I think you're the best man for the job. No harm will come to you. It's only a precaution to make sure you don't run."

"I know, I'm the male heir to the binding curse. Who is the female? The gibberish the Oracle gave us didn't answer anything. Am I to remain chaste until the day a Wayfarer female child not of my brother's line is born?"

He smoothed his mustache thoughtfully. "I'm as clueless as you. But the Council is revisiting the original version of Aquila's prophecy. We'll wing it with the Oracle thing. No other Oracles have shown themselves in the Carn line, or any other."

"I knew my future was uncertain before today, but this is downright silly. I can't live in fear of being forced to marry someone in hopes it frees us."

"What were her last words? I couldn't hear her? I'm hoping you did, and then maybe we can make sense of them and find answers."

"She said, 'lead with your heart, do not follow.'"

Davidson put a palm to the middle of his forehead as if trying to stave off a headache. I understood, I felt one coming on, too. "Why are these things so hard? I truly think the Oracles and fortune tellers write technical manuals on the side," said Davidson.

"Come on, we've a reception to attend to," I said, grinning.

The next three and a half hours were long. Once I arrived, I helped to hold the broom for Guy and Kensa to hop over for good luck. Next, I made my toasts to them, and removed the fasting cord after the dancing and the cutting of the cake. What made the night uncomfortable for Davidson and me was the constant flow of women who now threw themselves at me. I'd suddenly risen from a nobody to celebrity, because every girl dreamed of breaking the binding curse. By the end of the night I felt dirty and embarrassed by the things the girls did and said, with Davidson at my side through it all.

I got so many phone numbers and room maps it was comical. I managed to stay off of the dance floor, except for one dance with my new sister. She seemed mystified by the attention as well. Though, like my brother, she had also carried the burden of the prophecy throughout her whole life. I can't imagine what it would have been like to know people had begun fighting for the right to marry her the moment she had been born.

The night started to wind down, and I had a duty to show my brother to the bridal suite. I made a promise to Davidson to meet him at my room afterward. Kensa had made her way to the room earlier and enough time had passed for me to escort Guy.

"Are you ready for this?" I asked as we walked up the stairs.

"Are you kidding me?"

"Yes, but I don't know, maybe you've got stage fright."

He shoved me. "You're not funny."

"Are you sure? I feel like I am."

He rolled his eyes. "Are you going to be okay?"

"Why wouldn't I be?"

"You forget, I carried the burden for most of my life. It isn't easy. At least I knew to whom I'd be married. I never had to deal with the stuff you had to deal with tonight. Man, those girls had no shame."

"On the upside, I got more girls' phone numbers than you," I said.

"You're funny."

"I'll deal with this. You worry about your bride. I'll be fine."

When we reached the door to the bridal suite I knocked lightly. A muffled, "Come in," answered me.

I opened the door to see Kensa's mother Elbrel standing on the far side of the massive bed. Kensa had the sheets pulled up to her neck and her cheeks were bright red. Seeing the coast was clear, I shoved Guy into the room. He stopped on his side of the bed and looked at Elbrel. She nodded and joined me. We waved them goodnight and shut the door.

Elbrel and I spoke briefly, and I left with a high opinion of her as we went our separate ways. I made my way toward my room.

Davidson waited for me. "I regret doing this to you. I've already sealed the window in your room, and once you're inside, I'll seal the doors. It will be impossible for you to leave without me knowing."

I wanted to smile. He couldn't know that I planned to leave in a while to go grave robbing. "I understand. Good night, Davidson, and no hard feelings."

"Good night."

I entered my room, and he closed the door behind me. A minute later, I sensed a pressure as he sealed the doors. I had my reasons for being so agreeable: I didn't want him to put a tracking spell on me. If he did, I wouldn't be able to find Hilda's body when I left to locate the dark object she'd used to curse me. For now, I planned to sleep for a couple of hours. I figured two-thirty in the morning would be the best time to visit the old crone. Everyone who was up late for the Mabon holiday should be starting to head home around that time.

Over the years, I'd discovered that my familial signet ring could be charmed to do any number of things, besides be a calling beacon. I'd charmed my ring to heat up to wake me instead of an alarm clock, that way no one is alerted by the sound. I hit the pillow and fell immediately into a deep sleep.

## CHAPTER ELEVEN

### Late August 1988, Santa Cruz, California

Sometimes I'd get days on end with Lydia, other times I'd go a week without seeing her. As summer ended, I knew I wanted to be able to talk to her year-round. During our times apart I experimented with different ways for us to communicate. My answer came one day as I talked to Rowan while we played chess in the park, sans Lydia again.

"How did you get here if Lydia flew and you weren't on the plane?"

He walked back and forth across the stone tabletop, looking at the chessboard. Our games had become more challenging as the summer progressed.

He laughed before calling his next move. *"Easy boy, the Muninns are old and we know the entrances to bridges long forgotten by men."*

I tilted my head looking at him. "Excuse me?"

"*Shouldn't you focus on the board?*" he asked.

"I think this is more important. Explain, please."

He got into the position I'd come to think of as the pose of pride. He knew something I didn't, and he wouldn't give it up easily. "*How well read is your Norse mythology?*"

"Not good."

"*Well, I suggest you read up, then we can talk. But for now, let us finish our game.*"

I resigned myself to the fact that he wouldn't tell me anything until I did as he requested. He kicked my butt in that game and the next. I quit early to go to the library. I didn't tell him, but the chicken knew.

At the library, I checked out a couple of books. One on Norse mythology, and a history book. I planned to fill my brain with as much as I could.

Luck happened to be with me when I got home and found myself alone. I hit the pantry and fridge then headed to my room. Around two AM, I thought I had figured out what Rowan was talking about.

The next day I waited for him at our spot; we were in the middle of one of Lydia's longer absences.

He landed without a sound on the table. "*I know that look. Okay, fire away so we can get to our game.*"

"The mythology talks of Yggdrasil, bridges, and Bifröst. My theory is Earth, and its land masses are most of the nine realms, with the rest being hidden places, celestial or underground. They're tied together by bridges if you know where the entrances are, and the right bridge can take you anywhere fast."

"*Oh, young one, you never disappoint. Yes, you're correct. There are bridges; one between Cornwall, near Connecticut, and a couple of other places in the states. It's how I got here. But I'm not to speak of these things.*"

"You're saying we don't know of them?"

"*No, there was a time I understand the Kind did, but the knowledge has been lost.*"

"Will you show me how to access these bridges and navigate them?"

## CONVERGENT LINES

*"Did you not hear me? There is no way you would make it through."*

I laughed, "I don't want to go through, I simply would like to send messages through, tiny pieces of paper. Would that be a problem?"

He stared at me out of his left eye. *"This should be okay if you swear you never plan to traverse the bridges."*

"I swear."

*"Is this so you can communicate with Lydia?"*

"Yes."

He made a raspy noise. *"I can't wait to see what you came up with."*

"I've outdone myself this time. I assure you."

*"Too much talk. Where is the game?"* I set up the board so he could humiliate me again. Well into our third game, on Rowan's turn as he paced his usual route around the board deciding on his move, he suddenly squawked and shot into the sky.

He circled above me as I attempted to figure what the problem might be. Suddenly, I was grabbed from behind. I jumped, scared, but then heard familiar laughter. Rowan landed to glare at Lydia. Somehow, she'd managed to sneak up and scare us both.

"Sorry, I couldn't resist."

"How did you sneak up on Rowan? Me I can understand, but him?"

"He loves games and puzzles. When he's focused, I can sometimes sneak-up on him." She started laughing. "One time I got him a pack of the metal disentanglement toy puzzles. He *had* to figure out how to pull them apart. I didn't see him for days."

He glared and plumped his feathers in the wind. *"I'm out of here,"* he said as he squawked and flew off.

"I thought you couldn't come today?" I asked.

"Didn't think I'd be able to, but my grandmother had a sudden change of plans and took off somewhere. I overheard her on the phone; she got excited. Something about a baby girl being born. The Elder Council called a meeting for late tonight and she wanted to be there."

"Um, I bet my parents will be going too. You know why, don't you?"

"No," she said with a shake of her head. "I stay out of the politics."

"They think the baby Marrak who was born a couple of weeks ago will break our binding and return our powers."

A look of confusion crossed her face.

"You know about the May Binding of 1645?"

"Yes, on May 1, 1645, the church sent seven priests dressed in white across the countryside of Connecticut in which they bound the Kind and the effects were felt throughout our world."

"Yeah, that's the one. My dad claimed they couldn't do it in Cornwall because of the Church of England. Whatever they did here seemed to work everywhere, though. You remember the prophecy from the Carn family before the binding?"

"Some. I figure they chose Beltane because of the importance of the holiday to us. Sometimes I wondered if the binding really did that much to us. I often think the magic has drained from us because we're two thousand years removed from the fae sealing the gates and the disbelief in magic of the people on the outside."

"You're right, but most Kind believe in the prophecy. They believed a girl would come from one of three families, the Blyghs, Marraks, or Wayfarers. The Blyghs had a girl a couple hundred years ago. They married her to the first-born male of a warring family. Not only did she not break the curse, but she died in the fighting. That left the Marraks and Wayfarers. The chances of a Wayfarer child with only four males left seem unlikely. Thus, everyone has been waiting for a Marrak girl."

"I would hate to be her."

"No kidding. She is why everybody is freaking out."

"I think it's a load of bollocks," Lydia said.

"I bet this is the social event of the century. My parents are going to try and score a bride for my brother."

Lydia's eyes widened with shock. "Your family would betroth him to an infant?"

"You bet they would, leaving him at least twenty years in celibacy waiting for her."

"Will you suffer the same kind of fate?"

I shook my head. I was lying, but more to myself. If I didn't admit to it, maybe it wouldn't be true. "He's the first born, with all that comes with it. Though my parents will be reluctant to marry me until he marries."

"Sometimes I wish I was one hundred percent human. There's just too much to deal with when it comes to our society."

"I know what you mean," I said.

She'd taken Rowan's place during our conversation and she eyed his pieces on the board. She picked up and moved the rook. I made my move and smiled, gazing up into her bright eyes. Being this near to her felt right. I didn't have to pretend to be something I wasn't or be on guard as I had to be in every other situation in my life.

She scrunched her face up as she considered her next move. I loved it when she did it. "Lydia."

"Hmmm," she said without looking up from the board.

"Do you know when you're going back to Cornwall?"

"Not exactly, sometime around the Mabon. What about you?" She made her move.

"We need to be back home on the nineteenth. A little over two weeks from now."

"Probably the same day for me. The good news is I bet we can spend most of that time together unless you have something going on?"

"Are most of the social events over with?" I asked.

"From what grandmother said, yes. The next parties and gatherings are on Mabon and in Kind cities."

"You know, I always wondered how we ended up living so close to each other. I mean, it's not like there are a lot of Kind out this way."

"My grandma says she bought the house here several years ago to be in the perfect weather for at least part of the year. You know, in the glorious sun and surf. Though I never see her in the sun. But there are more Kind out this way now. Otherwise my grandmother wouldn't be able to drag me to so many boring luncheons."

"My dad bought this house before I was born. He told me he wanted his kids to know what it's like to live by the beach and in the sun. I'm glad your grandma brought you here. The sun agrees with you. Look at you with your glowing tan and me with my pasty white skin and sunburn."

She laughed. "Can we run by my house and pick up my swimsuit? It's beautiful today, and I want to bodysurf."

"Yes. Can we stop by my house, too? I'll get my stuff."

"Yeah, let's go."

"We haven't finished the game yet."

"I just did. Checkmate."

I rolled my eyes. "You've been playing Rowan for years, haven't you?" She bobbed her head up and down as she bit her bottom lip. I picked up the chess pieces and put them away.

We spent every day together for the next two weeks, from early in the morning until the sun went down. Sometimes Guy would make an appearance and join us in the water. I started packing my camera and taking lots of pictures.

· ৡ ·

Rowan pecked at my window at sunrise the day before I was to return home, waking me from pleasant dreams. I stumbled over to the window, almost tripping over my skateboard on the way.

"Can you come now?"

"Yes, but why?"

"She's leaving in a couple of hours."

Without another word, I dressed and grabbed my things. Loaded up, I snuck out the front door without disturbing the sleeping house on the quiet Sunday morning. He led me to the beach, near the pier.

"Good morning."

"Hi, glad you could make it." The sun had begun to peek up from the east. She sat on the towel with her bare feet in the sand.

"Do you know what I'll miss the most about California?"

"Me," I said with a giant smile and hope.

"Of course, you. But I'll miss sunrise and sunset on the ocean, the feel of sand, the warmth of this place."

"Please tell me you'll be back next year."

"I will. My grandmother is happy with me. She wants me to be a fashion accessory for her summer social scene."

I pursed my lips as I doubted anyone could be so cruel.

"You think I'm kidding, but I'm not. That's how she said it, as if I were the newest handbag or pair of shoes."

"Really?" She nodded her head. "Doesn't it bother you?"

"No, not if it means seeing you."

I sat next to her, took my shoes off, and set my feet next to hers in the sand. I wrapped my arm around her. We sat there for a second, an hour, some immeasurable amount of time, which ended in real life but not in my mind. With the sun overhead, she stood and I knew she had to go.

"Wait here a minute." I put my shoes on and ran up to the boardwalk to buy two bottles of Coke from a vendor. The vendor yelled at me as I ran off, smiling, "No glass on the beach!"

Lydia watched me approach with a look of confusion. I reached into my backpack and pulled out a bottle opener and my sketchpad. I set the sketchpad down and opened the bottles, careful not to bend the caps. I handed her a bottle and lifted mine. "Cheers," I said and we toasted each other. We drank in silence and I knew she was curious about my actions.

When she finished hers I asked for the bottle back. She handed it to me, and I began scooping sand into the bottle. I stopped when I got to where the soda would stop. Grabbing one of the caps I forced it back on. Once secured, I tipped the bottle upside down as Lydia giggled, thrilled with my idea. The sand in the bottle shifted showing tiny shells, sand, rocks, and little piece of seaweed. I repeated the process with my bottle.

Out of my backpack I took a black marker and wrote on the bottles, "September 1988, Santa Cruz, CA, G&L." I handed a bottle to her. "Now we both have a reminder of today."

"You're the kindest soul I've ever known, and the funniest," she said, giggling.

"Well, the surprises are done yet. I've one more for you."

"I can't wait to see it."

I picked up my sketchpad and turned away from her to write on one of the pages.

"What are you doing? Let me see," she said as she tried to look around me.

"Stay there. Trust me, it will be worth it." I wasn't looking at her, but I know she fidgeted and rolled her eyes behind my back. I finished my note and turned around to look at her.

"After I show you this, I'm giving you this sketchpad. I've bespelled every page so when you remove a page out of the spiral it will do this."

I tore the sheet out and lay it flat on my hand. On its own, it began folding itself, until it looked like a butterfly in my palm. Its wings fluttered, and it flew into the air, and glided on the breeze for a moment. She gasped, her hands going to her mouth. The butterfly flew in a couple of spirals before heading toward her.

"Hold your hand out for it to land."

She did, and it landed in her palm. The butterfly fluttered its wings a couple of times before it began unraveling. Within seconds, the page of my sketchpad with a drawing of us together sat in her hand.

She gasped again and read aloud the short message at the bottom of the page.

*To Lydia,*
*My best friend. May you always remember us together on the beach.*
*The best summer ever! Santa Cruz, 1988*

She squeaked a couple of time and threw her arms around my neck as she kissed my check. "You're the best!"

I blushed, as I always did when she kissed me. All too soon she released me and began examining the sketch. "So this is how we can communicate?"

"Yes, I've written a spell into the sheets with instructions on how to navigate between us. You can also stick something onto the page, like a photo, and it will come to me, too."

"I don't know what to say. I don't have anything to give you in return."

"You already gave it to me."

"I did?"

"Yes, your first summer vacation and you."

"You're too good to me."

"No, you deserve this, and more. Let me have your skateboard and the bottle."

She handed her things over. I opened the sketchpad and placed both into a page. "The pages are also bespelled to store your things for you. It won't weigh any more than the notebook, and the stuff will keep. Just remember to take your stuff out before you send it to me. If you run low on pages send me a note, and I'll send you one back with a new sketchpad."

We stood, and I handed her the pad. She stared down at the page with the skateboard and bottle, tears welling in her eyes. She hugged me again, tighter this time.

"I don't want to leave you."

"I know, I don't want you to leave either, but if we don't start back soon, you'll get in trouble with your grandma. I don't want to do something which will risk you being able to come here next summer."

She nodded and held the open sketchpad in her hand. I reached down, picked up my things, and put them in my pack. I grabbed her towel, shook it out, folded it, and handed it to her. She placed it in the page with the skateboard and bottle.

We walked hand in hand down the boardwalk. As we drew near the arcade, I heard the song, "Under the Milky Way Tonight" playing. The song which played the first time I saw her.

"Do you think it's a coincidence that song is playing now?" she asked.

"Not a chance."

"Think we have enough time to get a picture in the photo booth? We should have done it earlier."

I glanced down at my watch. "It's ten thirty."

"We're good on time. My grandmother told me to be home by eleven."

We went over to the photo booth and took four different strips of pictures. I let her pick her favorite two, and I took the others. We ended up running most of the way back to her house, making it with no time to spare. She jumped up, kissed my cheek, and gave me a bear hug. When she pulled away, I blushed again, and she laughed. "I hope you never stop blushing when I kiss you."

I blushed harder.

"Goodbye, for now," she said.

"I'll miss you and your chicken."

She blinked at me, absorbing what I'd just said. She roared with laughter once she figured it out.

"Don't tell him, please."

"I will not tell him you called him that." She smiled, all teeth, "He wouldn't forgive you. He has a sense of humor, but not when it involves his pride."

"I know."

She was still smiling as she turned to leave. I managed to grab her hand and, for the first time, I initiated a hug. I closed my eyes, enjoying the moment. She smelled of sunlight and a warm breeze, with hints of citrus. I let her go and felt her absence.

## Samhain, 1988, Ravenswood Boarding School, Cornwall, Connecticut

Not hearing from Lydia had been killing me. Tired of waiting, I took matters into my hands. The dorms were empty. Everyone else was out celebrating Samhain. They were all out at the bonfire. It gave me the perfect opportunity to send her a message.

Grabbing my sketchpad, I ripped out a piece of paper and wrote my spell on the side, adding an instruction to fill in the page with black ink. The words disappeared into the page. Within seconds, an ink spot formed in the center of the sheet, spreading outward to the corners, and to the opposite side. The inky blackness swallowed all the white of the page.

I'd learned the trick a few years earlier while drawing something that had a large black area. Tired of coloring, I bespelled it to turn black instead.

I rummaged through my art supplies looking for my white colored pencil. I had to dump the whole bag of pencils on my bed; it was half the size of the others. I sharpened it. After thinking for a few minutes, I decided to keep it short and casual. I didn't want to come off as desperate.

*Hi Lydia,*

*I hope school is tolerable, and Rowan is enjoying his library. Haven't heard anything from you, concerned something is up? Things are the same here, as always, boring. I miss you, California, and your chicken.*

*Happy Samhain.*
*Gray*

I looked down at my message; basic, a little sappy, but not desperate. One more word was all it took to cause the paper to shift, fold, tear, and rearrange. This creature took longer than the first one did, a bat being a more complicated creature than the butterfly. Fully formed, the bat fluttered its wings just above my bed. I gave it the final instruction, "Go. Seek her out." The bat hovered for a couple seconds before taking off through the crack in my window.

I decided I didn't want to go to the celebrations. Instead, I would shower, then go to bed. It was nice to have the bathroom to myself for a change. I could take a shower for as long as I wanted and not worry about it. My roommate, Tristan Tremayne, had gone to the celebrations and wouldn't be back for hours. Being Samhain it was customary for us to stay out and celebrate until the witching hour of three AM, though some would stay up until sunrise for All Saints Day. This wasn't a problem since there wouldn't be any classes the day after the holiday.

Many of my classmates would use the powers of the holiday to imbue spells they had created with more power. I couldn't care less. My mood since leaving Lydia and California had been sour at best, angry at worst. I finished with my shower, climbed under my covers, and fell asleep. I left the window open about four inches letting in the cold of the night. Bundled under my blankets, it didn't bother me at all.

At some point in the night, I jerked awake, as though I'd suffered a bad dream. Soon I realized I hadn't, but a white owl was flying in circles around my bed, begging for my attention. I sat on my bed for a while watching him fly around, amazed at the magic. The owl waited for me to invite it to land. At last, I gave in, saying, "Come to me."

Upon landing, the paper unraveled until two sheets of white paper sat on the bed. I smiled, happy for the first time in more than a month.

*Hello Gray,*

*Sorry I've been slow to write, but we have a new headmistress, and she isn't very nice. I now have a roommate; a distant cousin named Jessy Rosdew. She isn't that bad, but I get almost no time with Rowan, and I haven't dared until now to write you one of your messages, for fear someone would see me. But I've been planning. I've included a scary story for you. With the celebrations tonight I was able to get off to the woods to send this. I can't wait to see what the messenger is. I miss you something terrible. School is boring and no fun. But I've news, good news. Grandma is going to let me come for the next few summers, until I graduate. She said she's happy with my social introduction and if I keep it up I'll marry well. Yeah, just what I want to hear. Hope you like your gift. Have a happy Samhain.*

*Love, Lydia*

My heart skipped a beat she said, *Love*. I set aside the letter and read my gift: a short tale she had titled the "Soul Catcher".

# CHAPTER TWELVE

### Mabon, 2:30 AM, Cornwall, England

I ran hand in hand with Lydia into some nearby woods, both of us hampered by our costumes. Somehow, we'd managed to get away without anyone noticing. Each step became harder because of fallen trees and other forest debris. At last, we stopped by the trunk of a large fallen tree. Pushing my cape out of the way, I sat and pulled her onto my lap. She giggled.

Her breath hit my cheek as we stared at each other for a long time. At last, I made my move. I closed the distance between us until our lips were inches from each other. I gauged her reaction. She didn't flinch, and I took this to mean she wanted the same thing. I closed my eyes as our lips touched. At first, I didn't know what I was doing. For a moment it felt awkward, but as I relaxed, years of dreaming took over. We kissed, soft and light.

There was only us, nothing else. Her lips parted and I took her invitation and deepened the kiss. Time had lost all meaning as she wrapped her arms tight around me and we both fought not to breathe. She was mine at last, and I'd never let her go. I'd fight any battle to keep her, no matter the cost. I pulled back from the kiss and looked at her. She struggled to catch her breath, and her lips were plump from my kisses. Her cheeks flushed as she stared right back at me and smiled. I started to pull her back to kiss her again. As she neared, Lydia changed, blurred until the girl in front of me with lips puckered to kiss me was Hilda. I pushed her off of my lap and she fell back onto the forest floor, laughing.

I shot up in bed, breathing hard, perspiring, and still able to hear the laughter echoing in my head. Pain exploded in my lower left arm, as if I'd been bitten or stung. In a panic, I looked around for the source but saw nothing. My ring burned my finger. To be this hot it must have been heating up for a long time. I tapped it with my finger, and said, "Stop."

I considered my bad dream as I got out of bed and headed to the bathroom. In the years since I'd last seen Lydia, I'd never dreamt of her at night. Every day, all day, in my daydreams but never at night.

In the bathroom, I flipped the light on and splashed water on my face. My arm still hurt so I examined the area. There, on my left wrist, a red mark was forming. Weird. My heart raced in my chest. Repeatedly I told myself Hilda was dead. It was just a nightmare. Back in my room I grabbed my cell phone and checked the time. Almost three AM. If I were to do this, I needed to hurry. I grabbed the clothes I'd worn earlier in the day rather than spend time looking for new ones. In record time I was ready, but with one big problem: I needed a glamour. I couldn't take any chance of someone seeing and recognizing me. With my artistic abilities one would think I'd be able to master glamour spells, but, no, I sucked at it.

What to do? After all, I was going grave robbing. I'd never been to the building they were keeping her in. Her body had to be in the basement of the Coven House, the place we use as a church, but usually more for ceremonies and meetings. The Death Rites are done twenty-four to forty-eight hours after death occurs. My father once explained it to me when one of my grandparents had died. Since we're part fae and part human, our souls are different. We have souls from our human side, whereas the fae don't; they're earthbound. Because the Kind are a hybrid of the two we have a heavier life force. It means it takes much longer for our souls to leave our bodies, so they need assistance. The necromancer who conducts the ceremony has a lot of control over the spirit, and black magic can result. At least one KIC member must be present at the ceremony. In the case of Hilda, I expected there would be several.

An idea struck, which required me to visit my closet at home. I rushed to the bathroom and jumped through the mirror into my closet in Connecticut. In the corner of the large walk-in closet was a wall mirror. I reached into my safe and I felt around for a cape. When I say safe, it's what I mean. I'd drawn a spell on the mirror years ago, creating a large pocket inside. The spell allowed only myself to reach in. Now I know you're wondering, what would happen if the glass shattered? I found a way around the glass breaking, I added another spell to make it unbreakable. My hand felt the velvet of the charcoal colored cape; I pulled it out.

One summer, years earlier, I'd been exploring Europe on a backpacking trip. During my journey, I traveled through Romania. A strange place full of magic and magical beings, including witches not related to the Kind. We don't mix; I don't know why. To my knowledge, it isn't against the law, it just isn't done. It's rare for us to interact in any manner. I looked into it after my trip and could only find a handful of examples throughout our written histories to indicate any interactions.

As I traveled about heading to Bran Castle, I encountered a small caravan-type wagon. It's the type which you would expect to find a gypsy fortuneteller at, and that's what I found. She sat alone outside by a small fire on the side of the country road. As I neared, she looked up from her knitting.

"It's about time you got here," she said looking right at me.

"Excuse me?"

"Come over and join me, Grayson Penrose." She pointed to a chair opposite her, which I swear hadn't been there a moment before. I swallowed as I wondered, *How did I find myself in this situation?* I'd gone on vacation to be alone.

"I've been expecting for you for a very long time," she said in accented English. She had magic. I could feel it, and it wasn't of Kind origins. How we, the Kind and another magical being sense one another is a mystery. Perhaps it's an evolutionary thing, which came about to protect ourselves from other magic.

"I evoke the hospitality clause. No harm shall come to you. Sit."

I sat down in the offered chair with great hesitation. "Who are you? How do you know my name?" I said with the tone of a back-talking teen.

She laughed. "Grayson, I'm a gypsy with a talent of foresight. I saw you a long time ago." I lifted an eyebrow in surprise. "You're very special. But I'll get to the future later. Would you like some tea?"

The day had been cool, almost cold, and the offer of hot tea sounded good. "Sure."

From her side, she pulled out a teacup and a canister with loose tea. She plopped a spoon full of tea leaves into the cup, topping it off with water from the pot. Done, she set the cup aside to steep. It felt awkward sitting there, yet I waited for her next directive. In the world I'd grown-up in, the world of magic, I learned early to never underestimate a magical being based upon looks. She might be old, but for her to look this old meant she'd survived a long time. If she wanted to read my tealeaves, I wasn't going to object.

"Drink up, it will rain soon and the temperature will drop," she said after several minutes. We sat together as I drank and watched the fire, and she knitted. The tea she gave me was good, fruity with hibiscus and a hint of citrus. I finished and sat the cup aside. As I did, she rose, and hobbled over to the cup. She picked it up and began to look at my leaves. For a long time, she turned the cup, looking at the contents as she smiled. She returned to her seat with the cup and looked at me.

"There's much I cannot tell you, but you're on the right path. Don't give up hope, follow your heart, be true to yourself, and take this." She pointed to a folded piece of gray cloth which had been sitting next to me on a pile of rocks. "My gift to you. You should find it useful in the coming years, a cape of glamour."

"How does it work?"

She laughed, "It's brilliant. The wearer shall throw a glamour to even the strongest of witches around them. But what's interesting, is the glamour is unique to each person whose eyes should fall upon you. They see what's needed to forget or ignore you. Say you were a bank robber and two police stood next to you as you wore the cape. One might see a homeless man while the other might see a young child."

"Please don't take this wrong, but why would you give me a gift like this? It has to be rare and expensive."

"What do I need with money?" she said with a wave of her hand. "But I do want something: enchant a sheet of your sketchpad for me, one that only I can reach into."

"That's all you want from me?"

"Yes, child. The cloak is rare but so is what you can offer me. I work in trade, a barter system. You offer me something I've not seen before."

I did my best to cover my surprise and set upon giving her what she desired. I finished bespelling the page and handed her the sheet of paper. The old gypsy stuck her hand in the page, happy. I picked up the cape, twirling it as I did. With the button secured, I looked down at it. It appeared to me as a charcoal cape. I looked up to ask her what she saw … and she was gone, along with all evidence she had been there. I turned around looking for her. Nothing. I continued on my way with the cape in my bag.

I was thankful now for the cape. I fastened it in place, remembering I also needed gloves. I pulled a pair of leather gloves off a shelf. Slipping them on I rushed back to my bathroom at Kolon; I had lost too much time already. I picked up my marker and began to write directions on the mirror. Using my connection to the KIC computers, I had found a map of the town. I was in Cornwall, England, but the Kind live apart from humans. We enchant or spell areas to keep humans from our places. Being free of humans has allowed us to use our magic without worry of them witnessing.

 The Coven House is located in the center of Cornwall, several miles from me. We had passed through the town on the way to the house, and the original KIC offices had caught my attention. It's similar to the human's Capitol building in the United States, complete with a large-scale obelisk out in front. I'd seen pictures of it for years and had hoped I could tour it while here. Lucky for me the obelisk had been cut from a solid piece of rock and polished to a mirror-like shine. I was not sure if this would work, but I decided to try it. In the past, I have used highly polished surfaces as a mirror to enter or exit. I hoped this would work the same.

 With the instruction in place, I walked into the mirror. The *in-between*, as I call it, is a strange place, a place between worlds. Every time I open a portal I go through a different *in-between*. Sometimes it's a large place, other times not. Once I even found a land, one I have claimed. When I'm not at work I'm usually there. This time I found a dark hallway of stone and dirt, more of a tunnel than a hall. As I surfaced at the opposite end, I looked out from my vantage point. A dark street lit with moonlight awaited me, but I felt like I wore dark sunglasses. I pushed my hand through the side of the obelisk to the outside. Confident this would work, I stepped out.

 On the sidewalk in front of the KIC building, I caught my breath. Until I left the obelisk, I had not realized how thin the air was. I gave myself a moment to catch my breath before I started for the Coven House, which sat behind the KIC building. It took a few minutes to find it; the building and grounds were much larger than I expected.

 Deciding it would be best not to approach the front of the building because of security, I circled until I found a side entrance with a keypad. The KIC owed their ability to use electronic devices like this to me. Years of schooling in the human world in my mid-twenties had helped me to develop spells and magic to shield the electronics from our electrically charged selves. I made a fortune. Many referred to me as the Bill Gates of the Kind. I made more money than my family, but I didn't care. This same knowledge would help me break in and shield myself from the video camera, which no doubt monitored the halls of this place.

Hiding from a video camera feed isn't the same as glamour, which is lucky for me. At the keypad, I hovered my palm above the surface, careful not to touch it. I inverted a long, complicated spell I'd created for PenTech to shield the electronic devices from magic. Speaking a spell in reverse will undo the spell put on it. As I finished the undoing spell, a popping hiss came from the pad, and it began to smoke. The door lock disengaged and I opened it. Security would be here soon.

As I walked through the door, I began to say the undoing spell again. Any electronics nearby would be fried, including the video feed. Just inside the door, I found a second door with STAIR-WELL printed on it. I needed to go down; I opened it and ran down the stairs. After considering where they would hold Hilda, I concluded she would be in cold storage. This would probably be in a basement, away from the public parts of the Coven House. I had reached the landing between the flights of stairs when I heard a door above me open and the sound of footsteps and creative cursing. I pressed myself against the wall to wait them out.

The upper door clicked closed, and I ran the rest of the way down. To my relief, there wasn't another keypad. The lack of real security surprised me. While humans might not find dead bodies valuable, the Kind had different ideas on the matter, especially the darker side. At the door, I stopped, opened it, and peered out into a dark hall. Darkness and silence greeted me. Out into the hall I went. Security would be doing a sweep after they barricaded the door I had come through, so I didn't have long.

It would take too long to check each of the several doors lining the hall. I needed to find cold storage. The fifth door on the left had a plaque, as I got closer I could see COLD STORAGE engraved on it. I stopped and listened. Nothing. I pushed, but found it locked. Kneeling to be level with the lock, I pulled a pen out of my pocket. It's my favorite pen and doubles as a wand focus for me. With the silver tip touching the lock, I forced my will and said, "Unlock."

I heard the tumblers move. I stood and pushed again just as I heard someone in the stairwell. I hurried into the room and looked for a place to hide.

The room could have come out of a TV morgue scene. On the wall to my right was the large cooler with several small latched doors for bodies. In the middle of the room, several stainless-steel roll-around tables sat empty. To the left was an open closet door.

I rushed into the closet, which turned out to be filled with cleaning supplies, and closed the door with a little click. I got into the corner behind the door.

I held my breath as I heard two voices nearing.

"Damn security system, do we need to look through every room?" a male voice said.

"You know the protocols."

"Was this door unlocked?"

"I don't remember. We'll lock it on the way out; don't forget or we'll hear about it tomorrow morning."

"Yeah. Did you check the closet?"

"No, I'll get it."

The doorknob rattled and the door opened. I held still hoping my cape would help if he saw me. A large flashlight beam shone in the dark corners of the closet.

"There's nothing in there."

"I told you there's no point. How long between when the malfunction happened and when we got there? A minute, maybe a little more? Who would want in this creepy place?"

"Yeah, yeah, but we have a job to do. Come on, let's finish this. I want to continue with our game."

"Sure. But you're locking the door." I heard the door open and I relaxed ... and my foot bumped the mop bucket. *Smack!* The mop handle hit the floor.

"Damn it! What was that?"

"I don't know. It came from the closet."

One of them returned, pointing the flashlight beam at the floor. "It's a mop handle." The man walked into the closet, knelt, and picked up the mop, as he stood, he backed into the door causing it to open wider, concealing me further from view.

"Nothing to worry about. Let's go."

I heard the door squeak open and the key in the lock, locking me in with Hilda. It took my heart a long time to quiet itself. I waited almost five minutes before moving again.

Despite the risk, I turned on the lights. There was no way I would be alone in the dark with Hilda. My skin crawled at the thought of what I planned. I hoped they hadn't taken her clothes and things away from her yet, or this might get messy.

I wondered which cooler housed Hilda's body. There were three rows with four doors each. My guess was they didn't have many bodies here, so the middle row of drawers would be the easiest. I started there. The first one I checked was empty, but not the second. A sheet covered the body. Under the sheet I found an old man. I closed the drawer.

I tried the third door to find another sheet. The air felt heavy. This was her, I knew it before I looked. I held my breath, and looked beneath the sheet to see her dark, dead eyes staring up. She still had her clothes on. I imagine they threw her in here because the wedding and events of yesterday took a bit more precedence than her death.

I shivered, as I pulled out the drawer to reveal the rest of her. She looked strange, pale in a long, dark dress. Her brown hair had been styled in an up-do and she was still wearing all her jewelery: dangling pearl earrings, a gold watch, and several rings. If it weren't for her eyes being open, she might look like she slept. There was one strange thing I couldn't make sense of, a dark singe mark around her neck. It looked as if she'd worn a necklace with a large charm under her dress and the necklace had burned her.

Around her waist, she wore a belt with several small pouches. Hesitant to touch her, and thankful for the gloves, I reached for the belt. I popped the snap closure on the first pouch. Inside I found several different rocks and gems. Certain that what I looked for wasn't here, I moved on to the larger of the two on the side nearest to me. There I found money and other common items one would expect in a purse. I put everything back and walked to the other side.

A single pouch waited to be examined on this side. I hoped what I was looking for would be there. I doubted she'd risk keeping a dark cursed object in her house where another might happen upon it. No, on her person was the best place.

The snap on this pouch didn't want to open. I jerked it hard and fell backward. The force caused Hilda's head to tilt to the side just enough to "look" at me. I shivered, cursing at the creepiness of this. I stood back up, and finally managed to get it open, except it looked empty. To be sure, I reached in and my hand rubbed something. I wrapped my finger around it and pulled it out. In my palm, sat a black velvet drawstring satchel. The velvet bag felt dirty and oily, even through my gloves; I wanted to drop it. It had to be the dark object.

A small noise caught my attention. I looked back at Hilda in time to see her mouth opened, the sound of cracking bone filled the room as a dense, black mist escaped her gaping mouth. I fell backward into a stainless steel roll-around cart, which slammed to the floor with a clatter. I scrambled away, as the mist dissipated. Dead bodies weren't supposed to do that. My heart pounded in my chest. It would be a miracle if security didn't come back because of all the noise.

I sat on the floor for several minutes trying to compose myself. My brain came back online after the fear left me. The best thing to do would be to get out of here and leave no sign of my visit.

Robbing the dead isn't for the faint of heart, I told myself, and set the bag aside. I put the sheet in place and pushed Hilda back into her drawer. With time running out, I hurriedly put the bag in my pocket and looked about for a mirror. Nothing, I'd have to use the stainless steel. The wall on the far side of the cooler had enough exposed surface for me to use. I stood in front of it checking my reflection; I could see myself. Not as well as I liked, but it might work. I tried, but the spell wouldn't take. It must be the metal. I'd never tried metal before. Guess I don't have a metal affinity.

I headed for the door, unlocked it by twisting the deadbolt, turned the lights off, and peeked out in the hall. Dark and empty, just how I like my halls. I decided it would be best if I left the way

# CONVERGENT LINES

I'd arrived. Before I left, I took my pen out and locked the door, wanting to leave as little evidence of my presence as possible.

Back in the stairwell, I check my watch and found it was close to five AM. I climbed the stairs to the main floor. A tentative peek told me I was close enough to the outer door to twist the deadbolt without exiting the stairwell. I opened the door, reached out, and unlocked the deadbolt. The door opened easily and I ran into the night as another alarm sounded. Free at last, I ran along the trees and bushes to hide myself. I hurried through the grounds of the KIC, until I came even with the front of the building. There, I stopped and peered around to see if the area was clear. Two figures stood near the obelisk. I ducked into the bushes and watched them. How would I get out of this? I couldn't walk back to the house it was too far, and the moment I did Davidson's alarm would sound. I'd have to wait this out and hope I didn't get caught.

# CHAPTER THIRTEEN

### June 1989, Santa Cruz, California

My family arrived in California early the next year, leaving me to wait for Lydia. Through the school year, we communicated with greater frequency as summer neared. Sometimes it became almost daily. I had to send her two more bespelled sketchpads so we could continue to communicate. We'd started playing games of riddles or puzzles on the back of the pages. I even played long-distance chess games with Rowan.

At one point she let me know the Muninns had contacted Rowan to find out the nature of the strange flying objects using the bridges. He had requested I send one, a raven, to his grandmother Muninn so she could see the message for herself. I did; sending a note to her for the use of the bridges. Once delivered it returned to a raven, which she could control.

Lydia had instructed me to go to the forest on the outskirts of my schoolyard on the Ostara holiday. At first, I didn't understand. But once I saw the shadow of an enormous bird, I did. She landed on the ground next to me. It was a good thing I was in a clearing or she wouldn't have been able to land. Rowan is large for a raven, but Muninn is a giant in comparison. She eyed me for a time before speaking, through her beak, not through telepathy like Rowan.

"I wished to see the boy my grandson talks so much about."

I bowed to her. "I am honored to meet you. I consider myself lucky to have met Rowan. But to meet you, too? Fortune has shined upon me."

"A quick tongue, too. You're interesting. Rowan has shared his library with me, and I must say I've not seen one as talented as you in millennia. I'm pleased you have a good heart. You renew my faith in the Kind. It has taken a beating up until now."

"Your compliments mean much to me. I adore your grandson."

She laughed and cawed. "You call him chicken?"

I blushed. "Just a little poking fun."

"It's fine. It's the jibe we pass among ourselves. I must go before I'm missed or discovered, but I wished to bring you something."

She held her right leg out to me. "Around my claw, you shall find a charm, a raven's claw on a leather thong. It's for you; a gift from us for your kindness. Something we haven't bestowed upon a human in centuries."

I knelt by her right foot and pulled the charm free.

"You honor me. Doesn't Lydia wear one?"

"Yes, she does, but it came to her through her family. Though had she not had one we would have given her one as well. She treats my grandson well."

I put the necklace around my neck and felt the power in the charm; a lot of power. I bowed to her and said my goodbye. "Muninn, if I may be of assistance to you for anything, please let me know."

She laughed. "Careful! I may take you up on that for my library."

"Anytime."

She bowed to me and left.

## CONVERGENT LINES

To pass the time waiting for Lydia, I'd call my new friend and roommate from school, Tristan. He'd started at Ravenswood at the beginning of the year, the first Tremayne to ever go to a Kind school in the U.S. At first, they were worried about putting a Tremayne with a Penrose, but I assured them I had no problem with him. In fact, I was curious about the vampires of the Kind.

Turns out I was the last one they tried to put him with. They'd tried everyone else and no other family would allow their son to board with him; they were too scared. When they moved Tristan in I didn't find him scary, but I'd never seen anyone in our culture like him before. His skin was a caramel color and he had the brightest green eyes. The Kind were thirteen families in the countryside of Cornwall, England going back thousands of years. Diversity is non-existent with us. Looking at Tristan, I think it might have been to our disadvantage.

The Tremaynes have an affinity for blood. Thus, many consider them vampires, but they're not, in the true sense of the meaning. They have the distinction of being the most reclusive family in our world. Sometime in the 1600s they up and left England and Connecticut, preferring to settle in New Orleans, and left the rest of the Kind behind. They are another family that was aligned with the dark fae before the closing of the gates.

The administrative people who brought Tristan stayed just long enough to feel like they'd done their job and ran off. I wasn't sure what to say to him at first. *Would questions about him and his family make him more uncomfortable than everyone else already had?*

"My mother is Creole and a Voodoo priestess."

I blinked at him not sure what to say. While not outlawed, I'd never heard of a Kind member mixing with another of magic kin.

"Sorry, I didn't mean to make you feel uncomfortable."

"It's okay. I know they forced you to take me. I promise, I'll stay out of your way."

"I volunteered."

It was his turn to look surprised.

I offered him my hand. "Let's start over. I'm Grayson Penrose, but I prefer Gray. If you use my full first name, I'll assume I'm in trouble."

He almost smiled as he shook my hand. "I'm Tristan Tremayne, son of the notorious Victor Tremayne and Olivia. I've spent my entire life until yesterday in New Orleans and I feel like a fish out of water."

"It's nice to meet you, Tristan. I'll help you adjust. I've spent my life dealing with these idiots and can help make the transition easier."

"I haven't felt very welcome here."

"No, I don't imagine you have. Kind society isn't forgiving and they don't like change."

"I'm glad you're my roommate Gray, I think we can be friends."

"Me, too."

· ☙ ·

I had a gift for Rowan. I'd made a unique chess set; each piece drawn with care. My side, the white side, was made up of a cast of humans, each one different, with the pawns being people who annoyed me, to the better pieces being people I liked. For example, the knights were my brother, the bishops my father and the rooks my mother. I, of course, took the role of King and Lydia was the Queen.

On the black side, or the raven side, I made mynah birds the pawns, magpies the knights, jays as the bishops, and crows the rooks. Rowan was the ravens' king and queen. It was his unique set to play with. He would be thrilled.

I'd been there two days, forced to do stuff with my family. On the third day, I got up early to go down to the pier to watch the sunrise. If she wasn't here yet, I wanted to be where I felt closest to her. I rode my skateboard, thrilled to do so for the first time this year. Later this summer I'd be able to get my driver's license. My dad felt it an important skill to learn. Who am I to complain, but even after getting the license I'd travel mostly by skateboard around Santa Cruz. It made no sense for me to have a car, and wouldn't until I got out of my KIC service years from now.

## CONVERGENT LINES

I waited in my usual spot on the beach, and waited on the sunrise. Someone sat down next to me. I turned to see Lydia with a smile. I reached out to hug her, but all I managed to do is tackle her in a big bear hug. I'd hit the awkward stage of growth where controlling my legs and arms was impossible, or my giant feet. Over the winter I'd shot up three inches, and now stood at six-foot three.

She laughed hard, in between laughs she managed to get out, "Gray, let me up. I can't breathe."

I fumbled off her, and she put her arms around me in a more acceptable hug. The other hug was better. "I didn't think you would be here yet," she said.

"I thought the same thing about you."

"I got in yesterday morning, but grandma had afternoon lunch plans for us with her friends. I came hoping you would be here because I can't come tomorrow. The good news is I can stay all day."

"Good, so can I."

I put my arm around her and we watched the sun come up. Being with her again felt like coming home. She'd changed. Her hair was longer, and she wore it in two long braids with a blue bandana worn as a headband. As usual, she wore cutoff jean shorts, a blue tank top, and a light blue hoodie. Always shades of blue, just like her eyes.

"Where's Rowan?"

"He's somewhere up north with the Muninns. They called him just before we left. I imagine he'll get here in a few days."

"I met his grandmother. She gave me this." I held up the raven's claw charm.

"Good, I'm glad. It's similar to mine, but without the weird stone."

"Can I see yours?"

She nodded her head and took it off. Hers hung on a chain instead of the leather cord. They looked identical, excepted for the patina on hers from age and the strange stone grasped in the claw. It was a smooth stone, about a half-inch around, and it changed colors from purple to green and then red.

I asked, "What kind of stone is it?"

"I've asked a couple of jewelers and they think it's an uncut alexandrite. They say it's a rare gem from Russia."

I handed the necklace back to her. "It's pretty, how did you get it?"

She refastened it around her neck. "When Rowan came to me he brought it, said it had been returned to them in trust until the next owner could claim it."

We resumed our summer routine easily. Rowan didn't arrive until almost three weeks later. He found us on the beach one afternoon, as we body surfed in the hot sun. He wouldn't, or couldn't, say what he'd done. Lydia said it was the longest he'd ever been away from her.

After we finished swimming we headed to the park to play chess. Rowan hopped around, excited. I opened my bag and took out a wooden box with ornate carvings of ravens and trees on it. It had a brass hasp and corners, and Rowan's name carved on it.

His eyes widened. *"What's thissss?"*

"Just a little something I made for you this winter."

He hopped on top of the box and began to eye the carvings. His claws made little clicking sounds on the wood. He tilted his head to the side to examine it.

*"You've outdone yourself."*

"Thank you."

Then Lydia said, "Hop off, the suspense is killing me. Let me open it so we can see what's inside."

He didn't respond. Instead, he hopped into the air and soared around us as she opened the box. She gasped as soon as she opened it, and he landed to look in. They peeked in the box, then at me and then back to the box.

"This is unbelievable," said Lydia.

He must have agreed for he hoped up and down repeating, *"Yesss."*

I smiled and reached over to the lid of the box where the board was stored. It stayed in place with two twisting metal flaps, which I moved aside to cause the board to come away from the lid. I unfolded the board, I sat it in the middle of the table. I lined the white pieces up on my side of the board, followed by the black pieces on his side. As I placed each one he eyed it, taking in the details. I'd almost finished when she beat me to the black king.

She looked at it and smiled. "It's you, with a crown." She held the piece up for his inspection.

"Yes, it is. But put it on the board, I wish to begin playing and break it in with my first win."

I rolled my eyes, "As if that's going to happen. I'm going to win this one."

He squawked with laughter as I made my first move. A quick game ensued, one in which the chicken did beat me. I bowed out, humbled by my loss, and Lydia took my place. The next game Rowan wasn't so lucky. She bested him. With the match done she came over and gave me a giant hug, then she planted a kiss on my cheek.

"The kiss is a thank you from Rowan."

He cawed. *"No, it isn't. My thank you was the hug. She claims the kiss."*

I turned to him and puckered my lips to send kisses his way.

*"Gross. I think I'm going to be sick,"* he said and he gave me his back, as Lydia and I laughed.

· ◈ ·

Every moment of the summer ended up being special to me. I felt like I knew them both well and I couldn't imagine my life without them in it.

In August I celebrated my sixteenth birthday with a large party at my family's house. They invited a ton of people, which made it easy for me to sneak Lydia in. My parent didn't notice, but I made sure not to spend too much time with her. I didn't want to draw attention to the fact we were friends. My parents would freak out over it and not allow me to see her anymore.

Such is the life of Kind teenagers; it's why we had separate boarding schools for girls and boys. My brother spent the rest of the time with her. He had come to spend a couple of weeks with us around my birthday. It was the first time I'd seen him since the previous September.

She gave me my birthday present after the party. Somehow she'd managed to get concert tickets for us to the Cure and the Cult later in August. We made it to both shows, though we had to sneak out to do it. For one of the shows Guy had to cover for me and I almost got caught. Thankfully, he managed to distract my mother from going into my room.

Having Guy around turned out to be fun. He seemed different. I don't know how to describe it, but he seemed more … mature maybe? He said his time in service hadn't been as miserable as he'd thought it would be. A lot of it had been interesting, even fun. Lydia and I incorporated him into our daily plans of going to the beach or playing chess. We just kept Rowan a secret. Lydia should have reported having a familiar, but from what I understand most who do have familiars avoid reporting it when they can. They see it as giving the KIC a weakness to be used against them. Of the laws, rules, and regulations, not reporting your familiar is probably broken the most.

The summer passed too quickly. It seemed like one minute I was greeting her on the beach and the next I was saying goodbye. I hated it. Over the summer, we'd discovered a large bookstore, a music store, a comic book store, and a movie theater. When we got bored hanging out on the beach, we'd head over to one of the stores or go to the theater and hop from movie to movie. We made it to Disneyland again, and several of the other amusement parks, too. She loved the roller coasters. Not me, but I tried to keep up appearances for her.

# CHAPTER FOURTEEN

### Mabon, 5 AM, Cornwall, England

I watched the two figures near the obelisk. No doubt they were security or KIC guards. Both appeared to be smoking cigarettes; probably on break. Their attention was focused in my general direction, because of the alarm. They started to move in my direction, when I heard a noise behind me. I gulped, doing my best not to panic. I didn't have a choice, I'd have to trust in the cape. The men continued on the path toward me. I veered to the side but saw no recognition of my presence. As they neared, my fear got the better of me and, not looking where I was going, I tripped.

The men shined a flashlight on me and one exclaimed, "It's only a cat."

The light flicked off and the two guards walked past me as I lay on the ground. My attention turned to the now unattended obelisk. I jumped up and ran to it. I slid to a stop as I neared and jumped into my portal. Once inside I fumbled for the marker and wrote the spell to close the portal. As soon as I emerged from the bathroom mirror, I stood atop the vanity panting, trying to catch my breath. I knelt and put my feet on the floor, then turned and shut the portal for good on my side. I wanted no trace I'd ever been there.

Before I got comfortable I needed to put the cape in my sketchpad in case I need it again; it wouldn't be good to get caught with it. I found my sketchpad and placed the cloak in its pages. Done, I sighed with relief and shed my clothes for a shower. I felt dirty. Under the hot water, I scrubbed my skin hoping to take away the feeling of wrongness. It didn't work.

I wrapped a towel around my waist and got out of the shower. A thought occurred to me; I'd never looked at what Aquila had given me earlier. The pants I'd worn earlier in the day were on the floor near my feet. I picked them up, to looked in the right, front pocket. In the pocket I found something the size of a marble at the bottom.

I pulled it out and looked at the white mass in my hand. *What is it?* Curious, I unwound the twine holding it together. The knot proved to be stiff, but with a tug, it came loose and fell away. I removed a piece of cloth which was old and yellowed with time, and when unfolded a piece of fabric about five inches square sat in the palm of my hand. On the yellowed side I could barely make out a faded signature. I pulled it closer to examine it better. After debating for a minute, I concluded it had to be Aquila's name. I dropped the cloth as I tried to flip it.

I knelt and picked it back up. The inside of the cloth was a detailed drawing of a raven's claw; it was the claw Muninn had given me years ago, which I'd lost. On one corner of the cloth Aquila had written: *1+12=13*.

I rubbed my temples wondering if things could get any weirder?

It was after five AM. I needed to get back to bed. Davidson would sleep in so I could get some rest, but first I had to deal with the dark object. If I kept it on me someone might sense it.

## CONVERGENT LINES

It was time to open the bag.

I lined the counter with some tissues to catch everything; I didn't want to leave a trace. I dumped out the contents of Hilda's bag: ash, rocks, sparkly fine powder, a black feather with a lump of something heavy. A feather? Why would there be a feather? I shook the bag to make sure it was empty, and then set it aside. I pulled out my pen-wand and used it to pick apart the things so I didn't have to touch them.

I decided the small rocks were onyx. The sparkly dust seemed to be ground-up crystals of some kind. I moved on to the black lump. Wrapped around the object several times was something which looked like fine string.

"Damn it!" I said dropping it into the sink. *That's hair, and probably my hair. How would she have gotten my hair?* I thought as I rubbed my chest.

I poked at the object again with my pen, unable to make sense of it for a minute. It was like a salt crystal, but dark and foggy, with something encased inside. I shifted my focus and picked up the tissues, again careful not to drop anything. I carried it into the bedroom and threw it into the fire, along with the bag it had been in. Like water, fire is good at purifying things, and while it might not destroy the onyx and small rocks it was the best way I could think of to be rid of it. Back at the sink, I turned on the hot water and let it run over the object. What was left was a dark, misshapen rock, about three inches across.

Unsure of what to do, I touched it. The object felt dirty and oily as the water ran over it. I picked up the soap, lathered some in my hand, and cleaned it. Once I'd washed and rinsed it I held it up to the light. Encased in a cloudy crystal-like substance, I could just make out the shape of something I never thought to see again. I swallowed. *How was this possible?* The feather now made sense. Inside the crystal, which seemed to melt away like salt, was my long-lost raven's claw from Muninn.

I needed to hide this in my sketchpad before I left, along with Aquila's note and anything else magic on me, in case the KIC or Davidson took me into custody. They'd search me and I'd have a hard time explaining any of this.

I grabbed the encased claw and the note, and stored them in my sketchpad. Finished, I put the pad on the nightstand. Sunrise would come soon. I let my eyes droop and I drifted off to sleep.

While I slept, dark shadows chased me. There I stayed for what didn't seem long before a pounding thud on the door roused me. I sat up rubbing my eyes. Between my late-night adventures and jet lag, Cornwall hadn't been much fun. The thud sounded again. I turned the alarm clock on the nightstand; it read 8:32.

"Come in," I yelled.

Sounds came from beyond the door. It must be Davidson, eager to get back home. To my surprise, my father walked through the door.

"Come on, get up. There's much ado this morning."

"What?"

"Someone broke into the Coven House last night and stole Hilda's soul. Davidson will be tied up for a while so you're under my custody. I'm starving."

I blinked at my father as I tried to process what he'd just said. I hadn't done anything to Hilda's soul. *Did someone break in after me? Crap! The soul of the most powerful necromancer was missing. What if someone had plans to use her for black magic, or worse? Damn it, of course they do, why else would you steal that evil woman's shriveled black soul? What if the black mist which escaped from her mouth was her soul? Shit!*

"Also, your brother is getting ready to leave on his honeymoon. Wouldn't you like to say farewell?"

"Of course. Are there any leads on Hilda?"

"No, but if someone got away with Hilda's soul, we're all in trouble. Honestly, the KIC is clueless. Nothing like this has happened in memory. I can't believe they didn't have her under guard or some protection."

I shook my head, wondering that now myself. If I'd had help and more time to plan I could have gotten in without them ever knowing. I thought back to her body. It hadn't looked disturbed. I desperately wondered if I'd left anything there which might tie me to her. I racked my brain and came up with nothing, unless they had someone who could time travel or read objects. Hopefully, the gloves I wore would stop them from being able to read any objects I touched. Those were rare talents, and something I should have thought about before I had broken in.

I looked up at my father to see he watched me.

"Are you okay?" he asked.

"Yes. Jet lag, late nights, lack of sleep, and the whole of my people's future on my shoulders might be the cause."

My father sniffed and twisted his mustache to the side. "When you put it like that, I'm sorry I asked."

"Could I have a few minutes to change?"

"Sure. Meet me downstairs and I'll tell your brother you will be there soon." He left without my answer. Ten minutes later I found Guy and Kensa surrounded by a big group of well-wishers. He looked up at me and smiled as I descended the staircase.

"Don't you look happy? Like a man without a care in the world." I said to Guy.

"What an apt description. Thanks for taking the weight of the world from me."

"You held it for too long anyway. You were making me look bad. Besides, there's this beautiful redhead who caught your fancy, how could you balance both?"

"Oh, Gray. It's not that bad," Kensa said. Guy's brows lifted. "Well, it is that bad, but you'll get used to the attention … after a while."

"A long while," Guy mumbled.

"Mostly it's just waiting. If I were you I would try to avoid Kind events, and shopping…" She bit her lip as she considered. "Maybe it would be best if you didn't leave your house for the next couple of years."

"Thanks, you two. If I wasn't worried before, I am now. Go, have fun. You both deserve it. I'll be fine … I hope."

Guy laughed and pulled me into a hug. I was happy for them. He released me and I turned to Kensa and kissed her cheek.

"Hurry back, so I can get to know my new little sister."

"You're so adorable. I happily claim you as my brother," she said.

Someone yelled, "Your car is waiting."

They left and the crowd in the hall dispersed. I went to find my dad and breakfast. He was sitting at a table in the dining room, with a cup of coffee. The room smelled amazing, of bacon, eggs, and coffee. I sat down next to him and a waiter appeared with coffee and a full plate. I dug in, hungrier than I'd realized. The food disappeared into my mouth faster than I'd have thought possible. As I sat my fork down, I heard a commotion by the door. I turned to see Davidson entering the dining room with several people in tow.

Spotting us, he headed for our table and sat in an empty seat.

"Please," he said to those following him. "I need to eat and make some phone calls. Let's meet around one and I'll address all of your concerns then." Several looked as if they weren't going to accept his terms as a server sat a cup of coffee down for him and he ordered food.

"I'm done, let me eat and figure things out. Now please, leave me in peace." Some of the people began to move. Three of them stayed for a couple of minutes as if they thought he would reconsider.

Once they finally cleared the room, Davidson put his face in his hands and sighed.

"That bad?" I asked.

"Yes." He picked up his coffee and downed it. An attentive waiter stood nearby refilled it as soon as the cup touched the table. Davidson reached for the sugar.

"I hope this isn't about me," I said.

"No. People want to know about you. Now that Aquila named you, your reputation is quickly soaring to rock star status, with every available female your fan."

I rolled my eyes.

"You can't be serious, Davidson?" Dad asked.

"I am. If I were you, I'd consider doing some expansions on your home's protection spells. Gray isn't going to have any privacy if this continues, and I'm sure it will. With an eligible bachelor named who can break the curse, every female now dreams of being the one to help him."

My father looked dumbstruck. I knew I'd get more attention after this revelation. I sipped my coffee to find it cold and bitter. I winced and set the coffee aside. The waiter picked the cup up without invitation and carried it away. As he departed, I marveled at the fantastic service here. He then returned with a new cup and sat it in front of me, refilling the contents from a fresh pot. I raised my brow in surprise. "This is the best service I've ever had."

"Thank you, sir, I consider that the highest of compliments. Especially from you." He bowed to me and walked away.

Davidson laughed. My father stared at him. "What's the matter?"

"Did you not see the reaction the waiter had to him? *That's* what I'm talking about." He sobered and began to finger his mustache.

"Dear Lord, I bet this means we're going to have a real problem with women throwing themselves at you."

My eyes grew large as I looked at him. "What do you mean?"

"Well, I've heard at least three separate titles for you this morning. The Guiding Light." He rolled his eyes at that. "Pathfinder, and my personal favorite, the Lodestar. I nominate the last, it has a nice ring to it."

"Honestly, Davidson. How can you find this so funny?" My dad asked.

"It's our new burden, we might as well laugh about it while we can. It will likely be a real pain most of the time."

The two of them went back and forth for a while. I'd considered having more attention, but the attention of the Council, not of others in the Kind. I didn't want women throwing themselves at me. Yeah, I know, "woe is me." Suddenly I'm the most desired man in our society, what's not to like? I hated everything about this. I didn't want the attention of others. I loved my privacy and didn't want my hard-won freedoms lost. It didn't take long before I tasted blood. My father and Davidson were close to fighting. It was time for me to intervene.

"Please, let's let this go. We can deal with it later," I said.

A plate of food arrived in front of Davidson and he dug in. I let him eat for a minute before I asked.

"Davidson?"

He swallowed a bite of food. "Yeah?"

"Is what my father said correct? Did someone steal Hilda's soul?"

He took a sip of coffee and picked up his fork and poked at his eggs. "I'm afraid so. The alarm at the Coven House sounded twice within an hour."

I looked at him in shock. I was sure he'd report there had been more than the two alarms. Surely someone had broken in before or after me to steal her soul. I might be guilty of grave robbing, but I didn't rob souls.

"Do they have any leads?"

"No," he said as he shook his head. "The only thing they have is two guards near the KIC office who responded to the second alarm; both saw a cat. We were hoping it might be a shifter or potion, but there's a problem with the reports of the two guards. One said he shined his flashlight on the cat and saw a black cat with yellow eyes. The other guard said he saw a big, feral tomcat with long brown hair."

I almost sighed with relief, but didn't dare.

"This can't be a shifter. We're wondering if there's some spell that could be the culprit."

"Is there any way to track her soul?" Dad asked.

"No, not with the necromancer we have left to us, no one is powerful enough. If Hilda had been alive, she probably could have." He rubbed at his temple. "We have everyone we could think of come and try to reconstruct what had happened. A psychometrist tried objects and door handles with no luck. We had a Carn scry to see if they could see anything. The people assigned to bring the body to the Coven House didn't do a proper exam of where she died or her body. It's possible she could have lost it before she ever reached the Coven House. They're over at Hilda's hospital room trying to reconstruct the scene to see if black magic was involved in her death. It's probably too late, the magic would have dissipated by now."

"Is this really your concern?" my father asked. "After all, this is Cornwall and there's a dedicated Council here."

Davidson let out a long breath. "There's only one Council member here right now, and she's the oldest. I'll be the one to research this until tomorrow, when someone will relieve me. It also means you're here until tomorrow, Gray. You're still in my charge."

I eyed him over the rim of my cup of coffee. "Fine with me. Do you mind if my father is my guardian for the day? I'd like to take a nap and see some of the sights with him."

He looked to my father. "If you agree, I am fine with it. I just ask you both to return before dark."

## CHAPTER FIFTEEN

### June 1990, Santa Cruz, California

With our constant communications throughout the school year, we'd been able to figure out when we could meet. It would be at sunrise at our usual spot, the earliest day we could, even if it meant we couldn't spend the whole day together. We managed to meet each other on Thursday morning, only a few days after school let out.

I beat her there and saw her approach. She wore a white Siouxsie and the Banshees T-shirt, with Siouxsie's black eyes staring out, cut-off shorts, and her hair in two ponytails. The things I'd sent her in my letters from the human world were having an impact. From where I was, I could get music, clothes, comics, books, and junk food that she couldn't. Because of this nearly every time I wrote her, I'd send her something. She sat down and leaned into me.

Now I know what you're thinking, how can you be watching the sunrise while facing the ocean on the West Coast? Easy, it's cool to watch the first rays reflect off of the water, and it's even better when the tide is coming in. This morning it was colder than I'd have liked and she felt warm against my side. I reached around her and put my arm on her shoulders and kissed the top of her head.

She curled into my side and we stayed like that until the sun was up. After the sun had risen, we walked along the boardwalk, hand in hand. She had to be back home no later than noon. Before she left, we stopped at the photo booth at the arcade for pictures. As she left me to wander the beach alone, Rowan landed on my shoulder.

"Been a while, old friend. What do you say to a game of chess?"

I noticed he carried his pack.

"You're on. Do you have your board?"

"Forevermore."

"Oh, you're so funny."

He cawed and bounced on my shoulder. *"Gitty-up, Gray, my stallion! To the park, we ride."*

"I should never have given you a TV and VCR. Let me guess, you're watching old westerns?"

Caw, *"Yup, I lived in the Old West; loved it. You forget I'm an old bird."*

I eyed him. "So are your feathers a glamour? Are you featherless from your feathers falling out and causing feather pattern baldness?"

*"You're not funny, sir. Though, sadly, you think you are."*

"I know I am, and I'm here for my entertainment, not yours. I find my sense of humor rather charming. In your old age you must not be able to appreciate us young whipper-snappers."

He shook his head and sighed in disgust. *"It's a good thing I like you and you're a decent chess player. Otherwise, I'd find me a new partner. What does she see in you?"*

I laughed hard, appreciating our banter. "I sure have missed you."

*"I'm sure you have; how could you not? Hey, did you bring bribery food so I'd play with you?"*

"Yes, you unappreciative chicken."

"Ah, that's just low. How about the loser has to walk along the boardwalk doing the chicken dance?"

"You're so on." We continued our banter to the park and through several close games. But I'm happy to report that Rowan in the guise of a chicken clucked his way down the boardwalk with my laughter as a soundtrack late that afternoon.

The summer turned out perfect. As it progressed, we would sneak out at night to join up and light a small fire on the beach. With a little magic it was easy to hide us from the sight of non-Kind. We'd meet a few times a week and roast marshmallows. Most of them turned out to be for Rowan. That bird has a taste for all things junk food. Later in the summer Guy joined us, too.

Lydia was fifteen, and the prettiest girl I'd ever seen. Often the surfers would take notice and hit on her. I'd have been jealous, except she always looked like a deer in the headlights when it happened. After the first few times she learned to use me, which I didn't mind at all. She'd walk up to me and put her arm around me or grab my hand and introduce me as her boyfriend. Oh, the things it did for my ego.

My seventeenth birthday came and went. She gave me a poem she'd written for a gift, titled "Gray." I loved it.

This summer, I felt like I'd finally outgrown my awkward period. It became rare for there to be anyone taller than me at the beach, and the surfers started to steer clear. The downside was that the non-Kind girls started paying too much attention to me. It drove Lydia nuts. She might have been little, but she was sassy and told more than one girl off. My ego soared to new heights.

We both knew that discussing a relationship would get us nowhere. Our fate rested in our families' hands. There were many nights I'd dream of running away to live in the human world. To be free to pick a career, love whom I wanted, and have freedom. As summer progressed I got to spend more time with Guy, as Lydia's responsibility to her grandmother's social calendar kept her busy. Guy seemed happier then I remembered him being. He liked the path our father had taken in politics.

The next year he would be given more freedom than either of us had experienced before. I had plenty of freedom during the summers in California, but I wasn't about to tell him. The things Lydia and I did, for the most part, I kept from him. The two of us escaped to the various amusement parks, to see movies, even going as far as being extras in a couple of films, to driving up and down the coast with my father's car.

Lydia took pictures of our adventures to San Francisco and Catalina. There were also lots of concerts, plays, and even the symphony at the Hollywood Bowl. One night I made us fake IDs, and we got into Whisky a Go Go to see a band. These were the best of times, from June until early September with her. Things were changing for the human world and ours. The Berlin Wall had fallen, the USSR had started to collapse, and technology increased to a point it was becoming a real problem for the Kind. We tend to have strange effects on technology. The older I got, the more I impacted technology. For me, this became a fascination. I wanted to know all about human technology and if I could adapt it for the Kind. My father noticed and encouraged this in me. He said it came from the Penrose genes.

The summer ended earlier than I'd have liked. She had to go back to Cornwall at the end of August for a wedding in her family, which would happen on Mabon. Her grandmother had to be there for the planning.

She managed to get out of the house the night before she left. We spent it on the beach in front of the fire. Just before sunrise I helped her to get back into her house without anyone noticing.

The next two weeks would have sucked had it not been for Guy. He got our parents' permission to take me camping in Northern California. This was my first real camping trip, and Guy taught me a bunch of magic, natural magic, in the woods. He also started teaching me about the Penrose affinity for fire. By the second night, I was able to light the fire without the use of matches. Over those two weeks, I found I could call fire to me in many forms, or stop a fire from spreading. I seemed to be able to do things even my father couldn't do.

Guy seemed impressed. The fire gift hadn't come easy for him, producing fire was forced, but he discovered something interesting about himself during our trip. He could see magical beasts. I couldn't until he pointed them out to me.

Our trip reaffirmed something I had always noticed, and wondered if my brother did, too. Being brothers, our magic should be similar, as it usually is with siblings. What usually differed was the strength of magic. But I had no doubt my brother had powerful magic, it just wasn't the *same* magic.

We went deep into the wilderness for the trip and something about the area we'd picked, or were drawn to, appeared magical. Perhaps there were ley lines? He showed me how to use a pendulum to find ley lines, which could amplify my magic if I found the right spots. He gave me my own pendulum, a heavy silver one on a silver chain with a rose charm at the end.

The time spent with my brother camping sealed our bond, and for the first time since we were young, we were close. As Mabon of 1990 dawned we arrived back in Santa Cruz to meet with our father and return home for the celebrations.

# CHAPTER SIXTEEN

### September, Cornwall, England

I took a nap for most of the morning, and that afternoon my father took me on a tour of the Kind's town of Cornwall. A separate area located within the human's Cornwall, but protected from humans. He even took me to the KIC offices, and I stood next to the obelisk I'd used the night before.

My mother joined us for dinner at a local restaurant, called the Silver Moon. I enjoyed my evening with them. Whatever had been causing the problems between my parents for years seemed to have changed with the revelation about Guy. Even her attitude toward me had changed. Perhaps something good would come out of this yet.

After a large meal and sampling several of the local ales, I retired early. Davidson didn't seal me in this time; he was probably too busy. I expected we'd be off to the States in the morning, which is what I wanted. No more Cornwall for me. I'd rather return home.

After a good night's sleep, I awoke early and found myself too lazy to get up. A knock sounded on the door. "Come in," I said.

Davidson opened the door. "I hope I didn't wake you."

"No," I said as I sat up. "Been up for a few minutes, just being lazy."

"Well, it's early, only a few minutes after seven."

I studied the clock on the wall behind him, surprised to see he was right.

"It sounds like I'm here for another day. We're having problems getting into her house. Apparently, she has several spells in place. We have one of her sons coming to help us out." He sighed, and run his hand through his hair. I knew what was to come.

"We can't return until tomorrow. Sorry."

"It's fine, but I wonder if you would mind if I roamed the town again today? I promise I'm not going anywhere. I'd like to see if some old friends are here."

"Sure, I trust you. But please be back early again. I'm holding a fleeting hope we can leave this evening."

"Great. Have fun with your breaking and entering."

"Yeah, yeah," he said, and he waved his hand on the way out.

At first I wasn't happy about my situation, but then I realized this would give me time to look through the papers I'd stolen from Hilda's house.

I got up, showered, then went and grabbed something to eat. There was no one else about while I ate, except for the service staff. Afterward I found myself back in my room. I decided it would be easiest and best to do this at home. I grabbed my sketchpad with my things, and headed for the bathroom. I spelled the mirror portal to my closet in the States and peeked out into my room. In Connecticut, the time difference made it sometime in the middle of the night. We didn't have staff living in our home with us, but to be safe, I took my wand out and said, "Anyone home?" I flicked my hand with the wand toward the open door of my room. The spell returned a couple of minutes later in the form of a globe of blue light. I was alone. If the orb had been red or orange, it would mean someone else was in the house.

I sighed, thankful for the peace. I'd still need to be careful. Someone could see me turn on a light. I left my room and ascended the stairs, using the moonlight from the high windows to find my way. In my study, I closed the curtains and turned on a lamp. At my desk, I set down my sketchbook and sat in my comfortable leather chair. It felt good to be home, even if it was only for an hour. I flipped through the pages until I found the files from Hilda's office. Open to the page with the file I reached in and pulled it out.

The file on Lydia was thick and comprehensive, with candid photos throughout. Lydia in her school uniform was a sight to see. She looked incredible in a navy pleated skirt, white shirt, and knee high socks. My teen self wouldn't have handled this well. It was bad enough having sex forbidden to us, but images like this would have tortured my hormones.

In the file, I found what I expected, school paperwork for the years at Skol Hus. I think Skol Hus means something like magic school in Cornish. There were notes of her behavior, observations, and report cards. Year after year, the same report. Lydia seemed a typical, well-behaved student with average magic skills for her age. From five until thirteen the notations remained the same. A few months before I met her the first interesting report from her creative writing teacher appeared. Mrs. Eden Marrak wrote a note to Hilda saying Lydia was very talented with language and the written word. She believed Lydia would be good at charms and spells in the coming years.

This notation looked like it had been referenced many times, as if Hilda had taken an interest in it. Things changed in late 1988; some incident, but not with Lydia. Her cousin Jessy had something happen, and the school said they wouldn't allow her to attend classes there anymore because they didn't trust her to room with anyone. Hilda arranged for her to stay with Lydia. At this point she started asking for more reports on both, and limited the school teaching them magic. Strange things started to appear in the file at this point; here random newspaper clippings were inserted. Old stories seemed random, except for the commonality of the events all happened at Skol Hus. Of the seven articles, three were about accidental deaths of students. Two were deaths of elderly staff members, and the rest were of magic gone wrong, accidents. In the columns of the pieces were her notes in some strange shorthand, a combination of Cornish and maybe … French? I couldn't decipher any of the notes. I spent at least an hour trying to make some guess at the reason for the clippings. I arranged them on the table in order of events, in categories, and anything else I could think of. Nothing.

The reports from the school seemed to get more frustrated in Lydia's last two years. I stopped and turned back to the beginning of the file. It occurred to me I hadn't seen a birth certificate, baby photos, pictures of her parents, or anything about her early life. Flipping back through I didn't find anything. She'd told me her parents had died in a car accident, but there was *nothing* about it here. I set the file down and thought about what I knew of Hilda. Her death announcement would go out in the *Daily Arcane* soon; maybe I'd get some answers about her age, how many times she'd been married, and how many children she'd had. With that information I could get into the KIC system and research further. My position and knowledge would let me do this unnoticed.

I looked down at my watch. Sunrise would soon happen here. I had to get back to Cornwall. I put everything back in the folder, marking my place so I could pick it up later. I stuffed everything back into my bag, turned out my light, and headed back to my closet to return to Cornwall.

I walked into the mirror and came out on the other side in my room at the Kolon. In the bathroom, I heard a sound out in my room. Curious, I leaned against the wall by the door, listening.

"He isn't here," said a male voice.

"No. I don't think he's involved, but as soon as I find him again, I'll have him shadowed. We can't take any risks." He remained quiet for a minute, and I realized he was talking on the phone to someone. I risked a peek around the corner, I saw Davidson's back as he faced my bed.

"Damn it. There's no reason to put him under arrest. Doing things like that will ensure he doesn't cooperate with us. Better to leave him free and follow him. If he has secrets, we will find them. He's smart, too smart. I also suspect he may be one of the most powerful in our world, but he refuses to show his powers. If we're to find them out it will be through watching him. I'm in charge and I've decided to do it this way. If he gets away, I'll take responsibility. You can tell that to the rest of the Council."

My heart pounded loud in my chest and I breathed in shallow breaths. If I wanted to get one last thing done I needed to get out of here before anyone saw me. When we got back home I'd have to consider my situation further and come up with a plan. There was no way I would be a prisoner or slave to my people. I would run if necessary, but it was not my preferred option.

"No, we haven't made any progress on her house. To be honest, I don't think we will, either. Several of her family members have tried, and let's just say, it hasn't been pretty. A few people had to go to the hospital."

He listened to the other person. "No, I've no idea where the power for this is coming from. Every one of us is at a loss. She was old and had no problem using the blackest of magic. Her house library contains lots of lost knowledge. We need in there. Though with the responsibility of Grayson I've decided to hand off her house to another member and come home in the morning. When we arrive, I'll head straight to the office with him. No, I won't forget, and I won't lose him. Yeah, 'bye."

As the call ended, I heard him leave the room with heavy footfalls. I dared a peek into the bedroom to see him walk through the door to the hall. If I wanted to get to *her* I'd have to get my cape again, I opened my sketchpad and found the page with the cloak. I pulled it out, unfolded the velvet fabric, and fastened it around my neck. After last night, I knew it worked. With sketchpad in hand, I headed out of my room.

I encountered no one in the hall. At the top of the grand staircase I stopped, there were several people below. I took a deep breath and descended the stairs. Half way down I noticed Davidson talking to my dad next to the door I needed to go out through. A full-blown panic attack hit me. Committed I continued forward. As I neared them, the door behind Davidson opened. A distant

Penrose, one I'd been introduced to but couldn't remember his name, came in. He held the door and said, "They need you again, Davidson."

Davidson turned to look right at me, then to the man addressing him.

"Show me where," Davidson responded as he followed the guy out the door. I followed on his heels, and right on passed my father. He didn't even spare me a glance. It was so weird to walk around as if I were invisible. I wondered how the cape would disguise me if I spoke. Right now probably wasn't the time to find out. Davidson and the man with him walked off to a waiting car.

The black sedan sped off, kicking up dust.

"Can I help you, sir?" A servant asked.

"Ah, yes. I need to go into town."

"I can call a car for you or you may borrow one of the loaner cars."

"I'll take a loaner."

"But of course, what's your name?"

I saw no problem now with getting away or being discovered, I figured I could use my name. "Grayson Penrose, and I should only be a couple of hours."

"Yes sir, it isn't a problem," he said as he handed me a set of keys. "These are for the white Mercedes. You will find a map in the side of the door. Is there anything else I could help you with?"

"No. You have been more than helpful."

"Thank you, sir."

I opened the door and attempted to sit in the driver's seat. The seat had been set for someone much shorter than me.

"Please, let me help," said the servant. I stood back as he adjusted the seat for me. When he moved away, I easily got into the car and he shut the door. I turned the key, the engine roared to life, and I pulled out. I'd driven a similar C-Class, but in the States. This one felt weird, everything being opposite.

In town, I found a busy parking lot and pulled in. I brought up the GPS on my phone and punched in Jessy's address. I hoped she would be home and willing to talk to me. From what Lydia had told me about her, it could be a problem. She sounded terribly shy.

## CONVERGENT LINES

While I'd never met her in person I'd heard rumors about her more than a decade earlier; the worst kind of stories for someone in the Kind. According to the rumors, her family had tried to arrange a marriage. The groom must have been from prominent line, or perhaps it may have been Jessy. She went before the Oracle, probably Aquila, and in front of everyone, received the worst of news. The Oracle wouldn't approve the marriage based on an unequal match. It wasn't said outright, but everyone believed it was her. The male, whose family name I couldn't remember, had a high position within the KIC. I'd heard she'd been disowned by her family, though not banished, but left with no one to live with on the outskirts of the Kind. When I'd heard about it, I wished I knew her personally and could help.

I pulled out of the parking lot and headed east. The GPS said nine minutes to her home. The city thinned and I found myself on a country road again. As I followed the map I saw several cars ahead on the left and smoke. As I neared, I noticed a fire truck and ambulance. So many cars surrounded the mansion I slowed, pulled close to the shoulder so I could pass. On the other side of the fire truck I could see the cause of the smoke. A large house smoldered.

Off to the side, stood Davidson, surrounded by firefighters. The house had to be Hilda's. I cursed my luck, though I should have expected Jessy's house to be near Hilda's. She was a Rosdew, after all. Fortunately, everyone seemed more interested in the fire, and paid no attention to me.

Not far past Hilda's house the road curved and I entered a forest with dense trees on both sides of the road. I rolled the window down, enjoying the woody smell. The day had been bright, no clouds in the sky, and warm. Not what I'd expected of autumn weather in England. I breathed in deep of the smells and relaxed. I didn't know what tomorrow held, but I finally knew the answers to several questions. My future, while still hazy, had gained some definition for the first time in years.

Whatever my fate with the Council, I decided to have faith. I had the power. The Kind needed me, not the other way around. If they wanted me to do something, they'd meet my terms. Sure, they could throw me in jail or try to force me into marriage, I simply wouldn't consummate it. After going this long in my life without sex, I could go for a bit longer. Though I didn't relish the idea. The binding would only break for me if, what Aquila said were true.

The female voice on the GPS interrupted my thoughts, *"Your destination is in eleven hundred meters on the right."* The forest next to me appeared thick with no houses in sight. I began to slow the car as I approached a sharp curve in the road.

*"Your destination is on the right."* As the road straightened, a small clearing, with a house set off the road, appeared. A dirt track wound to the house. The term road didn't apply to the rutted and worn path which lay before me. I made it far enough off the track as not to be a hazard. Destroy the car or park it and walk? I parked the car.

Deciding it was best not to go in disguise, I removed the cape, folded it, and put it in my sketchpad. I noticed her file and wondered if I should have read it first? No, this way if she asked I wouldn't be lying. In the Kind world, one learns quickly to tell half-truths or avoid answering, too many natural lie detectors around.

I shut the car door and began to walk. The house was small but loved. Several minutes later I realized the house sat much further back from the road than I'd thought.

The gardens were beautiful. Jessy must have an affinity for growing things. Late blooming flowers surrounded me in the flowerbeds. Smells of earth and sun flowed into my nostrils as I breathed in deep. Heather and lavender stood higher than my knees, and the smells were heavenly. Like so many humans and Kind, I spend too much time indoors. Part of why our magic is disappearing, in my opinion, has been everyone's move away from the earth. We no longer sit out every night and watch the sky or trek through the forest, except on rare occasions. The heart of a witch is of the earth. How can one remain connected to the earth without spending time with her? It's a question I struggled with often.

I climbed the wooden steps to the door. As I knocked I wondered at my reception—would she speak to me? Behind the door, I heard shuffling. Guess I'd find out soon enough. The door cracked open as far as the chain would allow. One dark brown eye with a blond corkscrew of hair hanging over it peered at me.

"Hello."

"What do you want?" said a thickly accented voice.

"I'm looking for Jessy Rosdew."

"The news of Hilda has been received. You may be on your way."

"This does concern Hilda, but not her death. I'd like to speak to you about your cousin, Lydia." The eye narrowed with suspicion.

"Are you Grayson?"

"Yes, and I need to speak with you in private. Please. I'll be quick, but I think you'll want to hear me out, and I've something for you."

The door closed. After a second I heard the chain move. I'd at least get to tell her my story.

"Come in," she said with her arm outstretched to the inside of the house.

"Thank you." I risked thanking her; I wanted her to feel like she was in control here and I needed her help, because I did.

As I entered, my eyes had to adjust to the dark room. The sunspots started to disappear from my sight after a few moments. I found a small cozy sitting room surrounded a well-used hearth. It seemed my eyes took longer to adjust than usual; several times I thought I saw things out of the corner of my eyes.

"Have a seat," said Jessy from behind me. "Can I get you something?"

I wondered what she looked like. I'd never seen even a photo of her.

"No, your counsel is all I seek." My attention turned to the small girl who followed me. I say girl because she seemed no older than seventeen, even though she had to be close to forty now. I searched her face hoping to see a resemblance to Lydia. She shared her cousin's small stature, but the similarity ended there. She had brown smoky eyes, pale freckled skin, and a mop of curly strawberry-blonde hair. Dressed in light colored jeans and a white tank top, she was too thin. Her button nose twitched in a rather cute manner.

She giggled as she sat in an old wooden rocking chair opposite me. "If you're looking for a resemblance to my cousin you won't find it."

"Caught," I said unashamedly. I was desperate for a connection to Lydia. Her cheerful disposition helped me relax.

"What brought you all the way out here? I'd ask why you're in Cornwall, but I know of your brother's wedding."

I swallowed, finding my throat dry. "I came to see you. Things, weird things, have been happening the last few days."

"Yes, I imagine finding out our race is dependent upon you could be a hard thing to deal with."

"It is, but I'm here to talk about something else … Your grandmother put a curse upon me." I reached into my backpack and pulled out the dark object, holding it up for Jessy to see. Her eyes grew large.

"I'd ask you if you were sure, but I can feel the dark magic flowing off that thing. It feels like her."

"It does?"

"Yes."

"I only met her a few times."

"Then how do you know she cursed you?"

Over the next hour, I explained everything, even my breaking into the Coven House. She listened to me, with only a few questions to clarify points. When I finished, she asked for the dark object. I handed it to her. She examined at it for a few minutes.

"The claw inside belongs to you? It has special meaning?"

"Yes, the necklace was a gift to me, and a prized procession. I thought I'd lost it the last time I saw Lydia."

She seemed shaken. "Why come to me? You take a great risk telling me these things."

"Because Lydia trusted you, and I've no one else to go to."

"The black mist you saw come out of Hilda's mouth was her soul. She must have anchored it to the dark object." She sighed, "I bet she figured you would feel the curse lift and come in search of the object, thus freeing her soul. You are sure you didn't feel the curse when she placed it on you?" she asked.

"I've been told it hurts, and I can't think of any time in the past I felt unexplained pain."

"I'm sure she cursed you, but … why? There wasn't anything for her to gain, and to maintain one for a quarter of a century takes great power." She lifted the hunk of resin with the claw in it toward me.

"Here, take this back. I hate the way it feels."

I did so. "I know. Do you have any idea where I might be able to find out what the curse was?"

She bit her lower lip as her fingers played with the wooden handle of the chair. "I don't. What happened all those years ago haunts me to this day. Hilda was an evil, vile woman. She knew nothing of love, longing only for power for herself."

"Were you around when …" I didn't get to finish my question.

"No," she said as she shook her head. "I had lost favor with Hilda before everything." Her fingers continued to fidget, and she seemed to watch something near the fireplace.

"Before I left for the wedding, I broke into Hilda's old house in California." Her head whipped up to look me in the eyes and her hands stilled.

"I went in looking for the cause of the curse and any information I could find." While I'd shared secrets, I hadn't shared everything.

"You managed to get in?"

"Yes, only her bedroom seemed to be hexed. I also took several of Lydia's old things. I hope you can forgive me, for wanting her stories and pictures."

"No, you deserve at least that."

"I managed to get into Hilda's office and I took several files." Several expressions played out over Jessy's face. I reached into my backpack and pulled out her file. "One of them had your name on it." I handed it to her. She took it with big eyes.

She looked so scared, as if Hilda's ghost had haunted her long before she died. "Please, don't tell anyone of our discussion today.

I brought the file to you, and I want you to know I haven't read it, I swear. But I'm keeping Lydia's."

"I won't tell anyone you were here or that we talked. Thank you for giving me this. I always wondered what she knew of me."

"Did Hilda have a familiar?"

She blinked up at me and cocked her head to the side, just like Lydia used to do. For a long moment she seemed lost in her own head.

"No. I never saw one or heard any rumors. I'd even say she wouldn't have kept one if she did. Sacrificing a familiar brings a lot of power. The kind of power she would have wanted."

From my pocket, I pulled out a business card and handed it to her. "I'm going to go. There's my number. Please call me if you think of anything or if I can help you. Lydia cared about you, and I know things haven't been ideal for you. If I can help, please let me."

She nodded. I headed to the door and turned to look at her one last time, and for a second, I swear a man stood next to her; a ghostly figure. I rubbed my eyes and looked back to see Jessy focused on the folder in her hands. I shut the door behind me and walked back to the car, maybe something positive would come from today.

## CHAPTER SEVENTEEN

### June 1991, Santa Cruz, California

Lydia wouldn't arrive as early as she had last year. Her grandmother had plans which kept them another two weeks in Cornwall. Guy wasn't here yet, and only my mother had come with me to California. My dad wouldn't follow for a while. It would be just my mom and me. At best, we had a strained relationship, most of the time we were barely on speaking terms. The norm held true for now. Ever since I can remember I'd wondered what I'd done to my mother, why did she not like me? I didn't have any real answers to that question, and I didn't dare ask my family.

After years of considering, I'd come up with an explanation, I think it's because I'm a male. Yeah, I know in most of the world a boy is preferred, but not among the Kind. A female means more power, thus more power for the family. In the days of old, your family became your Coven, and together the power gained by this is what made humans fear witches and magic. When families worked as Covens, it led to vendettas.

The Kind usually take the last name of the parent which your magic most resembles. In my case I have the Penrose name because my magic is closer to my father's. Guy took the Penrose name, too, but it's because his magic didn't fit into either of my parent's abilities easily.

In earlier times, you would live within your Coven's holding. For a married couple, the decision was often determined upon which one was the more powerful after the marriage to decide which Coven you would join. Spouses would usually adopt the last name of the family they were conscripted to. Because the females were usually the more powerful members, male children were often lost to their birth family once they married. If one was lucky they would marry into a Coven which was allied with their birth Coven. Allies became important, but if you were from warring Covens or were a peace offering, rarely did things go well.

Families could be split apart with this approach. Your will was not your own, the decisions of the Coven would rest upon the Pennaeth, most often an older, widowed woman. She would usually have one male advisor and one female. They were referred to as the Tri-Pennaeth. The Tri-Pennaeth were chosen by force and sheer power, proven during magical duels. While this system prevailed, black magic ran rampant, with weaker members of the Coven often sacrificed to perform the magic. Vendettas arose from fighting for dominance, the splitting of families, or over magical artifacts and knowledge.

As most of Europe dealt with the Black Plague, the Kind lost most of its population not to sickness, but to fighting and sacrifice for black magic. The Coven system allowed for spells to be worked in tandem, to create more powerful magic. It also attracted the attention of humans.

The old ways favored the strong, enslaved the weak. It also brought attention to the Kind because displays of power and mass destruction are difficult to hide. Once this was the way of the Kind's world. Thirteen separate Covens, each vying to be the most powerful. About a thousand years ago, the Kind saw the start of our new system, with the Elder Council and laws designed to hide us from human attention. We lost many of our members in the early days because of the fighting. That, combined with our powers and longevity diminishing, brought about change. The Binding of 1645 made the laws and enforcement of the laws important to our survival. It had made strengthening the bloodlines into an almost-breeding program, a focus of the Council.

Our current system might not be perfect, but it was better than the old ways.

Engrossed in a *Wired* magazine I didn't notice Lydia's approach. She finally had to shout at me to get my attention. Startled, I looked directly up into her blue eyes.

She smiled at me. "Are you going to say anything?"

I shook my head, pulled her down next to me in the sand, and held her tight. She leaned into me. Everything felt right, except something was off with her. Outwardly she seemed happy, but I could tell she wasn't.

"What is it?" I asked.

"Nothing."

"Don't do that. Tell me what's wrong."

"It's my grandmother."

"What? Is she sick?"

"No, she's starting to scare me."

"What do you mean?"

"She's watching my every move. Even at school, she has a ghost tailing me."

I pulled back and stared into her face and realized she'd been crying. "I don't understand? Did you upset her? Has she found out about Rowan?"

"If I upset her I don't know how and I don't know why. The spirit doesn't know about Rowan. It's because of Rowan I know about the ghost. He spends most of his time in the library you created, only leaving it while I'm in class."

"Is it following you now?"

"No, it appears to be tied to the school's building. To get away from it I go outside. It's the only way I can send you messages or get yours. But I don't know how much I can get out this summer to see you. She's up to something."

"Why didn't you tell me this before?"

"I didn't want to bother you."

"You aren't bothering me."

Rowan landed on the table next to us. *"She told you?"*

"Yes. What are your thoughts, Rowan? Why would she be watching her so closely?"

*"I don't know."*

"Is there anything else weird?"

He tilted his head to look up at Lydia, in a manner which made me think he might be prodding her.

"What?"

"She doesn't want me instructed in many forms of magic. The headmistress is mad, and I think she plans to go to the KIC."

"Did you have a hard time getting away?"

"No. I don't think she feels there's much of a chance of me meeting other Kind here and she thinks of humans as lowly creatures. I've taken to bribing the staff at the house; they like me and fear her. When she's away they tell her I stay about the house reading or go to the beach and come home early. She seems to believe them thus far, but who knows."

"I'll teach you. This summer, and what little time we have next summer, I'll show you the stuff you're missing at school. Rowan, think you could find a place suitable to give her lessons, away from humans?"

*"Yes. I like this idea. I shall find something today for you."*

"Good." He took off, disappearing into the sky.

I pulled her into a hug. "We'll figure this out."

She spent the next few hours with me, and I told her all about my life in hopes of taking her mind off her troubles. She left early to make sure to be home before Hilda.

Rowan tapped on my window, waking me. It had been almost a year since he'd done it, but it woke me faster than my alarm clock. I let him in. A frigid, wet breeze blew in, and I got back under the covers.

"I found a place, but we'll have to wait until tomorrow. She's going to some annual luncheon with Hilda and the weather is terrible."

"What did you find?"

"An unused warehouse. It's secure, but you should be able to get in."

"Good, is it close?"

He tilted his head. "I think. Your sense of distance is different than mine. I can fly there in under five minutes."

While I wasn't sure of the exact distance, I'd bet it was a couple of miles. Which would be manageable on skateboards. Now that we had a place to practice I needed more information.

"Do you think Hilda is using black magic on Lydia?"

"Yes. She isn't above using anything to get what she wants, even the darkest of magic. It's why my grandmother watches her. Let me tell you a story; one I've not shared with Lydia."

"I'm guessing I won't like it?"

He shook his head. "His name escapes me, but I know he would be a relative of yours, though a distant one. He lived more than a hundred years ago and was the most eligible bachelor of his day. You know the Rosdews and Nancarrows have a very long history, some good, some bad, but they consider themselves allies."

He made himself more comfortable next to me.

"Hilda, as I heard it, had lived through her first husband, or two, by then. She had already had children, but due to her powers and the fact she had proven to be fertile, the KIC wanted her to remarry. She had her heart set on a much younger man, a Nancarrow. Evidently he was a heartthrob of the time." He puffed his feather out.

"He must have spurned her advances or his family said no. He'd been powerful, and the KIC wished to keep him happy, but she wouldn't let it go. Somehow she arranged an alibi for herself."

"What do you mean alibi?"

"They found his body, still living, but barely, and without his spirit. Within a week his body died. To do that caliber of black magic, you *would need to be close. She was in the States and he was in Cornwall when it happened. It's one of the great mysteries within the Kind. His spirit was never found. Many believe she destroyed it; something very powerful necromancers are said to be able to do. But here's the point, don't mess with Hilda."*

I had heard some of the stories before, but not linked to Hilda.

"Then what's your guess about Hilda's interest in Lydia?"

*"I think Hilda wants something from Lydia."*

I thought about his story for a while. "On that, we agree."

We hung out in my room all day. I went to get us something to eat, and we resumed playing chess and cards while he filled me in on the gossip and the year at school.

· ꩜ ·

Early the next morning Lydia and Rowan met me at the beach, and he led us to the warehouse he'd found. We skated there. I could have driven us, but I didn't want to risk a car in the area. The warehouse he'd found ended up being about two miles from my house. It was surrounded by a chain link fence, but on the back side someone had cut a hole in it. A basic padlock secured the door. I searched around to see if there might be any video feeds. At one time there might have been, but not now. The padlock hadn't been opened for some time and showed signs of rust.

"Come here, watch me do this," I said.

She came to the top of the metal stair platform in front of the door. I grabbed my favorite pen and put the tip inside the lock. "This is my wand. It's something meaningful to me which helps me focus my energy. I insert it into the lock and focus."

I focused my energy and said, "Unlock."

The padlock *clicked* and flakes of rust fell. Next time I'd need to bring some oil for the lock and door. I removed the lock, and hung it on the nearby hand rail.

"I can't believe you unlocked it, and we're breaking in."

I turned to her and smiled. "Come on, I draw something and it becomes real isn't hard for you to believe, but using magic on a lock is? Besides, breaking in is an excellent way to learn some magic."

"I see your point. Let's see what's inside."

"Oh, now you're okay with this?"

"Come on, let's not stand out in the open." She brushed past me into a dark room. I closed the door behind us after Rowan flew in.

With the door closed, the room became too dark to see. I opened my hand, and a ball of fire appeared. Lydia jumped. "How did you do that?"

The ball of fire hovered above my palm, when I moved my palm, it moved. "I'm a Penrose. I have an affinity for fire. My brother taught me how."

"Doesn't it burn you?"

"No."

She watched the ball of fire as I used it to look around the room. There were several old chairs scattered about, many upside-down or broken, and one filing cabinet with the drawers open. It was hard to tell from this room that we were in a warehouse.

"Come on. We'll need something more open."

She followed me through the open door into a hallway. It took several minutes to find our way out of the maze and into a large open space. Puddles of water spotted the floor along with the occasional two-by-four. Light streamed in from the windows lining the wall where it met the roof. I took our skateboards and put them and my backpack on the one wooden table. This room would work just fine.

Rowan flew around the room looking for a hole large enough for him. He must have found one in the back corner because he disappeared for a minute and then reappeared.

"Rowan, would you stick around? I may need your help."

*"Yes."*

"Before we start we need to figure out your wand."

"Can I use a pen like you?"

"I don't think that would work for you. While you might like to write you use a typewriter most of the time. No, I'd like something you would connect with more, to make this easier for you."

*"I know,"* Rowan said as he landed on her shoulder. *"Take one of my tail feathers."*

"I'm not going to start plucking your feathers."

Rowan shook his head. *"Just take one of my long tail feathers. I'm a magical beast and your familiar. It will work, and besides, I regrow feathers fast. Just be gentle."*

I was happy he had learned to project his thoughts to both of us. The one-sided conversations I'd heard were at best weird, but usually uncomfortable. He turned around giving her his splayed tail feathers.

*"Pluck away."*

The expression on Lydia's face hadn't improved.

"He's right, it will be magical on its own, and you'll connect with it," I said.

She rubbed her face as she tried to decide. She looked at me, pleading, but I gave her no recourse. I watched her as she took a breath, then reached up and plucked a long tail feather. For Rowan's part, he squawked and flew away. While I'm sure it wasn't pleasant I knew he was playing it up. Her face turned red.

"He's teasing you. I'm sure it didn't feel good, but he will live."

*"Lighten up. Plucking a feather doesn't hurt me,"* he said to calm her.

"You dirty little chicken," she yelled at him. "How dare you let me feel guilty for hurting you!"

He bowed his head in shame.

"Let's get down to business," I said.

Most of the day was spent showing her different spells, from simple things like summoning, to defensive spells. I didn't spend too much time on any of them with her. I wanted to know if the feather worked for her as a wand and where her abilities lay. Some of the simple spells were a challenge for her—I suspected Hilda had long been holding back on her training—but she excelled at defensive spells. She would easily surpass me in defensive magic. Cursing and defensive arts had never been Penrose strengths. We were better at traditional means of war, such as sword fighting or hand to hand combat.

## CONVERGENT LINES

Every time she could get away, we'd start by practicing magic. The first few weeks we went over the basics. Her affinity with Rowan's feather was as strong or stronger than mine to my favorite pen. But after the end of the first week, she wanted to give up.

"I don't want to do this. I've spent the last hour trying to summon my skateboard to me. It's on the floor, flat on its wheels, and it still won't work. I don't have any abilities."

I sighed, "It's harder because no one taught you these things early. You have the abilities, but it's like learning a foreign language, the older you are the harder it is."

"Can we quit for today?"

"Let's try this again, without your wand. You need to be proficient at this in case you don't have your wand and need something. If a human had you trapped, you'd need this."

She gazed at me with her arms wrapped around herself, looking defeated.

"One more time."

"Fine," she whined.

I didn't like being hard on her. "I had a thought last night. Your father was a Rosdew, right?"

"Yes, my grandmother was his mother. Or the few clues I have say."

"Do you know what family your mother came from?"

She blinked again and looked as if she might cry. "I don't know ... maybe. My grandmother let something slip recently. She was upset and talking to one of her daughters."

"What did she say?"

"Something about how she 'never approved of that damn Teague,' 'never should they have been allowed in the family,' and 'it's why they're both dead now.' She had to have meant my parents. It's all I can figure, no one else I know of has died."

The Teague family is the largest Kind family. They're like our middle class, and fulfill many of the basic roles, like teachers.

"Sorry. I didn't mean to upset you. The reason I asked is, if you knew we could figure out if you had an affinity for your mother's magic. I don't have any of my mom's abilities. Guy got those powers."

She sniffed, "That's okay, you got the cool abilities."

"That's what I tell myself."

I gave her one more hug and released her. "Another tough question, do you have a Rosdew who can teach you spirit magic? I can't help you with that. You might very well be a powerful necromancer. It might be why Hilda doesn't want you trained."

She seemed surprised. "You think so?"

I nodded.

"I never thought about it that way. You think she might be afraid of my magic because I might dethrone her as a necromancer?"

"It makes sense."

Rowan chimed in, *"Good theory."*

"I don't know her well, but I don't think I'd be wrong in saying she's power hungry and wants to be the center of attention. It isn't a far step to guess she would hurt anyone she saw as competition, or stop them before they became a threat."

"If your theory is correct, I need to learn magic, and quick. So she can't control me."

"Yes."

I thought about the combination of magic she could have, spirit magic from the Rosdews. From the Teagues she could have foresight, abilities with teaching others, and strengths in charms and spells.

"Let's try it again," I said.

She walked over to the table and put her feather down, then returned to her spot.

"Let's start with your hand out to the skateboard," I said as I walked around her. "Visualize the skateboard coming to you and say something aloud, like 'come to me.' The wording isn't as important as your intent. It doesn't even matter the language. Soon you'll get to the point where you can do it without words."

I raised my hand to the skateboard and had it zigzagging toward me to stop right in front of me.

She lifted an eyebrow. "Wasn't I supposed to do that?"

"Yes, sorry." I sent the board back to where it had been.

"Show off."

I shrugged. "Try it." I stood to the side. She closed her eyes and extended her hand; after a moment she said, "Come to me."

The skateboard jumped straight into the air and fell, flipped, and moved farther away from her. I laughed, I couldn't help myself. She opened her eyes and looked at the board. Before she could run, I grabbed her.

"It's okay. You made tremendous progress."

She stopped squirming in my arms. "Really? Then why are you laughing?"

"Well, you missed the show. You went from zero to a hundred there. We just need you to back off some. You have plenty of power; you just need confidence in yourself. Let's try it again, with your eyes open. Just try to set the skateboard right." Her eyes shined with tears. She seemed so fragile, and I wanted nothing more than to protect her. I hugged her and kissed her cheek, stopping before I did something else.

"You've got this. I know you can do this, so does Rowan. I need you to know you can. Relax, we have time."

She'd laid her head on my shoulder. Like me, she longed to be touched and loved. We'd both known such cold existences. Whenever we were near each other we were usually touched in some manner. Not in a sexual way, but in a reassuring way.

I set her back down on the ground, but I still had my arms wrapped around her. I lifted her right arm in mine and lowered my mouth to her ear.

I whispered, "Tell it to flip over."

She took a deep breath and closed her eyes.

"Open your eyes and look at the board."

Her head nodded ever so slightly. I supported her arm, palm out, she said, "Flip over."

The board flipped over with a slam, then flipped again, so the wheels were in the air again.

Her shoulders fell.

"Don't panic! Try again. Imagine it in your mind … in slow motion."

She cleared her throat and took a deep breath. "Flip over, onto your wheels." At first, the board teetered, and then very slowly it flipped over and settled gently on its wheels. She covered her mouth in surprise.

"See, I knew you could do it." She turned and jumped up into my arms. We hugged as I twirled her around, laughing.

I don't know how long Rowan squawked, but his caws and voice finally pierced through to Lydia and me.

"*Someone is in the parking lot and heading toward the unlocked door.*"

I cursed and ran to grab our stuff from the table as she ran and grabbed the skateboard. We'd mapped out the warehouse in case we should ever need a hiding place. We both ran to the far side of the room to a corner created by drywall which hid a metal stairwell, with cinderblocks on one side and drywall on the other. It went up to a catwalk which ran the length of the warehouse. At the top of the stairs we could see most of the warehouse, as well as see out the windows along the tops of the walls. We were easily thirty feet off of the ground here, which would make it difficult for anyone below to see us.

We knelt quietly as the metal door opened. They'd found where we'd come through.

"Rowan," I whispered. "How many?"

"*Three total. Two are now in the offices. One stayed outside.*"

Right then I could see a large man in a suit looking out into the room.

"Hey Jeff, do you see anyone?"

He looked around, taking in the warehouse. Just then, I noticed Lydia's hoodie was still on the table. Hopefully, he wouldn't see the lump of blue cloth.

"It looks undisturbed. It was probably just kids playing with the lock, but let me check the back." He started toward a set of double doors in the wall which partitioned the warehouse. He opened the door and walked into the darkness of the other side.

As soon as he was through, I stood and I whispered, "Come to me!"

Her hoodie flew into my hand, and I hurried and knelt back down just as the guy walked back into the room ... and stood in one of the spots where he could see me. His head snapped to our hiding place.

I whispered a curse. He started our way and had almost made it to the stairs when Rowan squawked loudly and landed on the floor not far from him.

"What is that?" yelled the guy in the office.

"It's nothing; just a crow. We must have holes in the roof."

"Nothing else?"

"No, let's go." He started walking back to the offices but turned back to look at Rowan. "A really big crow." Rowan squawked at him and he scurried off.

Then we heard it, the padlock snapping shut and locking us in. I turned to Lydia.

"We're locked in." Her eyes widened in panic. "Don't worry. We'll figure this out."

"Can't you just unlock the padlock?"

"I'm not sure I can. You need to be able to see it. I might be able to get it to unlock, but I don't know how I'd get it to move and unfasten," I said.

"If you can unlock the padlock I will get the door open," Rowan said.

"Rowan, will you see if they're gone? I'm going to go work on the padlock," I said.

Some fifteen minutes later we were outside, very lucky to escape without being caught.

·  ✥  ·

We got just over two months to practice her magic. The final days of summer had come, and she would leave any day now. We'd returned to the warehouse after almost being caught, practicing several times a week for the rest of the summer. No one bothered us again. By the end, I felt Lydia could protect herself against most things, though she wouldn't be able to do anything against Hilda's black magic.

Lydia and I met at the beach; the first time all summer. The temperature was in the mid-nineties, a surprise for the first week of September. We didn't start school until after the Mabon holiday in mid-September. To us it was like the Labor Day weekend holiday; it marked the true end of summer.

I skated down to meet her, wearing my swimming trunks and a plain green T-shirt because I thought we might surf. I sat down in the warm sand, and waited.

It was nearly a half hour before she showed. As always she scared me; she moved so quietly I wanted to make her wear a bell. She wrapped her arms around me from behind and I jumped.

"That's so not funny, for the millionth time."

She laughed hysterically. "Maybe not for you." She smiled up at me with her one dimple and I was lost. No matter how many times I saw her she had the same effect on me.

She was dressed in cut-off jeans and a tight baby blue tank top, and I did my best not to stare at her with my tongue hanging out of my mouth.

"I need to go change. I'll be right back. Watch my skateboard?"

I rubbed the back of my neck and nodded. She had her beach bag slung over her shoulder as she wandered off to change.

Laughter sounded in my head. *"It's a good thing she doesn't take advantage of you. She has you wrapped around her finger."*

My cheeks flushed as I realized again how bad I was at hiding my feelings for her. "I don't know what you're talking about," I said in my mind back to him. I wasn't sure where Rowan was.

*"Keep telling yourself that."*

"Why are you here anyway? I thought you needed to do something."

*"I do, but I came to see how you will react. Then I'll go."*

I looked around trying to find his hiding spot without any luck.

"React to what?"

He answered my query with more laughter. I glared at the sand, wondering what he might be talking about. I stood up, ready to go after the bird and choke him until he told me what was up. My steam ran out, as my eyes landed on Lydia. Every single thought in my head scattered. I lost the use of speech and perhaps bodily functions. She came toward me in the smallest blue bikini I'd ever seen. She stopped in front of me and said something, but it sounded like gibberish to me.

*Don't look down, don't look down,* became a mantra in my head. Unfortunately, I forgot about thinking things too loudly.

*"Why don't you want to look down?"* His voice in my head trailed off as he figured it out and laughed. I looked to a palm tree off to my left, where he sat watching us.

"Do you have a death wish, bird?"

"Is he taunting you?" she asked me.

My focus returned to her and my shyness returned in full force. "Yes, he is. Are you trying to kill me? Because you're doing a good job."

She batted her eyelashes at me with a look of complete innocence. "If you don't like my new swimsuit I'll go put my clothes back on. But we'll have to do something else because it's the only suit I've got." She turned to walk back to the changing room.

I can assure you my reflexes have never been so acute as they were in that moment. I caught her before she could finish turning. She smiled at me.

"So you like it then?"

"'Like' isn't a strong enough term for how I feel about your suit."

Surprising me, she jumped up and wrapped her arms around my neck. I grabbed her so she didn't fall. She went to kiss my cheek but I turned just as she did and she kissed me on the lips. It was quick and she released me from the shock of it. She looked up at me sheepishly. In the span of five minutes I'd seen more of her than I ever had and she'd kissed me.

There's a belief among the Kind that our soul resides in our breath. With Lydia being a Rosdew, this is paramount. Their element affinity is the spirit. Now you may say she has kissed me before, which is true, but never on the lips. It's taboo. You can kiss if you're married but not in public and never with sex magic. In a society ripe with necromancers, one never wants to expose one's spirit.

I'm not saying necromancy is bad *per se*, for there are several legal, useful abilities for those with this dark gift, such as contacting spirits and death rites, so I don't fear it, but neither do I want to be close to it. The few times Lydia and I had touched upon the subject she had indicated she had no powers in that area, much to the disappointment of her grandmother. Though we didn't know for sure because she hadn't been instructed in spirit magic.

We spent the rest of the day at the beach until late into the evening. It would be the last time we got a full day together. She left the following week, and during those days we only managed a few hours together. As I hugged her goodbye my worry for her grew.

## CHAPTER EIGHTEEN

**Late September, Cornwall, England**

Deciding to make things easy for everyone, I returned to the Kolon. No pushing Davidson's trust of my father or me, they'd been best friends for too long. The first thing I saw happened to be my father and Davidson at a small table, with coffee. They shared a look of relief as soon as they noticed me. I felt my heart drop in my chest. I'd hoped they'd both trusted me more.

Yes, I'd been pursuing my agenda, but it didn't run contrary to theirs. While I felt very confident in my abilities with magic and at work, my self-esteem, when it came to relationships, was insecure at best. Years of hiding my skills with magic had resulted in amazing bluffing skills, which extended to cards, sports, and business. My strength would come from me and me alone knowing I had an out, a place I could go where no one could find me. With a fake smile on my face, I went to meet my jailor.

Davidson stood. "Gray, my boy, join us. I've news."

I bet we could return home, at last. A stray thought drifted through my mind: now that he'd seen me again, I'd have a tail. Hopefully, they wouldn't put a tracking spell on me. A tracking spell would, in fact, make my life difficult. Best to keep to my plan and cooperate with them.

A servant brought another wooden chair to the table for me.

"Would you like coffee or tea?" the servant asked.

"Tea, but not Earl Grey, sorry I don't like bergamot."

"Of course. Milk or sugar?"

"No, just the tea."

"Did you have a pleasant afternoon?" Davidson asked.

"Yes, I did. I got to see a few old friends. Since this is my first trip to Cornwall I wanted to see everything."

"Guess I didn't realize that," he said as he tilted his head back to drink the last of his coffee. As he set the cup down, he seemed to consider something. "You didn't do the KIC service, did you?"

"No, I went immediately to Stanford to start into my computer science degree. I stayed there for almost ten years before returning to Connecticut."

"I know you were rightfully busy. Hell, we'd not be where we are as a culture without you and that time well spent. I asked because if you had done your KIC service you would have spent some time in Cornwall." There had been invitations to come to Cornwall, both family and business, but I didn't like to leave my comfort zone.

I considered his comments. It wouldn't be the first time I felt left out. So many of our laws and traditions had been reinforced during those years, and I'd discovered it made it difficult for me to understand or communicate with others of the Kind.

"I didn't know KIC service included serving time here. Sometimes I'm a little behind because of missing my service."

"Maybe. But don't worry. The service you provide from working in the human world is worth more. You'll be serving your people again by breaking the binding, too."

The servant appeared with a tray, and I was thankful for the interruption. He placed a large teapot on the table in front of me.

"Are we returning home in the morning?" I asked.

He glanced up from his coffee. "Ah, yes. It's part of the good news."

"Good. I've got a lot of work waiting for me back home. Taking this much time off will have put me behind," I said. I wanted to see his reaction.

His face scrunched up in an expression of someone who just drank sour milk. "Yes, well … ah, there's just no other way to say this: it will be a while before you'll be able to return to work."

Time to play dumb. I lifted an eyebrow in confusion. "I don't understand, Davidson. You just agreed my work is important to the Kind. Why would I be kept from my business?"

He ran his hand down his face. "I didn't think about interrupting your work."

My father with narrowed eyes said, "This will need to be addressed with the Council. We'll cooperate with whatever the Council decides, but some consideration should be given to our sacrifices and the work the Penroses do for the Kind. We aren't asking much."

"Of course, we should be able to work around this. We'll try to get the Council stuff out of the way as soon as we get back so as not to interfere with your work."

"Sure, and if it takes a little longer I might be able to work around it, I just need some flexibility. So, did you have more news?"

"Yes. It isn't about you, but it does make my life easier. They managed to get into Hilda's home today. Guess we just had to pick the right daughter and granddaughter. Hilda's one of the few in the Kind with too many children to choose from."

"How many kids does she have?"

"I don't know how many, but several. She'd been married four times and produced children with each marriage. We tried at least seven relatives before finding one who could get through. I hear they even made it through to the library."

"Good, I'm glad you don't have to worry about her anymore."

"So am I. From what I saw, most of the family seems relieved she's gone. They're in a hurry to be rid of her. They're donating her home and everything in it to the KIC."

"What would possess them to do such a thing?" Dad asked.

"If you'd been there today, Jowan, you'd understand. Everything she owns has a dark, sickly feel to it. To be honest, I think the only reason she wasn't convicted is no one in the Kind would have been powerful enough to do anything about it."

"Are you saying she was that powerful? No one could match her? I find it hard to believe." Dad said. While he didn't like Hilda he'd always thought her abilities were exaggerated.

"Well, she had the largest knowledge of black magic. Raw magical strength versus black magic isn't a competition. If someone was willing to make the sacrifice required, then you're looking at someone with limitless power." Davidson put his hand in his hair and pulled until it stood on end. "So, yes … no … we don't know. But no one is willing to take a chance. The spirit magic of the Rosdews is a multipurpose magic. No one wants to share the darker, more powerful side of it. What they can do, we can only guess at."

"How did her spirit leave her body so quickly? I thought they weren't able to remove a spirit from our bodies until twenty-four hours after death?" Dad asked.

"We don't know. We consulted with other necromancers, but they seem to agree that a strong talent can do it, but the magic ability has been lost, like so many others. The necromancers saw no benefit in it, except to imprison the spirit to do black magic. One mentioned something I didn't know was possible, and I guess the main reason for the waiting period. According to him, he'd been taught a spirit could be split by doing the ceremony too early, perhaps more than split. He thought it might be possible to shatter it into many pieces."

I turned to him with big eyes as we all processed what he'd said. "Could it be someone seeking revenge on Hilda? To make her suffer?" I asked.

He blinked and fingered his mustache, "I hadn't considered that. It's an interesting idea; I'll share that one."

"Maybe someone who was too afraid of her in life and is now emboldened to go after her in death. Are there any necromancer suspects?" I asked.

"No. There are a fair number of Rosdews with those abilities, but no one is ratting out anyone on abilities. But the feeling among the KIC is that we don't believe there's a powerful enough necromancer to do this."

"Well, can't you just follow the black magic?" I asked, knowing the darker arts tended to leave a trail.

"That's the thing, she died at a medical center not far from here. She'd gone to the doctor for some pain she'd been having, and ended up being checked into the medical center where she quickly slipped into a coma and died. They didn't even get her into a medical gown before she slipped into the coma. Due to her age, it had been decided not to revive her, which, I assure you, broke no one's heart."

The lack of evidence was frustrating me. "Weren't any family or friends with her when she died?" I asked.

"Yes, a long-time servant. He tried to help us get into the house, but couldn't. Here's the thing; her body was picked up from the medical center, dressed in what she wore to the doctor's appointment, and taken directly to the Coven House. If the black magic happened anywhere, it would be at the Coven House where they would remove the spirit. But there are no traces of black magic at the Coven House. This whole thing makes no sense."

"Well, at least you can wash your hands of this now, and we can go back home," my dad said, unaware of what would be in store for me when Davidson and I returned home.

"Yes, the sooner I can be away from Hilda's mess the better."

"Now, Davidson, I thought our hospitality more than made up for Hilda," said Lowen Penrose, as he joined us at the table.

Lowen is my distant cousin and the current owner and caretaker of Kolon. He stood taller than my father and myself, and was about the same age as my dad. Lowen had earned a reputation as a heartbreaker.

Davidson rose from his chair, stuttering, "I meant no offense."

"None taken. I don't envy you the task of dealing with Hilda," said Lowen with a sniff.

Davidson visibly relaxed, and Lowen laughed. Since arriving, I'd seen little of my cousin. He'd probably been busy with arrangements and the running of the staff. I looked at my empty cup and reached for the teapot. Warm steam and the delicious smell of oolong tea drifted to my nose.

"Gentleman, I wonder if I might steal my cousin?" I turned to my father assuming he meant him, and then I realized he meant me. My dad just smiled.

*Why would he want me?*

"Join us in the library in about an hour," he said to my dad.

I picked up the tea I just poured and downed the contents. Like an obedient pet, I followed behind him, all the while I imagined scenarios for his interest in me. As we walked I studied my cousin. It's easy to understand why he'd earned the name heartbreaker. He wore a fitted British tailored black suit with a black and tan vest. Lowan reminded me of James Bond, the suave one from the sixties. Currently, he was widowed. His wife had died in childbirth around the time I'd been born. Despite pressure from the Council, he hadn't married again. The Cornwall Penrose heir being unmarried and childless was not something the KIC liked to have.

We wandered along several dark wooden paneled halls until he led me through an open door. Inside, a massive fire radiated warmth into the grandest library I'd ever seen. I stood in the middle of a Persian rug as I turned, taking in the room.

Overstuffed chairs were set in front of the fireplace, with a large ornate desk to the far side of the chairs. The rest of the room had shelves loaded with books, with another two floors above, accessible by ladder, which were similarly overflowing with books. The fire crackled behind me as my mouth popped open.

"Beautiful, isn't it?"

"Gorgeous."

He chuckled. "This is our family's ancestral library. Some of the oldest books within the Kind are here in this room. Today, I grant you full access. I'd have done it before now, but you haven't visited."

"You mean I could do research here?"

"Of course, this is our history, and you're welcome at Kolon any time. The house recognizes you and will open for you even if no one else is here. I brought you here today to offer you something I should have a long time ago. If you will join me on the third floor, I'll show you."

He made for the ladder and I breathed in, taking in the smell of fire, dust, and old parchment. This place was heaven. The room's decor reminded me of a British hunting lodge, with thick fabrics, tapestries, and hunting trophies mounted on the dark oak panels. He watched me from the second level as he leaned on the railing with both hands.

I climbed the ladder to the second floor, then waited on him to show me to the third. From this angle, the room was equally impressive.

"I should have had you and Guy over to stay with me when you were kids. I've corrected it with your brother, but somehow I think you'll appreciate this more." Lowen continued up the ladder, and I followed.

"So, cousin, why have you brought me here?"

"You know what a familiar is. Being Penroses, we don't have animal or spirit ones. Instead, we have ancestral guides, or connections, which assist us. That's why it's best to get one of these while young, though it will still be valuable to you." He lifted his arm to point to the rows of books.

"Behind you are the grimoires of the Penroses. Open yourself up and see if one speaks to you."

I felt my eyes widen with disbelief. I'd never heard of this practice. Curious, I opened my Third Eye completely. At first, I felt like I'd just walked into a rock concert in a bad stadium; sounds and feelings bombarded me. There are many words to describe what I had just done. In the Kind world, they tend to use the term Third Eye. I hadn't developed my skills with it, as I should have by now.

"Can you feel them?" I nodded. "Try to tune out the sounds and search for a path or a guide." Hearing and understanding him took me a minute. Tuning out my ears, I opened my eyes, which I'd closed. Before me, I saw things, ghostly things. A giant white dragon at the back of the library caught my attention. I saw parts of him down the rows of books, his head snaking down one, his belly down another, and his tail ending near Lowen.

I heard Lowen chuckle, "Say hello to the Pendragon; we protected him and in return he joined our family. He's a secret, and you cannot tell anyone about him. You, a female cousin you don't know, and I are the only ones who know of him."

"Hello, Grayson," said a deep, gravelly voice. I swallowed.

"It's an honor to meet you, Pendragon."

His head lifted and moved closer to me. "Lowen," graveled Pendragon. "Leave us for a few minutes please."

He nodded and left. I hoped he wasn't hungry. Could a ghost dragon eat me?

"Yes, but I'm not hungry."

"Great. You can read my thoughts?"

"Yes. You think I'm the big, bad dragon. Good, I like to start out in the predator position."

"Are you really a dragon?"

"So, philosophy it is. I'm many things. Whatever I desire, but the dragon is my favorite of the things I've been. What you see now is my essence. I stay around to protect what's mine, and as a Penrose, you are mine."

"Do you live here at Kolon?"

"I'm here when I need to be." This conversation seemed to be going in circles. "Walk up and down these aisles and look for the book which appears different from the rest. Not through your physical eyes, but through your mind's eye." I nodded and walked down the first aisle. The dragon watched me with interest. To my relief his ghostly body disappeared; I didn't want to have to walk through him. Then he did something even more disconcerting, his head alone appeared and floated behind me. He watched over my shoulder, sometimes making little sounds while smoke streamed from his nostrils. I felt like I'd just met the Cheshire Cat or Absolom from Lewis Carroll's tale.

I turned down the next row, observing the swords and impressive weaponry mounted on the back wall. After things settled down I needed to spend some time here. Down the aisle I walked, I didn't see anything stand out, though sometimes I'd feel a chill or warmth when I passed a book.

The last row seemed older and only had books on one side. I slowed, wanting to look carefully at everything. Nothing made itself known. At the end of the last row, I turned to my companion's floating head. He seems conflicted.

"I didn't see anything."

The head disappeared in a puff of smoke. I blinked.

"Follow me," said his disembodied voice.

"I can't see you."

I heard a sigh to my side. "Go back down to the bottom floor. I will join you."

Lowen sat at the desk by the fire. He watched me climb down. As I reached the main floor, he stood and came over to me.

"Well? Let's see what you got."

I gritted my teeth and said, "I didn't find anything."

His eyebrows shot up to his hairline, "Really?"

"Yes," growled Pendragon from the upper floor. We both turned to look up at the massive dragon. The body of the ghostly dragon, even with his wings folded, seemed to take up the whole floor. Which is saying something, as large as the library is. Pendragon snapped his wings open, launched into the air, and glided right toward us.

I dealt with the matter in the only rational way I knew … I ducked, grabbed my head, and squealed like a little girl. My squeal faded, and laughter filled my ears. Daring to peek, I saw Lowen guffawing at my reaction and Pendragon perched on the back of a nearby chair, chuckling. I glared at them. Pendragon had gone from the size of a monster to that of a large cat.

"You know, I did the same thing to Lowen when we first met," Pendragon said as his laughter subsided.

"Did not," Lowen quipped.

"Oh, sorry, you squealed like a pig and ran. I had to fight my predator instinct not to hunt you."

I watched the two of them as they began to resemble a tennis match. They continued squabbling like two brothers. With Pendragon distracted I took the opportunity to examine him in this smaller form. I decided he reminded me of Disney's Figment with bigger wings, except ghostly white and transparent, like smoke.

"I do not!" whined Pendragon. The change in voice drew me back to the conversion.

Lowen looked startled at the exclamation, and said to me, "You're having a conversation with him even if you don't speak it. He reads the louder thoughts in your head, especially if it's the only thing you're thinking about. Now share, what were you thinking which upset the overcompensating, pompous reptile?"

Pendragon stared off in another direction with his forelegs crossed angrily over his chest.

"I was just thinking he reminded me of a Disney World character named Figment."

Lowen cocked an eyebrow, "I'm not familiar with Figment. I tell him he looks like Mushu, which causes a similar temper tantrum."

He growled, a sound which was too loud to come out of his current form. "Figment is a little purple and orange dragon. Disney only has it at their Florida theme park. He's a Figment, a Figment of your imagination."

Lowen rubbed the brown stubble on his chin. "I'm going to have to search for images of him." He smiled. "This is the real Pendragon; a small, scaly ball of teeth and bitterness. But also my good friend and companion." Lowen turned to Pendragon, who looked bored. "What do you think about him not finding anything?"

"Troubling. Let him wander the library with his mind's eye to see if something pops out at him. Hell, even his brother found a book."

"He did?"

"I wondered if something might be off at the time. Your brother connected with a Penrose from the fifteenth century, Laden Penrose. He wasn't very good at magic, but he has the family distinction of killing more of the Wayfarers during their vendetta than any other. Irony, I find, is life's way of making its sense of humor known."

Chills ran down my back as I continued roaming the library. They stayed by the fire debating what might be wrong. Finished with the first floor, I climbed to the second. Nothing. I climbed back down to join them. I lifted my hands in the air as I approached to show them I hadn't found anything.

"Are we sure all books are here?" asked Pendragon.

"Yes, the only ones not here are with living Penroses." He sighed, "There's one book, a grimoire, that was destroyed in a fire centuries ago. Can't believe a Penrose witch was dumb enough not to bespell her book against fire." He shook his head.

Pendragon rolled his eyes. "I don't have any other ideas."

They continued their back and forth. I tuned them out and walked over to the fire to get warm. After I stood by the fire for a couple of minutes I realized how hot I felt, though I stood well away from the fire. A thought came to me: *This might be my third eye.*

"Yes," Pendragon said behind me. "You missed out on a lot of training, boy. Follow the heat. It means you're near a magical artifact." What he said made a lot of sense. With Lowen and Pendragon on my heels, I followed the heat. Around the back of the big desk, I noticed another bookshelf built into the wall; seven shelves loaded with old books. On the fourth shelf, at the end, a book shot sparks and glowed with all the colors of the rainbow. The heat, which had been almost unbearable, faded as I touched the book.

The two gasped as I picked the book up.

"There's no way that book is it," Lowen said, looking at Pendragon, who sat on his shoulder.

"Maybe we'll finally have answers. That book predates me by a long time and is number one on the mysteries I've wanted to solve. Tell me why you picked it, Gray?"

I studied the fragile leather bound book in my hand. "The heat I felt led me to this one and a rainbow of colors sparked from it. When I touched it, the heat disappeared, and so did the sparks."

"Interesting. Bring the book to the table. Be careful; as far as I know, it's the oldest book in here. Modern day people would argue that no one bound books when it was written," Pendragon said.

"Can I bespell the book to make it more durable?"

"Yes, we could probably come up with something," the dragon answered.

At the desk, I sat in the chair with the grimoire. Oiled, dark brown leather covered the book, with gold characters. The characters didn't resemble any written languages I knew.

A loud knock came at the door.

"Great," Lowen mumbled as he went to answer the door with Pendragon still on his shoulder. He opened the door to Davidson and my father. I watched as Lowen invited them in. As if on cue, Pendragon flapped his wings and rose into the air in full view of the new arrivals. They remained as oblivious as before.

"So, did you find a book?" Dad asked.

Lowen answered for me, "Yes, but he just found it. We're not sure who it belonged to yet. I'll need to keep him until dinner, if that isn't a problem?"

"Oh, no, not at all. Any guesses?"

Pendragon blew a big gust of ghostly fire at Davidson's backside. I felt my eyes bug out, afraid of his reaction. Lowen pretended not to see what he did, but I could tell by the twitch in his left eye he had. Davidson, for his part, jumped and looked at the fireplace.

"Davidson, are you okay?" Dad asked.

He seemed confused and dazed. "Ah, maybe. I'm not sure."

Pendragon's gravely laugh echoed in my ears and Lowen rubbed his face in exasperation.

"I think I might turn in for a while, I've had a rough few days."

My father nodded, "I think I'll do the same." They walked out together, Davidson rubbing his backside.

Lowen glared at Pendragon. "What?" he asked. This time Lowen growled. "I didn't hurt him, just got rid of them. Nobody outside of the family should be here for this."

"Usually, I wouldn't agree with you, but with this book …" Lowen waved at the book in front of me.

"What's so different about this book?"

"We don't know. Nobody can read it or make any sense of it. The letters don't resemble any known languages," said Lowen.

"I maintain it's a fae book, which somehow found a way to this realm before the gates were closed." Pendragon said as he crossed his forelegs across his chest.

"No, I still think it's a rune cipher."

"There is no such thing as a rune cipher. If they did exist I'd have encountered some in my long life," Pendragon said.

"Let's settle this. Gray, open the book and see what you think."

I turned my attention back to the book and opened it. The first page didn't give anything away. The next page, a title page from the look of it, had the same style of designs as the cover. Turning to the next page, I found more of the same, and I couldn't decipher any of it. I looked up at my companions, I shook my head.

"It has to be fae. I wonder if he should have picked the book up next to it?" Pendragon asked.

"Do you still have your third eye open?"

I didn't. Opening the cover, I flipped through the book. It remained the same, except sometimes out of the corner of my eye I could swear some of the words stretched. As soon as I focused on any of the designs, they would appear unchanged.

"It's the same," I said. The two started arguing. But something about this reminded me of my magic. As I turned the pages I came upon a beautiful illustration, a depiction Yggdrasil, the tree of life from Norse mythology.

That was it! The book reminded me of my drawing magic. When I write on a mirror the text looks normal until the spell is complete, then the text elongates and twists to form magic.

I reached for my pen-wand in my pocket as I flipped back to the first page. Pen in hand I wrote my spell. A simple spell, '*If this is my family familiar, please allow me to read from your pages.*' The ink ran and twisted before disappearing. After a minute, I turned the page.

The ink swirled to form, "*Hello, Grayson, I am Kador Penrose, and I've been waiting a long time to meet you.*"

I pushed the book away and stumbled to my feet.

"What's wrong?" Lowen asked.

"The book just talked to me."

They exchanged a look. "What do you mean the book talked to you? How?" Pendragon asked.

"See for yourselves."

They leaned over the chair I'd been sitting in. I walked over and stood in front of the fireplace. "The book looks the same," Lowen said.

Sighing, I walked back over to the desk to see they were right. Was I just seeing things?

I sat back down and realized I could read the page: *The grimoire of King Kador Jameson Penrose, the Dinistriwr Duw of the Dyfnaint and Gwarcheidwad of the Third Gate.* Dyfnaint was the Welsh name for Devon, England. We studied pre- and post-Roman British history extensively in school. The Romans were the main excuse cited by the Kind for the withdraw of the fae and the sealing of the gates.

I squinted at the page, as I thought about what *Dinistriwr Duw* could mean and *Gwarcheidwad*. Usually I could translate written Welsh. Most spells were written in Welsh or Cornish. But those three words weren't commonly used in spells. But *Duw*, I knew that one. God ... *Something* God. Oh! *Dinistrio* means "destroy." God Destroyer.

*King Kador Jameson Penrose, the God Destroyer and ... of the Third Gate. Gwarcheidwad?* Usually when I start focusing on translating my brain kicks in and I can figure out most words, but this one gave me trouble. I said, "*Gwarcheidwad.*"

"What?" Pendragon asked.

"I said *Gwarcheidwad*, one of the titles of the person this grimoire belonged to."

Pendragon said something back to me which sounded like someone choking. I looked at him, clueless.

"Guardian, you said guardian in Welsh. At least I think it's what you said. Your pronunciation is terrible."

# CHAPTER NINETEEN

### June 1992, Santa Cruz, California

I spent my first full day in California shopping. I loaded up with comics, books, and records for the summer. I still used vinyl even though CDs were taking over the market. Vinyl is analog-based with simple equipment. Most analog equipment uses simple technologies, like magnets and vacuum tubes. My magic didn't seem to effect magnets or their polarity, but anything sensitive to magnets seem to be affected by my magic. I had bought a Sony CD Walkman and shorted the thing out in hours. The more advanced the technology, especially if it had lots of circuit boards and little parts, the greater the chance the device would die from the effects of my magic.

At the end of the summer, I would be expected to start my mandatory two years of KIC service, much like some countries require their youth to join the military. School had become boring the last couple of years, so I looked forward to my service. At least it would be a change; our society and its stagnating ways were wearing on me. Why weren't we taking human technology and combining it with magic? If no one else planned to do this, I would. At the end of my two-year service, I planned to request leave to attend one of the human colleges, such as Stanford or MIT. I wanted to dedicate myself to studying computer science and figure out ways to shield the devices from magic.

I started by reading magazines about making PCs. I figured if I learned more about the components I might understand how I could make them usable to the Kind. I read about Bill Gates and Steve Jobs. My fascination started that summer with computers and other new technologies to come.

I returned home from my shopping trip to find my father had arrived. He took us out to dinner, and for the first time in my life I enjoyed my parents' company. During dinner, I told them both about my interests in computers. Both encouraged me. They said if I finished my service they would support my request to the Council that I be permitted to study computer science. According to my dad, no one had expressed any interest in this yet, but the Council was becoming more concerned about the matter recently. Computers were popping up all over, and the Kind needed to be able to interact with computers and not destroy them. Dad planned to make some calls and tell those in the KIC of my plans. It was possible they wouldn't want me to wait to finish my service.

When we got back home, I joined my dad in his library. We talked for a while before I got the nerve to ask him. He'd been drinking and was a bit drunk.

"Dad, do you know any of the Rosdews?"

He put his bourbon down on the desk and the ice clicked against the glass. "Where did that question come from?"

"Well, I've seen Hilda Rosdew around; she has a house near here."

His eyes widened. "Stay away from her. She's bad news."

I swallowed. "I'm a friend of her granddau ... ah, grandson," I hurried and corrected myself, hoping he didn't catch my mistake.

He sighed, "There's always danger in befriending a Rosdew.

The Rosdews, Blyghs, Nancarrows, Tremaynes, and Wayfarers all like to dabble in things which can cause a great deal of trouble for those around them. At least we don't have to deal with the last two much."

"Not true, I befriended Tristan Tremayne a few years ago in school. He's my best friend."

My father's eyed me as he asked, "Is he the Tremayne boy who started school about four years ago?"

"Yes, the first one to ever attend school in Connecticut."

"Interesting, I've only met one Tremayne; the one on the Council. Everything I know about them is from rumors. Is this boy of the Blood? Isn't that what they call it?"

"I think it is, but he's far too young to consider it. He's just like any other Kind teenager. Well, one with a very different accent and much darker skin."

"He's from New Orleans?"

"Yeah. He has interesting stories to tell, too. I am going to have to go see Mardi Gras for myself."

"Interesting. Perhaps we can go together. I've always wanted to see it."

"Maybe this next year?"

"Yes. Do you think Guy might go with us?" Dad said with a smile.

"I'd like that. Let me see if Tristan can get us an invitation."

"Promise me you'll be careful. I had to learn the hard way with a Nancarrow. Those families have different beliefs and morals."

"I promise."

"Now, I guess we should have an unpleasant conversation."

"Come on, we were doing so well."

"Yes, I know. But you turn nineteen soon, and you'll start your service, maybe even in the human world. Be careful, you will be tempted. It isn't worth it, trust me. If you were to become involved with a human female, it will end badly. Somehow the Council knows. It happened with one of your great-uncles; he fell in love with a human woman and she became pregnant. If it had been a century ago, the human would have been killed. But as it happens, it wasn't much better. They waited until the child was born, took the infant, and erased the memory of her from the mother. Your uncle endured years of punishment and the child was made to be a servant to the Penrose family."

"When will we step into the twentieth century?"

"You know better than that. If they weren't harsh, we'd disappear. But I'm not worried about you and a human."

I sensed something was coming.

"No, I think you have found someone in our world. Be careful. Keep it clean. If you go into the human world and come back successful, and we sign the contract for your brother …" He sighed before he continued, "I may be able to let you pick who you marry. I don't like having to do this with your brother, but if I didn't, things would be far worse for us."

"I know. But I could pick who I marry?"

"If you solve our computer problems and your brother becomes betrothed to the Marrak girl, the Council would probably allow it. They'd want to keep you happy. Who is she?"

"I can't tell you. But I swear I'll be careful."

He smiled and took a drink, "I know you will, it's why I haven't bothered you."

"Does mom know?"

"She might suspect something, but as we both know she's always focused on what's going on with your brother. Breaking the binding is everyone's focus. I hope you know, I love your mother, and while it might not seem like it, I'm glad we married. Until I met your mother, I hadn't met any girls in the Kind I liked. There were two human girls, but my father cut them out of my life so I wouldn't have the temptation."

"Did that upset you?"

"It did for a while, but looking back now I realize I was only physically attracted to them. They weren't a part of my life, nor did they understand it. It would have ended badly, and he saved me from it."

I understood what he meant, humans were different than us. Sometimes I had a hard time understanding what they talked about. Our worlds were completely different in so many ways. It would be like a fish falling in love with a bird.

The days flew by. July started, and still no Lydia or Rowan, and no message from either. Nervousness became my natural state. After seeing how scared Lydia was last year, I felt helpless. Feeling weak and helpless is the worst feeling in the world. Here I was on the verge of adulthood, with magical abilities, yet I felt no more powerful than a child.

As the days progressed, I began to have nightmares about Lydia. In the dreams, she was tied down to a sacrificial table, and she was unconscious. Dark shadows moved around the table, she had sunken eyes and several bleeding cuts. It got to the point where I feared to sleep because of the nightmares.

Desperation called for me to figure out some way to be proactive. No more of this feeling helpless. After a long night with almost no sleep, I made a decision. I wrote two letters, one to a friend, the other to someone I hoped would turn out to be a friend. There was great danger in this; by sending the notes I revealed some of my magic and myself.

The first one went to Tristan Tremayne in New Orleans in the form of a bat. I hoped he'd appreciate the inside joke. The note asked him if he could intervene with the Rosdews, or if he could get some information about Lydia. Though the Tremaynes hadn't been active in Kind society for centuries, they had once had strong family ties to the Rosdews.

The second note, in the form of a crow for spirit, went to Jessy Rosdew, Lydia's roommate and cousin. If she wanted, she could tell her family about me, and I hated to think of the consequences of that. But she cared about Lydia, so I took the chance.

Each message had a return message they could send back to me. I sent them off and held my breath. I hated waiting. At first I tried pacing, and then riding my skateboard, but it just led me to Lydia house. There were no signs of life. Returning home, I found it wasn't even noon yet. Deciding to risk it, I fell into a deep dreamless sleep.

*Tap, tap... tap, tap.* I shot straight up in my bed. *Rowan.* I ran to the window and threw open the curtains. I didn't recognize the black bird until I opened the window and it flew in; Jessy had returned her note. The paper crow flew to the bed and unraveled, the black paper bleached to white.

I stood by the window, afraid to read the response. As I neared the page, I could smell the scent of wet paper. In my hurry, I had forgotten to bespell the paper against weather. The ink ran a bit in places, but I could read it.

*Dear Grayson,*

*Thanks for sending me one of your messages. Lydia has shown me a couple of your creations. I wish it had been under better circumstances. Much to my family's shame I've fallen out of favor with Hilda. All I know is that Lydia left school on the last day of the semester, June third, with Hilda. I was under the impression they were leaving for California, but from your letter I see that didn't happen.*

*On hearing she didn't go to California, I risked going by my grandmother's estate. They are in residence, but something is off. I, too, am worried, but I don't know what else I can do. My mother won't help, and Hilda wouldn't see me. Please, if there's anything more I can do, let me know. Lydia is my only family who I care about. I'm here if I can do anything.*

*Jessy Rosdew*

With every word my heart sank. I knew where she was, but what could I do?

The clock next to the bed read seven at night. With nothing else to do, I went in search of food; I hadn't eaten all day. If I couldn't get to the bottom of this soon, I'd go to my father.

An hour later I returned to my room with a full stomach to find a bat flapping erratically around the bedroom. It amazed me how the spells I cast caused the paper to mimic the animals in appearance and manner. The bat landed on the bed and unraveled to a flat black sheet. Once again the black leeched from the paper so I could read its contents.

*Gray,*

*I appreciate your sense of humor. So did my father. Do not be concerned, he's going to help. There's nothing like a Tremayne when it comes to reconnaissance. Hilda is currently at her estate. She has accepted some social invitations there in California, but they're all next week. As for Lydia, we haven't been able to find out anything about her. My father said if it weren't for school records he would think her a ghost.*

*Who is she? No one outside of the school has records of a Lydia Rosdew, nor could we find anything related to the name Lydia in her age group in England. My father is calling in a favor. Someone is going to visit the Rosdew estate soon. We've kept her name out of things, only mentioned a granddaughter. We didn't want to put her on the KIC's radar. I'll call you, as soon as I know more.*

*PS--My father would like to meet you. Next year you'll need to visit us. Fair warning, you owe him a favor.*

*Tristan*

It was easy to envy Tristan, his family was close, without any secrets. For years, I'd heard stories; it's what made me want to meet them. The last two lines of the letter were something I'd been waiting a long time for: an invitation to New Orleans, and from the head of the Tremayne family. New Orleans is the only place in the world our Kind needs to have an invitation to visit.

The Tremaynes broke off from the Kind right after we arrived in the New World; soon after they left the Old World, too. No one knows why. Until Tristan came to school with me, there was only one Tremayne on the Elder Council. They removed themselves from Kind society long before the binding. One of the biggest mysteries was whether they were affected by the binding. Many of the families wondered how the Tremaynes had managed to separate themselves from the Kind without a fight. Their permanent seat on the Council was probably the reason they were allowed to leave.

Tristan is open with me, but says there are things he just can't talk about. It's ironic I'd turn to the Tremaynes for help, if they'd removed themselves from our society would they be willing to help? For as removed as they have become they are also the most connected. There was a time in our history when the Tremaynes were the judges, lawyers, and bloodhounds for the KIC. Rumors abound about their abilities to read the blood of anyone and know the truth.

The Blygh family is also like this and replaced the Tremaynes in many of these roles. Their noses and transfiguration abilities made them skilled at these trades. It also led to the feud between the two; Blygh means wolf, and Tremayne has come to mean blood.

From what I understand, Victor Tremayne had started what many would consider our version of a CIA. They specialize in espionage, and somehow, though they are now a world away from the Kind, they know everything.

With nothing to do but wait, I decided to try a spell Tristan had taught me. Our phone sat out in the hall and had a very long cord. Pulling it into my room, I took out my pen and used it to cast a spell on the ringer. If it worked, I'd be the only one able to hear it.

From my shelf, I grabbed my mountain of reading material and lay down on my bed to wait. The ringer woke me several hours later. I'd fallen asleep with a *Spawn* comic covering my mouth and nose. Jumping up, I answered the phone.

"Hello, is this Grayson?" a deeply accented voice asked.

"Yes, it is. Is this Mr. Tremayne?"

"'Tis. I've received news. Hilda has been taken in for questioning. They can't prove anything, but her home reeks of black magic. She'll be set loose by tomorrow, perhaps to think twice about whatever she may have been attempting."

"Did they find Lydia? How is she?"

"They did. She seems shaken but fine. I'm afraid we've brought her to the attention of the KIC. They detained Hilda more for the girl, whom they couldn't place, than the black magic. Who is she?"

"I've known her for years as Lydia Rosdew. She told me her parents died in a car accident when she was very young."

"They think she's human. No one gets a read on her and she seems to have difficulty with magic. May I have your permission to look into her background?"

"Yes. Do you think she's human? I know magic is difficult for her, but I've assumed it's because Hilda refused her training. She didn't receive instruction as a child."

"This mystery is very interesting. You've seen her do magic?"

"Yes."

"Hmm. I've never heard of a family not training their young, especially a female. There's another possibility … it happens with some of the families; she maybe a Halfling."

I swallowed. I had never considered such a possibility. I wonder if Lydia had? "Is there any way to tell?"

"A few, but most you wouldn't want to do. I could tell, if I were near her. But I'll be honest with you, of the possibilities here, that seems the least likely. The Rosdews, more than any other family in the Kind, hate humans. I know of no Halflings from their line."

"Would you look into it, Mr. Tremayne? Lydia believes her father is Hilda's son and her mother was from the Teague line. But again, she isn't sure. And Hilda won't tell her anything. I know I owe you a favor, and I'll honor it, and another if you can find out anything about her."

A rich laugh sounded through the line. "You owe me nothing, child. It's Victor, please. No one calls me Mister. You've repaid me tenfold, and I do not even know you yet. The friendship and loyalty you've given my son is worth a lifetime of favors from me. I look forward to meeting you. I'll do my best to get you the answers you seek. With one caveat, you might not like what I find, are you prepared for the possibility?"

"I care as much for her as I do for your son. Neither her past nor her bloodline will affect my opinion of her."

"Good, hold on to that, her bloodline might be the problem. But I believe you. You and your family are being extended an invitation to our Mari Gras celebration. It's the first time we have ever invited anyone from the Kind who isn't of the Tremayne bloodline."

"I am deeply honored and gratefully accept for mother, father, and myself. I'll have to check with my brother."

"Ah, the Penrose heir. I look forward to meeting all of you. I must be going, but let me know if you do not hear from her soon."

"I will, and thank you. Goodbye, Victor."

"Adieu," he said as the phone hung up. Excited, I went to my bed and wrote a note to Lydia, sending it off as soon as I finished it. Then I went back to reading. The next morning, I received a reply. As with most of her messages lately, she didn't reveal much, but she said she'd be here soon.

· ☸ ·

Unfortunately, her definition of soon and mine were two different things. It was five days before she arrived, and it wasn't her I saw, but Rowan. He came to my window on a rainy Wednesday.

"You damn chicken," I exclaimed as soon as he got in. The raven in front of me wasn't the one I'd known for years. He looked weak and much thinner.

"Thank you."

"What for?"

"You're responsible for the KIC coming, aren't you?"

"Yes. Why? What happened? Why have I not heard from either of you?" He shivered. "What's wrong?" I grabbed a towel from my bathroom and wrapped him up in it.

"Hilda held Lydia for a month in some protected circle, experimenting and keeping her under the whole time. After school ended we went to the estate just like we always do. But Hilda must have slipped something into her food. Once Lydia was out, Hilda bound her to a table in the middle of a monolithic circle. I was able to get into the circle before Hilda closed it and stayed in a nearby tree. Day in and day out she experimented with the darkest of magic."

"What was Hilda trying to do?"

"I don't know, but whatever it was wasn't working. She started getting frustrated and stopped feeding Lydia; I thought she would kill her."

"She tied Lydia to a sacrificial table outside for almost a month?"

"Yes, and kept her drugged to the point she didn't know who she was. I found myself trapped in the circle unless I wanted to risk leaving when Hilda did."

"How did she last in the elements that long?"

"A tent surrounded the table. But Hilda is free now, and the KIC are watching them. Hilda is supposed to provide documentation on Lydia soon. Never thought I'd say it, but I'm happy the KIC is watching her."

"When can I see her?"

"I don't know. She's weak and sick." He must have seen the look of concern on my face because he added, "Don't worry, a doctor is attending to her."

"Did the KIC find her in the circle?"

"No. Hilda must have had some warning system, and was able to get Lydia to her bed. She has several servants helping her. Here's the problem; she thinks a teacher at Lydia's school ratted her out."

I smiled. "Don't worry, it won't point to anyone at her school."

"How?"

"I called in a friend. A Tremayne."

"I thought they split with the Kind."

"Mostly they have."

"That may be the one family she won't suspect, or go after."

"It's what I thought, too."

"It's so good to see you."

"Right back at ya, chicken."

"You can call me chicken anytime."

"Why are you wet? I thought your grandmother's spell protected you?"

"Lydia isn't the only one who is weak. My abilities will return when I get better."

Our friendship and routines resumed. Lydia appeared under my window early in the morning two days later. I ran to her as fast as could and swept her up in my arms. I couldn't believe she was here. I buried my nose in her hair, inhaling the familiar scent of her.

"Let me go. You're hurting me."

"Sorry," I said.

"Thank you so much." She put her hand on my cheek. "You've got stubble. It looks good on you."

"No, it's you who looks good. I've missed you," I said as I put my hand over hers. Even though she was weak, she'd grown more beautiful. Her black hair hung loosely down her back and she was dressed in a white sundress and sandals. My hormones were firing on all cylinders, while thoughts of running away from there danced in my head.

With her hand in mine, I led her to the beach. I wanted every moment with her I could get. Rowan flew over our heads, and for the first time in so long, I felt relaxed, as if everything just might be okay.

Hilda left her alone for most of the summer, not even taking her to social events like she'd done in the past. This was fine with both of us.

With her late arrival in mid-July, the summer was a short one for us. We continued her magic lessons. Everything I could think of to help her protect herself, I taught her. Since she had another year of school left, I didn't want to take any chances. Arrangements were made to have Jessy keep a close eye on her. From what I'd gathered, the ghost Hilda put on her still followed them at school.

One morning as we sat on the beach watching the sunrise, I dared a subject I usually avoided.

"Lydia?"

"Yeah."

"Can you tell me anything more about your parents?"

She turned to me, I could see the pain in her eyes. "I've learned nothing more. I've even searched around the estate house when she's out. There are lots of photos of her family, it's big, but nothing related to me. I've even spent time in the library at school looking at the microfilms for newspaper articles on my parent's death. Nothing. I can't even figure out who my father might have been. From what I can tell all of Hilda's children are still alive."

"I don't want to ask this, but ..." She furrowed her brows. "Is it possible one of your parents was human? That you might be a Halfling?"

A long moment passed before she answered, "I don't know. Though I wouldn't mind if I was. Maybe then they'd let me go. I hate my existence. I wouldn't care if I couldn't do magic again."

Rowan added, *"She wouldn't have me if she were part human, and she has magic. The Muninns have been trying for years to find out anything about her. We found nothing. This reeks of magic, and not the light kind."*

"Sorry, I needed to ask."

She nodded and seemed to understand. As things turned out, that day in late August was to be our last of the summer. Hilda took off with her without notice. I didn't even get to say goodbye.

## CHAPTER TWENTY

**Late September, Cornwall, England**

"What did you say?" Lowen asked.

"I can read it. This grimoire belonged to Kador Jameson Penrose."

Pendragon jumped down off of Lowen's shoulder to land next to me. As he neared, I smelled a hint of humidity and smoke.

"It looks the same to me. What did you do?"

"I wrote in the book."

Lowen gasped. "The book is thousands of years old."

Pendragon turned and shot a short burst of fire at him. "He didn't ruin it; stop your silliness."

"My abilities with magic are directly related to my abilities to draw. My pen is my wand. I asked the book to allow me to read the text if it's my family familiar," I explained.

"Have you told anybody about your magic?" Lowen asked.

I shook my head.

"Smart boy. I've never heard of such magic. Pen, have you?"

"No, and as much as this hurts me, you were right. It's a rune or magic cipher. I never considered such a way to read a cipher. Lowen, have you ever tried drawing? Could you do what he does?"

"No, I doubt I could. My magic is similar in the ability to shield electronics as he showed me years ago. Though I lack any artistic abilities, I can assure you."

Pendragon inspected me. "What do you mean, the book 'talked to you'? Usually, the grimoire will flip to the page it wants you to read. That's the way this works. Sometimes, like with Lowen, he grasps the pages and begins to flip them, then it will stop at the appropriate place. It's like asking a search engine a question."

"Well, after I wrote the spell I turned to the title page. The text rearranged and said *Hello*, then Kador introduced himself and told me it had been waiting a long time for me."

Both of my companions looked at me like I was nuts. "The books aren't sentient. They're spelled to resonate with a Penrose with similar magical abilities," Pendragon said.

"I'm just telling you what I saw. When I sat back down I saw an ordinary title page."

"Flip through the book, let's see what happens." I did as Pendragon asked. Flipping slowly, the contents now legible to me, though it didn't stop on a particular page. When nothing happened, I tried it again. This time as I flipped certain words stuck out to me.

*"Tell the all-knowing dragon HE IS WRONG,"* the book said as I flipped.

"That isn't working; let's try closing the book and asking it a question," suggested Pendragon.

I did as he asked again, knowing it wouldn't be wise to repeat Kador's words to Pendragon. "Please show me a spell?" Nothing.

"Did you notice anything else about this Kador?" asked Lowen.

"Yes, the title page said he was 'King and God Destroyer of Dumnonia and Guardian of the Third Gate.'"

"I have never heard of the Third Gate or Kador. I'm beginning to think this book is much older than we ever considered," said

Pendragon, as he rubbed at the scales under is mouth. "Though the God Destroyer thing sounds familiar."

"It does?"

"I think it was from an oral history more than a thousand years ago. Damn it! All the old ones are gone. I would need to speak to the Norse, or at least a Muninn," Pendragon said tapping a claw to his chin.

The mention of Muninn caught my attention. "A Muninn? Why?"

"Because the Muninns are Odin's computer and surveillance system, Muninn even means memory." He stopped tapping his claw and looked at me before asking, "Why?"

"Well, ah, how do I put this without getting myself into a lot of trouble …?"

They exchanged glances and had some sort of silent conversation. Lowen nodded to Pendragon and walked over to the fireplace; he pulled on the wall sconce, which resembled a torch. The wall to the left side of the hearth moved to show a sitting room.

"Come, we need to talk," Lowen said, as he motioned me into the room.

I followed them and the wall closed behind us.

"This room is warded with silence and the ability to keep secrets," said Lowen.

When we walked in, the light came up to show dark paneled walls and seven wooden and green upholstered chairs surrounding a table, with a bar by the far wall. The fireplace came to life and mirrored the other side. The room smelled of whiskey and pipe tobacco.

Lowen went to the bar and pulled out two glasses and poured scotch into each. Next, he opened a panel in the bar; this appeared to be a humidor for cigars. Returning to stand next to me, he handed me a cigar and drink, and motioned for me to take a seat. Once I sat facing him, he pulled a box of wooden matches from his pocket and lit our cigars. We puffed on the cigars for a moment; Pendragon settled on the arm of his chair.

"You're going to have to tell me everything. As the head of the family it's my job to help protect you. From what little I've seen you're much more powerful and troubled than I would have ever suspected, even for the prophesied male. In return for telling me, I offer you my help and my silence. What we say in here cannot be repeated. We refer to this room as an *oubliette*. Many think the French word means a prison with only one door, but the true meaning is 'forgotten.'"

He reached for a box on the table, which I hadn't noticed before, and pulled it closer to him. With a flip of the latch, the lid sprang open to reveal an ornate dagger. He set his cigar in the ashtray and lifted out the dagger. With the blade in one hand and his other hand open, he said "Gyda 'm gwaed, chlym fy nhafod," and cut his palm. It took me a moment to translate, "With my blood, I bind my tongue."

The cut didn't appear deep, but several drops of blood welled in his palm. Replacing the dagger in the box he turned his palm downward so the blood fell onto the stone floor. It could have been my imagination, but the stones of the floor seemed to absorb the blood. I glanced up at him with big eyes. The corner of his lips twitched, and he took a handkerchief from his pocket to wipe the blood off his hand. He held his palm up for my inspection: no cut, only a couple of smears of blood remained.

"I assure you, I can never speak your secrets, even if I should want to. The dagger is bound to a spell, the oubliette, and blood. With my blood, I seal my silence. Pen isn't held to the same, but the room does seem to tie his tongue as well. You can release me from this if you wish, or you may give us permission to share with another. Now tell me your tale."

Over what seemed like several hours I relayed my life. Both remained silent through my explanation until I got to the exploits of the last few days.

"Can you go to your room and bring the file, the dark object, and your sketchpad?" Lowen asked.

I nodded, and he let me out to gather my things. While in my room I checked my phone to find several work-related messages. Per the time on my cell, only an hour had passed, and there was still another hour until dinner. With everything in hand, I returned to the library, and the waiting oubliette.

## CONVERGENT LINES

I set my sketchpad on the table and they studied it. "You're telling me the drawing is real, so the funny looking rock in the sketch is the dark object, and the image of the papers is the file?"

I nodded, picked up my pen and wrote their names on the page. I stopped before I finished Pendragon's name and looked up at him. "Would you be insulted if I called you Pen, too?" I asked, hoping not to upset him.

Pendragon eyed me for a long moment, it ended with him burping, and smoke rolling out of his nostrils. Lowen made an audible sound, which I took to mean disgust on his part.

Pendragon glanced at Lowen before saying, "Excuse me." He dragged out the phrase before looking at me and saying, "Yes, you may call me Pen. You are well educated in manners and etiquette. I'm pleased that you can see and interact with me. As you have most certainly noticed from the present company, I don't have much in the way of engaging interactions." The expression on his face looked very much like a smile, if a dragon could smile.

Though I'd only been around them for a short period, I had no doubt Pen loved to goad Lowen. If I only had one person who could see and talk to me, I'd do the same.

"Glad he was instructed in proper manners. It's more than I can say for some," Lowen added.

Pen rolled his eyes and opened his mouth to insult Lowen back. Before he could, I said, "Reach in and grab one of the objects." Lowen hesitated.

Pendragon jumped to the table. "I'll do it." He didn't bother reaching in, he just jumped into the sketchpad. One moment he was in the room and the next he became an animated sketch in my pad. He grabbed the dark object and jumped out onto the table. In his ghostly paws sat the dark object. Lowen and I bent away from the feel of it. In this room, the effects of the object were powerful.

"Bloody Hell!" Lowen cursed.

Pen turned the stone, examining the object inside.

"Is that your hair tied around it, Gray?" Pen asked.

"I think it is, but I have no idea how she got my hair."

"The hair ties it even closer to you. She created a fetish, a dark object, all for you. I haven't seen anything like this in a long time, perhaps since the Dark Ages," he said, holding it up to the light. "She must have had significant resources. Our problems are much worse than I anticipated."

"What do you mean, Pen?"

"She's a greater threat in death than in life. A powerful, dead necromancer, of whom no one can discover how her spirit escaped her body. I know the answer: Hilda did it."

"What the bloody hell do you mean?" asked Lowen.

"I know why they couldn't get into her house and why this object is so powerful. She tied her spirit to her home before she died. My guess is to at least two objects, this being one of them. The other object must be at her house and is the power source for the protection. I've no idea what you did or what she thinks you did, Gray, but you are number one on her list. And death will not stop this woman."

I swallowed hard and did my best to process what Pendragon just said.

"I can't believe this. Did she split her soul on purpose? Is she looking for a vessel to inhabit?" Pen nodded his head, agreeing with Lowen's assessment. "Put that thing back in the sketchpad," Lowen said.

Pendragon's arm hovered over the book until he dropped the object, and it returned to the page. The room became lighter with the object gone. Then Pendragon looked at me and asked, "I hope you didn't store the file next to the dark object for long?"

I shook my head. "No, I only put them together to bring them down." I reached in and pulled the file out.

"May I take a copy of the file?" I nodded. "We shall see if we can figure out anything from what's there. Pen, tell me everything you know about dark objects, and I want you researching all we have on the subject in the library. Also, anything of spirit magic." Pen nodded in agreement, but he seemed deep in thought.

"When I came to this plane, before the gates were closed, dark magic was common. My affinity has always been with the light. In those times, there were many magical humans and other races. But we were spread far apart and travel wasn't easy. Also, the sources of the magic varied widely. The Kind like to think their magic is only of the fae in source, which is true for the most part, but there are other sources, too: Druid, Celtic, Norse, and many other forgotten sources."

"Which do you think is the source of Hilda's?" asked Lowen.

"Not fae, they don't have souls. This is human magic."

"Now, Pen, the fae do have a sort of soul, an essence, but it's earthbound and is supposed to be swallowed by the earth from which they were born."

"Yes, you're right, but they cannot trap their essence, it's too wild. This reeks of the Druids. There has long been a belief that the Rosdews were of Druid origin, brought into the Kind by the dark fae for their powers. The whole concept of necromancers comes from the Druids and Celts."

Lowen chewed on his bottom lip as he considered the information. "Of course, this would have to go down that road. We don't have much, do we?"

"No," Pen said as he tilted his head to the side. "Ask Kador if he's versed in these matters."

I'd been holding the grimoire this whole time in my left hand. For some reason it felt comforting. Putting the book on my lap I reached for my pen. Before I could touch the book, Kador opened it to a blank page toward the back, and in giant letters, responded.

*"Yes."* Guess he had been listening to the whole conversation. How could this be if the book was not sentient?

"He--I mean, the book, says yes." Two heads swiveled towards me.

"Are you telling us the book is talking to you again?"

"I'm not lying to you." I held the book up for them to see the response. From the expressions on their faces, I guessed this to mean they could actually see it.

"Kador, are you a spirit trapped in the book?" Pen asked.

The answer *Yes* appeared repeatedly on the page. Pendragon glared at Lowen.

"We need help. What do you think about trying the old summoning? The moon isn't full, but it's more than three quarters," said Pen.

"Yes. Let's see what we can figure out before dinner, but I think that's the best idea so far. Kador, do you have anything to add?"

"*Do not let the dark object out, and do not try to release the object inside. It will free Hilda's spirit.*"

"Should I destroy it?" I asked.

"*No, that could also release her soul. She had to be planning this for years, and I believe she knows something we do not. A puzzle can only be solved with all of the pieces.*"

"Kador, you're wise. May I ask how long you have been in the book and who put you there?" Pen asked.

"*Thousands of years. I hold no grudge against the one who put me here. They did what they needed to do, to stop me. I am the first Penrose, and I see my story has been wiped out of existence. You hold a hope I might be able to explain a split soul, but I cannot. My soul is all here, and trapped by a powerful being. The Druids walked my lands long ago. Are there any left?*"

"No, the Christians did a number on the Kind, but nothing compared to the Druids. They bound us, but we eliminated all of them and most of their history and culture," said Pen.

"*Are there any markings on the dark object?*"

"Nothing that I saw," said Pendragon.

And I added, "No, only the velvet bag with rocks, which I think was onyx, crystal dust, and a single black feather."

"We'll try to summon the Muninn tonight. Perhaps she'll come and be willing to assist us, because of your connection. You'll have to go with Davidson in the morning, but Pen and I will follow you soon after. I shall be your counsel at the hearing. You're to cooperate with them in all reasonable ways. They'll want you to stay in the Coven House. Do this, but keep Kador with you, always. Tell them it is your sketchpad. Since you've carried one since you were a child, no one will question it. You're to go through your sketchpad and put your things in the back of Kador so you can access them. Also, there is a mirror in the other room, can you open me a passage to your home?"

"Yes, but I've never had anyone else travel the mirror passages with me."

"Let us go now and try. Then I'll take the file and make copies. I'll have your copy back to you after dinner. If you would, tear the sheet with the file and the dark object in it out of the pad and leave it here." I did as he asked and left the one-sheet on the table.

He opened the wall to the library and I saw the giant gilded mirror he wanted me to bespell. Marker in hand I walked over and wrote my spell to open the mirror to my room in the States. A slight wave in the mirror alerted me the spell had taken.

"Wait, come here." Lowen stood in the opening to the oubliette. I joined him back in the room. He had the dagger in his hand. "Give me your right hand."

Without hesitation, I complied, and he cut my palm, then his own. Joining our open palms, he told me to repeat after him. "Gyda gwaed fy hoffwn eich amddiffyn."

He released my hand and I felt a tingling sensation. "What did we just do?"

"'With my blood, I pledge protection.' It's a promise to you from me that I'm your advocate and will always be there for you. Now let's see this magic of yours. Come on, Pen, you're coming for this, too."

Pendragon bounded up Lowen's arm to sit on his shoulder. They followed me into the mirror. I was used to the sensation so it seemed normal to me. They were slow to follow. At first, I saw only an arm. Then he pulled it back. Next a leg, again he pulled it back. The words to the silly children's song played in my head, *You do the hokey pokey, and you turn yourself about.*

Finally, Lowen dared to walk through. He released the breath he'd been holding. Pen jumped up and down excited on his shoulder. Lowen gazed about my walk-in closet. "Is this your closet?"

"Yes."

"Can we leave this open?"

"Of course."

"Good, I'm heading back. I need some time and coffee to consider everything. Oh, one more thing: do you have a place to escape? A place you cannot be traced?"

"Yes."

His eyes narrowed, "You didn't tell me about it?"

"No."

"Good, you're not to tell anyone, including me. There may come a time when you'll have to disappear, and we cannot take the chance of anything or anyone being able to get to you. Your ability is one of a kind."

"What about the dark object?"

"I want to think about everything. I may turn it over to the KIC and make this their problem. What I have not worked out is how to explain how I acquired it. I wonder if it would have been better if you'd left it alone?"

"So do I," I said.

"No," said Pen. "The consequences of him leaving it were too great. They'd have tried to get to the object inside, unaware of the soul anchored to it. Then they would have learned of her interest in Gray. Think of trying to explain that."

"As usual, you're right. Are you ready to work?" Their conversation continued as they walked through the mirror and out of my hearing, James Bond and his dragon. I used the mirror in my room to return to my room at Kolon. Taking my sketchpad to the bed along with Kador, I began to remove everything from it. He sensed what I was doing because he opened up to the last few pages.

The first third of the sketchpad was filled with my things, including the stuff I'd taken from Hilda's house. When I finished he asked, *"May I look through your personal things? I need to learn about your time."*

"Yes, there's nothing that personal. Well, mostly, I did put the letters from Lydia in there. Perhaps you might be able to learn more from them."

*"You do me a great honor by trusting me. When things are settled, I shall return the favor and give you my story. When I do, I believe you will understand that we share more than blood."*

"I'm really looking forward to hearing your story."

It was time to dress for dinner. I changed my clothes. Dressed, I strolled down to dinner with Kador in my hand. The staff at Kolon outdid themselves on the dinner and desserts. Coffee and games went smoothly, and everyone left us before midnight.

"That was easier than I'd hoped. While we could wait until three, I would rather try this at midnight. Come with me," Lowen said as we started for the door, but he stopped at the coat rack and handed me one. "Here, put this on." He put one on, too. Pen fluttered above our heads. All through dinner Pendragon had sat on or near Lowen. Sometimes he would talk to me, and I'd pretend to answer by answering someone else. Lowen had done the same thing. It was like we were dancing around an invisible dragon in the middle of the room.

Lowen led me into a giant atrium off of the main hall. "If we go this way, we won't be visible through the windows upstairs. It will also put us closer to the clearing in the woods, which is the best place for a summoning. Are you sure she still owes you a favor?"

"I never collected, but when she finds out what happened to the claw, she might not feel so generous."

"Good point. Here." He handed me the sheet of paper with the dark object.

Earlier, in my closet, I'd grabbed a small military satchel, one intended for maps and correspondence, which I usually used for my sketchpad. Now Kador was housed inside, along with my dry-erase markers and pen-wand.

Lowen led us on a long trek through the forest; it took us almost twenty minutes to find the clearing. The moon was high overhead and lit the way. In the clearing, moonbeams reflected off several standing stones, like Stonehenge but smaller.

"Isn't this a Druid formation, Lowen?"

"The Druids were not the only ones to use these. This is a place of power and it will help us summon Muninn."

"What do we do to summon her?" I asked.

"I thought you knew how?"

"Not without the claw; it's how she told me to summon her."

The foulest string of curses I think I'd ever heard fell from Lowen's lips. Pendragon's brow lifted in surprise. "Did that make you feel better, Lowen? In all of our years I never knew you to be such a wordsmith. I'm impressed."

Lowen glared, and Pendragon said to me, "Don't worry. I think the claw will still work. The resin might mute the call, but if you try several times and wait, it should work. Let's just hope we don't wake Hilda."

"What do you mean, 'wake her'?" Lowen sputtered.

Pen sighed. "Her soul will probably begin to stir, but we're around seventy-two hours out from her death. She'll be weak, and it will take her time to surface. If all goes well, she won't wake."

"Bloody hell."

"Yes, if she does wake it will be bloody hell."

Lowen instructed me, "Take the object out, stand in the middle of the stones, and call to Muninn."

I went to the center of the stones. With a deep breath I pulled the encased raven's claw out of the paper. Holding the sickening object in the air, I called out, "Muninn, I summon you to me. I request an audience with you." I repeated the summoning. Nothing answered me. I waited for a time and tried again. At the end of the third time I dropped the claw, it had begun to heat up. "Shit!" I yelled. The object burnt my hand.

"Stay, something is happening," Pendragon said, but as if from a distance.

I searched the ground for the dark object, but couldn't find it. A circle closed in on me, a protective one, with a *pop*. When a protection circle closes, it is not something you so much see, as feel. I heard it close and felt the sensory deprivation begin. An artificial sense of silence, with the added smell of ozone. It must be why Lowen and Pendragon couldn't reach me, and I could no longer hear or see them. On the dirt below my feet, an outline of Yggdrasil glowed in the circle of the stone. Anything outside of the stone circle was pitch black, it made me feel as if I were all alone.

"You summoned me after all of this time, with a corrupted gift?"

Self-preservation kicked in and I bowed. Fear spiked in my belly and I hoped my voice didn't quiver as I said, "Muninn, please forgive me. I've tried several times over the years to summon you or Rowan, but received no answer."

"What happened to the gift I gave you?"

"Years ago, someone attacked me. I was seriously injured and lost my memory surrounding the attack. When I started to heal and remember, I realized the claw was gone, along with everything important to me." I was nervous and my words spilled out of my mouth in a rush. "Hilda Rosdew died three days ago, and I discovered she'd cursed me. I found your claw on her body, as the cursed object. She has anchored her soul and attached part of it to the claw."

Muninn hissed. "What has become of my grandson? He has been lost to us for almost twenty-five years."

"He has? I thought he was angry with me and that was why he wouldn't respond to my calls."

"Is this curse the reason I couldn't find you all this time? We have tried many times to locate you."

"You have?"

"Yes. Try summoning Rowan; you won't need the claw. Perhaps he's now released from whatever blocked him from us."

"Rowan, I summon you to me." I tried three times. No response.

"You found the claw in her possession?"

"Yes."

Muninn shook her head. "She knew."

"What did she know?"

"That you would summon me. The claw only allows one summons and is *destroyed*. At least part of her soul is now free to roam. She hoped you'd feel the curse break, seek the dark artifact, and summon me."

I sucked my breath in, "What does this mean?"

"One of the evilest beings I've encountered is now loose and looking for a vessel. You must find the other artifact and tell your people. She isn't confined by your rules anymore and she is much more powerful. Especially if she can release the rest of her soul and the parts of the soul combine again."

"Muninn, I'm so sorry. I didn't know."

"I do not blame you for someone else's evil. But stay vigilant, you will be her first target. Go, if I discover anything I'll send you a message."

"What if I need to speak to you?"

"Send one of your messages into the bridges for me. I shall get it."

"I will."

"Good luck. Try to return my grandson to me."

"I will."

Muninn launched into the air and the protective circle popped. Lowen and Pendragon stood right where I'd left them.

I explained what happened to them and tried summoning Rowan. I received no answer.

# CHAPTER TWENTY-ONE

### Mardi Gras, New Orleans, February 1993

My family received and accepted the invitation to New Orleans. No one in the KIC knew of our destination, on purpose. By not telling them it gave us all an excuse to not spy on our hosts. Better to ask for forgiveness than permission. Due to the time frame and the fact I lived in California now, I traveled alone to New Orleans.

I never made it to my first year of service. My father spoke with the Council like he promised, and they decided it would be better to let me attend a human university to study computer science. I started my freshman year at Stanford last fall.

This trip would be the first of many to New Orleans, but it was my first to anywhere in the southern U.S. Victor and Tristan met me at the airport. I'd never given any thought to Victor's appearance before I got there. Bram Stoker nailed an accurate description of him, and it made me wonder how old he might be. Could

Dracula be based on him? One of the rumors floating around about the Tremaynes is that those of the Blood were immortal.

Victor stood tall, with short black hair and black eyes, pasty white skin and dark clothes, everything I'd expect of a vampire. Except, he stood in the midday sun next to his dark-skinned son. On close inspection, you could see a resemblance.

"So you're the famous Grayson Penrose?" he said with a bright smile.

"Yes, and you must be the big, scary vampire I've heard so much about?"

His smile disappeared, and he looked around at the passing people.

"My secret is out? How will I manage?" We all laughed. From Tristan, I knew his father had a good sense of humor; he'd have to after Anne Rice wrote her novels. He was well known in New Orleans for his vampire shtick.

The flight bringing the rest of my family was more than an hour out, so we went to a nearby restaurant to wait.

"I've been looking into that matter for you for some time now. I am ashamed to say I have nothing for you. Until Lydia enrolled into the Skol Hus at five years old, there is nothing. Not even in the human world. It's as if she's a ghost."

"Did Hilda provide documents to prove who she is?"

"No. She either called in a favor or paid off the right people. As much as I'd like to point out she did this, I don't think it would be wise. Instead, I've another offer for you to consider. I can figure out her ancestry. I can tell which Kind families she shares the most immediate relationship with, if we meet in person and I taste her blood."

I stared him straight in the eye. Not easy to do, either, his eyes were black and disconcerting. "So the rumors about you being able to tell bloodlines are true?"

"Yes, I am of the Blood, and outstanding at what I do."

"This summer I'll talk with her, and figure out what she wants to do. But if she says yes, how would we do it?"

A big smile spread across his lips—maybe it was my imagination, but his teeth and fangs seemed sharp—"Return the favor, have your family invite Tristan and me for a party. A brief meeting is all I need to accomplish this. Hilda is a Rosdew. She wouldn't miss a chance to meet two Tremaynes. Might I suggest a masquerade party? That would make it easy for games of espionage."

"We'll invite you to a party even if Hilda doesn't want to attend. We are already planning a party to take place later in the summer to celebrate the formal announcement of Guy's betrothal."

"Perfect. So, tell me about how your school is going and what you think of California?"

The next hour flew by. Once my family arrived, Victor took us in a fancy limo to his estate in the Garden District, playing the tour guide the whole way. New Orleans was his city, a fact he was very proud of. Tristan sat at his father's side, quiet, as usual. It was a beautiful day in February so the windows were down and Tristan gazed out at the city. It had been almost a year since I had seen him, and I wondered how school might be. He'd grown a lot in that time. He stood over six foot now, with a close-cropped 'fro. After meeting his father, I decided his green eyes must have come from his mother.

We arrived at their estate. It had the look of something out of a movie. In front of the house, a woman waited for us with the staff. She had to be Olivia, Tristan's mother; her coffee-and-cream skin looked just like Tristan's. Dressed in flowing jewel colored skirts she looked the part of a Voodoo priestess. A male servant opened the car door for us. Victor, the first out, went to stand by the woman. As we approached, he introduced her, "This is my lovely wife, Olivia Tremayne, Tristan's mother and Voodoo high priestess."

Victor finished the introductions, gave us the grand tour of the house, and showed us to our rooms. My mother walked with Olivia. I could hear them laughing, something I was truly happy about. Who would have figured the Penroses and Tremaynes could get along? Not me, I thought this trip would have several hiccups.

Once we were situated in our rooms, Tristan stole me away to show me Bourbon Street and the sights.

"How's school?"

"Boring now that you're gone. I miss the trouble you stirred up and always managed to frame Stig Nancarrow for."

I chuckled. "He's my distant cousin, through my mom. As a kid I used to have to spend holidays with him. He's a bully and deserved it."

"The months are flying by. My dad wants me to do my two years of KIC service, then he'd like me to go to medical school down here."

"Is it what you want? I like your father, but he seems like the kind of guy that gets what he wants."

"He is, and I don't know what I want. I think the two years in the KIC will be good for me. I can help my family reconnect with the Kind; we need it. As for school, I haven't decided."

A door opened in front of us, and a guy came flying out, landing in the gutter. The bouncer who had thrown him out stood in the doorway saying, "Stay out!"

We laughed as the guy in the gutter stood up, trying his best to keep his dignity and failing. Together we continued down the street, sometimes being propositioned by women, sometimes by men, and cajoled by the vendors lining the street. New Orleans is something to experience. The streets were alive with the coming celebration.

He led us back to his house before dinner, promising a real show in the coming days. A servant opened the door to the house as we returned and I saw Olivia had been waiting for us.

"Tristan, my boy, let me steal yer friend, eh?"

"Yes, but be nice," he said looking her in the eye. "No scaring my best friend."

"Course not, cher."

"No knuckle bones," he said as he left us.

"Wouldn't think of it. So ya are the one?" she said.

"The one what?"

She flung her hand in my direction, "Humble, and cute, too. Allons, we'll talk."

She led to a room most people would use as a study. For her it looked like part sacrificial altar, part Voodoo doctor supply store, and part laboratory. The humidity in the room overwhelmed me, as did the strange earthy smells. She led me on a path past creatures in jars, vials of spices, all wallpapered in luxurious fabrics, to a table dressed in vibrant colored scarves, with a crystal ball at the center.

"You don't really use that?" I pointed at the ball.

"Sometimes it has uses. People 'spect it. Don't wanna let them down. Have a seat."

She sat opposite of me and pulled out a bag, which I suspected were the knucklebones. She leaned her face into her left palm, and examined me.

"Ya've been kind to my boy. A debt I shall always owe ya. There's power in yer family, but ya are the one. It surrounds ya; bet others don't notice?" Her accent was so thick I had trouble following everything she said.

"No one pays much attention to me."

"The Kind, I think ya call yerselves, but ya witches no matter what title ya use. Ya don't mix with others in this world with magic, nor do ya follow many of the traditions us other folk do. Yer aura is crazy, sometimes a rainbow, but ya like yer white and silver. Wonder what color it be when ya use your powers, hmm?"

What could I say to that?

"Ya asked Victor for help, and I gotta say, ya've posed the only questions I've ever seen him not be able to answer. It's drivin' him nuts. Ya be troubled by it, too. I'm gonna throw the knuckles for ya, but these are old and from magical sorts of beasts. Bones don't lie; they tell very harsh truths. Do ya wanna hear those? I don't use 'em often, and only for magic kin. It's yer choice and ya must decide upon three questions before I throw them."

Tristan hadn't told me much about his mother. I knew her to be a Voodoo priestess and an Oracle. If I wanted answers, she'd probably be the best bet to give them.

"I want you to throw them," I said.

The left corner of her mouth turned up in a half-smile. "I knew ya'd say that. Here, write a past, present, and future question on this paper, fold it, and don't show me."

The three questions came easy. I wrote them out and folded the paper in fourths.

"Hold the bag and think about yer questions. I need wine."

The purple silk drawstring bag was heavier than I'd have thought. With a big glass of wine in hand, she sat and held her hand out for the bag. She began humming a strange tune with her eyes closed, as she shifted the bones in the bag. For a full five minutes, she continued. I was about to interrupt her when she shook the bag violently and dumped the bones on the table. She glanced at them and sipped her wine.

She made little noises as she looked around the table at the bones, then she looked up at me. "This reading makes 'bout as much sense as tryin' to read a book backward. Everything is a contradiction with ya."

In situations like this, I do what I do with my mom, shrug and look innocent.

"Looking at these bones and the responses, I'd believe ya to be much older than ya are." She stared at me for a minute without saying a word. I wanted to squirm under the attention. "Let me see yer right palm."

Without hesitation, I held it out to her. "This makes no sense," she muttered.

"I'm left-handed." She held her hand out for my left hand. With my palm under her gaze, she made more funny sounds.

"Well, yer palm helped explain some of what the bones are showin' me. Let's discard yer questions. Yer life and influences are too great for simple answers," the wine thickened her accent even more.

"Ya've been on this path a very long time, for several lifetimes. Everyone and everythin' in this life is here for a reason. What the outcome will be I can only guess, but this life will resolve this path ya started many centuries ago."

"What path? Can you tell me anything?"

"No, but somehow, yer tied to other souls with a single purpose; an important one. Reading yer bones is like reading Victor's. Nothin's clear, but ya should follow yer heart. Don't let anyone force ya into something ya don't want. That's happened before. Ya won't resolve this if ya don't lead the way. That's pretty much it, except, and I prefer not say this, ya have many years to wander lost in the woods."

"What does that mean?"

"Ya won't find the path ya need for many years."

"Can you tell if I'll be able to help Lydia?"

"I can't tell. There is a blockage of some kind around ya; I can't see through it. Does that mean ya won't be able to help her? J'sais pas. What I do know is ya need to be careful."

I considered her words. It seemed nothing in my life had a simple answer or was easy. "Don't worry, I won't tell Tristan you brought the bones out." A giant smile spread across her face. "Have you done this for him?"

"No, it's bad luck for me to read my own son's future. I could affect it. Fate, or destiny, is a strange thing. Some people don't have one and are open to do what they will. Others are ruled by it, and some have only a few things in their life which are destin'd to happen. Ya fall in the second group. Because of this, ya will repeat the path until ya have finished, using yer own free will. If it makes ya feel any better, all of the truly great people I've ever met fall into yer group."

"I think I need to go upstairs before dinner and think about this."

"Remember, we're here if ya need us. Ya have people who care and will help. Don't forget it, for ya have a heavy burden to carry alone."

I nodded, agreeing, before leaving.

· ✶ ·

Our stay with the Tremaynes was great. They made sure I got to experience everything. Olivia even took me to meet a zombie, on the condition I tell no one. When the last day dawned, I felt sorry my time here was at an end.

On the last night, Victor and Tristan surprised me; they made me an honorary member of the Tremayne family. The ceremony did include blood, but not an exchange. Instead, a crystal champagne glass sat on the altar next to a dagger. Victor cut his palm first and let two drops fall into the glass, followed by the rest of my family, who stood and witnessed the ceremony. After everyone else, Tristan met me at the altar and cut his hand and mine. We joined hands and let the blood drip into the glass. Our blood joined together in the glass. Victor then said a long string of foreign words and the blood ignited into flame. I pulled my hand back and I saw my cut had healed. The flames licked the sides of the glass, dancing in dark red hues. When the fire extinguished, a red smoke billowed from the glass. I wouldn't be surprised if the term "blood-brothers" comes from this ceremony.

Tristan picked up the glass and brought it to me. It no longer appeared as a typical champagne glass, instead the base had taken on an almost black color, which faded to blood red, before turning clear near the rim.

"This is yours, whenever you need one of us just drip a couple of drops of your blood and say the name of the Tremayne you seek."

"Thank you," I said, honored by the gift bestowed on me.

# CHAPTER TWENTY-TWO

### September, Cornwall, England

Lowen took me to the study to warm up with a scotch by the fire. There is something to be said about being able to sit in front of a large hearth with someone else and enjoy the silence. It had been so long since I had been able to be so open about the burden I carried. Instead of judgment, I found in Lowen, Pendragon, and Kador, a caring ear, friendship, and brotherhood.

"There are a couple of other things I need to tell you this evening before you leave. First, well, I'm not thrilled to be telling you this, but I think the Council will want you to marry a young Blygh girl. She's the most likely candidate, my sources tell me. Currently, she's twelve years old," Lowen informed me. I coughed on the sip of scotch I had taken.

"Now don't panic, that gives us time. It's a good thing for everyone, well, except your libido."

"No way."

"Relax, like I said, it gives us time. To be honest, I figured it would be sooner, so consider yourself lucky. Now, I want you to go home and do what's asked of you. I shall be your counsel. I'll step in if they ask anything too outrageous or want to keep you under guard. Of you being the *Guide*, I've no doubt. Because of this I want you to think back over the years to every time you have received a prophecy of any kind. Write it down as close to the original as you remember. Send them to me and I'll forward it to Pen, but I want both of us aware of everything. No matter how trivial."

I looked at him and held up my empty glass, his cue to refill it. His brow lifted. "You know, part of life in the Kind involves arranged marriages. Think of what your brother went through."

He picked up the scotch and poured, I urged him to pour me a strong one. I sipped it as I considered his comment. Lowen was right. Guy had carried his burden for over twenty years.

I still held Kador in my hand. I opened his book and flipped to the pages I had stored my things in. I took out the scrap of fabric Aquila had given me and shut the book. I set the fabric on an end table. "Here, this is something Aquila gave me."

Lowen's brow lifted in surprise. "Do you have any other things in there related to your future?"

I shook my head, then reconsidered. I flipped the book open again. "Kador?"

"*Yes.*" Appeared on the page.

"Have you encountered a fortune ticket with the name …" Damn it! What was his name? Zoltar came to mind, but that wasn't it. I had held onto the stupid ticket I'd gotten from the arcade fortune teller the day I met Lydia. I usually had it with my photos and old ticket stubs from my times with her. "Oh yeah, Balthazar."

Kador was silent for a minute. Then an image of the ticket appeared on the page. I reached into the page and grabbed it. "Thanks, Kador," I said as I closed his book.

Lowen, with Pendragon on his shoulder, approached me. "Is that from someone named Balthazar the Great?" Lowen asked.

In answer, I handed him the ticket.

"Wow, I always thought he was just a story," Lowen whispered in awe.

"Seriously? Balthazar the arcade fortune teller is someone you have heard of?"

Lowen chuckled, "Yeah."

"Who is he?" Pen asked.

"When I was a kid, my mother used to tell me stories about him. Julia, my mother, was from Connecticut and came here when she married my father. She claimed she knew him, a human or something with magic that was cursed. I used to think it was just a story. If you ran into him, it means you're the Guide. He was a powerful oracle, and some would say sage."

"How come I've never heard of him?" Pen asked.

Lowen didn't respond for a moment, he seemed lost as he read the card from Balthazar.

"I forgot about him. Pen, why don't you do some research on him? See if you can find anything online." Lowen said as he handed the card to Pen.

"When did you get this from him? And have you run into him any other times?"

"I've only seen him the one time. It was at the arcade on the Santa Cruz Pier, June 8, 1988."

His eyes narrowed in confusion. "How do you remember a date so long ago?"

"Easy, I encountered him a few minutes after I met Lydia." Lowen's right brow rose. Pen looked up at me and cocked his head to the side.

"Did you noticed your name is printed on the card?" Pen asked.

"Yup. When I encountered him he was at the back of the arcade, and unplugged I might add. I sensed the magic coming from him. Without power, his booth lit up and I put a coin in him. I figured it was probably bad luck to ignore him. The event was so unusual I held on to the card."

"Well, I think I'll make a copy of both and return them to you. Think about it, see if you come up with anything else like this." Lowen said.

"I will."

"Now, a time will come when you will need to disappear," he continued.

I sipped the scotch, which burned all the way down my throat, but in a pleasant way. "I've planned for it."

"Good. I don't want to know where, but when I need to reach you how should I do it?"

The numbing effects of the scotch were starting; I'd soon pass out. "Take a dry-erase marker and write your note backward on the mirror, like Leonardo da Vinci, on the bathroom mirror in my room here at Kolon. I'll check it regularly."

"Fine. If you disappear, I'll bespell the bathroom so only Pen and I can enter."

"I'll respond by leaving you a note, and open a passage to the location. Be aware, I'll have a backup plan to escape if it comes to this."

"Good. You're definitely a Penrose, and I'm happy to call you family. Now go to bed, you need to be up early."

After everything, I was more than ready for sleep. I said my goodbyes and headed for bed. Half-drunk, I just stripped to my boxers and threw my clothes into a pile on the floor as I jumped under the covers. Sleep found me moments later.

・ ෴ ・

The sun shined into my room hitting my eyes. I woke up feeling as if I'd just gone to sleep. I knew I wouldn't be able to go back to sleep I got up and got my things together. No matter if Davidson was ready or not I intended to go home.

I looked around and noticed something seemed off; my clothes were arranged nicely on a chair, also I had no hangover. With as fast as I had downed the scotch the night before, I had expected some trouble this morning. I rubbed the sleep out of my eyes and wondered if I still might be drunk? Deciding I must be nuts, I headed for the shower.

Ten minutes later I emerged from the shower with a towel wrapped around my waist to hear a knock on my door. On the other side, I found Davidson. "Can you be ready to go in an hour? I want to go home."

"Sooner. I can't wait to get out of here." He gave me a funny look. "I'm not planning to run. I just want to go home."

He left me to pack and get dressed. Once I was done, I went to look for Kador, but I couldn't find him anywhere. I thought I'd put the book on the nightstand before laying down the night before. Concerned, I went in search of Lowen. I didn't need to look far, he was with my father in the main hall by the foyer.

"Good morning," I said. They greeted me and continued their conversation as I grew restless.

"Pardon me, but could I steal Lowen for a few minutes?"

Lowen's eyebrow lifted in a questioning manner. I nodded in answer and followed him to the library. As soon as the door shut, I blurted out, "Someone was in my room and took Kador."

His eyebrow appeared stuck in the same position. From upstairs I heard a gravelly response to my statement.

"I was in your room last night, to check on you. What I didn't expect is how easily you left your most precious possession unguarded and easy to grab. Hilda will soon be strong enough to touch the physical world and take what she wants. You've got to be more careful, especially now with Hilda on the loose."

I watched Pendragon on the banister of the third floor of the library. He stared back at me.

"You mean you didn't bespell the book with some protection? A cloaking spell? Perhaps a disguising spell? Nothing? Gray, I expected so much more of you," Lowen said.

I flushed, realizing both were right. "I screwed up. But in my defense, I'm not very good at those spells."

"Definitely a Penrose, the little magics and black magic seem to escape us. Pen, might you be able to assist with something."

In response, Pendragon launched off the banner and glided down in circles to land on the desk. His claws clicked on the wood of the desk and the humid, smoky smell I identified as "Pen" filled the air. A loud noise sounded. All three of us looked around the library for the source. Pen's eyes went to the bag by his feet. He tilted his head as the sound came again, then swiveled his eyes to me.

"Your king calls."

I blinked. What? My king? Oh, Kador.

I grabbed the bag and took out the grimoire. It jumped and vibrated in my hands. "Okay, Kador, I get the message."

Without waiting, he flipped the book open. A series of angry rants filled the page, insulting and demeaning me for leaving him exposed. Pen hopped up onto my shoulder to look at the pages and laughed. "Your king has a rather filthy mouth."

"Sorry Kador. But I'm no good at the spell we need for this."

"May I try something?" Pen asked.

"Sure."

"Kador, may I apply magic to your vessel? I wish to see if I can do something," Pendragon asked.

*"YOU MAY,"* appeared in large letters on the page.

Pen flew to the mantel of the fireplace and grabbed two items before he returned. Both went in a bowl on the desk. He picked up the larger of the two, which looked like a small dried out branch.

"This is a limb from the Rowan tree." He picked up the next object. I knew what it was without being told. "A piece of sage. I'm going to burn both of these and use the ashes to loosen the lock on Kador. It won't release him, but sometimes simplest is best." He shot a long burst of blue flames from his nostril to the bowl. Both objects incinerated instantly into a fine white ash. Next, he placed a plate over the bowl.

"Let's make sure there isn't anything smoldering in there before I place it in the book. The book *is* bespelled against fire, but best not to test an old spell."

After more than two minutes he lifted the lid, and with bowl in hand, he dumped the contents into the open pages of the book. With a flip of his claw, he closed the book with a thud and a white cloud of ash.

"How will we know if it worked?" I asked.

The grimoire flew open in a cloud of dust with a loud noise.

"I'm not sure your experiment worked," Lowen said.

*"Nor am I."*

I looked up at them. "Who just said that?"

"Said what? I just said I didn't think his experiment worked."

"No, not that." This time, I heard a cough. "Seriously, who is coughing?" They appeared more confused. But I had a thought.

"Kador, is that you?"

*"Grayson? You can hear me?"*

"Yes," I said.

"What's the matter?"

"I can hear Kador."

They narrowed their eyes at me. "Have either of you ever known someone with an animal familiar?"

Both shook their heads. "Unless you count Pen, no. And he isn't really a familiar. Just some of us can see him."

"Not true, you can speak to him telepathically."

They exchanged a look.

"Is that how Rowan spoke?"

"Yes."

A knock sounded on the door. Lowen answered the door to let in Davidson.

"Gray, can we head out?"

"Yes. I just forgot I left some of my stuff down here." I went to the table and picked up Kador.

*"Grayson, can you still hear me?"* Kador's voice sounded rough and unused with a strange accent.

"Yes, I can," I thought back to Kador, not wanting to alert Davidson.

Lowen, with Pen on his shoulder, walked over and gave me a friendly hug and said his goodbyes. "Davidson," Lowen said holding his hand out to him.

"Your hospitality has been appreciated," Davidson said as they shook hands.

"Of course, but I'll see you tomorrow."

"You will?" Davidson seemed worried.

"But of course, as the family head I will be Gray's counsel."

His comment didn't seem to sit well with Davidson, though he tried to hide it. Lowen had a reputation in our world of being a whiz at business, and even more resourceful at politics. In the human world he would be like a businessman and lawyer turned politician. Nobody wanted to go against him.

"I look forward to it," Davidson said in a higher than usual voice.

We left for the airport. In my backpack were my tablet, cell phone, a few personal items, and a book I intended to read on the way back. Once on the plane, I got a drink from the staff and sat in the window seat, reading. Davidson looked tired. He sat a couple of rows behind me and fell right to sleep.

Maybe an hour had passed when I heard Kador's voice in my head. *"When you finish your book, may I read it?"* he asked.

"Sure. Have you read the books and things I got from Lydia's house?"

*"All of them. I'm bored in here and need more information about your time. The books here are strange. Is the world that different?"*

"No. What you're reading is fiction; made up stories. I can get you a whole bunch of history, mythology, and other books to read. It will prepare you for our world better. Have you ever read the Christian Bible?"

*"No, what's a Christian?"*

"Really? You predate Christ?"

*"I guess?"*

"How are you able to read and understand them?"

*"Easy, a simple translation spell. But not all concepts make sense to me. Of the things you loaded into my book, I grasp Sandman and the Endless the most. Eternity, endlessness, and being trapped, that I understand. Or maybe having the pictures with the words helped."*

I laughed. "Interesting … I wonder if I can give you other things to help with the quiet and loneliness. Would you like to be able to listen to music? Or watch moving pictures that tell stories?"

*"Such things exist? What magic is it?"*

"No magic. It's human inventions."

*"You lie to me."*

"No, I don't."

*"I'd love to see a woman. Thousands of years without sex or companionship is not living."*

I laughed out loud. "I'll be able to help you out more than you can ever imagine with this. We'll have to figure out if you can get an internet signal in there."

*"What's this you speak of?"*

## CONVERGENT LINES

"I'll explain later, it will be easier to show you."

*"Thank you."*

"For what?"

*"Finding me."*

# CHAPTER TWENTY-THREE

### August 1993, Santa Cruz, California

In May of 1993, I became the first adult Kind to play a video game console. To my surprise the Nintendo continued to work. When I was younger and played with Lydia in the arcade it didn't count because of my age and abilities. Though more powerful than most Kind at my age, back then I hadn't attained my full magical powers. Now, and every year until I hit about fifty, my power would grow. If I married the right person, my magical powers could grow even more.

At the end of May school finished and I headed to our place in Santa Cruz, earlier then I'd ever been able to go before. I brought the Nintendo with me for the first real test: would it hold up to my father playing it? Or what about several Kind in close proximity? I intended to find out. Over the summer, I also planned to buy my first whole computer, one I didn't put together, and discover if I could shield it for my father. Baby steps, I told myself.

I found myself alone for nearly two days, waiting for my parents. I'd grown accustomed to living alone, it would feel weird to have others in the house again. The thought of seeing Lydia overwhelmed me. Much of the reason I worked so hard at solving this problem found its roots in my feelings for her. Doing this would guarantee a secure place for me in Kind society, with the intention of being able to choose her as my wife, and to let us live as we wanted. No matter how long this took, I would do it.

Our correspondence continued as it had in years past. From the tone of her letters I believed things were no better than before. The subtext told me she was holding back. We both wondered if someone could intercept our messages. Because of this I'd added a line to make the text invisible to everyone but the two of us. If the notes were intercepted they would appear as a curiosity. Yet Lydia still held back, maybe because she'd become afraid, or someone or something watched her while she wrote the notes.

The contract with the Marraks for the betrothal of my brother was due to go before the Council for approval soon. Somehow my parents, despite great odds, managed to get the contract. The prophecy didn't say which family the male would come from, and many other powerful, and equally likely, families were in competition for her.

If the contract got the Council's approval, my father might let me try to marry Lydia. Though there would be great odds against a Penrose acquiring a betrothal to a Rosdew. If I could have my mother, a Nancarrow, obtain the contract, then it might happen. The real challenge would be getting my mother to approve and seek the contract for me. This meant my mom would have to like and consider Lydia as a viable candidate. With Lydia's background and bloodlines being an unknown this would be a problem. My mom could be difficult and a snob, especially about bloodlines. But she did have a weak spot for Rosdews and, maybe, my feelings.

For all that my parents did to obtain the contract for Guy, I know they didn't want him to have to marry someone he didn't know and to wait so long. Years ago, when my brother took me camping, he revealed something our mother had shared with him.

"When I was young, my mother, your grandmother, had me go before Aquila. She told me I'd give birth to the *Guide*, the male child who would break the Kind's binding," Guy had quoted our mother to me. This went far to explain my mother's actions. He thought our mother felt the need to protect him from the Kind and secure him the bride he would fulfill his destiny with. If Guy's theories were true, then my mother might agree.

Which was why my work on computers was so important. But as I said, I'd made amazing strides. No one knew of my accomplishments yet either. I planned to show my father when he arrived. The advancements I'd made in less than one year's time was enough to ensure a large role for myself and my family in the future of our society.

Yes, the Council had been worried about computers, and cars, but they were coming to the conclusion that we wouldn't be able to overcome this problem. In the last year, the Council had considered a ban on Kind flying. With onboard computers appearing on planes, the fear was a real concern.

At this point certain guidelines were in effect for Kind planning to fly. The first was no flying in small planes or near the wings on jets. Only a mother and child could sit together, to lessen the power concentrated in one area. No wands or magical objects could be on your person or in your carry-on. These items needed to be in checked luggage for safety. Another recommendation was a sedative for the flight; when we sleep our magic doesn't seem to affect our surroundings as much.

I was confident I'd have some power in directing my future. If this worked I would use it as a bargaining chip with my parents, Hilda, and the Council. Lydia was of age now, and I had no intention of waiting any longer. Before year's end we would be betrothed or, better yet, married. Of course, her wishes would be the final piece; hopefully she would pick me, and not because she felt I was the only way to escape Hilda.

When she arrived, I would tell her of my advancements and plans. I would get her away from Hilda, and we could see about getting her out of KIC service, too. She would be with me if that was what she wanted.

My parents arrived on time. To my surprise, I was excited to see them. The next couple of days we spent going over my advancements with computers. The Nintendo worked, and worked well. I've never seen them so happy. They were so impressed I took them to my condo to show off my computer. It worked for them, and I even got to show them the internet.

My father made an immediate call to the Council. Within three days they were on my doorstep. Over the course of the next few days I showed Davidson Gwyn, Sowenna Penrose, and Samantha Rosdew my progress. By the end of that time I knew my plan had worked. The Council would be financing me lavishly and I could make my demand: allow me to marry who I wanted. No one seemed surprised by the request, but I was told they would need to discuss it with the rest of the Council because of my bloodline. If it was agreed, I would be free to choose who I married.

Lydia's name didn't get mentioned. This would be a process, and I expected them to come back with a counter offer. What did surprise me is that neither of my parents seemed surprised. I had discussed this with my father so his reaction seemed understandable, but my mother didn't seem surprised, either. This alone scared me. I figured I'd have a fight on my hands with her. The Council left and we returned to Santa Cruz. Rowan waited for me.

He hopped around on my bed.

"How were things this last year?" I asked after telling him about the events of the last few months.

"*Quiet, but something is wrong; I don't know what. Lydia is still weak, and magic is even harder for her than before. Jessy is out of favor, and Lydia is not to have contact with her now. She's completely isolated now. And she won't be going into KIC service. Instead she's to move in with Hilda as a servant.*"

"This is worse than I imagined. Has there been any talk of marriage?"

"*None. It seems to be her goal to isolate Lydia for some reason. I hope you accomplish your goal with the Council. Remember, it's a high-risk game of chess you play, though you do have the upper hand. You'll probably get what you want, it's only a question of when.*" He tilted his head and went on, "*I don't think Hilda will agree. Perhaps down the road when you've become successful. But there is something she wants from Lydia. For some time I've wondered if she has some information we don't. For years Hilda has watched Lydia and Jessy. She probably arranged the trouble with Jessy, which landed her in a room with Lydia. That's about the same time the ghost began watching them, reporting the movements and actions of the girls to her. At some point she decided Jessy wasn't it, thus she has no more use for her. Lydia is her focus now, and whatever she wants, she thinks Lydia has it."*

"What you say makes sense, but what could it be? What could she want with a girl she has deprived of magic?"

"*I don't know.*"

"Does she know about you?"

"*No. Of that I'm sure.*"

"I'm going to approach my mother to handle the negotiations with Hilda. A Nancarrow would be someone Hilda will negotiate with, at least."

"*You don't understand what I am saying. She wants something Lydia has or something she thinks Lydia can do.*"

I looked at him as my sense of accomplishment leeched out of me. The only answer would be to run, but now that the Council knew what I could do, they would hunt me down and I would lose Lydia. Rowan must have read my face.

"*Sorry.*"

"All I can do is move ahead and try. Tell Lydia I'll meet her tomorrow on the beach."

Rowan nodded and flew out the window. I sat down on my bed with the weight of the world on my shoulders.

A knock sounded at my door. Surprised, I got up and opened it. There stood my mother. "May I come in? I'd like to speak with you."

Shocked, I opened the door wider and held my hand out in a welcoming motion. She came in and sat on the bed. Whatever her motives, I sensed she wanted me to close the door.

"I was rather taken aback by your request to the Council. It made me realize I'd not been paying much attention to you. Scratch that, I've never paid you much attention. I don't know you. It became apparent to me last year when you started at Stanford. For this I'm sorry. I love you, but have never made it clear to you. Can you forgive me?"

I worked as hard as I could I keep my face from revealing the shock I felt. Questions started in my head, *Who are you?* and *What have you done to my mother?*

"As strange as this might sound, I've always trusted you, I knew you wouldn't get into trouble, and you're smart. But the time has come, who is she? You wouldn't have asked the Council if you didn't have someone in mind. I'll help; it's the least I can do."

My eyebrows lifted, unable to hide my reaction. "What if you don't approve of my choice? There's a good chance you won't mind her family, but she isn't a direct line."

"If I think we can get the Council to approve, I'll help. Who is she?"

"A Rosdew."

Her mouth popped open, and her eyes widened. "You want to marry a Rosdew? I need to meet this girl. Tell me about her family."

"That's just it. We don't know. Her parents died when she was young."

"Then how did you meet her? Who's her guardian?"

"She comes here in the summers. I met her six years ago. And before you ask, I've never done anything with her."

"No, I wouldn't think you would. Why don't you want to tell me who her guardian is?"

I cleared my throat, "Hilda Rosdew."

The look on her face said everything. "You ask for a miracle. Is it the granddaughter, the one with the black hair? Sorry, I forget her name. I've met her a couple of times at parties."

"Her name is Lydia, and yes, she's the granddaughter."

"We are on good terms with the Rosdews. My mother and Hilda have been friends for years. Let me think about this while we wait for the Council's decision. When dealing with the Rosdews things should be done with great caution. Does anyone else know about you two? Is she old enough, and is there an arranged marriage for her already?"

"No one but Guy, and before you say anything, he is always lecturing me about being careful. She's eighteen and just finished school, though there are no plans for her to enter the KIC program. No arranged marriage that we know of."

"Yes, it's common for the Rosdews to avoid the KIC if possible. I'll do my best to help," she said as she got up to leave. To my surprise, she stopped in front of me and gave me a hug. "I'm proud of you. I'm sorry I've never said it before now."

"It means a lot to hear you say it."

She smiled as she walked out, the door clicked behind her. A cool breeze blew in from the open window, it lifted the light sheer curtains. Rowan sat on the window sill looking at me.

"You heard that, huh?"

*"I shouldn't have doubted you. I would've never thought you would have your mother's support."*

"Yeah, I wouldn't have thought it either."

*"You should tell Lydia; it's your news."*

"Yeah. Here's to hoping things keep going our way."

# CHAPTER TWENTY-FOUR

**Late September, Connecticut**

Somehow I knew before the airplane doors opened that the KIC guards were waiting for us. No doubt they were there for me. I felt Davidson stop in his tracks. He hadn't known they would be here? Interesting.

Kador sensed my unease, *"What is it?"*

As my feet reached the tarmac in front of our hanger, Kador seemed to comprehend our situation. I stopped at the bottom but moved aside for Davidson. I didn't need magic to sense his anger. A man about my age separated from the others to approach us. His brown uniform identified him as someone from law enforcement. As he neared he looked more like an old sepia tone photo, with a brown uniform, brown hair and eyes; he seemed flat, with no contrast.

"Petrok, what's the meaning of this?" Davidson demanded.

Once I heard his name, I recognized him. He'd been a couple of years ahead of me in school. He and Guy might have been friends at some point.

"I was instructed to meet both of you here and take Grayson to the Coven House." He approached slowly as he assessed me.

"This is ridiculous. Who instructed you?"

"My orders came from the top: Arthur Wayfarer."

I felt dizzy. So, I was to be a pawn already?

"You know the Kind law. A Wayfarer cannot make a ruling over a Penrose or vice versa."

"In this he can. My orders are to offer the Council my judgment. First, I shall assess his chances of fleeing or being non-cooperative. Second, I'm to evaluate the best way to secure such a valuable asset." Petrok's sneer concerned me.

My parents were supposed to arrive later that night, but Lowen wasn't coming until tomorrow. I took a deep breath. Best to appease them; give them a false sense of my cooperation.

"It's okay. I'll comply," I said. His sneer turned to a painful smile. A shudder of fear ran cold along of my spine.

"Well, since you're offering, would you mind letting me put these on you?" He held out a small rust-colored, metal chain. As my eyes focused upon them I realized they were manacles.

I cursed a long stream of foul words in my head, causing Kador to realize the problem.

*"Is he metal-touched?"*

"Yes," I shouted in my head.

A stream of strange words fell from him. I must say, we lost the expressiveness of that language when we switched over to English.

*"Give me permission to see through your eyes."* I blinked thinking about his request.

"How?" I thought to him.

*"Say 'I grant you permission to see through my eyes,' but it has to be said out loud. Just whisper it!"*

"I grant Kador permission to see through my eyes," I whispered, no one seemed to hear me.

"Petrok! Really! He doesn't need those, he has been cooperative with me every step of the way. I trust him completely. Heavens, I've known him since he was born. Gray single-handedly saved the Kind with his advances in technology." I could understand Davidson's sentiment. His power seat is water and I know he has difficulty with metals, especially iron. I imagine metal cuffs would be the worst punishment he could think of.

*"Let him do it. What he does will not affect me or our bond, plus I suspect you possess some of the same abilities as me. Metals didn't bother me as much as it did others with the fae blood. I believe it's why you're successful in your ventures in the human world. It will dull you, but if we have to get out of it we can."*

"Go ahead. I mean if you're that worried my 'superpowers' will hurt you …" The look on Petrok's face went from one of triumph to insult in less than a split second, and Davidson turned to me surprised. "Hey, I don't care. Whatever makes the Council feel better. You guys need me more than I need you."

Petrok moved closer to me, and with a look, indicated I should lift my wrists. My point had been made, and he made it apparent that he understood by snapping the manacles hard and tight around my wrist. Once they were on I waited … I didn't feel any different. He gave the chains between my hands a yank. It woke me from my stupor. His actions caused a cut on my left wrist, deep enough for blood to begin dripping.

"Kador? Can you hear me?" I thought.

*"You aren't affected by metals. You must have inherited this ability from me. While it might not affect you, you'll not have an affinity with it. Metal to us is like it is to humans, a tool."*

"Not so confident now, are you?" he said with a thrill of triumph.

"Excuse me, but would you please release my charge," said a deep voice I immediately recognized.

Petrok turned his attention to the new arrival.

"If I'm not mistaken you have spilled his blood, and his blood is my blood." The expression on Petrok's face said it all. Though unknown to most of the Kind, Victor's stature, charm, and power resonated with others.

"And who would you be, sir? You're interrupting Council business."

"I am Victor Tremayne, and I am Grayson Penrose's stand-in counsel until Lowen Penrose arrives. Now, remove those barbaric things. What is this? The Middle Ages?"

Petrok's mouth opened wide with a loud pop. The other officers moved away and the atmosphere became tense. With the Tremaynes being absent so long, rumors had turned to legend.

Victor stood proud, with Tristan at his side. My friend had grown to be nearly as tall as his father, but the couple of inches he lacked were more than made up for in width. Not to say he's fat, far from it, his muscles made me think of comic book superheroes and made me very glad we were friends. I felt no shame in admitting he could kick my ass.

Petrok seemed to gather himself. He strode up to Victor with his chest puffed out like a proud bird. "What business would a Tremayne have with a Penrose?" he said as he crossed his arms. "Perhaps you would like to tell me who you *really* are?"

Victor stood as still as a statue, though rage seemed to radiate off him in waves. His eyes never left Petrok and for the briefest of moments they appeared to glow a bright red, like blood.

"Enough!" Davidson said as he moved in between the two men. "Petrok, I've been expecting Victor. Grayson has a long-standing relationship with the Tremaynes and they're here to assure his safety. Remove the bonds and allow him to go home."

"On whose authority?"

"Boy, you forget your place. I'm on the Council and outrank everyone here. Arthur's little trick didn't go unnoticed like he thought it would. Now, do as I ask or it will be *you* spending the night in lock-up," he said as he frothed around his mustache.

Petrok returned to remove the chains, and he made no pretenses of being happy about it. Once the chains were off, he and his reinforcements left.

"Victor, Tristan, it's nice to see you again," Davidson said as he held a hand out to each of them.

Victor took Davidson's hand and shook it. "Did Lowen tell you I'd be coming?"

"No, but the way I see it right now, Gray will need all the allies he can get."

"Yes, he will. Where do you fall?"

"Gray is more like a son than my own. I held him the day he was born and have been there since. No one in the Kind would be better to guide us than him. But he'll carry a burden, become a walking target for enemies, and women who want to be the one to help him break it."

Victor's face turned from a blank stare to a smile. "You're a Gwyn, full of sunshine and light. It isn't in you to lie or deceive. It's a good thing I'm here."

Tristan and I started laughing, Davidson stood for a moment unsure of how to react. He soon figured out Victor was not joking.

"It will take someone like Grayson to get the light and dark together."

We spent a few more minutes discussing things while we waited for Henson to arrive.

# CHAPTER TWENTY-FIVE

### Summer 1993, Santa Cruz, California

The sand felt cold as I waited for Lydia on the beach. Minutes before sunrise I spotted her. In a rush, I jumped up, happy to see her. As she neared, I could tell things were bad. She wore a smile and jumped into my arms. Holding her, I knew my first impression was not wrong, she'd lost weight. Too much weight. She settled her head on my chest, trying to hide her sobs.

"What's wrong?"

"I can't believe I'm here."

"Did she hurt you again?"

"No, but things have never been the same since last summer. I swear, every day I just become more tired. All I do is sleep, and it's never enough." Tears rolled down her cheeks.

"Come, sit with me, I've news. Good news." Over the next hour, I told her of my adventures from the last year. While I'd communicated with her through letters, I'd never told her too much; I didn't want to give her false hope. Now I had the full support of the Council and financial backing.

Together, we planned for the future for the first time, and she seemed to relax. We were planning a huge masquerade ball on my twenty-first birthday in August. The celebration had several purposes, my step into adulthood, the announcement of Guy's betrothal to the Marrak girl, an excuse to invite the Tremaynes, and to announce my success to the Kind. With these things, I felt good about our chances with Hilda.

Lydia listened to all I had to say. When I finished, it seemed as if our lives were about to change for the better. She left soon after, but we planned to meet later that night on the beach. Rowan stayed behind with me.

"Do you think we'll succeed?" I asked him. He circled my head as we headed toward my house.

*"You've accomplished much more than I'd have thought possible."*

"Are you hungry?" I asked.

*"Starving."*

I stopped and got us some food from one of the street vendors. He did the little dance of excitement when I sat his large chili cheese dog in front of him. Suddenly I wasn't hungry. I felt as if I'd swallowed a bunch of butterflies. Instead of eating my chili cheese dog I watched an exuberant Rowan eat his. He didn't look at me until he was finished.

*"You planning on eating that?"*

In answer, I pushed my hot dog towards him.

*"What's gotten into you?"*

"I think I'd better go home and have a discussion I've been dreading."

He cocked his head to examine me out of one eye. *"You go to your family?"*

I nodded.

He cawed, *"I wouldn't want to be you right now."*

I grunted. Now that I'd seen Lydia, another conversation needed to happen, now.

## CONVERGENT LINES

"Get it over with. May I suggest telling your mother to start the gossip mills running about the successes of the Penroses? If Hilda hears these things she'll be more interested."

I considered his suggestion as I said goodbye.

At home, I found my brother alone. He sensed my mood and bugged me until I relented. To my surprise, I found an ally. Next, my father arrived, and my brother won him over. By the time my mother showed up, several hours later, we were united. It was after dark when my mom came in.

"What are all of you up to? Should I be worried?"

My dad answered, "No. Gray plans to make his move, and you, my dear, are his advocate."

My mom's right brow lifted, and she seemed relieved. "It's already done."

"Excuse me?" I asked, in complete confusion.

"I just came from a party at Hilda's. I met Lydia and spoke in private with her." My mom stared at me. "I like her, though it will be a challenge to get the KIC's approval." She walked over and sat on the couch. "I opened the conversation with Hilda. She has heard about Guy's betrothal to the Marrak heiress and of Gray's progress. It's in the early stages of the intrigue, and a betrothal was not mentioned ... But rest assured, I'll gain it."

I began to wonder who this woman in front of me might be.

My father smiled. "You never disappoint, Jessamine. Do you think we can buy the Council members who pose a problem if we agree to them appearing before the Oracle?"

She returned his smile, and for the first time I think I saw genuine love and appreciation between my parents. Maybe they were more alike than I supposed.

"Have you done your part, Jowan?" she asked.

"Of course. Davidson has agreed to argue the point if we concede the Oracle and deal with Hilda. Though, what of the girl's line? Did you inquire?"

"She's from one of Hilda's oldest children. She came from a recognized marriage, a marriage Hilda opposed. It means she originates from a pure bloodline. Hilda won't say which families.

She's been married three or four times. All Council-approved so it should be okay."

"Then it doesn't matter. With Guy's marriage, our family has fulfilled our duty to our people," Dad said.

"Don't forget Gray's contribution, too," Guy said. My brother is amazing, the fact he backed me in this, considering his future, made him the best brother I could ever have.

"How long do you think this might take? I ask because Hilda is less than kind toward her and I'd like to get her out of there as soon as possible."

My mother looked at me. "Yes, I can see you're right about her treatment." She tapped her finger on her bottom lip as she thought. "I'll ask to foster her."

I blinked at my mother, not sure how to respond. Fostering in our society is an old practice, but not very common anymore. To be honest, I didn't know what it entailed.

"Are you sure? It a big undertaking," Dad asked.

She continued to look at me. "Yes, but do you understand what it will mean for you, Gray? Do you even know what it involves?"

I shook my head *no*, and looked to Guy. He shrugged.

"You'll have to move out, and all interactions between the two of you must be chaperoned. It's very much like a pre-engagement deal. Meaning if Hilda agrees and the Council approves, she'll take your room, and I'll treat her like a daughter. She'll appear in society with me and all decisions about her future are mine to make while she's under my care, except for marriage, of course."

I swallowed. Would having my mother instead of Hilda be any better? Of course, it would. Moving out for the summer wouldn't be a big deal.

"I'm for it if she agrees."

"I've got to meet this girl," Dad said.

"You will shortly." My mom looked to me, "Get ready." I nodded and went up to my room to start packing.

## CONVERGENT LINES

I reached the bottom of the stairs and set my things to the side before I went to join them. As I opened my mouth, someone knocked on the door. I looked at my parents, then glanced at the door. My mother got up to answer it.

"Prepare yourself. You're going to have to impress the most corrupt being I've ever encountered."

*My mom had arranged everything already?* She opened the door, and I heard someone address my mother before she invited them in. Guy patted me on the back.

"I hope you understand the events you just set into motion."

The look of terror on my face gave me away.

"Shut your mouth, smile, and nod your head a lot. Let mom lead. Got it?"

"Ah … Yeah. I think."

He sat back down on the couch. When I went to join him, he glared at me and motioned for me to join my mother in the entryway. I went to my mom's side. There I got my first real look at Hilda. She wasn't what I expected.

The woman before me stood maybe two inches taller than Lydia. She was fragile in appearance, with small features and bones. Her eyes were dark, her skin pale, and she had long mahogany hair; I found her attractive. If she'd been human, I'd have guessed her age to be somewhere in her forties, but I knew the woman in front of me had to be closer to three hundred.

Lydia stood behind Hilda with her head down in a meek pose.

"Hilda, I'd like to introduce you to my youngest son, Grayson James Penrose. Grayson, this is Hilda Rosdew, a long-time friend of your grandmother and myself."

I bowed to her as I said, "It's a pleasure to meet you."

When I stood tall again, she looked at me with interest. "Jessamine, you didn't tell me how handsome he was. I don't believe I've ever seen him before."

"Probably not, he has always been my quiet, artistic son."

"Hello, Hilda, it's nice to see you," my father said.

"And you, Jowan. May we come in?"

"Of course, where are my manners? Please, come in," Mom

said. She led the way into the sitting room, and I followed. My father stepped aside; I think he wanted a look at Lydia. His curiosity betrayed him as he examined her. Once we were all situated, Hilda introduced Lydia.

Lydia looked up and played her part well, but I knew her well enough to know she was nervous. Hilda seemed at home, as if society and drama were her specialty, though I bet my mother could match her. They bantered back and forth for a while, with my father knowing where his cues were. It was if my parents had danced this dance before. I guess they had, when they'd scored Guy the most desired female in our world. For my part, I did my best not to be awkward, though I'm sure I failed with my fake smile. Hilda's eyes narrowed on me. It was time for my interview. I wished my mother had prepped me for this.

"So, tell me, Grayson, how did you meet my granddaughter?" Lydia froze. She must have told her something and if my story didn't match hers we could have a problem. I cleared my throat as I awaited an answer to come to me, and, to my surprise, it did.

*Tell her you met Lydia on the beach a couple of years ago,* Rowan's voice said in my head.

"I met her a couple of years ago on the beach."

"I was with him. Sometimes she would join us on the boardwalk or for a movie," Guy said coming in to help. I knew he'd saved me, for he just declared himself our chaperone. Smooth, maybe my brother was just as practiced at the politics and drama as my parents.

"Oh, Lydia, why didn't you tell me you knew Guy, too?"

She looked at her grandmother before answering, "Sorry didn't think about it. Yes, Guy was there, too. I'd meet them in the park by our house maybe once a week and play chess with them. Both are good players."

"Good, I worried about her out in the human world."

"Both boys told me they knew Lydia, and when they were doing something with her," my mother mentioned to keep up the lie, though it wasn't a real lie. We had told her … earlier that night. If Hilda's lie detecting skills were good, the truth of that should get pass her.

My turn. Time to tackle the subject we'd been dancing around. It was time to propose.

"I'd like to marry Lydia. It's forward of me, and not our custom, but my parents have agreed, and the Council is open to my choice. You and the Council have final say, but you won't regret it. I'm making strides with technology. With the full backing of the Council, I'll be able to provide a family, bloodline, and name for Lydia. Will you consider my offer and allow my mother to foster her?"

She smiled, as did my parents. I made the right move.

"You're very straightforward; a good trait in a man. Your success has reached my ears already. I have given the Council money to invest in you. I've businesses which will benefit greatly from your progress. So while I had not met you yet, I've known who you are for the last year. You very well may be the most eligible bachelor in the Kind society behind your bother. Lucky for you most of our society hasn't yet realized what you've accomplished. But it won't be long." She looked at Lydia. "I'll agree to the fostering, from now until your family's party on your birthday. If things go well, I'll expect a contract."

I hoped I didn't look too shocked.

"I'll have our lawyer draw up a temporary contract for the fostering and have it to you within the week. When you've signed it we can all go before the Council for approval," my mother added.

"It's agreed then. I shall have her clothes delivered tomorrow."

"Don't worry, I shall take her shopping. It's our responsibility to provide a wardrobe for her."

I looked at my mom, surprised, but I guess Lydia was now my parent's daughter for the next two months.

"My little Lydia, look at you. Marrying into one of the best families in the Kind. Your parents would be so happy if they were here. You've made me proud," she said as she set a hand on Lydia's shoulder.

The Lydia I was seeing tonight was entirely different than the one I'd seen before. Not necessarily in a bad way, and I imagine she thought the same of me.

"Give me a hug. You can come by the house anytime. I suppose you'll want to stop by for some of your things. But I'm tired and it's getting late. I should go."

"Yes, grandmother," she said as she stood and hugged Hilda.

Hilda smiled at me the whole time. I smiled right back knowing she had plans for us. And whatever those plans might be, they weren't good.

She left us in an awkward silence. Guy excused himself. He was probably grateful his role was done for the evening. That left the rules, which would be forthcoming.

"Jessamine?"

"Yes, Jowan, I'll do it." Then to Lydia, "Gray is going to be moving out in the morning. Tonight he can stay in the guest room on the main floor. You'll take Gray's room. It's clean and not too masculine. I hope you'll be happy with the accommodations."

"I'm sure I will be," she said, still in her formal mode.

"Lydia, you can drop the behavior you've had with Hilda. It must be tiring. I want to get to know you."

"Okay."

"Now, for the ground rules. You two aren't to be alone. You must be chaperoned at all times. Gray will spend most of his days here, but will leave every night. You'll take up my social schedule with me and I shall introduce you to society as my new daughter-in-law. You'll also start to show me your magic; I'll supplement your education. Do you understand the terms?"

"Yes, but it's my turn to be honest. I've not received formal training in magic. My grandmother didn't want me to." Gone was the timid Lydia, in her place stood the beautiful, honest girl I loved. What she'd just done took guts. She didn't know my parents or what their reaction would be. No contract existed yet, and she could find herself right back at Hilda's. There was a time, I'd have thought my mother would send her back, now I was not so sure.

My mom's brow lifted. "I'd heard rumors, but I had assumed they were lies. Hmm, though there is some sense to what you say. Hilda wouldn't want competition."

"I trained her." My parents looked at me.

She told my parents over the next hour about Hilda, school, and the black magic rituals Hilda had performed on her. They listened, and didn't seem to pass judgment on her.

"Where are her strengths? I need information so I can work with her," Mom asked, looking at me.

"She's good with defensive and offensive spells. She's fast and quiet, too."

"Do you have any guess as to which family your mother was from?" Mom asked.

Lydia's face was blank as she answered, though her voice sounded timid. "I was young when they died, and my grandmother doesn't speak of them or like me asking. I've heard her mention a member of her family whom she speaks of in the past tense and with dislike."

My mom answered, "A Teague? I know one of her children was married to a Teague and died."

Lydia nodded her head.

"Were you born in Cornwall?" Mom asked.

"I believe so," Lydia replied.

"Have you seen anything to give you a hint of her bloodlines?"

"No, but I do think she's a Rosdew, though I had no way to help her learn her any spirit magic. There's Victor's offer. He could tell us her closest bloodlines if he meets her and samples her blood."

Lydia didn't look happy about the idea.

"If it tells you who your family is, it would be worth the sacrifice. The decision is yours. Though under no circumstances is Hilda to find out about this," mom added.

Soon after, mom took Lydia upstairs to settle her in my room. My dad didn't say anything until they were gone. I wondered what he thought about her. Did he approve?

"She's beautiful."

I regarded the stairs. "Yes, she is; inside and out."

"You have my complete approval."

"I hear a but—"

"Yes, there is one. It's a feeling, and one I can't shake or articulate. But I trust my gut. You've started down a long hard road with an unknown ending. With Guy I know he has years to wait, though he'll be fine because his path is straightforward. Yours isn't. I think I've always known this. When I'm honest, I always thought it funny you were the second born."

"I don't know what to do with that, Dad."

"Nor do I."

# CHAPTER TWENTY-SIX

### October, Connecticut

I didn't sleep. I just lay in bed for hours staring at the ceiling. I had hoped returning home to Connecticut would help my mood, but it didn't. Even from my room in the tower I could hear the commotion below. Everyone must have arrived and were waiting for me to make my appearance. I wouldn't be leaving any time soon if I had my way. Or so I thought until my closet door opened and Lowen and Pendragon walked in to stare at me.

"Don't be harsh," Pen warned Lowen. "He has a hell of a few days ahead of him. Not to mention the events leading up to now."

Lowen sighed at Pendragon. "I know, but he's got to be in top form for this. The game of intrigue is afoot, and it's called your life. Now tell me, did the Tremaynes arrive already? Bring me up to speed."

I wanted to groan and throw the covers over my head. But then my sense of self-preservation reared its head and I told them of my homecoming.

"I'm sorry I missed it," Lowen said when I finished telling him.

"I think I'd like to spend the day with Gray. I'll be his direct counsel," Pen said.

"I agree. I suspect there are things we don't know. For that matter, there may be more players in this than just Hilda. It appears we have the Wayfarers, and possibly others in play. We may be severely under-prepared for the trap we're about to walk into."

"What do you mean?" I asked.

"I didn't think Arthur had it in him to pull a stunt like that. I'm sure someone else is behind it. Rumors are floating around." Lowen's face held no emotion, which told me how bad it must be.

"What rumors?"

Before he answered he cleared his throat. "There may be a couple of girls up for the role of your wife."

I felt the color drain from my face.

Lowen clapped his hands as he said, "Come on, get showered and dressed. Put on a good suit. We're going before the full Elder Council."

· ॐ ·

There are days in your life you look back on and wonder how you survived them. This was one of mine.

Not long after I made it downstairs to greet everyone, Davidson showed up with our great aunt Sowenna to escort us to the meeting, which was to be held at the Coven House. They expected a full house and were preparing additional seating when we arrived.

Pen had taken up residence on my left shoulder, and I carried Kador's book in a black side-slung bag to make it harder to notice against my black suit. Before leaving my room, I granted him the ability to see through my eyes so he could observe everything. My counsel would be an ancient trapped king and an invisible dragon.

We were early, so we managed to beat the crowds. They sat my family, my counsel, and me in a back room. While everyone talked, my mother sat down next to me.

## CONVERGENT LINES

Quietly she said, "I'm so sorry. I really screwed things up for you. I should have known you were the one and prepared you." Tears filled her eyes. I knew she felt guilty, but right now I felt guilty for making her cry.

"I'll survive."

"No, you shouldn't be here, you should be a father by now and married to *her*."

It surprised me that she alluded to Lydia. She'd avoided the subject for more than twenty-years.

"Mom, please don't cry. I need you here. I need you to be the Jessamine Penrose who arranged my brother's impossible marriage, and the woman who went head-to-head with Hilda Rosdew. Please. Assess the situation and tell me what's going on; you'll know better than anyone."

She sniffed. "There's something you aren't telling me."

Damn it. She was good when she applied herself. Lowen was watching us from across the room, and Pendragon relayed his instructions. *"Tell her of the curse. She needs to know, but don't reveal the rest of your hand. I especially need your mother's social intellect. There's no one better. To do this, you must tell everyone in this room of the curse and Hilda."*

I nodded and stood. "Can anyone do an anti-eavesdropping spell?" I asked the room.

Victor snapped his fingers and my ears popped. "It also locks the door and slows time," he said. "The floor is yours. I suspect you have something to say."

"Yes, I do. I've been holding out. The day before Guy's wedding I discovered I'd been cursed."

"Why didn't you come to me?" My mother's face looked betrayed.

"Because we were in the middle of the biggest event in recent Kind history. It would have also put him in the midst of an investigation. One which may have pointed a finger at his brother," dad added.

I'd not considered Guy falling under suspicion. Once everyone knew he was a Wayfarer they would have assumed he knew and cursed me to try to break the Kind's binding himself.

"It wasn't Guy, and it happened before he knew about his father. I know who did it and had the proof until yesterday."

"You never disappoint with the intrigue. You've given me the most excitement I've had in years. It must have been Hilda. Please go on," Victor said with a smile.

Everyone turned back to me as I nodded.

"Start with how you knew you were cursed and go from there; leave no detail out," dad instructed.

"The morning Hilda died, I got up to shower and was suddenly in terrible pain. I knew immediately that it was caused by a curse lifting from me. I didn't know who could have cursed me until I met Davidson for breakfast. He'd received the call about Hilda's death. I knew then."

"Okay, but where did you get proof?" Mom asked.

"I broke into the Coven House and robbed Hilda of the dark object she'd used to curse me. That's how I know."

Everyone's face in the room, except for Lowen's, had a look of shock.

*"Damn. You go for the drama, don't you?"* Pendragon said from my shoulder. I felt a light flutter as he adjusted his weight.

*"This is entertaining,"* Kador said.

*"Better than most daytime soap operas,"* Pen said. The two of them were distracting me and starting to get on my nerves.

I continued, "Davidson took me to my room. I managed to mitigate his sealing spell. Then I waited an hour to make sure no one would be awake, and I slipped out."

"But how did you get to the Coven House? It's so far from the Kolon," Dad asked.

I walked right into that.

"I loaned him a car during his stay; it's how he went into town," Lowen said coming to my rescue.

"I used the Mercedes he had loaned me, and my phone to map it. You forget it's my knowledge which makes it possible for us to use technologies. Once I got to the Coven House, I shorted out the security system and got in. I found her without any problem. They must have been in a hurry when they brought her in. Nobody seemed to think of extra security."

"What did you find?" Mom asked. I think she knew where this was going. I needed to be careful.

"In one of the pouches on her belt, I found the necklace Lydia had given me years ago. It was encased in a dark resin, wrapped with my hair, and stored in a satchel with some ash and several strange rocks. Her mouth also popped open and a black mist escaped."

My parents looked at one another as if they were sharing a silent conversation.

"What? Do you suspect something? Share; now isn't the time to hold back," Lowen said.

Mom answered, "This makes so much sense now. All those years ago so many things were off: Gray's memories, which I don't think he has fully recovered yet, Hilda's strange behavior while he recovered, and his panic when he discovered the charm was missing. It's like he lost her all over again."

I went on, "Then I showed the object to Lowen. We were trying to figure out what she'd done and accidentally destroyed it, unleashing part of Hilda's soul. It was Hilda. She'd trapped her soul in the charm."

My mother gasped audibly and Victor's eyes widened, just as someone knocked on the door. Victor held a finger to his lips as he snapped his fingers. Again, I experienced a popping in my ears.

"Yes?" Victor asked.

"May I come in?" It was Davidson.

"Of course," Victor replied.

Davidson opened the door. "Sorry to interrupt, but the Council meeting will start in fifteen minutes and they won't let anyone in until we have Grayson safely in place. A warning, we have more than a hundred of people lined up to get in."

I swallowed hard, hating how public my life had become.

"Come with me, Grayson," Lowen said. I stood and walked to his side. As my counsel he would be with me throughout the proceedings. We walked out into the hall and headed to the Council room, and my fate.

I sat at a table in the middle of the floor looking up at a half-circle dais and table where the thirteen members of the Elder Council would sit. Lowen sat next to me, in the middle, with Victor on the far end to offer him counsel. Behind me sat my parents and Tristan. The crowd sounded large, but I didn't dare look over my shoulder; my nerves were frayed already. We'd been waiting for twenty minutes when a door to the side of the platform opened, and Davidson stepped out. In his hand, he carried a gavel, which he banged against the table to bring the proceedings to order.

"Silence, the Elder Council in now in session. Any disruption will result in immediate ejection from the meeting."

Behind him, the other twelve members started filing in. Everyone was dressed in black and ranged in age and gender. Some I recognized, several I didn't. Over the next thirty minutes, they introduced each member and the agenda. As the Council finished intros Lowen stood, and interjected, "Before we get into Grayson's situation, I have some information which has come my way."

"This should wait until later. Right now Grayson is our most pressing issue," Davidson said with an stern look on his face.

"I beg to differ ... Hear me out. I'll be quick," Lowen said.

Sowenna Penrose, a Council member stood, "I second Lowen having the floor. He told me something of this matter, and I agree it's more pressing." She sat back down in his seat, while Davidson fingered his mustache with irritation.

"Proceed, Lowen. With great haste."

Lowen walked around our table to stand before the Council. He reminded me of a high-powered lawyer in some movie. "Grayson came to me to disclose some information—information I asked him to withhold. As family head it would have been my responsibility to deal with it. This event happened before the revelation of the last few days. It seems I should now brief the Council."

"What are you referring to?" Davidson asked.

Lowen pursed his lips before he answered. "Upon Hilda's death, a curse she had placed on Grayson was lifted."

Three ... Two ... One ... Chaos.

Mayhem erupted from the audience. Lowen appeared rather

amused, as did Victor; they exchanged smiles. It took Davidson and the guards almost ten minutes to get everyone calmed down again.

"Lowen," Davidson said louder than he probably intended. "Care to explain yourself?"

Lowen, who had sat back down in the chaos, stood to relay a well thought-out and highly entertaining story. Most of it true, if no one asked for a timeline. He covered most of it, making a convincing case. Only the break-in and dark object were left out. If he revealed those details Davidson would know I slipped past him, and they'd have more info on my magic. They would also know who broke into the Coven House.

Once Lowen finished he sat down next to me, and the questions began. Not of him but of me. There is no way I could have made it without slipping up if I didn't have my two silent counsels. Pendragon and Kador were great. Lowen let them ask me questions for a while before we were going around in circles without revealing anything new.

"At this point I think it would be best to move on to the matter we came here for today. I decided to alert the Council to the curse, so we all had the same information. Every question we have asked Grayson, I have asked, and many more. I've looked into the matter without being able to discover anything new," Lowen said.

"Yes, I think it best. Grayson, will you rise, please," asked Davidson, acting as the Council's voice. I rose to my feet.

"You know why you're here today, correct?"

"Yes."

"Aquila Carn stated upon her death that you were the *Guide* foretold in that prophecy. Is this correct?"

"Yes."

"You may sit." I sat as Davidson called Christopher Carn, who came forward.

"Were you present at the prophecy reading with Grayson?"

"Yes, I was. My grandmother Aquila; Grayson, Jowan, and Jessamine Penrose; Guy Wayfarer; and you were also present. Aquila stated Grayson would bring the end of the binding, before she died."

"What else did she say?"

"Years ago she told me I'd know him when I saw him and I'd bring him before her. To Grayson she said little." He pulled out a piece of paper to read from. "The first of her comments was, 'You're a handsome one, powerful, too.' Next, she said, 'It's you. Don't worry, in the end, you'll have everything you want. I didn't know you would have such a good heart; hold on to it, for you have a rough journey ahead of you, Grayson James Penrose, you are our Guide. We've waited a long time for you. You shall lead us in breaking the Kind's binding.' She ended with 'Guide with your heart, do not follow.'"

Gasps sounded behind me and Davidson slammed the gavel down to silence them. "Did she hesitate?"

"No."

"Do you believe Grayson is the *Guide*?"

"Yes, I do think he is."

"Did she say anything about the female?"

"At that meeting, no. When Grayson's brother appeared before her earlier in the day, she stated the girl had been born, but she didn't know anything else."

Davidson motioned Christopher to hold on a moment as a female Council member to his right leaned over and spoke in his ear. He nodded after a moment. "Would you read your Grandmother's original prophecy from the 1600s?"

"Of course." From his other pocket, he pulled out another piece of paper. He read, "A binding will come from seven in white. It will tightly bind the Kind, shorten lives and cull all the Kind's magic. For centuries, it shall remain until the time of dwindling faith. A first-born male from the light shall unite with a female from a family denied female children. Together they shall join to unravel the Kind's binding and restore balance. Through him we shall find our way, he will be the *Guide*, but she is the crux."

I'd never heard the original prophecy before. Strange that something so pivotal to my life had been withheld for so long. As with most prophecies it made little sense, unless you viewed it with hindsight.

"Did Aquila have any insight into the prophecy? It sounds like most prophecies, confusing and short on explanation," Davidson asked.

"No. A prophecy is meant to be instructions, the people we assign the roles to are to decide its meaning and result."

Davidson's bushy brows lifted. "How honest of you."

I wished I could laugh. He just admitted I had the power.

*"You're stronger than you know. It doesn't mean you'll get everything, and chances are you'll deal with or face something horrible. But you'll come out better on the other side."* I looked at Pendragon as he sat on my shoulder.

*"He's right,"* Kador added.

"My head is too crowded. I don't need two of you in here." I heard answering laughter in my head.

"Though there's one thing Aquila would write over and over in her altered state. Our family long thought it might be related to her main prophecy," Christopher said.

"And that is?" Davidson prompted him.

"She would write $1 \neq 13$ and sometimes other strange mathematical equations. We'd find pages full of scribbles with those written on it. Sometimes there were variations, though the numbers, one, two, twelve and thirteen appeared in all. When confronted with the sheets she wouldn't answer, instead she'd become fascinated with them and start scribbling on the sheets again. It could be entirely unrelated. She was old and I think she had lost her mind. Hosting the Oracle takes a toll, especially for more than four hundred years." He took some sheets from his bag and held them up.

"We'll keep it under consideration. Leave the papers and we'll look them over. I now open the floor to the Council members for questions."

Silence remained as the Council members looked at one another until Arthur Wayfarer spoke up, "Okay, I accept Grayson Penrose"—He popped the P with disdain—"is the male. Who the hell is the female? Hasn't that always been the question?"

The room erupted in chaos again. Davidson banged the gavel for silence, fights spread through the crowd. He called in the guards and emptied the room of everyone but Council members, witnesses, Lowen, Victor, and me.

Davidson rubbed his head as Lowen stood. "If I may address the Council as Gray's advocate?"

Davidson waved his hand in a motion to continue.

"Does the Council have a list of possible females born after Kensa?"

The member looked at one another before Davidson answered, "No. We were all so sure Kensa Marrak was the female."

"May I suggest you take a week or two to collect the names of possible girls born since Kensa, and we start there? Let Gray return to work; we all know how important his work is for all of us."

Davidson opened his mouth to respond and Lowen held his hand up to stop him. "Victor and I will be his guardians. We offer our services, one of light and one of dark. Gray is of little concern for the moment. We know who he is." Lowen ran a hand through his thick hair before continuing. "Now, are there other prophecies related to this one? Ones we haven't heard yet which might give us some direction?"

My mom stood. "I have added information. Aquila foretold a prophecy about me before Christopher was born."

"Is this right?" Davidson asked.

Christopher eyed my mother for a moment before answering, "I know nothing of what she speaks."

"Over twenty years ago my prophecy secured the engagement of Guy and Kensa."

"Oh yes, please continue, Jessamine. I'd forgotten, and I believe you're the only one present who would know anything of it," Davidson said.

"As a child, my mother took me to see Aquila. Honestly, we didn't expect anything, and if she did tell you something it could be a heavy burden. It's why I didn't allow my sons to go before her. I was eight, and she did her creepy floating thing. There were four people present, including myself."

"What did she foretell?" Davidson asked.

"I was young, and I'm not sure there is a record of it, but I believe it was, 'Jessamine Rosen Nancarrow, you shall bring us the

## CONVERGENT LINES

male, the *Guide* to find the way. Guide him and he shall know her.'"

Davidson fingered his mustache. He asked, "That was all? Are you sure you got everything right?"

"Yes, my mom would repeat it over and over again."

The Council members began to talk to each other. I looked at her and smiled.

"Jessamine." She looked up to see who addressed her.

"Yes, Arthur."

"Who was present during the telling of the prophecy?"

"Aquila, my mother, Hilda Rosdew, and myself."

I watched my mom's face, as the realization set in. Hilda had heard the prophecy.

"Did Hilda take an interest in this?" Arthur asked.

"At the time no, but other events make a lot more sense now."

"Such as?"

She looked like she wasn't going to answer him. "Jessamine, you must answer his question," Davidson instructed her.

My dad stood up next to her. "May I answer it?"

"Yes," Arthur said.

"Over twenty years ago, once we had gained an arrangement between Guy and Kensa, Jessamine procured an agreement with Hilda for Gray to marry one of her granddaughters. It seemed easy at the time, almost too easy for dealing with her. We started plans for the wedding," my father's voice cracked.

"Arthur," Davidson said.

"I did the paperwork and got the approval for the marriage from the Council. With the agreement signed, and at the announcement party no less, Hilda pulled the contract, right after someone savagely attacked and nearly killed Grayson at the party. Before he even awoke from his injuries, the girl had run away from Hilda. She died in a tragic accident."

"Gray has never fully recovered from the incident," Mom said in a quivering voice. "He threw himself into his work. Which is where he's stayed for more than twenty years. Yet here he sits waiting for a marriage to be forced upon him for the good of the Kind."

My dad wrapped an arm around her for support.

"Is this true, Grayson?" Arthur asked, his face unreadable.

I'd long since become numb; I didn't care anymore. "Every word of it. The answer to the next question is, I don't know what happened for much of that night, nor do I have any idea who attacked me." The last few words were a lie I hoped no one would pick up on. Lowen stiffened.

"*Careful,*" Pen said in my head. When we were in public Pendragon spoke to us through telepathy, less chance of someone over hearing.

"*He pulled it off. No one but us caught it,*" Kador said.

Arthur tilted his head. I couldn't imagine what he was thinking. "I'm sorry, I'm not trying to be rude. I've nothing against you or any Penrose, despite the rumors. But I wonder, as small as this world is, why didn't I hear about this? How did you even meet Hilda? Your family lives here and she lived in Cornwall."

I stood to address him. "There's a good reason; at the time of the events I lived in California. My parents have a summer home in Santa Cruz, not far from Hilda's."

He seemed more confused. "Hilda had a home in California? Are we talking about the same woman?"

"The Penroses and Rosdews were some of the first families to have vacation homes away from us. I can't imagine why," Davidson added. The Council members laughed, they all knew how rough it could be living under our rigid culture.

"I had no knowledge of Hilda's history with Grayson. In a way, the curse makes sense now," Arthur said.

"How does it make sense? That happened more than twenty years ago, and Hilda's granddaughter is dead. What is to be gained by a curse?" Davidson asked.

Arthur chuckled, "Spoken as someone who never dealt with Hilda. I am sure she had a reason, though we'll probably never know it."

"I don't understand," Davidson said with drawn together brows.

Arthur sighed. "Hilda was vindictive, spiteful, vengeful, and every unpleasant thing you could conceive of. The only surprising thing is there weren't more curses lifted with her death. Though … anyone cursed by her is probably too afraid to come forward."

I became fed up with them talking about my life as if I wasn't there. I decided to change the course. "What my mother said is true; my life has never been the same since the summer of 1993. I have no desire to marry. I'd rather be left alone to my work. Nor do I plan to run. If I did, I'd spend the rest of my life running. To be honest, I'm too tired to do that and have nothing worth running for."

Arthur nodded. "I understand. I've lost loved ones, too."

"I've a couple of questions for the Council if I may?" I asked. Lowen's eyes darted to me with concern. "Once the females are known, how will we know which one is the right one? What are you doing to address Hilda's missing soul?" Davidson looked uncomfortable and no one bothered to answer my question, so I decided to push it further. "I know Lowen explained to the Council about the possibility of Hilda herself being behind her missing soul. If she is, she must have allies, have something planned for us. Arguing over who I should marry seems like a waste of everyone's time right now."

"We don't know," Davidson said. "That's the honest answer. For now, you may go home, under the guardianship of Lowen and Victor. We'll let you know when we have more."

# CHAPTER TWENTY-SEVEN

### August 1993, Santa Cruz, California

Over the next two months, I had very little time with Lydia that wasn't in the presence of my family. The summer was terrible, but Lydia had a home with my family, and they adored her. We began to plan for our masquerade party, with a Carnival theme.

Rowan found himself in a similar situation to myself; he got almost no time with her. He ended up spending many days and nights with me. Sometimes I think he longed for the time Lydia and he used to spend together under Hilda, though I knew he was happy for her.

As the party neared, negotiations about our marriage contract started. Things were going very well, and my parents thought we might be able to marry before the end of the year. The week before the party, I talked Guy into going shopping for a ring with me. I already knew I wanted to get her a sapphire ring. Guy said he knew a place.

"Why do you know someone who sells jewelry?"

"I don't know her. She's a gypsy and a friend of a friend. She has a curiosity store, and there's a back section with magical items which she sells to Others and Kind."

"So you're telling me she's Other? A gypsy witch?"

"It's what I've been told. I went in there once. She had some weird stuff, but she also had beautiful old jewelry."

"Okay. We can always go someplace else if we need to."

I had money I'd been saving for years. The Council also provided me with a sizable monthly stipend when I went to college. I never came close to spending all of it. I figured I'd take my savings when I finished school and start a company.

Guy drove me to a part of town I'd never been to before. He parked the car in front of an older building called Curio. The name spread across the large display window in gold, cursive letters with the tagline, *A little of this, and a little of that.*

We got out and went into the store. Inside it was dark, and the brass bell above the door announced our arrival. A woman came from the back room, through a beaded curtain behind the register. She was beautiful, with curly red hair spread wildly around a pale face with freckles, and blue eyes. She dressed as a gypsy in flowing purple skirts and a lavender peasant blouse.

"Hello, Guy."

"Hi, Tina."

"Who is the cutie with you?"

"Tina, this is my younger brother Gray. We're here looking for a sapphire wedding ring for his fiancée."

"I might have just the thing in the back room. Come on."

He started after her, and I followed a moment later as my eyes adjusted to the dark. The shop had a strange assortment of things, from a giant stuffed grizzly bear wearing a fez and smoking a cigar by the register to insects mounted on the wall, and all kinds of different skeletons scattered around. I hurried to catch up. Guy stopped suddenly and I ran right into him, almost knocking him over.

"Ouch!" Guy said angrily.

"Sorry. Are you okay?" I asked.

"Yeah."

Tina turned to walk back the way we'd come. "Give me a minute. I need to get the keys for the cabinet. I thought they were in here, but no." Guy watched with appreciation as she walked away.

"Redheads, huh?"

"Yeah, redheads. I sure hope Kensa turns out to be one. I wouldn't mind if she looked like Tina."

"Who is Kensa?"

"Kensa Marrak, the girl I'm to marry in like twenty years."

"Oh, sorry."

"I know, can't believe I can't see her until a couple months before we marry."

"Ouch!"

"I know. Get this, they put a spell on me, too. It will stop me from having sex."

I looked at him, surprised. "When?"

"A couple of weeks ago. There is an upside though."

"There is? I don't see how."

"The Council has agreed to allow me certain sexual acts a couple of times a month from the Bleujan girls. Though they're going to go to great lengths to make sure I don't become too attached to any of them."

The Bleujan family has an affinity for sex magic. They were the one family in our world with a progressive sense of sex. But from what I understood it was a bit *too* progressive.

"You're taking one for all of us. You know that, right? I appreciate you for it."

"Thanks. Though it's not bad. Just lonely."

Tina returned, keys in hand. She stopped and looked at us. "Did I interrupt something?"

"No," Guy said as he blushed.

I looked down at the case and saw all kinds of jewelry, most appeared to be old, but beautiful. The silence in the room caused me to look up from the case. Tina watched Guy, and for his part, he squirmed under her attention. She asked, "You're worried about your arranged marriage."

His eyes narrowed as he looked at her. "How did you know?"

"I'm an Oracle."

"You are?"

"Yes, the Kind doesn't have the market cornered on that."

"What are you? I mean what group do you claim?" Guy asked.

"A little of this and a little of that; I'm a hodgepodge of things. But I'll give you this because you brought Gray to see me; I've wanted to meet him." She looked at me as if she were sizing me up. She turned back to Guy and said, "You have a long wait. It will be worth it. You will love Kensa. She happens to be everything you could ever imagine and want. Even a redhead."

Guy turned several shades of red, and I tried not to laugh.

Then she turned to me. "I have a ring for you. It's old, ancient, and Lydia will love it." I looked up at her, surprised. She batted her eyelashes and said, "I told you: I'm an Oracle."

"I believe you."

She fussed with the key for a minute before getting the cabinet open. She pulled out a tray from the bottom, which had been hidden. "I've been holding onto this one for a long time. I've been told the ring was fae-made."

She handed me a delicate silver ring with an oval stone in it.

"It's a sapphire cabochon set in silver."

I examined the ring, taking in the details. The band had scroll work around the shank which looked Celtic in design. And it was old, I could feel the faintest traces of magic as it seemed to warm it my hand. The sapphire was a clear, dark blue and as light shined on the curved surface a star formed. I looked to see if there was an inscription. There were faint markings, which circled almost the whole ring. But whatever it said I couldn't read it.

"Do you know what the inscription says?" I asked.

"No, but if I were to guess I'd bet it's a spell."

I slipped the ring on my pinky and watched the light play on the stone. Without a doubt, I knew this was the ring.

"I'll take it."

She smiled. "It's a lucky ring, and if I'm right, the stone will glow a little when Lydia puts it on. Be careful with it. The ring has magic and might not act as you expect."

"Are you sure it's safe?"

"Yes." She put the ring on. It remained the same. "The ring isn't meant for me. See, it doesn't glow. I know it will for her, I've a feeling this ring is crucial. I just don't know why."

I handed her my credit card, and she said, "I'll clean it up and box it for you. But don't you want to know the price?"

"No, whatever it is, I'll pay it."

⁂

Guy agreed to help me after dinner. He got rid of my parents and promised to be our chaperone. As soon as my parents were gone he threatened both of us. "I'll be in the next room. No funny business. Don't mess with the sexually frustrated guy who isn't gettin' any for at least twenty years. Got it?"

Lydia's eyes bulged out of her head.

"Ah, Guy? Virgin ears here." I pointed to both of us.

"Yeah, yeah, and it better stay that way." He walked out of the room, leaving us alone.

"Is he always like that?" Lydia whispered?

"No. We were out earlier and met a witch, probably of gypsy origins. Guy was drooling over her, and it turned out she's an Oracle. She told him he would be hard up for twenty years, but his wife would be everything he ever wanted, even a redhead. He was really embarrassed."

"Okay." She bit her lip. God, I loved it when she did that. "Why did you guys meet with a witch? Where do you even find one?"

"Guy took me somewhere to look for something." I sat next to her at the kitchen table.

"What?"

I reached into my back pocket and pulled out the little white box. I set it on the table in front of her. Her eyes followed my every move and settled on the box with a look of confusion.

"I went to find this," I said as I pushed it in front of her. "Open it."

She sat staring at the box. I heard a tapping on the glass door. As she continued to stare at the box, I let Rowan in.

"*I didn't want to miss this,*" he said, as he landed on the table next to the box. He looked at the box with one of his eyes before saying, "*Aren't you going to open it? The suspense is killing me.*"

Tentatively, she reached for the box. Her finger rested on it for a moment. Rowan's impatience showed as he danced about and squawked at her. I panicked, worried Guy would hear, but he had the TV turned up. I glared at Rowan, whose attention was on Lydia. With great care she opened it and gasped. Her eyes found mine.

"Marry me, as soon as possible."

Tears streamed down her face. I took the ring from the box and I knelt before her as I held it out. "Lydia, will you marry me?" I dragged each word out. The tears flowed and her hands covered her mouth.

"*Say yes. Don't keep the poor boy waiting any longer.*"

Her hands came away from her mouth and she whispered, "Yes."

"What was that? I couldn't hear you?" I prompted her.

She rolled her eyes and Rowan laughed.

"I will marry you."

She held her hand out to me and I slipped the tiny ring onto her finger. It fit perfectly. For a second she examined the ring before she jumped up and threw her arms around my neck. I laughed and kissed her.

"What's this?" With Lydia in my arms I turned to see my parents looking at us. To my relief, mom didn't look angry.

Rowan. Crap.

"*I heard them and left,*" he said.

To my parents I said, "I can explain."

Lydia let go and I made sure she made it safely to the ground. She bounced on the floor and went to my mother with her hand held out. "He got me a ring."

My mom looked at it. "He did. Where did you find this? It's gorgeous. Look, I think it glows. Is it magical? Can I see it?" Mom asked.

Lydia tried taking the ring off. "It won't come off."

"Don't worry, Lydia. It recognizes you as its owner since you just accepted Gray's proposal. It won't hurt you and I bet should you need to take it off you'd be able to. It's fae made, and old," Mom said.

"Guy took me to this store in the old part of town. A weird store with some gypsy owner."

"Curio?" Mom asked. "And Tina? It's perfect. You found her a very rare gift. A Tynged ring; it glows because you're the owner of his love. I've heard of them, but never seen one."

"What does Tynged mean, mom? I don't know that word. Welsh, right?" I asked.

"It means 'fated,' in Welsh," she answered.

Lydia touched the stone with her other hand and closed her eyes. "It's old, and it feels like it has emotions stored within it."

"Good, your psychometry is getting stronger," Mom said.

"You know Tina?" I asked.

"We both do," Dad answered. "Tina has been around for a long time. Don't know what she is, though it's Other. It was meant to be Lydia's if Tina gave it to you. Did she charge you?"

"I gave her my card, so I assume so."

He laughed. "There won't be a charge."

· ꙮ ·

The next couple of days passed in a blur. I worried because I didn't know what would happen after the party. My parents had decided to rent out a reception hall and hire catering staff for our masquerade. The number of guests quickly escalated to a point where we couldn't accommodate all of the people at our summer home. Pretty much everyone from Connecticut was invited, and many, like my cousin Lowen, were coming from Cornwall.

I dressed in my costume, minus my mask, at my apartment down the street from my parent's house. I was to meet everyone there and then we'd head to the reception hall. It felt weird walking down the street in the midday sun in my costume. Thankfully there were few people about and the day was rather mild.

At the summer house, the place was utter pandemonium. Mom wasn't ready and in a panic. Lydia sat in her costume on the couch, watching everything with a smile. She looked gorgeous in an empress-waist dress. It was bright blue and exposed her neck and cleavage. She'd swept half her hair up on her head with the rest falling down her back. My heart beat so fast every time I saw her. I couldn't believe I'd be able to marry her soon. She looked up at me.

"You look handsome, birthday boy."

"Nothing compared to you." I hurried to kiss her before someone came in. She put something in my hand. It was cold and felt metallic. "What's this?" I asked.

"Open your hand and find out."

I did, and in my palm lay a silver band. I picked it up to see markings very similar to the ones on the side of her ring. She picked it up and slipped it onto my finger. "Thank you, I love it."

"Good. I got it from the same shop you got mine. Seems Tina was saving it for me. Strange woman, but nice. I can see why Guy likes her."

I pulled her in for a hug.

"Oh, you're here. Did she give it to you?" my mom asked.

I held my hand up while I held Lydia with my other arm.

"Will you take Lowen and Lydia to the reception center? We'll follow in about twenty minutes."

"Sure."

· ꙮ ·

We were walking around the grounds when we came upon Hilda. Thankfully Lowen had remained with us. During the last two months, Lydia had only seen her grandmother a couple of times at parties.

"My dear, give me a hug and let me see your costume."

I felt Lydia stiffen.

"Grandmother, it's good to see you," she said as she let go of me to hug her. Hilda pulled back quickly, making me think the hug was for appearances. Hilda grabbed Lydia's chin to examine her.

"Your costume and hair are better than I expected. You look appropriate for this evening."

"I'm happy you are pleased," she said as she started backing up to me. Hilda seized her left hand before she made it out of reach.

"What is this lovely ring?" she asked as she examined it.

I answered for Lydia, "It's an engagement ring. Now that our agreement is signed it seems only fitting she have a ring."

"Of course. You have wonderful taste, Grayson. I guess this is your night. Happy birthday, and congratulations on your betrothal! I couldn't be happier about having you in my family."

Hilda did not look her age. Tonight, she wore a Victorian era dress, though much more revealing than most from that time period. From the detail of the costume I was willing to bet it was one she had owned back in the Victorian era. The dress was burgundy velvet and gold satin, which dripped down her in tight layers, the center piece being the burgundy corset. Her dark hair was pulled back from her face, with a gold and crystal diadem topping her head. Yet it was the thick golden cord around her neck that disappeared between her cleavage which caught my eyes. The effect was a V pointing at her chest, but something dark seemed to weight the necklace down. Who knew poison was so beautiful?

She seemed to lose interest in us as she began talking to Lowen. They started off in the direction of the bar, and as soon as they were out of earshot I asked, "Lydia?"

Her attention was fixed on her grandmother's back. "Yeah?"

"What is at the end of the necklace your grandmother is wearing?"

She turned to me and blinked. "I'm not sure. She never takes it off. It's some kind of charm."

"You've never gotten a look at it?"

"No. She always makes sure it's hidden. But it's heavy and black. With it being my grandmother, I bet it's something long dead. It's strange how something so evil can be so pretty, isn't it?"

"That's exactly what I was thinking." Lydia stiffened, and I realized my mistake. "Of course, she's nowhere as beautiful as you."

She looked up at me, I think to see if she believed my response.

I didn't worry, because it's true. Whatever she found in my face seemed to be a sufficient answer.

We wandered into the grand ballroom to find a string quartet setting up to play for the party. The caterers had finished and the rest of my family had finally arrived. The next hour went by in a rush as my mother sent me about to do tasks for the party.

Dad called from the bar, "Gray, come here." I made my way to his side and he offered me the barstool next to him. "Gray, you've made me very proud. You have done well for yourself. Happy birthday." He slid a glass of what I suspected was whiskey to me as he held his aloft in a manner to indicate he wanted to toast me. Though I'd had wine and beer before, I'd never had whiskey. I picked up the glass, sniffed it, and repeated his gesture.

"Cheers," he said as our glasses clinked together and I repeated it to him. He threw the contents back, swallowing it down in one gulp, so I copied him. I immediately wished I hadn't. It burned and I began coughing. He smacked me on the back a couple of times, laughing.

"Don't worry. It will take the edge off your nerves tonight."

"I thought whiskey was supposed to taste good?"

"It does when you don't chug it down," Victor said. I turned to see him and Tristan. They were dressed in period clothing with lace-cuffed silk shirts, cravats, vests, tailed suit jackets, knickers, white stockings and buckled shoes. What differed were the colors, Victor's vest and jacket was blood red, while Tristan's was emerald green. Both looked like they had stepped out of an Anne Rice book.

"Victor! Tristan! Have a drink with us. Bartender, another round."

Tristan came up to my side and held his hand out to me. I took it and pulled him in for a hug. "It's good to see you; I'm glad you're here," I said.

"It's good to be here. Any excuse to come to California. Oh, happy birthday and congratulations. Do I finally get to meet her?"

"You will shortly."

"Yes, I too want to meet her," Victor said.

My father handed each one of us a drink.

Victor held his glass aloft and said, "This time, I'd like to make the toast. Here's to Grayson, a wonderful man, one who will do many great things. May you know great happiness and success in the coming years." He clinked his glass against all of ours, before adding, "Sláinte!"

This time when I drank the whisky I sipped it and found the taste interesting. Across the room, I caught Lydia's eyes and signaled her to join us. She walked the length of the ballroom in her graceful way, her skirts swirling around her.

"This is her?" Tristan asked as she approached.

"Yes, that's my Lydia."

Victor turned to watch her as she neared. They bowed to her when she reached us.

"Lydia, what a pleasure it is to finally meet the girl I've heard so much about, and who has made my adopted son so happy. I am Victor Tremayne, and this"—he held his hand out to indicate Tristan—"is my 'other' son, Tristan, Gray's best friend."

She curtsied. "It's a pleasure to meet both of you. Gray has told me much about both of you, and his trip to see you in New Orleans."

"Perhaps once you're married you'll visit us, too," Victor said as he kissed her hand. "You aren't what I expected."

"How so?"

"Well …" He rubbed the back of his neck uncomfortably. "Sorry, I didn't mean it the way it sounded. I thought I'd be able to tell more from you once I met you. I usually get strong indications as to a Kind's bloodline when I'm this near, but I get nothing from you."

"Has this happened to you before?" she asked.

"No, it's what makes me me. People expect me to know. Did Gray tell you the other way I'd be able to tell?"

"Yes, and I might consider it, but not right now."

He stiffened and his eyes grew cold. Lydia read him and knew immediately Hilda stood behind her.

"Well, you must be Victor Tremayne. I've been looking forward to finally meeting you," she said.

He bowed to her and took her hand to kiss it. "Hilda Rosdew, I presume. The pleasure is mine. Please allow me to introduce my son, Tristan."

Tristan repeated Victor's actions. "A pleasure to meet you."

Hilda looked at Tristan with curiosity. She'd probably seen few with his coloring, especially in the Kind.

"Would you join me at my table?" she asked. "I'd like to get to know you better. My father used to be friends with Gavin Tremayne, and I used to hear stories."

"We'd love to join you, and I've plenty of stories about Gavin myself." Victor took Hilda's hand and led her off. I felt like sighing with relief.

The other guests were starting to arrive, and the room seemed to fill almost at once.

# CHAPTER TWENTY-EIGHT

### October, Connecticut

Days passed and I settled into an uneasy rhythm. Lowen would come to work with me, and from my office he continued to run our interests in England. Plenty of Kind members from most families worked for me, but for the most part their tasks were menial. He had been my partner and financier, along with my father, when I started the company. He had his own room in our house and I opened a mirror portal to take him to his library in Cornwall. Victor had also taken up residence with us, but Tristan had returned to New Orleans.

Every day new rumors abounded. I let them worry about the intrigue while I worked and thought about Hilda. As far as I was concerned, she was my problem. A week after the Council meeting, Lowen and Victor grabbed me, taking me to the Kolon. Lowen had excused his staff while he'd been in the States, so the house was quiet. I realized it was serious when Lowen took us into his oubliette. After the dagger ceremony, we settled in to compare notes on that August night in 1993.

Both had been there, but we didn't discover anything new. Except for one thing; Hilda had been with my mother for most of the night. Including during the attack.

"Guess it's time to tell you why we're here in Cornwall. We"--Lowen indicated the three of us--"are going grave robbing. Hilda has been buried and we plan to exhume her. And something you aren't going to be happy about ... We need to exhume Lydia, too."

I went cold. "We can do it alone if it's too hard for you."

"The hell you will!" I yelled.

"I've come across some info at last," Victor said, looking at me.

I perked up, knowing what he meant in an instant. "After all these years?"

"Yes."

"What?"

He pursed his lips. "It's just a theory. With Hilda's death, her life's history has been easier to access. Our mistake was making an assumption."

"Which assumption?"

"That Hilda's son was Lydia's father."

My mind ran a thousand miles an hour. "Oh. So you think that she was born to one of Hilda's *daughters?*"

"I need to examine her to see if my summation is correct. I should be able to tell."

"Okay. Once this is done will you share?" I insisted.

He nodded.

"Then let's get this over with."

· ꙮ ·

We did what anyone who is going grave robbing does; we dressed all in black and grabbed shovels.

"I must say this again: Gray, you have the most interesting life. I've never been grave robbing before, but I can now check one more thing off of my list," Victor said. His morbid sense of humor seemed fitting for a vampire.

## CONVERGENT LINES

We arrived at the graveyard in Cornwall, which was surrounded with magical security.

"Victor, I believe this is yours?" Lowen said.

A strange smile twisted his face as he sniffed the air. "Ah, what a good night to go a-grave robbing."

I shook my head as he disappeared from right in front of me. I jumped, but Lowen seemed unfazed as I heard Victor's laughter on the wind.

"You know, I find it surprising what we can find mundane, living in the Kind," I said. This time Lowen laughed.

Victor appeared from the shadows. "It's done. I'll have to put the wards back up when we leave, so no one will know we were here."

"How did you know how to take them down?" I asked.

"Easy, I put them in place."

I should have known. He led us through the graveyard seeming to know the layout. There were thirteen parcels, one for each family. We headed straight for a large mausoleum with *Rosdew* in big gothic letters above the door.

"If she's in a mausoleum why did we bring shovels?" I asked.

"Hilda is. I doubt she put Lydia here. Besides, it's better to be prepared. Honestly, who goes grave robbing without shovels? It's like going to a duel without a gun," Victor said, grinning.

"Can you do your hocus-pocus on the mausoleum and get us in?" I asked.

"Yeah, about that. The only way to open the door is with Rosdew blood, and I don't have any," Victor said.

"Then it's good thing that I do," Lowen said, and got both of our attention. "Don't ask; it cost me a lot, and I'm not going to tell you the price or how. Some things are better left unsaid."

"Agreed," Victor said as he held out his hand for the vial of blood. Lowen removed it from his coat pocket. Victor uncorked the vial and took a whiff and started nodding his head as he puckered his lips. "Strong Rosdew blood, too. Whatever you did, it must be shameful."

Lowen glared at him. They were turning out to be great friends, not something I'd have expected. Victor put his finger to the lip of the vial as he tipped it. He coated his finger in the blood and wrote the runes for *Open*. The door slid to the side with the sound of rock grinding on rock.

Once inside, I called a ball of fire to my palm to light the mausoleum.

"Nice and handy. Can you do that, too?" Victor asked Lowen.

"Yes."

We looked around the large tomb. Open shelves lined the wall. Most had decomposing bodies resting on them. Her body sat in the middle of the back wall. We neared it together.

Surprisingly, she looked nearly the same as she had years earlier, when I'd first met her. Except for a wide streak of white in her hair on the left side, that I hadn't noticed the other night. I'd been in too big a hurry and nervous.

"I only met Hilda the one time at your party, but I did know of her long before. She was a force in our world for centuries. Strange that such a little, fragile-looking woman could cause so much trouble."

"Why are we here?" I asked.

"Good question," Victor said. "I wanted to make sure she was dead, not mostly dead."

"I understand the concept in the movie but fail to see how 'mostly dead' applies here."

He laughed. "With Hilda, take nothing for granted. She could have used black magic to seem dead. Hell, she could have anchored a small part of her soul to her body and to other objects, with plans of resuming it later."

My lips curled in disgust. "It's possible to do that?"

"*Yes. A Druid once faked his death in my lands. When I found out I killed him personally, and permanently,*" Kador said.

"You care to share?" Lowen asked.

"How did you know?"

"You still get a far-away look when you talk to Kador."

"He said a Druid faked his death on his lands centuries ago

in the manner Victor described. When he found out about it he killed him, making sure he couldn't return."

Lowen bit his lip before asking, "I plan to research my library and several others to see if we might figure out a way to release you, Kador. I would like to be able to record your tales and knowledge."

*"Tell him it's his if he can do it."*

I relayed his words. "So how do we tell if she's faking it?" I asked.

The glint in Victor's eyes scared me, and I stood back as he pulled a stiletto blade out of his coat. "A quick stab to the heart should do the trick. Few things can survive it, plus it's the anchor for our soul," he said as he plunged the blade home. To make sure, he twisted it a few times.

"Nope, she's dead. Which makes me wonder what she could be up to. What I wouldn't have given to have gotten into her library before the idiots blew it up and released the other part of her soul."

I stared at him. "Do you think she broke her soul into more pieces? And could she be whole yet? Maybe watching us?"

"No, the only other place I thought she could put her soul would be here, with her body. As for if she's whole yet? I don't know enough about spirit magic; blood is my specialty," he answered, but it felt like he was holding out.

"Go ahead, tell him; he needs to know," Lowen said.

"Know what?"

"Kador, what are your thoughts?" Victor asked instead of answering me.

*"What he doesn't want to tell you is that she probably has solidified. She'll be looking for a vessel, or somehow has figured a way to tie her soul to an object or person, which gives her mobility. Typically, a spirit needs an anchor. Though with her, I bet she had the vessel prepared before she died. She could be anywhere. Even here, though that's doubtful. She probably doesn't know of your abilities, especially to travel as you do."*

I repeated his words to them.

"Very good, Kador. I'm thrilled we see things the same way," said Victor.

"What's the purpose?" I asked.

"Simple, immortality. She's trying to find a way to live forever. It was no secret that she was seeking this. Though the real question is at what cost and does she have other motives?" Victor said as he stared at Hilda with a strange look.

"What is it?" I asked him.

"The burn round her neck troubles me. I expected her to still have the necklace she always wore."

I looked at the mark, as I thought back to the first time I'd noticed it. "Yeah, she did always wear a necklace, a very thick braided cord. And I noticed the burn when I got the object off of her in the Coven House. What happened?"

"I don't know. There was a rumor once that she had a powerful magical artifact. Perhaps that's the cause? Anyone have any theories?"

Lowen shook his head.

*"Any thoughts as to what the artifact might have been?"*

I repeated his question out loud. Victor tilted his head to the side as he examined the burn. He reached down and unbuttoned Hilda's top. Lowen grunted and turned around.

"Damn it! I never figured you for having a thing for the dead? Gross. I don't think I can work with you any longer." He shivered and mumbled, "Vampire."

Victor laughed. "Stick around, Lowen, I'll show you a whole new world." His fingers worked nimbly without ever seeming to touch her skin.

"Interesting," he murmured, and pointed at Hilda's body.

I leaned over to see. Between her breasts where her heart would have been, if the witch had one, was a black hole. Victor's dagger stab mark lay just below the hole.

"What?" Lowen asked with his back still turned.

"See for yourself, Lowen," Victor said as he moved out of the way. Lowen turned and stepped closer to look at the hole in her chest.

*"What's going on?"* asked Kador. I let him see through my eyes so he could see for himself.

## CONVERGENT LINES

"What the bloody hell happened to her heart? And why didn't this information get out?" Lowen asked.

Victor stood off to the side with a far off look on his face as he rubbed his bottom lip with his index figure. "Your questions are my questions. I doubt they knew what happened to her heart, but how I didn't hear about this is concerning," Victor said.

"I know." Both men looked at me. "I imagine she was good at glamours. I doubt anyone noticed because of a glamour. I mean, really? Do you think anyone was brave enough to do a thorough examination of Hilda's body? They wanted her buried, and old age was good enough for every member of the Elder Council, which lived in fear of this witch. We can see it now because the power source has faded. Plus, that's the same dress she was wearing when I last saw her."

*"I think you're right."*

"Yes, I like your answer; a glamour. You are also right about no one looking too hard. The question would be what was the power source? It couldn't have been your dark object. It would have had to remain with the body. I don't like this."

Victor flicked his hand and re-buttoned her top.

"Come on, let's start our search for Lydia. We can discuss this later in a more secure, and warmer, place," Lowen added.

As they started for the door, I lingered, still looking at her. A sound in the corner made me jump. I turned to see a rat scurry away. As the rat ran out the door I had a thought … Not for the first time, I wondered: Could Hilda have had a familiar? A chill ran down my back and I ran to catch up with the others.

· ॐ ·

Pendragon hadn't come with us. It was too dangerous for him. He can see spirits and they can see him. We didn't want him revealed, plus I'd taken him to Hilda's house in California earlier in the evening to see if he'd have any luck finding anything of interest. Her hexes didn't work on him, and we were worried the Council would be searching for the house ever since I revealed its existence.

Victor could see Pendragon, which we discovered soon after the first Council meeting. He explained Pendragon was just a fuzzy outline to him and he only heard the occasional word when he spoke aloud. Victor could see him as a side effect of being of the Blood. He also regularly saw ghosts and could sometimes commune with strong spirits. Lowen decided, not long after I revealed everything to him, to include Victor. We needed his help, help only he was uniquely capable of providing. We experimented with a few spells until Victor was able to see and hear Pendragon clearly.

I followed behind them as we started the search for Lydia's grave. I'd never seen it and wondered if it would even be here.

"Are you sure she's buried here?" I asked. They stopped and looked at me.

"I thought she died here. You mean you don't know?" Victor asked.

"How would I know? I was in a coma when she died. As a matter of fact, I returned to Santa Cruz for the first time last week."

Victor rubbed his neck, thinking. "Her body has to be here. The Council wouldn't let a Kind body not be checked out after death; especially a Rosdew."

He had a point. We continued looking. A half hour later, Lowen called us to a small stone slab on the back side of the Rosdew mausoleum. It was opposite the wall where Hilda rested inside the crypt, which also faced the wall of the graveyard. Only about three feet separated the two. Lowen shined his light on the plaque.

It read *Lydia Rosdew, February 9, 1975–August 22, 1993*. I couldn't believe my eyes. In all these years I'd not seen anything which made her death so real. She was dead, and stuck behind Hilda in a corner of the graveyard where no one would ever notice her. Tears filled my eyes.

"Are you sure you're okay? We can do this without you," Lowen asked.

"I need to see this. It will make it final."

Victor pulled the vial of blood out again and repeated the runes. The stone plate moved. In a hole barely big enough for a body, sat a skeleton. Lowen and Victor looked at each other as if they were talking.

## CONVERGENT LINES

"What?" I insisted.

Victor knelt down to look at the bones. They were bare, except for a few pieces of cloth. Satisfied, he stood and used the rest of the blood to close the slab. "Give me a couple of minutes and I'll explain. I need to check a few more things."

"Come on, let's talk after we get Pendragon," Lowen said.

We made it back to Kolon, and just like the first time, I felt dirty. No more grave robbing for me. At least this time I didn't take anything. I sat in the oubliette next to the fire. Lowen had lined the walls with mirrors, so I could open portals here, where the chance of someone finding them diminished. They'd gone to get Pendragon from Hilda's house while I waited.

Pen came through the mirror first, followed by the other two.

"How did it go?" I asked.

"Not bad. She had a store of books I've stolen to add to our collection. Probably not as good as what she had in her Cornwall home, but it's something," Pendragon said.

I noticed they each carried a heavy box with them. They put the boxes down and we all sat around the table.

"So?" I asked.

"It's Lydia," Victor said.

"Are you sure?"

"Yes, I'm sure her mother was Angelica Rosdew and her father was Ian Teague. Her mother died in childbirth. Her father lived on a few years only to die of some illness."

"Why wouldn't Hilda talk about them to Lydia? And why did Lydia think her dad was Hilda's son? This doesn't make any sense."

"Hilda strongly disagreed with the marriage. According to what I learned, it was Angelica's father who approved the marriage. Hilda had plans for her powers, but Angelica didn't have the stomach for it. The way I heard it, she wanted nothing to do with Hilda's inherited powers."

I thought about his theory; while not perfect, I could believe Hilda would swear off a child who refused her abilities.

"There is more. That has to be Lydia's body. It was badly damaged and is consistent to how she was said to have died. Also, most of her left hand was missing, including her ring finger." Victor reached into his pocket and pulled out what looked like a newspaper clipping. He unfolded it and handed it to me.

"Pendragon found this."

I took it and read. The article from the *Daily Arcane* had three small paragraphs, with a picture of Hilda instead of Lydia, and only mentioned her name once. Per the article, Lydia had committed suicide. It said she probably didn't mean to, but she'd run away after Hilda had decided not to let her marry. She'd fallen from the Cliffs of Sorrow & Pain to the water below, a common location for suicides. Apparently, the cliffs are located on Hilda's property, not something Lydia had ever mentioned. The Cliffs of Sorrow & Pain are well known in Kind folklore. Some horrible event happened there a long time ago. The rumor is if you're angry, depressed, or suicidal you should stay away from the cliffs. They're known to lure Kind and humans to their death, like a siren. There are all kinds of rumors as to why, but I don't know if anyone really knows. If Lydia was upset, this would make sense, because I couldn't see her doing this.

"You didn't know?" Victor asked.

I shook my head.

Victor rubbed his chin and added, "The Cliffs have always been near the Rosdew's holdings. Hilda must have taken the land for herself and built on it after I left. I'm sure she found the suffering and deaths of others useful to her spells."

"Are the Cliffs important?" I asked.

"Maybe," Victor continued. "There are many tales about the Cliffs being cursed. Some claim the Cliffs of Sorrow & Pain call out to those suffering, like a beacon, resulting in their deaths. As weird as this sounds, I don't think Hilda wanted Lydia dead. No. She had plans for her."

I agreed with his assessment. Then I voiced something I'd always wondered about, "What about Rowan? If a Kind dies with a familiar, does the familiar die, too?"

Victor blinked at me. "I hadn't considered the raven. I've not known many with a familiar. Lowen?"

He shrugged. "I don't know. Pendragon, it's your turn."

Pendragon puffed smoke before answering, "I'll have to research it, but it would make sense why no one has seen him or been able to contact him."

*"In most cases, yes. It appears it was more common in my time for familiars. They died with their host. Their souls are tied. But ... if a witch sacrifices the familiar for magic purposes the bond is permanently severed and they can never join with another. The witch will live on after their familiar, in cases of sacrifice."* I told the others his answer.

"Here's my question, why did she break the engagement in the middle of the party? Is it because I was attacked?"

"Have you ever heard what happened at the party after you left?"

"No. Something else happened?" I asked puzzled.

"You left with Lydia. While you were gone everyone's attention was on Guy and his in-laws as they signed the engagement paperwork."

"I knew they would. It's why I was able to get away with Lydia."

"There was much fanfare, and right after the signing of the contract something happened. Like a shock wave, which felt amazing. Everyone's powers surged, and have increased since then. It's why everyone thought their engagement actually was the one," Victor said.

"I don't understand. I must have been out of it when that happened because I don't remember it."

The events of this night were starting to wear on me. I could only numb the pain for so long. I wanted a drink; screw that, I wanted the whole bottle.

Victor continued, "Well, not long after the shockwave, Hilda, for some reason, seemed upset. I couldn't find you so I started searching. I smelled your blood. Which is how I found you. You were near death and Lydia was nowhere to be found. I carried you back, and when I reached the reception hall with you in my arms, Hilda was arguing with your parents about breaking the contract."

"Yeah, and that's when your parents saw you in Victor's arms. They rushed you to the hospital, and I cleared the partygoers out. I watched Hilda leave, alone. The last time I saw Lydia, you two were going outside, into the gardens. I made inquiries of others at the party and after, but no one other than Hilda saw her, as far as I knew. Then a few years ago, someone applied to work at Kolon, a woman who had left the service of Hilda and wanted to become part of my house's staff. She claimed she saw Lydia when she returned to Cornwall with Hilda. She saw Lydia the night before she died," Lowen said.

I tried to process everything they were telling me. None of it made sense. "Has anyone ever gotten my mother or father's experiences of that night?" I asked.

"Haven't you asked them?" Lowen asked.

"No. It's an unspoken rule in my family not to discuss that night in any way."

Lowen rubbed his cheek, lost in thought for a moment before he responded, "I think it would be best for you to discuss that night with you mother, father, and brother. I doubt much new information will come from it, but I think it will help to bring closure, for them and you. Wait for the right time to bring it up. I also think you should try and get Davidson's memories from that night," Lowen said.

I agreed with his advice, and decided I would need to act on it.

"I had a thought earlier: Did Hilda have a familiar?" I asked.

Victor answered, "I considered the possibility. If she did she hid it well. Familiars are common within the Rosdew family. They are also not shy about using magic to get one should they want one."

"Did you discover anything else about Lydia?"

Victor shook his head. "But Pendragon said he had something. Pendragon, will you take it from here?"

Pen's nostril's smoked. Lowen's brows were raised as he looked between the two of them. He must not have heard this yet.

"I found ... uh, I found the rough outline for her curse on you," Pen said.

"Spit it out dragon, the suspense is worse than the truth," Lowen growled.

Pen's eyes narrowed on Lowen. "Said as someone who doesn't know what I found."

"Exactly! Tell us already," Lowen said.

"Please, Pendragon, tell me. I want to know."

"Hilda *had* found out about Lydia's familiar. I do not know if she knew about him being a Muninn, but she knew he was a raven, the notes indicated this. The original purpose of the curse seemed to be about cursing or separating Lydia from her familiar. At least that was the first thing she had written down. Later it changed to you. But ..." Pen flapped his wings and gritted his teeth together, his lips open. He seemed visibly frustrated.

"But what?" I asked.

"I don't know exactly what she intended. Her shorthand is very hard to decipher."

"Yeah, I saw her shorthand in the file I grabbed on Lydia. It looked like Welsh and something like French," I said.

"It isn't French. It's some dead language which I have not been able to transcribe."

*"Give me copies of it. Perhaps it is an ancient language from my time."* Kador said.

I relayed Kador's offer to Pen. "A great idea. I will do so. Anyway, what I think she was trying to accomplish in the early stages of the curse, is to make you forget about Lydia, and perhaps make everyone else forget her, too." I blinked. "This is the part that I really don't want to tell you." He flinched, before continuing, "I think she intended the forgetting part, but there is some indication her plans changed again. The curse didn't become about just forgetting Lydia, instead it looks like she made it about revenge."

"I'm sorry, I am not following you," I said.

"The last entry in the journal differs from the rest, her writing is harsh, like she was mad. I'm guessing this took place after the party. Perhaps on the plane back to Cornwall or once she arrived here."

"How would you have anything from when she arrived back?" Lowen asked, frustration dripping from every syllable.

"I managed to get into her Cornwall home last night," he said.

Victor's brows shot toward his hairline in surprise. My mouth popped open, but I thought Lowen was going to shoot fire out of his mouth. "What do you mean, 'you got into her house last night.' It's under heavy guard, warded and hexed."

Pen did his best to look innocent. "I've got skills."

"Hold your anger for a minute, Lowen. It's justified, but I want to hear this," Victor said.

Lowen growled.

"I can transport, sometimes. Especially over short distances. I managed to get on the grounds, and from there I managed to get in. I didn't tell you because you would have insisted on coming along; I couldn't have gotten you in. I promise, it wasn't bad. The security was too lax."

"You and I are going to discuss this later," Lowen said.

Pendragon's face looked like that of a child just reprimanded by a parent. "I didn't bother with the library; instead I focused on her room. My decision was because of Gray's experience in California; with Hilda's room being the only one with a hex."

"Interesting. You're saying she had a hex on her room?" Victor asked.

"Yes, but it did nothing to me, once I became even less corporeal. I managed to grab more than ten of her journals. The witch was so paranoid she also hexed each of the journals. These are her most recent journals, and written in a more difficult shorthand."

I interrupted, "Pen. What did you mean about revenge? And don't think I haven't noticed you're avoiding the topic. You're willing to incite Lowen's anger rather than tell me," I said.

He sighed, "You're right. I think she decided, probably after Lydia's death, to not make you forget her, instead she decided to …"

"To what?" I asked.

"To corrupt your memories of her. To make you so focused on your memories of her that you would become unable to function. I think she was trying to drive you to the point of suicide. She wanted to punish you, Gray. She was willing to spend years, and a lot of power, to hurt you. From this alone I'm positive Lydia is dead, and she wanted you to pay for it."

I stared at Pendragon. Was he saying my memories of Lydia weren't true?

"What made you conclude that, if you are having such a hard time reading the journals?" Lowen asked.

"I can't read all of her words, but many of the ingredients, and the sketches, were for spells about memories. That I could decipher."

"Are you saying my memories of Lydia are false?" I asked.

"Some of them, maybe all of them. It's possible you two never even liked each other."

"But how can my family, or Lowen and Victor, have memories of her?" I started panicking.

"It is possible Hilda managed to plant the seed in you of Lydia and it became a shared false memory for everyone."

This had to be the cruelest thing I had ever heard of.

Victor sucked a breath in, loudly between his teeth. "That's harsh, even for her. But it explains a lot. With this theory, it might be possible Lydia never existed, that she planted the whole thing. It's possible Lydia isn't the reason for the cruse. Perhaps she is covering your true memories," Victor said as he ran a hand through his hair.

"No!" I shouted. "Then explain the photos I have, the stories and notes from Lydia?"

"Gray, it's possible Lydia existed, or maybe there was someone else that you remember *as* Lydia, and Hilda planted this story in your head to match the pictures. It's very possible Lydia was human."

"Then explain Rowan and Muninn!" At this point I was shaking with anger.

"Relax. What they are telling you is a possibility, a strong one, but not the only one. And I know you won't want to hear this--but the only way to move forward, now that you have this information, is to let her go. She's gone. At this point, does it really matter?" Kador said.

I swallowed hard and sighed, knowing Kador was right. "I know, but there's one more question."

"Okay, what?" Lowen asked.

"How did Hilda get my raven claw from Muninn, which I was wearing that night, and never took off?"

*"Whoever she hired to beat you to death grabbed it,"* Kador said.

I stood and walked into the mirror back to my room in Connecticut. I couldn't deal with anything else.

# CHAPTER TWENTY-NINE

### August 20, 1993, Santa Cruz, California

As the official opening to the party, my parents introduced me and bragged on about my accomplishments. Being the center of attention isn't my thing. Once they toasted me for my birthday and accomplishments, they announced my engagement to Lydia. She joined me in being the center of attention for a time, and she looked just as uncomfortable as I felt. Finally, the dancing started and we were free. In a while, it would be my parents' and Guy's turn, as the big announcement about his official engagement was made.

We danced. Then we spent time with Tristan. He didn't want to be the center of attention either, which is exactly what Victor was for the whole of the party. He embodied what was thought of as "our" monster. He fulfilled the role because he drank blood, lived in secret from an already secret people, and was ancient. In the time I'd know him I'd never gotten a straight answer as to his real age, nor would Tristan spill the beans.

Since this would be my last night with Lydia for who knew how long, I wanted to sneak away and have some time alone with her. The party posed a possible distraction for this to happen. Carefully, I led Lydia from the dance floor to one of the doors and out onto the patio. We'd almost cleared the door when I saw Lowen watching me, not far from the exit. His eyes narrowed so much I could see it through his mask. Afraid we'd been caught, I stopped.

To my shock he nodded his head and flung his arm out in a motion which said "go." Without further hesitation I grabbed her hand and pulled her through the gardens, into the foothills, and a small forest which boarded the reception center's property.

Lydia didn't say a word, she just followed me. At last we came to a small clearing where a tree had fallen; I sat on the trunk. She stood looking down at me with her hand still in mine. With a gentle tug I pulled her into my lap. She giggled softly in my ear as she took off my mask.

"Why did you bring me out here? Do you have nefarious reasons?" She paused, and I wasn't sure she was okay with my plans. Then she smiled and said, "Please say yes."

"Perhaps. After all, except for the brief time I got to ask you to marry me, we haven't been alone all summer." I pulled her mask free and set it on the tree trunk.

"I know."

"Is Rowan nearby?"

"No, it's just us."

"Good." I wrapped my arms around her bringing her closer to me. I felt her breath on my cheek. Lines became crossed in my mind. What did it matter anymore? I had done everything asked of me and so had she. We were engaged, so nothing but time stood between us. I closed my eyes and brushed my lips against hers to see her reaction.

Her breath hitched and she relaxed in my arms. A kiss and the mingling of breath is considered taboo in our society for all but married couples, and even then, only in privacy. Sex is more acceptable, and even used for magic, after one's virginity was gone.

## CONVERGENT LINES

I kissed her, soft at first, until she opened her mouth. I took her invitation and deepened the kiss. Her arms wound around me as she held me close. I'd always heard the first experiences with sex and love are forever imprinted in your memory, I knew now how true the sentiment was. I kissed her until I lost my breath, pulled away long enough to catch it, then started to kiss her neck.

She was the most intoxicating thing I'd ever known, and I knew I'd always love her, no matter what. She became imprinted inside me in a way I'd never be able to erase. Kissing the nape of her neck, I moved along her shoulder until I pushed the soft strap of her gown out of the way. Time didn't mean anything right now; there was only Lydia and me.

I wish I could say more, but suddenly things started to get fuzzy. My skin crawled and I was in great pain, though a different kind of pain from how I felt when I woke up later. Sometimes I get small flashes of events afterward; mostly I remember lying on the ground looking up at the night sky with dark shadows around me. I also remember I heard a scream, and I don't think it was me.

In the following year I got drunk a lot to numb my pain, and the sensation of when you pass the moment of too much alcohol describes how I felt. Tristan once called it "time traveling." It's how one minute you can be talking away having a great time, then the next thing you remember it's hours later; you can't account for the time in between.

There are flashes of memories I chase through my dreams and waking memories, to no avail. Kissing Lydia's neck as she held me is my last memory of her. In later years, I'd seek out people with magic, or try potions, dream readings, and even human hypnosis, to try to recall the events of that August night. Nothing worked.

The next memory I have involves pain. Great pain. The doctor told me, once I was on the mend, it was a miracle I had lived. Something or someone had beaten me to within inches of death. I'd broken at least five ribs, my right femur, nose, cheekbone, and had a compound fracture of my right tibia. I'd also ruptured my spleen and I had internal bleeding all over. And I'd needed more than one hundred stitches to various parts of my body. The doctors said my condition rivaled the worst car accident they'd ever seen.

Victor later told me, "I found you when the events of the night started to go awry. Hilda argued with your parents to withdraw your engagement. The Council members said no, and I think they would have sided with you if you fulfilled your promise of seeing the Oracle. She knew she was losing. About this time, I started my search for you."

He seemed very distressed as he told me this story in the hospital. I'd been there for two weeks at that point, and I'd regained some of the memories surrounding the events. No one would talk about Lydia or what happened to me. My family would check on me, but quickly left. Victor was the only visitor who talked with me.

"I used all of my abilities to look for you after I couldn't find you in the ballroom. Tristan helped me, too, yet we still couldn't find you. It wasn't until Lowen, who had been distracted by Hilda's request, noticed my distress. He told me you two had escaped out onto the grounds of the reception center. Do you remember any of this yet?"

I answered honestly, "No."

"Lowen, Tristan, and I kept looking for you, as your parents argued very publicly with Hilda. Her demands made no sense, and I knew something was terribly wrong. Outside we found nothing. It wasn't until the winds shifted that I smelled your blood, a large quantity of it. I found you face-down in the dirt and leaves, well into the tree line of the surrounding hills."

He paused and watched me as emotions played in his eyes. "When I got to you I was sure you were dead. Hell, you *were* dead. I used a magic I shouldn't have, but I regret nothing, it's not in my nature. Through those means, you are here today."

I moved my left hand, my dominant hand and the only functioning one, to rest it on Victor's hand. "Thank you," I said, acknowledging debt owed to him.

He nodded, understanding. "I picked you up and carried you back to get help. Once you were safe, I went to search for Lydia. I caught her scent for a moment, near a fallen tree with your scent, then it was gone. Your brother, Tristan, Lowen, and myself looked through most of the night. We didn't find her." Tears ran down my cheeks as he continued; I knew what was to come. "Hilda left the reception hall about the time we found you. She seemed disinterested, and didn't ask about Lydia. She left alone, and as far as we know Lydia didn't return home. What we do know is that Hilda returned to Cornwall the next day."

"Has there been no news of Lydia at all?" My emotional pain started to match the physical pain of my broken body.

"We didn't know anything until two days ago." He paused. "We have received word that Lydia has died."

"What?" I whispered, stunned.

"A Council member called and confirmed Lydia has died in an accident and no further information would be forthcoming. A private matter of the Rosdew family, was all they would tell me."

My brain wouldn't accept what he told me. I had to be dreaming. The amount of pain I felt convinced me I wasn't.

"Hilda is claiming Lydia was a Halfling sired by one of her sons and kept hidden to hide their shame. Davidson and I have been fighting for an investigation, but the Council members are siding with Hilda and claim you should be thankful; you were almost married to a girl with no magic. What would you like to do? If you want, I, myself, shall go and investigate. You're my son, and I don't want you to suffer."

"I don't know … What do I say to what you've told me? If she's gone then why am I still here? I don't want to be."

He squeezed my hand. "I lost my first wife. We didn't have any children, though it made no difference. I walked the shadows for decades, a shade. I know you won't believe me now, but one day you'll look up and see the world in color again, though it will be a very long time. Tristan and I are here for you, you're my family and it pains me to see you like this. Your parents are outside. They were going to do this, but I was closest to the events and they thought you'd want this from my lips."

"Yes, I prefer the truth. Even if it's harder to take."

I spent a month in the Kind hospital. They tell me I went to a human hospital to be patched up in California before I was flown home and treated by Kind doctors. In the human world, my recovery would have probably been more than a year, with physical therapy and such. It still took nearly two months with magical healing.

I missed the first semester of school directly following my injury and my parents didn't want me to return to California, even for school. I wouldn't hear of it.

As soon as I was able, I returned and threw myself into my schoolwork. I never returned to our house in Santa Cruz, though I spent most of the next ten years studying computers and technology at Stanford. The first moment my parents dared to leave me alone, I went to the reception center where we'd had the party.

I waited until the building had closed for the night and broke in. Inside there was nothing from the events of the masquerade remaining. Next, I followed our path into the trees. No sign remained, and it looked vastly different from that night in August. The leaves had fallen and winter had set in. While California winters are mild, it still changes the environment. It took me a while to find the fallen tree in the dark; when I did, I sat for hours where I'd last held her.

Heartbroken, I got up to leave, moving some of the forest debris on the ground as I stood. There, I saw something blue under the leaves. Reaching down I pushed the leaves aside to find Lydia's mask. I sobbed and searched the area, looking for anything else. After several minutes, I gave up. I keep her mask in my sketchpad. I still have the ring she gave me on our last night together, I wear it on a chain around my neck, so it's always close to my heart.

I returned to school and worked tirelessly. During those years, I avoided Connecticut and my parents. Instead, I took my breaks in New Orleans. Tristan also decided to go to a human university after he finished his KIC service. He became a doctor and decided to work in pediatrics.

Tristan and I spoke several times a week in those years. Sometimes I'd call him in the middle of the night because I just couldn't function and he'd talk me down. I'm here today because of him.

## CONVERGENT LINES

Victor's words to me about being a shade were truer than I could ever have imagined. For years, I'd wake up in the morning and not remember for a while. When I did, it was like reliving it all over again. I survive now because I've trained myself to be on autopilot and not think about those events too much. Alcohol, drawing, school, and music were all I had in those days. Duran Duran's *Wedding Album* on constant replay. Even now hearing "Ordinary World" or "Come Undone" can take me back to those days. While sad, I found comfort and strength in that music.

It was during this time I made the big discovery about my magic. One morning, right after I moved back to my condo, I awoke face down in my bed, still dressed and covered in ink. Going to the bathroom, I stared at my sorry reflection and saw the proof of my sad existence: too little sleep, too much alcohol, and not enough food. My eyes were sunken, and ink smudges covered my face. I didn't like the person who stared back at me. At least four days' growth of whiskers covered my chin, and my head hurt. I had started drawing again to take my mind off of things. Mostly pictures of Lydia or Rowan, but when I tried to reach in, I'd find nothing but a flat sketch.

I had two black Sharpies clipped inside my shirt pocket. I used my reflection to reach for one. Once in hand, I stood as still as I could and started drawing on my reflection. After a few minutes, I'd drawn myself in a suit, wearing a bowler hat with a black mustache and eyebrows. I laughed hysterically at something which probably wasn't funny at all.

Enjoying myself, I stepped to the side and then back a few times. My stomach hurt from laughing, so I braced myself on the counter, and the laughter died. Every morning the pain would return in full force as soon as I allowed my mind to wander back to her. Usually memories of the beach with her at sunset flowed through my mind. When they did, I would feel the piercing pain in my heart. I picked up the marker again and wrote: *Take me far away from here; to another world.* When I finished, the mirror's surface moved like a wave in the ocean. At first, I thought I'd lost my mind, which just made things worse.

I'm ashamed to admit that I considered killing myself. I looked around the room for something to help me accomplish it. But my eyes kept returning to the mirror. I realized that if I shattered the glass I'd have my pick of tools. The voice of reason began to speak, saying, *You know what happens to those who choose this path. They end up as a shade, trapped to walk the earth for eternity. It's the surest way to create a ghost.*

But I'd made up my mind. I hefted a soap dish and decided it would work. I slammed it against the glass. To my utter shock, my hand passed right through the mirror. Afraid, I pulled back and fell onto the bathroom floor. Wide eyed I stared at the mirror, which looked like it usually did, if you didn't count my doodles.

Feeling even more pathetic, I stood up and touch the surface again. My hand passed easily through the glass. Curiosity gripped me, and without another thought, I jumped onto the bathroom counter and walked into the mirror. Passing through the reflective surface felt like walking through thick liquid, but I remained dry.

Inside I found a strange world: a mirror reflection of my bathroom. I stood looking back at my bathroom for a few moments until I realized how thin the air was in this space. If my sense of self-preservation had been working, I would have returned through the mirror, but it wasn't; instead, I walked to the door in this reverse world and looked into the hall. A dark doorframe was the first thing I saw. Feeling daring, I stuck my head out the door. To my left, I saw a solid dark wall. To my right, a tunnel with a light at the end. At this point, I began to wonder if I was dreaming.

The tunnel went on for about a half-mile, but it was worth it for what I found at the end. There was another door ... which opened into the bedroom of a grand castle. Light came from sunlight filtering in through the windows of the room. I say a "castle" because of the stone walls and the furniture. It's what I'd expect from King Arthur's time, with tapestries and a massive canopy bed filled with velvet fabric and fur. I touched the bed and found my hand passed right through it. Perplexed, I stared at my hand as I tried to figure the puzzle out.

Confused, I looked around the room and realized the problem.

The room was a reflection cast from the mirror of the bedroom on the other side of the mirror. Deciding to test my theory I went to the mirror and tried to pass my hand through. My hand met solid glass. I stood back, scratching my head as I tried to process this through my hangover.

If writing on the mirror got me here, then maybe I need to open a portal into the other room? Shrugging my shoulders, I said out loud to no one but myself, "What have I got to lose?" I think this is the point where I started talking to myself. Say what you will about it, but I maintain it helped me keep my sanity.

I pulled the cap from my Sharpie and wrote on the mirror: *Allow me entry into this room.* Again, I saw the wave move across the surface. Without thought of the repercussions, like was I about to enter someone's house, I walked into the mirror. I felt the same strange thick liquid feeling as my foot stepped onto solid ground in the room I'd glimpsed through the mirror.

I took a deep breath and smelled fresh air and the sea. Excited with my discovery, I set about snooping through the castle. On this side, I noticed the dust and the fabrics beginning to fray. No one had been here for a long time. I felt emboldened, so I left the bedroom to find I was in a castle set on a cliff overlooking the sea. But that wasn't what was weird. Everything seemed off, the colors, the light, and even the plants. The colors in this place looked too vivid, as if over-saturated.

I didn't see or hear any animals or birds. Nothing in the area led me to believe anyone had been here for hundreds of years. After several hours exploring the surrounding hills and the castle, I decided this must be another dimension. During my time there, I decided I liked it, and I claimed it for myself. With a bit of TLC the castle would be livable again. With extension cords, I could run electricity and make it my refuge from the world.

· ✾ ·

One day I woke-up in California and realized I'd done everything I could there. The time had come to leave. I returned home to Connecticut and started PenTech. At first, I made tech only for the Kind. Though, with time, the shielding I'd perfected against magic found uses in the human world with governments and military companies. I was now the CEO and developer of new products. I earned more money than I could ever use, and owned nothing but my memories.

# CHAPTER THIRTY

**October, Connecticut**

I went to my bedroom in Connecticut when I returned from grave robbing. My sleep was anything but restful. Most of the night I spent tossing and turning, with strange, vivid dreams. I woke tired, just after seven in the morning. I headed to the kitchen for coffee where I found my mom making breakfast. Seeing her at the stove as she made eggs was a surprise.

"Have a seat." She nodded her head towards the table. "I'm glad you're up. You saved me the trouble of waking you." I sat down at the table and she put a cup of coffee in front of me. "What time do you need to be at work?" she asked.

"I'm not going to go in today. Lowen is working, and I didn't sleep well last night." I would bet money Lowen didn't expect to see me at work today. Which made me wonder, *Why wasn't he down here? Maybe he went into the office early?*

Mom brought two plates of eggs and toast over to the table. She set one in front of me and took the seat opposite of me. "What was the problem last night?"

I looked up at her as I shoveled a big load of scrambled eggs into my mouth. Not sure how to respond, I chewed my food to give myself time. I swallowed and took a sip of coffee before saying, "Bad dreams."

"I can understand you having bad dreams with everything going on. Tell me about them. Maybe it's your brain trying to tell you something."

My dreams had been vivid, and I remember at least some of them. But, it was silly, and kind of embarrassing.

"What?" she asked. "Oh, one of those dreams?"

"What! NO."

"Then what's the problem?"

"It was silly ... and kind of embarrassing."

My mother rolled her eyes at me. I'd never seen her do that. Wow. "Tell me. I promise it will stay between the two of us."

I looked at her warily, "Okay. I had a dream last night that I was having my fortune read by a bear."

She blinked at me. "A bear? Maybe you shouldn't have told me."

"*Mom.*"

"I'm just kidding. What kind of bear?"

"A giant grizzly bear. He wore a red fez, and smoked an endless chain of cigars. He had a deep baritone voice, too."

She started laughing. I did my best, but it was no use, I joined in. Glad I hadn't told her that at one point he started dancing.

"That's funny. Did he give you any good advice?"

I stopped to think about it. "He talked to me, though I can't remember anything he said."

"Well, it sounds like a silly dream, probably summoned because of everyone reading your fortune lately." She stood and grabbed our plates taking them to the sink. "Why don't you go back to bed. I'll find Lowen and tell him you won't be in. You'll have the house to yourself, because I've a lot of things to do today."

"Thanks."

"You know …" she cocked her head to the side and put a hand to her cheek, "I remember a grizzly bear. Well, he was a stuffed bear, but he wore a red fez. He stood in Tina's shop in California. Tina … Now that's someone I haven't seen in a long time. I wonder if she still has that shop?"

I looked at my mom, with my mouth open. She didn't notice, instead she grabbed her keys and waved goodbye.

I sat at the table for a while thinking about my mom's offhand comment. How could I have forgotten about Tina? I went upstairs and showered. There was no way I could sleep now. Dressed and ready, I sat on my bed talking to Kador. Do I dare go see if I can find her?

*"What do you lose from trying?"* Kador asked.

"Nothing." I tried to find her store Curio, online. I didn't find anything. This didn't mean she wasn't around, as magical beings usually shied away from technology.

"Well, Kador, would you like to go to California?"

*"Cala … what?"*

I laughed as I stood up, "California. I give you permission to see with my eyes, and hear with my ears."

*"Let's go. I love seeing your world. It is interesting."*

"You're going to be seeing mostly the human world today." I opened a portal to our vacation home in Santa Cruz. Once there I called a cab with my cell. I remembered the part of town, but not the exact address of her store. The cab picked me up in front of the house.

I stared out the window during the drive to let Kador see the sights. He had some interesting commentary, especially about the scantily clad women we passed. I bit down on my tongue for most of the ride, because I was tempted to answer Kador's rather raunchy comments out loud. I guess if I'd been trapped in a book as long as he had I'd be excited at seeing females, too.

The cab dropped me off near the spot I remembered the shop being. I paid in cash and started walking. Everything was different.

The area had been gentrified. I walked up and down the streets looking. After a while I was sure the store was gone. I found myself back on the first street again.

"It's not here anymore." I said out loud.

"*Are you sure?*" Kador asked.

"You've spent the last hour walking up and down the street with me. Nothing is the same. No, I'm sure it's gone."

"*I may have been trapped in a book for a long time, but I doubt much has changed when it comes to a glamour.*"

I stopped and looked down at his book in my hand. "What do you mean?"

"*Tell me you know how a glamour works?*"

I paused a moment, then said, "It keeps others from seeing something's true form or disguises it completely from anyone who's not supposed to see it."

"*Aye. And…*"

"And what?"

"*There is another application for glamour too. Try asking to see the shop. Make sure to state your need. It very well may be the shop isn't located here, but a doorway to it is. To find the doorway you must ask and have a valid reason to see it for the glamour to reveal it.*"

I'd never heard of that. "Okay." I looked around the street and saw a few random people about, none close enough to hear me.

"I need to find Tina, she summoned me in a dream to her shop, Curio." Everything stayed the same. The sun went behind a few dark clouds and the street fell into shadow. I looked down both sides of the street again, nothing appeared different.

"*Be patient.*"

I started to think of a retort to Kador when I noticed a neon light flashing in the window down and to my left. I read the sign, which said *Open*. The rest of the window said, Curio. *A little of this, and a little of that.*

Tina was still here.

I opened the door to a cloud of incense, and the bell jingling, announcing my arrival.

"Well, it's about time. I'd almost given up on you." I followed her voice to find her standing under the giant stuffed grizzly bear with a red fez on his head. She patted his belly and winked up at him. "Thanks, Harry. You still have it, you big ol' bear." Tina stood there in all her glory, with her fiery red hair and swirling skirts.

"You sent Harry into my dreams?"

"Of course I did. You haven't come to see me, and we need to talk. Come on," she said as she waved her hand for me to follow.

*"Damn! You didn't tell me she was hot,"* Kador said.

Tina looked back at me with a smile that made me think she might have heard Kador. *Great. This should be interesting.* She led us to the back of the store to another door. She opened it and flipped a light switch to show a room with blank white walls, concrete floor, and a round table with several chairs. A crystal chandelier hung low over the table, which was covered in colorful purple and pink scarves.

"Have a seat," she said as she sat in the chair closest to the door.

I rounded the table to take the seat opposite. The wooden chair was too small for me, and made my knees hit the table. I sat Kador's book down next to me.

"Why did you summon me?" I asked, daring to look her in the eyes. Her eyes were a clear blue surrounded by enough freckles to make her look innocent. She looked just as I remembered her, though it had been more than twenty-years since I'd seen her.

She bit her lip. I focused on her body language and noticed she looked as nervous as I felt. "Having foresight doesn't make life easy. I can't control how and when I see things. Hell!"--she threw her hands up in the air--"I have no control over how it manifests, either." She probably hadn't planned on it, but her confession made me relax.

"Then why am I here?"

She pursed her lips and looked at me for a moment, before she said, "You are constantly on my mind lately. I don't see anything about your future, but I have a strong feeling I need to talk to you. I know there has been a lot of commotion in the Kind world. What's been going on? I bet it's focused on you."

I told her everything. She remained silent, only asking for clarification on a few facts. It took a while to bring her up to speed.

"Well, you've been busy."

"Not by choice," I said.

"It is never by choice. The few meant to impact the world usually don't get a say in the matter."

"Why were you interested in meeting me all those years ago, when my brother brought me here?"

"Because I'd been seeing you for years. You play an important role among the Kind. I don't see your future like I see most people. No, with you I just get feelings. Like I thought you might be the 'Guide' the Kind's prophecy speaks of."

"I really just want to be left alone."

She reached across the table and covered my left hand with hers. "It will be hard for you to hear what I'm about to say, but it needs to be said. We all get stuck on something. You long for someone lost to you. The time has come to change how you look at your life. Exorcise Lydia's ghost from your memory. Be thankful for the time and love you shared, but let her go."

*"Listen to her,"* Kador said.

"You needed to experience the things you did so you would be ready to take on the role meant to be yours. Most of your memories of Lydia are pleasant, let them be. Does it matter if they happened or not?"

"You might be right."

She sniffed. "I've watched you through the years, you know? Most of the time in the background."

"Should I be flattered you told me you stalked me? And what does 'most of the time in the background' mean?"

"I did have one vision of you needing something, so I brought it to you. In Romania."

"That was *you*? The hag in the caravan with the cloak?"

"Yeah, that was fun. I see the cloak worked out for you. Keep it with you, you'll need it again."

I rubbed my hand down my face as I tried to be mad. "What are you? Some kind of fairy godmother?"

She laughed. "Yes, Gray. I'm your fairy godmother." I started laughing, too.

"Hey, something you said to me years ago has really bothered me."

"What's that?"

"The ring, you said it would be important. It's gone. We found Lydia's body last night and it wasn't there. I get the feeling Hilda didn't have it, either."

"Good question." She took a big breath and looked like she might say something, then stopped and bit her lip. For several minutes she seemed to consider her response. At last she said, "I know at the time that ring was meant for Lydia. It didn't mean it would work out. Young love rarely does. Do you still have your ring?"

"Yes." I pulled my necklace out from under my shirt. There on the chain was my silver Penrose charm and my engagement ring. I unclasped the chain and handed the ring to Tina.

She held it in her palm and closed her eyes. For a while she stayed like that. Finally, she opened her eyes and handed the ring back. "You never discovered who it was that attacked you?"

"No."

"I told you the ring was important, and I think it is. I think, and this is speculation, but I think the ring is important for your journey. The sapphire ring is part of a matching set, and sooner or later it will return to you. It might also give you a missing piece to the puzzle."

I considered her. She hadn't led me astray yet.

"May I borrow Kador for a few minutes?" she asked.

I blinked at her. I'd left him out of my tale earlier. *How did she know his name? Maybe she could hear him?*

*"It's okay. Let me have a few minutes with the pretty lady."* I rolled my eyes and handed his book to her. They left the room, while I replayed our conversation in my mind as I waited.

A few minutes later the door opened and Tina returned, carrying Kador and a big smile.

"Did you two enjoy yourselves?"

*"Aye,"* Kador said. Tina giggled.

"You and I aren't done. I'm here to help."

"What? I just come find your store when I need you?"

"No. Kador has my cell phone number. If Harry visits your dreams or you find yourself thinking about me, call."

I took Kador back and shrugged my shoulders. "Okay."

"Oh! And figure out how to release Kador, would ya? He needs to come out to play."

# CHAPTER THIRTY-ONE

### Mid-October, Connecticut

The call I'd been dreading came. It took more than two weeks, but the Council wanted to meet with me. This was to be a private meeting; they didn't want a repeat of last time. How they were going to make it happen became the problem. Everyone was waiting, hanging on to every bit of gossip, hoping for a clue to when the next meeting would be, which ruled the Coven House out. My house was out since it was watched day and night.

We finally settled upon my company's headquarters. They chose a Thursday morning, which also happened to be the day of the first snowfall. The full Council showed up to face me in my own boardroom. My parents, Lowen, and Victor sat with me as we waited to hear my fate.

My mom sat to my left and offered a comforting hand, with Lowen on my right tapping his fingers on his suit sleeve.

"We've called you here because we have completed our research," Davidson announced. "At first it seemed there was only one possibility, a young girl born to the Blygh house. Our search through the other families turned up nothing, until yesterday. It turns out there was another daughter born to the Blyghs, she's twenty and lives in Cornwall. Her name is Alis Blygh."

The door to the boardroom opened and two women came in. The first was a much older woman. She wore the brown uniform marking her as a member of our police. With her stood a girl with dark brown hair, amber-gold eyes, and freckles on very pale skin. She stood tall at probably five foot nine; she was dressed in a black sweater and jeans.

"May I please introduce Alis Blygh to the Council," said the woman with her.

Alis curtsied to the Council and offered a greeting. I stood, knowing my role.

"Alis, this is Grayson James Penrose. Grayson, this is Alis."

"Hello, Alis."

She smiled and I noticed she had dimples on both cheeks and a beautiful smile.

"Hi, Grayson."

"Please call me Gray."

"Gray it is then."

"Alis, we were in such a hurry to get you here we don't know anything about you. Can you tell us about your family, are you betrothed, have you ever been before an Oracle?"

"My father was Gerard Blygh. He passed away about ten years ago. I came along rather late in his life. My mother, who will be here later today, is Kate Rosdew. For the most part, I've been living with my father's family as I've been doing my KIC service. I am not betrothed. As to your question of the Oracle, my mother would have to answer."

I swallowed hard, and I know everyone at the table knew the implications of what Alis had said. She was probably Lydia's cousin, close or distant.

"Why couldn't your mother come with you?"

"Oh, she's sorry for that. But she's in charge of my late grandmother's estate in Cornwall."

Davidson's eyes grew big as he finally understood the situation fully. He shuddered as he asked, "Are you, ah … Are you Hilda's granddaughter?"

"Yes."

"I'm sorry about your loss, and understand now why your mother isn't here yet. I believe we met at Hilda's home; wasn't it you and your mother who helped the KIC get inside her home?" Davidson asked.

"Yes, that was my mother and myself," she answered.

"You've been very helpful to the Council concerning your grandmother. Bailiff Teague, will you take Alis to her family's home and get her settled? I understand she has just arrived and was kind enough to join us immediately. Alis, we'll be in touch tomorrow."

"Of course." Alis followed her guard out of the room and I sat back down. Lowen looked at me with sympathy.

"At this time, I believe I should make the Council aware there's a good chance Alis was related to Gray's first fiancée, Lydia. She was also Hilda's granddaughter. They were probably cousins. This seems rather cruel considering the circumstances surrounding Lydia's death," Davidson told the Council.

"I agree," said Victor.

"I second it," Lowen added.

A male member to the left of Davidson spoke up, "Do you realize how many children and grandchildren Hilda had?"

"We know, but surely there's more than one possibility. Maybe the Marrak line had another female?" Davidson asked.

"Victor, how about your family? Has a female been born in the last fifty years? Your family seems as likely as any other," another Councilman asked.

I wondered if he would answer. "The truth is my son is the only child born to my family in the years you are inquiring. We've experienced a very low birth rate, like many families within the Kind. If an eligible female had been born in my family, I'd be honored if Gray would marry her."

They started arguing, with most of the Council members involved. Tired of this, I stood. "Excuse me." I had to say it twice to get their attention.

"I understand you found someone you think fits the description of the female, but how will you know with Aquila gone? It sounds like another maybe; like Kensa and my brother. I'm sorry, but I'm not looking to be the Kind's sacrificial lamb."

"Don't you trust us?" a female member of the Council asked.

"Honestly, no. Would *you* like to be in my situation? What happens to me if you guess wrong? Will I be held responsible for your choices? If I were to guess, I'd bet my money on the Council placing the blame on me. Not to mention the choice of my marriage being taken away from my family and myself, taken by the Council without care for our feelings. I don't want to marry. I don't want the damn title of the *Guide*. Find someone else to fulfill your damn prophecy and leave me be." I sat down.

"We can't do that," Davidson answered. "The fate of the Kind rests with you." I rolled my eyes and crossed my arms over my chest. "We're doing the best we can. We'll have you come back tomorrow and both of you will go before Christopher. Apparently when Aquila died he received the spirit of the Oracle. We hope to have a better idea after."

I didn't like the idea of them discovering Christopher had Aquila's abilities. The result for me was a sleepless night. No one dared to approach me. I sat alone in my tower at home, mad at the world.

*"Try to relax. You need to be focused,"* Kador advised me.

"Why? There's no getting out of this, and you know it. My fate was sealed today; they've found some girl they plan for me to screw and hope it makes all of their lives better. I know there isn't the slightest chance of this working."

*"I think you're right. Prophecies are rarely straightforward. The harder we try to escape them the more we fall into it. It isn't hopeless yet."*

We went back and forth for hours. His companionship and concern did help me. After all, what's the worst that could happen?

I get married and lose my virginity? What if we didn't like each other? I guess we could live separate lives, then.

Early the next day, a knock sounded at my bedroom door. "Come in," I said. It did me no good to be mad at my family and friends.

My dad came in. "I'm sorry you have to go through this. I never wanted it for your brother or you." He closed the door behind him and came to sit on the edge of my bed. "Arranged marriages are the way of our culture. I'd hoped to find a wife you would like or love. After all, I do love your mother very much. Most of the marriages of my friends and family are happy ones. Though there are exceptions, like Davidson's son."

"Dad, you don't need to pacify me, I know you didn't want this."

"I'm here because I am worried about you. We're trying to come up with something to stop this."

"Stop what?"

"You from having to marry a Blygh girl. I told you once that several of the families in our world are different, like your mother's family. They have different values and ideas about life. The Blyghs aren't a good fit for you. Even Victor is worried. Hell, even the Tremaynes have a longstanding vendetta with the Blyghs. They don't mix well."

"I've known a couple, though not well. Is it as bad as you say?"

"Your mother is scared, Lowen has been on the phone all night long, and Victor disappeared to see what he could do. Does that answer your question?"

I stared at him, having no idea what to say.

"You need to dress. Davidson called while ago. We have to be there in an hour. Today, please hold your tongue. I know it's hard, but not everyone on the Council is a friend to us. We'll all be at your side. No matter what happens."

· ꙮ ·

The Council commandeered my boardroom again. There had been no sign of Victor. The Council members began to arrive and take their places. Next came Christopher, followed by Alis, a boy who looked like a male version of her, and a woman, who I assumed to be Kate, Alis's mother.

The meeting started.

"Will you please introduce yourselves?" Davidson asked the three newcomers.

"I'm Kate Rosdew, the mother of Alis, and this is her twin brother Alistair. They're my only children. Their father died years ago." Kate, dressed all in black, looked very much like her mother, Hilda.

"Kate, we were curious, have you ever taken her before an Oracle?" Davidson asked.

"No. I saw no need."

"Do you have any questions for the Council or the Penroses?"

"No."

"Okay, Grayson and Alis, will you come forward and stand by the whiteboard?" An order, not a request.

I stood, and Alis followed. She took up a place on my right. Christopher sat in a chair and turned to face us.

"Christopher, do you get anything?" As Davidson's question faded, I saw the smoke and strange glow coming from him, just like Aquila when I went before her. He stood and soon started to levitate. Dark smoke started trailing around him as his hollowed eyes looked at Alis. She stood still, looking right back at him without flinching at the sight in front of her; I couldn't say the same.

"Alis?" said a higher pitched version of Christopher's voice.

"Yes."

For a long moment, Christopher stared at her as if it didn't know what to do.

"It's to be this way?" he asked, elongating each syllable.

I blinked at him. "What do you mean?"

"There are many ways to fulfill something which is meant to happen. A choice is made."

I glared at him.

Davidson pressed on, "Are you saying Grayson should marry Alis?" The possessed Christopher turned to look at him. He flinched under the attention.

"Should? There are many paths; this is but one. The destination is the same. The losses and gains vary on each path. I have given you all I can. Make your choice and accept your fate."

Christopher sank to the floor as the possessing spirit fled. I caught him before he hit his head. It was easiest to let him lay on the ground, unconscious. On my feet again, I looked at the Council members who were looking at each other in confusion.

Christopher tried to sit up and hit his head on the chair. "Ouch!" His hand covered his forehead as he stood.

"Ah, good you're back with us, Christopher. Can you help us make sense of the Oracle's comments?"

He rubbed at the red spot on his forehead as he looked at the Council. "The feeling and impression I got were … I think 'confused' best describes it. The Oracle was perplexed by something, yet for a second, I saw the path. It will work."

"Are you sure? You don't sound convinced."

"The Oracle doesn't see the future in a linear manner, and it's confusing to me still. The path jumped around before it reached the end."

"What did you see at the end?"

Christopher looked up and bit his lip before he answered, "I didn't see something as much as I felt it: Grayson and power."

"Penroses, Blyghs, will you please leave us? We shall discuss the matter further and call you back in," Davidson said, dismissing us.

We all filed out and kept to our own groups in the hall. Victor was waiting for us. Lowen grabbed him and my dad, leading them off to talk. I stayed with my mother. She watched Alis with curiosity.

At that moment, I knew my fate. They'd have me married to her on Samhain, just over a week away. The time had come. I'd control my own future; I would run. As I considered my options someone called my name. I turned to see Alis's twin brother.

"Hello." He held his hand out to greet me. I took it.

"Hello. Alistair, right?"

"Yes. I wanted to meet you. Come here, Alis, you might as well meet him, he's probably going to be your husband."

She came to his side. "Hello, Gray," she said as her mother came up to my mom.

"Hello, Jessamine, it's been a long time."

"It has. Weird way to get reacquainted."

"Yes, forced arranged marriage. How lucky we are to have the great, almighty Council deciding our children's fates." The amount of sarcasm in her voice startled me.

"I was sorry to hear about Hilda."

Kate sighed, "No you weren't; nor was I. I've been helping the Council clear her estate to be done with it. Sorry, don't mean to be so curt. This has been a hard month for me. I'm sure it has been for your family, too."

Alis glared at her mother. She didn't seem to notice, neither did my mom. Alistair did, though. I couldn't decide if she might be upset with her mother or perhaps thought her rude? She noticed me watching her, and she smiled.

I wondered how I should feel about her, a stranger and, possibly, my soon-to-be wife? Numbness was the only thing I could conjure. Victor, Lowen, and my father returned to join us as we waited for the Council. My mother did the introductions. It was easy to see she and Kate had known each other at some point, probably though Hilda. The Council kept us waiting another half hour before they called us back into the boardroom.

"We've come to a decision. It's the will of the Elder Council that Grayson Penrose and Alis Blygh be married on Samhain," Davidson said.

Kate stood, resting her hand on her hip. "Can we leave? I'm going to have to start the arrangements immediately, and I'm jet-lagged."

"Of course," he said. The Blyghs filed out of the room.

Something told me I hadn't heard the worst of it yet. "May we go as well?" my mother asked. "I'll have a lot of preparations to make too, and I'd like to get Guy home in time for the wedding."

"You may, but Grayson must remain."

"Why?" I asked, nervous now.

Davidson was playing with his mustache, not a good sign.

"What is going on?" Victor asked, suspicion thick in his voice.

"Grayson is to have a hex placed upon him; one which will keep him from fleeing. Only until the ceremony," Davidson answered.

Nope, they weren't done. Oh, my life, it just keeps getting better and better.

"Who is to do this hex? For I'm sure there's only one of you on the Council capable of doing it. We all know that would not be a good idea," Victor said.

"You're right. It's why he'll perform it now, in front of witnesses."

Surely they weren't going to allow a *Wayfarer* to hex me? Victor looked at me, and I saw the flash of red in his eyes.

"Let me do it." Victor hissed.

"No, you're too close to him. We can't trust you in this matter," Arthur said.

My mother wrapped her arms around me, and an argument broke out between my family and the Council.

"Stop! I'll allow it if you will all stop fighting."

For the first time in the meeting, I heard Kador in my head. *"I'll make sure it's only a hex to keep you from fleeing. I might be able to weaken it, too. You must grant me your sight."*

I turned my head and whispered, "I grant you my sight."

"What?" Mom asked.

"Nothing." She released her hold on me.

Arthur looked at me and asked, "May I approach you? You may have Victor at your side to verify I only do as the Council instructed."

"Yes, you may."

Victor came to stand next to me as Arthur approached. At about six foot, with dark hair and gray eyes, Arthur didn't seem very intimidating to me. If I wasn't mistaken, he seemed nervous.

He stopped about two feet from me and lifted his palms. From his lips, a long line of ancient Cornish and Welsh poured. At the same time, I heard similar words in my head. At first, I didn't understand until I recognized the unique accent. Kador was speaking a matching hex.

In Arthur's hand, an almost invisible ball formed, spinning fast. With each syllable it increased in size until it resembled a coconut. I watched in fascination, knowing he called forth wind, as I would call fire. He reminded me of my favorite cartoon character, Aang, from *The Last Airbender*. Though if he was Aang it made me Zuko, and a part of the Fire Nation. The ball of wind spun in his hand faster and faster as he looked up into Victor's eyes.

"Does my hex meet with your approval?"

Victor's lips curled, and his dimples showed. "Fascinating, it's been a long time since I've seen air magic. You forgot to set a time limit."

"You caught that, did you? Davidson? What did we agree to for the length of time?"

"Until the morning following Samhain, after the wedding," answered Davidson. More of the ancient mixed language followed from Arthur, though Kador remained silent.

"Does it meet with your approval now?"

Victor gave a quick nod. I gritted my teeth; sometimes hexes hurt. He lifted his right palm with the swirling ball as if he had a baseball in his hand. He pulled back and threw it at my chest. I almost flinched but held my ground as the ball slowly came toward me. Just as it would have made contact with my chest, it exploded in a giant ball of flames throwing us all to the ground.

It took me a couple of seconds before I was able to lean up on my elbows and look around. Victor had managed to recover faster than me and sat crouched, looking at the now unconscious Arthur. Confused, I looked down at my chest to see smoke and a couple of singe marks. Then I heard the laughter inside my head.

"Did you do that, Kador?"

"*Of course, it serves that bastard right.*"

I noticed all eyes in the room were on me. Victor had a look of, "How the hell did you do that?"

Not sure what to say, I did the only thing I could think of; I stood, stuck my bottom lip out and shrugged my shoulders. All eyes turned from me to Arthur, who sat up and rubbed his head.

"What the bloody hell just happened?"

Victor answered, "You got knocked on your ass by a Penrose without him lifting a finger or saying a word. Impressive, Gray, I've never seen anything like it before. I guess the Council *won't* be hexing you."

I made it home with no hex upon me. No one else would risk it after what happened to Arthur. Instead, they hexed the house. Over the next week, I wasn't to leave the house without being in the presence of my guardians. Otherwise, I'd suffer some punishment, courtesy of the hex.

Late in the evening after my parents were asleep, Victor and Lowen met me in the library in my tower.

"Don't run. At this point don't reveal your powers. I've been informed the Council's number two mission besides the wedding is to discover your abilities," Victor said.

"I know, I overheard Davidson on the phone in Cornwall admit as much."

"Doesn't it seem rather convenient? There doesn't appear to be a viable female available for a while, then, magically, after two weeks, they discover one? And from the family who's already lost the one girl born in the last four hundred years because everyone fought over her and she became a casualty." Lowen paced the floor as he spouted his rambling thoughts.

"We'd have been in better shape had she been raised with her mother's family, the Rosdews, rather than her father's. My guess is her dad wanted her existence kept a secret. It's why her twin went with the mother. I bet if her father had not died she'd never have been permitted to do her KIC service," Victor said.

Back and forth, just like a tennis game, they passed around ideas and theories for most of the night. When I started to doze off, I decided to ask the only question I had at this point. "When will I know if I should run?"

Victor looked at me for a long moment before saying, "There will be no doubt in your mind about when to run. Listen to your gut. Let's wait until the time is right so we can get as many pieces to the puzzle as possible."

My mother worked furiously to arrange everything for my wedding on Samhain. We decided to have it at our house. She'd even gotten hold of my brother, who would return with his new bride in time. Tristan would be here for the wedding, too. He'd had to go back to New Orleans to work and to watch over his family's interests so Victor could stay.

My mother reached out to Kate for planning, and Kate coordinated with her, though she declined to have dinner or any other social events where Alis and I could spend time together. A very strange thing; most families would usually grant the bride and groom some time to get acquainted before the wedding.

As the wedding neared, I often found myself home alone. A couple of days before the wedding I was sitting in my room. I thought I was the only one home, when a knock sounded on my bedroom door. My mother came in looking uncomfortable.

"What's up?"

She sighed and came to sit with me on the bed. I set the book I'd been reading down on the nightstand.

"I want to discuss a couple of things you won't want to talk about."

"Okay."

"This discussion should probably have come from your father. But it's left to me because what I'm going to do he wouldn't approve of, and I'm not going to ask if he'll make an exception."

Which meant it probably involved darker magic, but for what?

She looked up at the ceiling, clearly apprehensive. "You've always been different from your brother. With him I knew I had to take certain precautions."

Oh no, I knew where the conversation was heading. I decided to head it off. "Mom, I know about sex."

She rolled her eyes at me. "I know you do. Though you never express a need for it, not since …" she trailed off, knowing better than to bring up Lydia. "I've been concerned for years, hoping you used your work as a substitute."

## CONVERGENT LINES

"I have, it's the only place I have some free will. What about sex?" She'd piqued my curiosity.

"I don't see any way for you to get out of marrying her. They may use magic to make you consummate the marriage. It's what I wanted to talk to you about."

My eyes widened in shock. "They can do that?"

"Yes, and they won't warn you. I'm here to give you two potions. One I want you to take no matter what. It's a male birth control serum. You're going to have to consummate the marriage at least once. After the one time, the law is on your side. This serum will ensure she doesn't become pregnant." She held a tiny corked bottle with a clear liquid in it.

I looked at it and took the bottle. "Thank you for thinking about this, it hadn't even crossed my mind."

"Trust me. You don't want a child with Kate's daughter, and a Blygh at that."

"Is she as bad as you say?"

"She used to be. Somehow, I think being married into the Blyghs might have changed her. Of Hilda's children, she is closest in age to me, and was a lot like Hilda when I knew her. My guess is she's now the most powerful Kind with spirit magic."

"What's the other potion?" She bit her lip instead of answering. "What?"

"Do you think you'll be able to ... to do it on your own?"

I mouthed an "O" and blushed. She had a point. I didn't know if I could ... "The honest answer? Probably no."

"Don't be ashamed. I'm not judging you. With Guy, I knew he'd have decades without. It's why we made sure he could experience at least some fulfillment. You had, then lost, someone. It's a broken heart, and nothing to be ashamed of. We each heal at our own pace, and with as long as our lives are we don't do things like humans. I also think it's a holdover from our fae blood. Their society moved very slowly."

I'd often wondered if something might be wrong with me, why I couldn't move past her. More than twenty years and I still felt like it had only been days. Though the bomb dropped about my memories possibly being false had rattled me in a way I hadn't conceived of. I felt relief. There was a possibility I wasn't broken, this information had helped me start to let go.

"This"—she held out another tiny corked bottle; this time, the liquid was a bright blue—"is an aphrodisiac, you'll be able to get through the night. It not very strong and it won't move you to do anything you usually wouldn't do, it will just make your body more willing. I also added a forgetting spell to it."

"I don't understand?"

She smiled at me. "Gray, you're genuine and feel very strongly about what you think is right. Are you going to stay in this marriage? Or fulfill your duty and go back to your life?"

"If I must go through with this, I'll do what I'm asked then go back to my life."

"Will you want to remember your wedding night? Especially considering how awkward it will probably be?"

I held my hand out for the bottle. She handed it over. "Drink both in something like a whisky just before you go to her."

"Thank you." She nodded her head and then left me alone.

# CHAPTER THIRTY-TWO

### Morning of Samhain, Connecticut

The morning of Samhain dawned, October 31st. I'd have the day to myself. We don't recognize Samhain until dusk, and the wedding would take place after nightfall. Our house overflowed with family and visitors. The wedding would take place in the backyard. It would be cool, but we planned for a quick ceremony; no handfasting and no special vows. We'd have a small wedding, and a short reception with several Council members, family, and friends present.

Days earlier the *Daily Arcane* had announced the Council's decision to the Kind. As a result, white ribbons and flowers were left at the gates of our house from our community. Everyone hoped the magic would return after tonight. I often wondered what people thought would happen. After all, there might be one or two people, like Victor, who were alive before the binding. Was our existence so horrible now? Was there a need to hope for more? We all have at least some magic and longer lives. Personally, I've always thought it bullshit. We're fine as we are, though I'm mostly alone in my opinion.

I spent the morning alone in my room. By noon I found myself wanting company so I went in search of some. In the kitchen, I found my mom and Kate coordinating the decorations and caterers. I didn't want to be involved with their activities; I went searching elsewhere. I couldn't find anyone. With the hex in place on the house I couldn't leave the property until the next morning.

Outside the weather seemed beautiful, and it was much better than sitting in my room sulking. I went to the gardens and watched the preparations. For a while, I sat at a table watching the comings and goings of the workers, until a man I hadn't seen in years appeared.

He waited by a wall of bushes lining the garden. Somehow he'd managed to get past the protection spells enacted for the wedding. Not surprising; I'd always thought his father underestimated him. Knowing he was there for me, I went to talk to Davy Gwyn.

"It's been a long time," he said.

"Yes, it has. What brings you out today?" I examined him. In height, we stood equal, though I bet I had forty pounds on him. His light green, almost silver, eyes watched me with interest, and I wondered again about his relationship with Davidson. Davy wore his long, pale, stringy hair loose, and in the sunlight, his skin looked transparent. For some reason, he'd always looked sickly and thin. He seemed to be a holdover, more fae than Kind. That, more than anything, was probably why Davidson tried to isolate him. Between his eyes and pale skin, he couldn't interact with humans; he looked too alien.

"You're what brings me out. I know we have a significant gap in age, but I think we've much in common. I came because I heard about your marriage."

"You mean doom?"

He laughed. "It's not the end. I've suffered a wife, picked for her beauty. Until I met her I never understood the meaning of the human saying, 'beauty is only skin deep.' I do now."

"Is it bad?"

"Hell, yes."

I rubbed the back of my neck, not sure what to say. When I was a kid, Davy would sometimes watch Guy and me, or we'd be stuck together for some event. He had to be about twenty years older than me.

"I've always known you were special. Don't know why. But when I was around you as a child, there just seemed to be something different about you. I didn't feel like that about your brother, or anyone else. I felt compelled to seek you out. I've been dreaming of seeing you for weeks."

"Really? What did you do when you saw me in the dream?"

"Just talked, though I awoke with an anxiety attack. I knew I had to see you."

"Have you had prophetic dreams in the past?"

"Yes, and I've ignored them and paid a high price. I'm here, and I'll be here tonight. I'm meant to be, for some purpose."

I bit my lip. A thought came to me as to why he might be here. "Can I ask you a personal question?"

He pursed his lips, and his brows rose. "Sure. You're the only person who is allowed."

"How old were you when your marriage happened?"

"In my mid-thirties, which is close to twenty years ago. My father thought it would do me good to marry well, even if it meant forcing me. Eva and I live separate lives."

"There's something you're not telling me?"

His eyes narrowed as he looked at me. "Yes … There was somebody else. No one, not even my family, knew about her. She's gone and I haven't recovered."

"You know the same happened to me? Were you there?"

He nodded his head. "My situation is a bit different. She's Other, not human or Kind. Her family made sure I'd never see her again, and we aren't exactly compatible."

My brows lifted in confusion.

"It's a long story."

I nodded, understanding. "How did you handle the wedding night? And did you go your separate ways right after?"

He looked mad, and I could tell he gritted his teeth. "My family used a spell to compel me. It's a common practice and a closely guarded secret. They don't want you to become aware of it until after you're married. It is sex, might not be great sex, but you'll live through it. The important thing ..." He sighed and suddenly seemed exhausted. "Don't stop paying attention to your gut and your head. A few days after the wedding, I realized someone had given me a strong love potion."

"Why?"

"I don't know for sure, but I wasn't the only one given the potion. I think both our parents hoped to rid themselves of two problems. There's a theory, that if both parties get the love potion it won't turn into hate. It's not true. Within weeks we were living apart and have been since. I recommend you do what you have to do tonight, and tomorrow, get as far away as possible." He laughed.

"What?"

"This is the longest conversation I've had in years. I'm going now. I'll be here later. I hope this works out. You were always a sweet kid, and one of the few people I ever liked. Sorry you're going through this."

"I appreciate you coming to talk to me, and being here later." I held my hand out to him, and he shook it. He turned to leave as the sun came out from behind the clouds, and for a second, it looked like his silhouette flickered. I rubbed my eyes wondering what had caused it? After a minute, I'd decided it was my imagination.

· ৯ ·

Dressed for my wedding, I paced my room. Lowen sat in a chair with Pendragon on his shoulder.

"I'm sorry. I found nothing in the laws or old stories to help you get out of this," Pen said.

"It's fine, this event was inevitable. I knew sooner or later I'd be forced to marry. Why should I get to pick? No one else does."

Lowen's lips drew together and his forehead wrinkled. "Doesn't make it right."

"Maybe we should try something different. Everyone is

convinced Alis is terrible. She seemed nice. Perhaps everything will work out?"

"Yes, this is your wedding night. A time for well-wishes. I wish the best for both of you. From now on we'll move forward with a different attitude. Pendragon, do you agree?"

"Of course," Pendragon responded.

"I think I'll carry Kador for you during the ceremony. I'll remain close enough for you to enable him to see through your eyes, which I suggest you do. I'd also recommend keeping your abilities from your new wife, at least until things settle down and we know what happened to Hilda."

"Okay. I don't know how I'd have done this without you."

"It's been our pleasure," he said as I handed him my bag.

"Kador, I give you permission to see through my eyes."

*"I must admit it's nice to see the world again."*

"Any time you want, let me know."

A knock sounded on my door. "It's time," Guy said from the other side.

We made our way to the garden and I took my place. Christopher Carn stood in front of me ready to officiate the wedding. The guests started sitting down and a string quartet began to play. As the minutes ticked by my heart pounded in my chest. Everything in me screamed at the wrongness of my situation. I picked up a change in the music and realized the ceremony was starting. I swallowed and turned to look. Tristan escorted a tall, dark haired girl dressed in a silver dress toward me. When they reached my side, the girl went to the opposite side of the aisle, and Tristan stood next to me. Next came Guy with Kensa. Once they reached us the music changed again and Alis started towards me on the arm of her brother.

Standing in front of a crowd and watching your bride should stir one to feel certain emotions. For the most part, I felt numb and my nerves felt raw. I wanted to feel happiness, excitement, hope, anything of the like, but it wasn't going to happen.

They reached my side.

Christopher asked, "Who gives Alis Lee Blygh to join with Grayson James Penrose?"

"I do; Alistair Blygh. I give my sister into the care of Grayson Penrose."

"You may join their hands." Alistair took Alis's hand and set it gently in mine, and then stepped back. I looked into the eyes of my soon-to-be wife. She looked beautiful, in a white and gold flowing wedding gown, with her dark hair up, except for the curls trailing down her back. Upon her head she wore a crown of flowers and gold ribbons.

"Today we come together to witness a joining, perhaps the most important to our people. Today Grayson and Alis come to bind their lives together, in hopes of break our binding curse. May their joining be happy and fruitful." The crowd cheered at his comments. "Grayson, would you repeat after me?"

I nodded my head in agreement.

"My blood to your blood, my soul to your soul.

I give you my body, that we two might be one.

I give you my love, until our life shall be done.

You can't possess me for I belong to myself.

But while we both wish it, I give you that which is mine to give."

Here it came, I had to do this. I opened my mouth and for a full ten seconds, nothing happened. I tried swallowing and tried again. My voice came out a whisper, but somehow I managed to say the whole thing.

"Do you have the ring?"

"Yes." I turned to Tristan, who held out the gold band. He set it in my palm, and I turned back to Alis.

I slid the ring home. His attention switched to Alis and they repeated the ceremony with her part. I lost track of time standing there, it didn't feel real, I felt like I'd entered a nightmare. I heard my name and turned to look at Christopher, the look he gave me led me to believe he'd called my name a couple of times. "Yes?"

"You may kiss the bride." I leaned into her and pressed a quick kiss to her lips. The guests behind us cheered.

## CONVERGENT LINES

A couple of hours later--hours which I didn't remember--I surfaced. The alcohol I'd ingested hadn't helped numb me. The dinner and other crap were over, leaving only the countdown to the most awkward couple of minutes of my life. Alis came over to me, as I stood to the side.

"Here," she said as she handed me a glass of whisky. She lifted her own glass. "Here is to this whole cluster being over with soon," she said. We clinked our glasses together. I downed the whole thing. Someone called her name and she walked away. I started coughing as I realized that what she had given me wasn't whisky, or at least not the one I'd been drinking all night.

A waiter came by and refreshed my glass. Careful not to draw attention I pulled both bottles my mother gave me out of my pocket.

I uncorked one bottle and added it, then the other. I lifted the glass to my lips and downed the contents in two gulps. If it tasted bad, I didn't notice.

Tristan came to my side. "Could I steal you for a moment? We need to talk."

My best friend was a man of few words. It must be serious if he wanted to talk here. I joined him in the corner away from prying ears.

"What?"

"I'm to let you know the Council decided against casting a spell to make you ..." he trailed off.

"Consummate the marriage?" I added.

"Yes. Instead they're going to do a much more public display."

"What do you mean?"

"They think it's fitting to do the unbinding ribbons. It's where they'll take your silk handkerchief and her ribbon. They'll tie them in a bow and display it in the middle of the reception hall. When you have finished, the two will untwine from each other, and we'll all know you did what you were meant to do."

My mouth dropped open as I considered this news. There would be no way around this. I hoped my mother's potions worked.

Tristan patted me on the back. "You'll get through this. It's not right, but you'll survive. Remember, you can always come live with me in NOLA. We'll protect you."

I smiled at him, thankful for the offer. Though I knew the Council would find a way around the Tremaynes if I went against them.

"It's just sex ... I hope."

He laughed, probably more from the look on my face than my comment. My father and Guy joined us. The time had come. Tristan drew me in for a hug. I hugged him back, thankful I had good friends.

"Come on. We've another thing with the Council in the other room," Dad said.

I followed behind them. Davidson, Sowenna, and Arthur stood together in front of us.

"Because of the importance of this joining we've decided to use an old tradition. It's called the unbinding ribbons. Will you hand me your silver handkerchief?" Davidson asked.

I pulled it from my breast pocket and handed it over.

He turned to Alis, "May I have one of the gold ribbons from your hair?" Alis nodded and her mother took one of the satin ribbons from her hair and handed it over.

Davidson gave my silver handkerchief to Sowenna, and the gold ribbon went to Arthur.

"Will each of you perform the charm for luck, happiness, and fruitfulness upon them?"

We all watched as the two did their magic. Both said long spells in old languages. Each added their little flair to it. Arthur's ribbon floated on the wind in an undulating motion, and gold sparks fell from the far end as he worked. The people around us gasped and whispered.

My great-aunt Sowenna Penrose, who had my handkerchief, had taken it and balled it up in her palm. As her fingers released it, she started speaking, and the ball of silver fabric became engulfed in a ball of white and silver flames as it floated over her palm. A steady stream of smoke puffed, creating different shapes. One appeared as a star, which took off like a comet. The next puff of smoke formed a heart and began to beat. The final shape was two people holding hands as they turned to each other and leaned into a kiss, before dissipating. Finished, they each handed their spell-bound cloth back to Davidson.

"Now, I shall knot these together." He entwined the ends of each, speaking a spell as he worked. "This knot shall remain tied as long as they're married."

Next, he took the pieces and tied a large bow as he spoke more magic. As he finished, the silver and gold bow began to float until it hung suspended under the chandelier. "The bow is tied and will remain until the union is complete. Once it is, the bow will untwine and the knot between the pieces will merge to form one, like the couple."

In my head, I asked Kador, "Will you be okay with Lowen?"

*"Yes. Take my sight and I shall give you your privacy."*

"Okay."

*"As everyone has said, you'll make it through this."*

"I know, but the closer I get to it the more I fear it. It doesn't make any sense."

*"No, it doesn't. Be careful, but do what you need to."*

I said the words to remove my sight from Kador. I stood facing the Council and I saw a strange look cross Davidson's face; I turned to see Davy standing behind me.

"Hi, Davy."

"Hello." Davy looked different than when I'd seen him earlier. He wore a black suit, which had a strange effect on his coloring. His hair had been combed, washed, and drawn back.

He held his hand out to me. I shook it.

"I wish you the best," he said as we shook hands. He held on longer than usual. He looked me right in the eyes as if trying to convey something. I felt it then; he wanted to slip me something. I grabbed the object before I withdrew my hand.

"What are you doing here?" Davidson said; the air in the room felt heavy.

"I came to wish a friend good luck."

"Really? You almost never leave the house. I didn't think you were friends with Gray. I didn't believe you had *any* friends."

"He is unique, I think everyone he has ever known likes him."

"I count Davy as a friend. He's always been good to me," I said and slipped the thing he'd handed me into my pocket.

"Davidson," said a stern voice from behind me. I turned to see Arthur Wayfarer.

Davidson's glare moved for Davy to Arthur. "What?"

"Leave it. This really isn't the time or place for this," Arthur told Davidson.

I felt like I had stepped into an alternate reality. Arthur was reprimanding Davidson about his own son?

People began to stare with curiosity. Taking advantage of the distraction, I stole a look at what Davy had handed me. It was a small piece of folded paper. I looked up to make sure everyone's attention was elsewhere before I opened it. Davy had written: *Run as fast and as soon as you can. Trust no one. It's from my dream earlier this afternoon. Good luck.—DG*

I stuck the paper back into my pocket as the hair on the back of my neck stood up.

"Gray, Alis, you should probably ... uh, go upstairs," Davidson said as he turned from Davy. He probably wanted to switch people's attention from himself to me. Davidson went back to glaring at Arthur instead of Davy. Davy seemed confused by the attention.

Wanting to be done with this I said, "Yes, I guess we should. You're always there to remind me of my duty to the Kind." I stomped off. Damn them all! I hope they all lost everything. Determined, and not caring, I marched up to my wife. I extended my hand to her, and she took it. I led her to the stairs and to the bridal suite my mother had arranged in the guest room of my tower. The time had come; I'd take control of the situation, and they wouldn't be running my life any longer.

# CHAPTER THIRTY-THREE

### Samhain Night, Connecticut

I pulled Alis the whole way up two spiral staircases to a landing with a door wide open in welcome. We stopped at the threshold and I asked myself a question: *Am I going to go through with this? If I am, then I should go the whole way.* The decision made, I turned to her awkwardly.

"May I carry you over the threshold?"

She blinked her dark eyes at me. "Yes, it's supposed to bring luck."

"So they say." Her height made it so that I didn't need to bend much to pick her up. With ease, I lifted her and carried her to the bed. I returned to the door to close it. Now what, I wondered? I scratched the back of my head feeling embarrassed.

"You aren't what I thought you would be," she said.

"How so?"

"You're accepting this marriage much more easily than I thought you would."

I felt my brow furrow with confusion. "Did I have a choice? Why would you accept it so easily?"

"I guess you didn't. I wanted this; it makes me the most powerful female in the Kind. I get to break the curse and marry the most eligible bachelor in our world. Why wouldn't I do this?"

"Because you don't know me, or love me."

She laughed. "Love? You really believe in that?"

"Yeah, I do. You're young to be so jaded."

She shrugged her shoulders. Still feeling bold I moved toward her, and she looked at me unflinching. I don't know why, but I found her fearlessness attractive. Standing close to her I looked down into her eyes, which looked back at me with curiosity. She lifted her hand and put it to my chest.

"Kiss me," she said.

I swallowed, leaned down, and kissed her. With her kiss, I felt a spark as though a switch had been thrown. My body erupted into flames; things I hadn't felt in years rushed through me. Was this me or the potion? Deciding it didn't matter, I deepened the kiss and followed my instincts. Let's say there's something to be said for what magic can do to take clothing off. With my body willing and hers, too, we found ourselves on the bed, naked. As each second passed I felt more aggressive and I couldn't figure out why. I didn't think the potion my mother gave me would cause this.

A haze engulfed me; my will wasn't my own. Something corrupt and wrong took hold of me. One moment I had Alis in my arms, the next, something ripped me from my body, throwing me against a wall. Unimaginable pain erupted through me. When I oriented myself, I could see my body entwined with hers from the other end of the room.

Angry, I tried to move, only to find myself stuck as I watched everything. I tried to scream. No sound came. My mind raced to figure out what was happening. How could I stop it? Focusing became hard as I felt this state, whatever it might be, fading. Sometimes I'd wake for a moment and catch flashes of events around me; time meant nothing in this hell.

After a while, I came to. The scene in front of me had changed enough to figure out time had passed. My body sat up in bed next to her as she spoke and caressed my face. Their lips moved, but I heard no sound. It didn't make sense. I watched them for a bit as they lay in bed together. Never did I want to watch myself like this. What was I saying? That wasn't me. Weak again I felt darkness descend, and this time I was grateful for it.

· ࿓ ·

If there are moments in life which you never want to forget, there are also moments you wish you could …

Someone hit me. I offered no resistance. Again it happened, but I felt like I was in a deep sleep. Something cold and wet covered me. I fought with everything I had. The only way I could describe the feeling is like when you're trapped underwater, deep water, and trying to reach the surface as you run out of breath.

I shot up, gasping. Air filled my lungs; the most incredible feeling. My breathing heaved for a minute as my eyes focused. When my brain registered the sight in front of me, alarms sounded, and panic struck me in full force. Hearing became the last of my senses to return.

The first thing I heard was, "What did you do to her?" I had no idea who had said it. Looking around I saw it was Arthur who had been speaking.

Arthur Wayfarer, Kate Blygh, Davidson Gwyn, Sowenna Penrose, Victor Tremayne, Lowen Penrose, Tristan Tremayne, Guy, my parents, they all stood looking at me. Most with anger, some with confusion, others with outright hate. My head swiveled taking in each of them. As I did, a picture began to fill my head. I was wet. I looked down to find the bed drenched in cold water, someone must have thrown it on me. But the other sight didn't make any sense. There was blood everywhere. My breath hitched even more; what had happened?

I turned to see someone was in the bed with me. Looking down I saw Alis with a gash in her neck. Her gold eyes stared lifelessly at my pillow. Screaming, I fell naked out of the bed onto the floor.

Someone came forward and slapped cuffs on me. Hyperventilating, I didn't fight, as I was dragged from the room.

· ☸ ·

Hours later I sat alone in a cell. They'd given me some clothes, a sweatshirt and jeans. Neither fit. Both were too small and did little for the chill I felt in my heart. A guard came by and silently left me a sandwich and a paper cup of black coffee. I took both and returned to the bed. The coffee was hot and bitter but helped, and I ate without tasting the sandwich. I sat alone for hours; at some point I knew dawn had come and gone. I had no desire to sleep. I never wanted to close my eyes again. I was too afraid I'd have nightmares of my wedding night.

Instead of sleeping I curled into a fetal position on the bunk where I felt more alone than I thought possible. What had happened to Alis? She hadn't deserved that. My mind replayed the whole day, over and over again. Nothing changed. Sometime near nightfall, I saw Victor standing outside of my cell, watching me.

"I'm not supposed to be here," he said at last. I just looked at him, not sure what to say.

He sighed. "Gray," he said my name as if he spoke to a child. "You didn't do this. I know this, and so do Lowen and Tristan. Your family doesn't believe it, and you have other friends in your corner. By friends I mean people who support you in the Council. I am working to figure out who our allies are. Here, take these clothes." He handed me some of my own clothes.

"Can you tell me what happened?" I asked.

"You don't know?"

"No. I can't even articulate what happened to me. I don't understand it, nor do I believe it."

"Alis is dead. The Council plan to put you on trial for murder." He laughed a humorless laugh. "Here's the thing, they can't kill you or punish you and they know it."

"Why?"

He laughed harder, "Because our magic is gone."

# CHAPTER THIRTY-FOUR

### All Saints Day, November, Connecticut

Victor left right after he dropped that bomb on me. I wished I had one of my sketchpads. I wanted to write my thoughts down, to record the tidbits of information which were running through my head and escaping just as fast. Something finally clicked as I paced the cell. I had become hung up on Christopher and the reaction the Oracle had to Alis. It had said, "It's to be this way?" That implied there were multiple ways. The other comment playing in my chaotic mind was, "There are many ways to fulfill something which is meant to happen. A choice is made."

If I took that comment and compared it with the other times my fortune had been read, it made more sense. The main theme which popped up again, and again in my fortune is, "Lead, do not follow. Do not let others make your decisions."

Okay. The marriage had been forced upon me. Perhaps the loss of magic was due to that? What if Alis's death happened because we were forced to marry? How I wished Kador were here.

I considered the other comment from the Oracle. When asked if we should marry, it responded, "Should? There are many paths; this is but one. The destination is the same. The losses and gains vary on each path; I've given you all that I can. Make your choice and accept your fate."

I paced faster, I felt like I was on the verge of a breakthrough. What was I missing? I ran my hands through my hair, frustrated. Possibilities? That's it! Aquila. Damn it! I wish I had Kador here so I could get to my things. Aquila's math problems. She saw different outcomes. This path was one of several? My hand was forced, something went wrong. The loss of magic?

Two guards came towards my cell. I stopped my pacing.

"Stand with your arms outstretched against the far wall. We're going to come in and cuff you. Don't fight or try to escape, or you will be hurt."

Without a word I went to the wall and did as they asked. I heard the door open and one of the guards jerked my hands behind my back and cuffed my wrists. It hurt, but I made no complaints. Once I was cuffed, I was led from the cell through a maze of quiet halls to a large, wooden door. On the other side, I could hear shouting. One of the guards opened the door and I found myself in the Council hall. They led me to a table. Victor and Lowen waited for me, while my parents sat with Tristan, Guy, and Kensa behind us in the general seating area. My mother's face was red and puffy as if she'd been crying; my father held her tightly to him.

I looked around the room to see the full Council, a few people in the general seating, with Kate and Alistair sitting at the table on the far side of the room from me. Kate looked at me with a look of pure hatred. I couldn't decipher Alistair's look.

"Grayson James Penrose," Davidson yelled like a drill sergeant.

He got my full attention. With a deep breath I found my voice, "Yes."

"Are you prepared to answer for your actions?"

## CONVERGENT LINES

I looked at Davidson, and said the only thing I could think of. "I was bespelled. I don't know what happened."

Chaos erupted among the Council as I took a seat. It was awkward and uncomfortable with my hands behind my back. Lowen leaned over and whispered, "You know our contingency plan? You'd better enact it."

I looked him in the eyes. How would I escape without magic?

Davidson banged his gavel and demanded order. Everyone quieted. I had a feeling they'd been at this since I'd been discovered the night before.

"Explain what you mean."

"I don't remember much after I got to our room. I carried her across the threshold and set her down. We talked and I kissed her."

"What did you talk about?"

"She said I wasn't what she expected, that she'd anticipated me to put up a bigger fight about marrying her. My response was that I didn't have much of a choice. She was happy with the arrangement."

"And?"

"I kissed her. Things get fuzzy from there. Parts of my memories don't make sense and seem crazy. You'd lock me up if I were to say them. But I will say this: it wasn't me who had sex with Alis, nor I who killed her."

"If you don't remember how do you know?" Arthur asked.

I took a deep breath, it wasn't like I had anything to lose at this point. "What little I remember was seen from the far side of the room, between bouts of consciousness."

"If it wasn't you, then who did it?"

"I was on the other side of the room, someone or something cast me out and took possession of my body."

Lowen and Victor turned to look at me with wide eyes.

Arthur laughed. "You expect us to believe you? Come on, there isn't anyone strong enough to do that. And why would they do something which took our magic?"

"I don't know."

"I don't sense he is lying. He believes what he's saying," Davidson said.

"May his counsel have a few minutes to speak to him in private? To see if we can help get more information?"

Davidson looked at the other members of the Council before he answered, "Yes. You may have fifteen minutes in the consultation room. Guards, escort them out and guard the door. He will remain cuffed."

They led our small group to a side room and closed the door behind us.

"Okay, we don't have long and we must be quiet," Lowen said as he came to stand close to me.

"Here's what happened to us: You went upstairs with Alis and were gone for roughly thirty minutes when a wave of power hit all of the members of the Kind, all the way to Cornwall, England. At first, everyone rejoiced, thinking the binding had lifted, and the celebration really started," Lowen said.

"However, Lowen and myself didn't celebrate, we were watching the thing no one else bothered to—the unbinding ribbons didn't untwine. Instead as time passed the spells which had been cast upon them seemed to be weakening. After an hour the bow had dropped a couple of feet," Victor said.

Their explanation didn't answer anything, only left more questions.

"By the time the ribbon untwined everyone at the reception was good and drunk. No one else noticed that the ribbons untwined completely. The bow and the knots fell to the ground. Victor and I, ran to your room and found it locked. That's when I tried to use my magic for the first time since the wave. Nothing happened."

"I tried, too. Nothing. So we kicked the door in. We found you unconscious, lying next to her body. You were unresponsive."

"Is that why I woke up wet? Someone threw water on me?"

"Yes, Arthur. He and a couple other Council members had followed us. They quickly took in the scene and figured out their magic was gone. Since then we've been arguing about what happened and what to do about it," Lowen said.

"Wow. I don't know what to say."

"Can you give us more details about what happened?" Lowen

asked, and I could see he hoped to find answers. "Can you tell us anything?"

"I took two potions my mother gave me before I went upstairs, but I suggest we not mention it to the Council. Things seemed fine when we talked. That changed once I kissed her. I remember thinking I'd caught on fire, I felt aggressive and couldn't figure out why. At first I wondered if my mother's potion caused it, then things got fuzzy. I think the fuzziness was my mom's concoction."

"The forgetting part?" Lowen asked. I explained about the potions from my mom and why I took them.

They both watched me silently. Lowen bit his lip, deep in thought, while Victor had a far off look. "The next thing I knew I was watching the scene from the other side of the room; my body with hers. I watched as they had sex. Except I'd fade out and come back. The scene kept changing. I watched my body without me in it, I tried screaming, but nothing happened, and I couldn't hear them. I do remember one other thing after: my spirit felt like it was ripped from my body; it caused the most unimaginable pain. I think the only reason I remember it is *because* it hurt so much."

Lowen started pacing and rubbing his temples.

Victor's brow lifted. "You've described something I've read about of some Kind spirits' experiences, ones who have had a near-death experience. It's also how the journal of Hilda's explained the spirit's experience.

"Pendragon found one of Hilda's diaries from her youth. This one journal wasn't in her shorthand, so we could read the whole thing. In it she describes some of her experiments into the darker side of spirit magic. Her description is very similar. She claims when a Kind dies their spirit hovers outside of their body, but is still anchored to it."

"Victor, are you saying it's possible for her to kick someone's living spirit out of their body and allow another spirit to possess it?" Lowen asked. My eyes widened at the thought.

"Yes."

Lowen seemed upset at these new revelations. He yelled as he asked, "How is it possible? The only one who could do this would be Hilda." He threw his hands in the air frustrated.

"I know," Victor said.

Lowen looked right at me and said, "You've got to run as soon as you can."

"Sure, let the guy in cuffs, jailed, and now without any magic, try to run away. I bet I'll get real far. Great plan."

A knock sounded on the door, letting us know our time was up. Victor leaned into me and whispered, "Are you sure your magic is gone?"

I looked at him as his words sunk in. It was possible. I hadn't tried to do magic in my cell, and now my hands were cuffed behind my back. I just assumed that my magic was gone, too.

Two guards entered to escort us back, the bigger one said, "Come on, let's go. The Council wants you back for questioning."

As we returned to the Council room, I noticed Lowen still wore my bag slung over one shoulder.

I whispered as we walked. "Kador, can you hear me?"

No answer. "I really need you," I said it loud enough one of the guards looked at me.

*"Gray."*

I sighed with relief. "You can hear me again?"

*"Yes, though I had to use magic to break through some sort of wall. Allow me to see and give me your hearing. I haven't been able to hear."*

The guard sat me down at the table again. I leaned forward and whispered, "Kador, I give you permission to see with my eyes and hear through my ears."

*"I can hear... Now, what's happened..."* his voice in my head trailed off as he took in the situation and realized I'd been cuffed. *"Guess I missed a lot."*

"Yes, you have. Please listen and catch up as much as you can. Do you sense my magic? Do I still have it?"

*"Of course, you do. It's how we talk and how you were able to make me see and hear. Why do you ask?"*

"Davidson," I said.

He looked at me. "Please, can I have my cuffs removed? The blood flow to my hands has stopped."

"Remove the cuffs. He isn't going anywhere," Davidson said. I had a feeling I no longer had Davidson's support. From knowing him my whole life, I knew he would be the most upset about losing his magic. If he believed I caused the loss of magic, he wouldn't forgive me.

A guard came over and took the handcuffs off. I felt pain in both hands and rubbed them together to get the blood circulating again. Lowen had the bag holding Kador hanging on his shoulder closest to me. With my right hand, I reached over and tugged down on the bag, which caught his attention. But he seemed to know what I wanted.

Lowen removed Kador from the bag and handed it to me. With as much grace as I could manage, I slipped Kador under my shirt and tucked it into my pants against my back. I had a plan now. I think I now understood the math problem facing me. Thanks, Aquila.

"Kador?"

"Yes?"

Stored in my things, there is a piece of old cloth, the one from Aquila with the sketch of Muninn's claw. Can you find it?"

*"Aye. What do you want with it?"*

"What does the math equation on the cloth say?"

*"Ah, Gray, I don't know what math is."*

Kador did predate algebra by several thousand years; it made sense he wouldn't have a concept of math like ours.

"On one of the sides is a list of numbers and symbols. Can you describe them to me?" I looked up at the Council, they seemed busy discussing something. Good.

*"I have it. There is the number one, followed by a cross, the number twelve, then two horizontal lines, with the number thirteen at the end."*

In my head, I visualized what he had said. $1+12=13$. *Oh, I think I've got this.*

"Grayson," Davidson said, pulling me from my thoughts. "We have several questions for you ..."

The Council started into me for the next several hours. I answered most questions honestly, seeing no point in lying. They didn't believe me anyway.

Kate Rosdew, Alis's mother, stood and gained the Council's attention.

"Yes Kate?" Davidson asked.

"May I have permission to question Grayson?"

"You may," he said.

"Grayson, you say your spirit was ripped from your body, correct?"

"It's the only explanation I have for what I experienced."

"My daughter, Alis, didn't have the Rosdew powers, nor does Alistair. As a matter of fact, both have their father's abilities. The Blygh's abilities are with transfiguration." I didn't understand where she was going with this. "I now have the strongest spirit magic within the Kind. What you're describing is ripping a living spirit from its body. This is a power lost to us. No necromancer, including Hilda, had that power. Please be honest, I wish to know what happened to my daughter. Why did you kill her?"

I looked Kate in the eyes, "I was honest with you. I did nothing to your daughter. My spirit was ripped painfully from my body. You say Hilda wasn't capable of doing this? I don't believe it. I think she freed her own spirit and anchored it to something. She is behind this."

"See, I told the Council he would blame her." I looked at Lowen and Victor. Neither looked at me. Something had happened while I had been locked up and I wasn't privy to it. She turned her attention back to me, and she noticed my confusion. "Hilda's soul wasn't missing."

"Excuse me?"

"Nobody bothered to have me inspect the body. Hilda's soul *was* there. When she knew she was going to die, she performed a spell to protect her spirit from being enslaved. It tethers the spirit just outside the body. It's a secret family spell. Had I been called, I would have been able to perform the death rite and release her spirit. Instead, no one told me until she was entombed. By the time I did perform the ritual, her spirit had withered away to almost nothing." My eyes grew large as I stared at her. Why was everything in my life turning upside down? I didn't know what was true anymore. "Hilda couldn't have done this to you. She is gone."

## CONVERGENT LINES

"She's correct, Grayson," Davidson said. "Several Council members and another necromancer were present at the ceremony and verified Kate's version of events."

"Also, I call into doubt your claim that my mother, Hilda, cursed you. Where's your proof? While I will be the first one to say my mother wasn't a good witch, her abilities were greatly exaggerated. She could not have cursed you in the way you have described. She didn't have that kind of power. No, it's just another one of your lies. Now tell us what really happened."

All eyes shifted from Kate to me. I sensed it then: doubt, from the ones who swore they supported me.

I took a deep breath before saying, "I can only tell you what I saw, felt, and experienced. If you don't believe me"--I shrugged my shoulders--"then I don't know what to tell you. As I said before this marriage, I didn't want it, and if something went wrong you would all blame me." I laughed without humor. "It's funny, there's this great prophecy which has been set on my shoulders. If I'm not mistaken, didn't the prophecy say I was the *Guide*? Yet no one--I repeat, *no* one--has let me make a single decision. So, if I did what you are accusing me of, how did everyone lose their magic? Do you really think I have that much power?" I sat back down in my seat.

*"Don't say anything more,"* Kador advised. His caution was unnecessary because I didn't intend to.

At last, Lowen asked if we could call it a day. The Council dismissed everyone. I was escorted back to my cell. With each step I worried the guards would notice I had the book. Lowen walked with me. We didn't say anything until they'd locked me in and gave me ten minutes with him. Once the guards were out of earshot, Lowen asked, "Can you hear him?"

"I can."

"Then Victor's theory is correct? Your artistic skills are still functioning?"

"Yes, they are; I shall take your advice. You remember my instructions?"

"Ah ... yes, I shall return to Kolon tomorrow and work with my research partner. Victor will probably go on walkabout soon. Your family will be returning with me to Kolon. I shall suspend

PenTech for now and cancel all orders until further notice." He rubbed his hand down his face. The stress was getting to him. "I believe you, Gray. So do your other supporters. But understand, there is doubt. Nothing is making sense right now."

"Did you know about Kate finding Hilda's spirit?"

He let out a long breath. "They told us just before they brought you in for questioning. Neither Victor nor I have had time to verify it, and if this happened before we inspected Hilda's body ... I would have told you, had we more time. But we need to find out what happened to help protect you."

"I don't believe myself. I don't know what happened or what is true anymore. Hilda isn't as powerful as I was told, my memories are false, and the best part, I may have just killed my wife."

"Gray, you need to get away from the Kind. No one should tell you what to do again. Only you know what's right, I believe that. You are free now, technically."

"What do you mean?" I was even more confused.

He smiled, "You're an adult at last, by Kind law. You were married, remember?" I nodded. "You're just a widower, like me. Now go figure things out. I would like my magic back, please."

"Can you still see Pendragon and communicate with him?"

"Yes. But I think it's his magic that allows it. You need to go tonight, if it's possible. I'm afraid of the things they're considering for you."

"There's one problem."

He tilted his head to look at me through the bars of my cell. "And that would be?"

"I need Victor. Tell him I'm curious if a vampire can still see his reflection. To prove this, he'll need my hand mirror."

Lowen's eyes looked off into the distance for a time. "Oh, I can see why you would want to know."

"Good."

"Of course. Until next time, good luck. The game is on, and we are missing far too many pieces."

"Yes, twelve to be exact."

"Excuse me?"

"I figured it out before the Council started questioning me.

## CONVERGENT LINES

Tell Pendragon we're missing twelve pieces. Let him work the riddle. This is the only thing I am sure about right now. Hell, I'm questioning my own innocence, and I was there."

He stood blinking at me in confusion.

"Time's up," the guard yelled.

"'Bye, cousin, happy research. And say goodbye to Pen for me."

He gave me a curt nod and left.

## CHAPTER THIRTY-FIVE

### November, Connecticut

I lay in my cell for hours. Kador and I talked; I told him every little detail and we bounced theories back and forth. We'd concluded: if I still had magic, I bet the rest of the Penroses did, too. Perhaps it would just take some time to return after the events of my wedding night. After all, I waited more than a day before I tried to use my magic. If I moved forward with that assumption, then I had a theory for Aquila's ranting. What if the math equations were for different solutions of how to break the binding? It meant there was a way to break the binding through one of several solutions, but that each family would have to break their own. If this were true, then Christopher's Oracle would make sense.

I had to wait for Victor. After that a blank canvas lay in front of me for the first time in my life. I was free. No one would tell me what to do ever again.

"You're still here?"

I sat up and looked to the dark hall and the other side of my cell bars. I could barely make out his silhouette.

"I thought I'd say goodbye." I grabbed Kador's book and flipped to the back page. There, among my many things, I located what I searched for. I reached in, grasped the handle, and pulled it out.

"I'm assuming Lowen explained how I'll communicate and to keep the mirror with you?"

He nodded.

"It won't break; I've put a spell on it." With the mirror in hand, I closed Kador's book. I neared Victor and held out the mirror in my hand.

"I feel I should warn you to be careful, play the role of parent to you, but you're a man, one with his own destiny to fulfill. One which too many have interfered with. Follow your heart and head, as a Penrose it should come naturally."

I neared the bars and stopped just opposite of him. "Thanks for everything, dad."

Even in the dark I could see him smiling. We shared blood and he'd always treated me as his son. I bent over and placed the small hand mirror on the floor. Before standing, I made sure it sat within Victor's reach. Certain he could grasp it, I stood and found his eyes, and without another word I jumped into the mirror.

· ☙ ·

I landed on grass, bending my knees to absorb the impact. Before me the ocean glimmered from the starlight of a clear night. I stood on a cliff looking out toward the water and the silhouette of a castle. I'd never had a name for this place; the place I'd found when I first went through a mirror.

"This is my home."

My brow furrowed. "Really?"

"Yes. I can't believe it still stands."

"Kador, I give you permission to speak with your own voice." It was sad this was the first time the command had occurred to me.

"Can you hear me?" he tested.

"Yes, I can. The reason it still stands is this isn't the human realm."

"What do you mean? Are you saying you can travel to the fae, even with the doors sealed?"

"No, this is an in-between place. I think it's in the realm of one of the Norse Bridges."

"Yes, that would make sense. He would cast it here."

"Welcome home."

"Its name is Cartref y Galon, or Home of the Heart."

"A good name. She needs work. I've done a lot over the years and we have electricity and internet."

I started toward the castle. For the first time in memory the weight of the world had lifted from my shoulders and I felt hope.

"Are you going to explain this internet thing to me?"

I laughed, "Soon."

---

I showed Kador around the castle so he could see its condition. Once I finished, I sat down and began to figure out what needed to be done. First I'd need to get food, and it would probably be safest to go to California, no one would think to look for me there. Though there probably wasn't anything to worry about. The Kind were powerless now, weaker than humans.

Our cities would be visible to humans now. My family and friends would be vulnerable. I couldn't let that happen.

I got up from the desk and went to the mirror in the study. I opened a portal to the bathroom in my room at Kolon. My family wasn't there yet, but they would be soon. With a marker and writing backwards, I wrote:

*Lowen, has your magic returned?*

*If it has, keep it under wraps. If my theory is correct, and Aquila's math problems were a guide, we're looking not for one curse or binding, but 13.*

*1 down, 12 to go!—G*

# EPILOGUE

### One week later …

I'd taken to staying awake at night, I only dared to sleep after sunrise. It didn't cure the nightmares, but they seemed more tolerable in the light of day. What plagued me about my dreams is they seemed unrelated to me or the events of my wedding night.

Kador didn't take much interest in my sleep patterns or my dreams. It wasn't until I awoke shouting that he took note.

"Gray? Are you okay?"

I sat in a pool of sweat feeling as if I hadn't slept a wink. "Not really."

A string of some language I'd never heard flowed from him.

"What was that?"

"You were speaking it in your sleep. A dialect of an old fae tongue, one often used by water or forest fae. Are you saying you don't know it?"

"I've never heard it before."

"I don't think it is the first time I've heard it. I think I heard you speaking it a couple of nights ago, too. What are your dreams about? I have not wanted to pry."

"Nothing I can articulate properly. Flashes of scenes I don't feel are related to me."

"Why do you think the dreams are unrelated to you?"

"The one consistent event in the dreams is water. Sometimes I'm drowning, but the next moment I feel like a fish. I have seen what I could only describe as water fae, other times it's sea creatures. It's all from my point of view, but I know it's not me. I've a fire affinity, not water."

"Interesting. Have you ever tried keeping a dream journal? Perhaps you have precognition by way of dreams."

To my knowledge none of the Penroses had much in the way of foresight. Sure, we could use things like tarot cards or dowsing, but it wasn't our strong suit.

"And I'm not one for writing. Drawing has always been my strength."

"Then draw the images. These dreams have meaning. Now get up. We need to go see a witch who *does* have foresight about your future."

I opened a portal into the parlor of the Tremayne's home. Olivia and Victor sat waiting. She squeaked, jumped out of the chair, and came running to me. She hugged me tight and I felt welcome, as I always did when I came to see my other family.

"It's good to see you," said Victor. "Our world is falling apart around us and you have a very large target on your back. I feel you should know, there are many who wish you dead. There is a real threat now. Do not for one second think you will be saved because of the prophecy."

Kador and I were certain of this possibility, too. Over the last week, I'd discovered I could spy upon others from the safety of mirrors.

"How are you? Any magic?" I asked.

"Nothing. It's the scariest thing I've experienced in my long life. I feel handicapped, human."

Olivia released me and I wondered how Victor couldn't hate me? To my surprise, he opened his arms to me.

"I've been so worried about you. Are you sure you are safe?"

I walked into his arms and got a big bear hug. It was clear Victor didn't hold any grudges toward me.

"How can you not be upset or blame me for this?"

He released me enough so I could breathe again and could look him in the eyes. "I love you, and couldn't be prouder. This isn't your doing. Don't forget that."

"He's right. Ya ain't responsible for the way this turned out. But, as I keep tellin' Victor, perhaps the best way for this to happen is to hit the reset button, start over." She started out of the room. "Let's deal the cards and see where they fall."

· ෂ ·

We were sitting at the table I first sat at years earlier in Olivia's study, I expected her to pull out the knucklebones. Victor sat to my right and Kador hung on my left side, with my sight and hearing, but able to speak with his own voice.

"The bones are more powerful," Victor argued with her.

"Trust me, I know what's best here. Do I question yer magic?"

"No, but…" She waved a hand cutting him off.

"What ya don't understand is I threw the bones for him years ago. The results were more confusing than yer readings. This calls for simplicity, with direct questions."

His eyes widened at her. She pulled out a black velvet bag and set it on the table. She rested her hand on it before speaking, "I've only used these twice before. My grandma gifted me these when I married. They're special and I was warned to only use them in dire times."

"Why have you never shown these to me?" Victor whined.

A faint smile appeared on her face. "Because ya would try to solve the puzzle of them."

"True."

She opened the bag to reveal a deck of cards the size and shape of a typical deck of Tarot. The backside was decorated with black and a white all seeing eye in a triangle, surrounded by several circles. She fanned the deck out in the middle of the table.

"Pick one, V."

His brow lifted as he reached to comply. From the center, he picked one and moved it to sit in front of him.

"Turn it over," she said.

He did. His face mirrored my response, confusion. A blank card sat in front of him. She laughed, but Victor was less than amused. I turned my attention back to the card and noticed a black spot in the center, where a second before there was nothing. The dot grew, with black arms reaching out to the edges, reminding me of a compass rose as it did. Within seconds the outline of a figure appeared to fill in with colors and a title. The Fool.

"In what way could the Fool possibly relate to me?"

She sobered. "This is a test. With one card, you're asking for the moment. The Fool couldn't be more fittin' for ya."

"In what way?"

"It means an ending, consequences, or beginnings. In the one card position it means ya are entering a new phase, and to enter it with caution. Could any other card be more appropriate?"

He rolled his eyes and nodded his head. "Okay. You're right, I shouldn't ever doubt you," he said.

"Oh, cher. Wouldn't be my V without questioning everything. I'd never begrudge ya that." She picked up the card and returned it. Her attention returned to me. "Pick up the deck, Gray."

I picked it up, stealing a look at the bottom card first; blank again.

"Shuffle 'em, get yer energy on the cards. Think about what's plaguin' ya most. This is for the immediate problem."

I complied, shuffling the cards as thoughts of my nightmares surfaced. For the first time, I could see the images clearly while awake. All of the visions involved water. As the imagines swam in my head one keep reoccurring, that of a golden scorpion.

I felt a touch on my arm, which brought me back. Victor eyed me with worry. "Are you okay? We called your name several times."

"Yeah. Sorry, just lost in thought."

They looked at each other, and I knew they, like my parents, were good at communicating without talking.

"What has yer focus so clearly? I need to know before we proceed. It could affect the readin'."

Sighing, I rubbed at my eyes. "I'm not sleeping well, just tired."

"Are ya having nightmares?" she asked.

"Yes."

"Your wedding night?" Victor asked.

I laughed without humor. "You would think so, but no."

"What does Kador think of this?"

"He is lucid dreaming from another's point of view," said Kador's deep, accented voice.

Olivia's chair screeched as she pushed it back, standing while looking around the room. Victor reached to reassure her.

"It's okay. It's his ancestral advisor. His soul is trapped in the pages of a grimoire, and apparently, he can speak for himself now."

"Why didn't ya tell me?"

"I've been a bit preoccupied as of late," Victor said with a faint smile.

She sat back down, though she still looked frazzled. "Could he be a precognitive dreamer?"

"I am having him start a journal. We should know soon," Kador answered.

"Pull one card. This is for the first problem we must tackle."

I did as she asked, taking the top card. The dot appeared and filled in just like it had before. The VII of Cups lay before me.

Olivia blinked and remained silent, not her typical response. "Ah, not sure what this means."

"What does the card usually mean?" Victor asked.

I hadn't spent much time on Tarot, except for a brief course in my early school years. It had only been meant to see if I had an affinity with them. I didn't, nor did I have any with most foresight methods.

"The Cups speak to emotions, yer inner self and the subconscious. This one is like the heart of the Cups. It usually means a lack of understanding or confusion about yer unconscious mind."

"It certainly speaks to our situation," Victor said.

The card began to leech of color. "Is it supposed to do that?" I asked.

She shook her head. "It never has before."

The card began to fill in again. I watched with interest as another card arose. The King of Cups.

Olivia let a long flow of strange words go. No doubt they were curse words, but I could only guess at the language. She started, "The King here usually means a person of authority, or someone who'll aid ya, will come into yer life." She looked to Victor before he could ask, "Not V. This is someone distant and reserved. It can't be V, these are water cards and both align with Scorpio."

"Excuse me? As in the astrological sign or a physical scorpion?" I asked.

"The astrological sign. Why do ya ask?"

"In my dreams, there is a scorpion which appears repeatedly."

She smiled showing teeth and dimples. "Why, Gray, my boy. Ye are a precognitive dreamer. Who in yer world does this describe?"

"The Marraks?" Victor asked.

I could see where he'd get them. They were aligned with Scorpio as a family. But it didn't seem right.

"Not the Marraks."

He made a face before saying something he looked disgusted with. "The Gwyns? Surely it cannot be Davidson?"

I could hear truth in the Gwyns. "Yes, it feels right."

"Nooo… there is nothing right about it. How the hell could your dreams be about Davidson? Sure, he helped some, but no."

I laughed at his reaction. "Wrong Gwyn."

"Then who?"

"Davy."

"The man at your wedding? The one who spoke to you before you went upstairs. He rattled Davidson's cage and Arthur's."

"His son."

"Interesting ... The outcast?" The card answered his question. Gone was the King and in his place sat the Hermit. "That's creepy," he said.

Chuckling I responded, "That means a lot coming from you." Always good humored he smiled. The card cleared again.

"Put the card back and shuffle the deck again. Think about yer future, keep shuffling until it feels right."

When I think of the future I see a blank canvas. Emotions only come in if I think of my family or friends. I set them down and turned over the first one.

"This should give us yer past."

The card filled in to show the last card I would have thought. The Devil.

"Mais! This makes sense! For ya I would expect the Major Arcana. In this position it means entrapment and a need for prudency. Ya been trapped by the decisions of others, which weren't right. Don't worry, it's not positive or negative."

As she finished the card faded to be replaced by the Chariot.

"These cards are connecting with ya. The Chariot means ya have a long difficult labor ahead. There will be losses, setbacks, and dead-ends, but ya should be victorious in the end."

The card bleached white again and remained so.

"Interesting. Why don't ya put the card back, and shuffle it again?"

I shuffled and flipped another card over. It remained blank.

"Shuffle it again, but when ya finish, set the card down ask, 'what does my future hold?'"

I repeated the act. As I set the card down I asked the question. The card didn't fill in. Instead the deck flipped, cards spilled all over. Everyone stood. In unison, the blank cards began to fill in. The first thing recognizable was the infinity symbol, which on this card was an ouroboros. Next, a hooded figure with one arm pointing to the sky holding a wand. The first card of the Major Arcana.

"Ah, Olivia? What is going on?" I asked.

"I've no idea," she said.

"Why do all of the cards have the Magician on them?" I inquired.

"That isn't the Magician. Look at them," she said pointing to the cards.

Feeling daring, I reached down and picked one up to look at it. As I said before, I'm not an expert, but I knew enough to know the card did bear a striking resemblance to the Magician. Olivia came to my side to look at the card.

"The Illusionist isn't a card in the Tarot but has the same meaning as the Magician. Though I fail to see the need for renaming it?" Olivia said as she rubbed her hand on her skirt.

"We would use the term Illusionist over Magician. An illusion is the ability to cast a believable image to fool others, an extremely rare talent long dead to us. Most often the image would be plucked from someone's head before being cast, usually a fear. It's how it differs from glamour. Whereas the Magician would be a human tricking others into thinking they could perform magic. I can see the need for a distinction," Victor explained.

"Yes, that makes sense, then. But this card isn't just based upon the Magician. No. I think it's combined with the Hierophant."

"I don't understand," I said.

"The Hierophant means self-confidence, success. In this spot it can mean uncertainty, and need for guidance. There are two distinct differences from the standard card, the title and the red cloak. The cloak is hidin' the figure from us. This is important. Sexual identity in the deck doesn't have the same meanin' as in life. Gender in Tarot represents ideals associated with the sexes. The one card, which is defined by this, is the Hierophant. I would read this aspect as the need to be careful of your motivations, don't let them be selfish. The gender of the Illusionist, or aspects of it will be determined by yer point of view."

My attention returned to the table to see the deck stacked together, as if waiting to be dealt.

"Take the card and keep it with ya. It might change with time."

I said my goodbyes. I needed to return to my retreat, to think about this new information and to sketch the images from my dreams. Then I could begin to figure out what's next.

THE ILLUSIONIST

# THE END OF:

## *Convergent Lines*
Book 1 of the Kind Mosaic

*Be sure to read:*

## *Deluded Lines*
Book 2 of the Kind Mosaic (Coming in 2018)

## *Side Lines: Kador's Curse*
Book 1.2 of the Kind Mosaic (Coming fall 2017)

## *Side Lines: King of Pain*
Book 1.3 of the Kind Mosaic (Coming fall 2017)

## *Side Lines: The Complete Works of Lydia Rosdew*
Book 1.4 of the Kind Mosaic (Coming 2017)

# A KIND MANUAL

# THE 13 COVEN FAMILIES

## ARUNDEL
**Meaning(s) and origin:** The name has come to mean, "Aristocratic." Unknown.
**Alignment:** Light
**Astrology Affinity:** Sagittarius

## BLEUJAN
**Meaning(s) and origin:** "Flower." Cornish.
**Alignment:** Light
**Astrology Affinity:** Gemini

## BLYGH
**Meaning(s) and origin:** "Wolf." Cornish.
**Alignment:** Dark
**Astrology Affinity:** Cancer

## CARN
**Meaning(s) and origin:** "Pile of rocks." Welsh.
**Astrology Affinity:** Taurus
**Alignment:** Light

## GWYN
**Meaning(s) and origin:** "White." Cornish.
**Alignment:** Light
**Astrology Affinity:** Pisces

## JERNIGAN
**Meaning(s) and origin:** "Iron famous." Breton.
**Alignment:** Middle, with dark leaning
**Astrology Affinity:** Libra

## MARRAK
**Meaning(s) and origin:** "Horseman or knight." Cornish.
**Alignment:** Middle
**Astrology Affinity:** Scorpio

## NANCARROW
**Meaning(s) and origin:** "Valley of the deer." Cornish.
**Alignment:** Dark
**Astrology Affinity:** Virgo

## PENROSE
**Meaning(s) and origin:** Pen=head and ros=moor. Cornish.
**Alignment:** Middle, with light leaning
**Astrology Affinity:** Leo
**Color:** Maroon
**Celtic Tree:** Holly
**Element:** Fire
**Talisman:** Dragon

**History:** One of the oldest families in the Kind. They have a strong affiliation with the light court and claim white royalty in their line. The Penroses usually have two family members on the Elder Council. They're almost always in creative fields, technology, or politics.

**Powers**: Invisibility or being able to transport between two places, artistic abilities (writing, music, art) infused with magic (a power which has faded), and telekinesis. They also have abilities with technology and regularly adapt human technology for the Kind. Known for being honorable, kind, and strong warriors based on fighting and strategy skills.

## ROSDEW
**Meaning(s) and origin:** "Black moors." Cornish.
**Alignment:** Dark
**Astrology Affinity:** Ophiuchus – The thirteenth zodiac sign, often used in antiquity as reference for extra-zodiacal indicators. Named for the constellation Ophiuchus, and known as the "serpent-bearer." Recognized between November 30 – December 18.

## TEAGUE
**Meaning(s) and origin:** "Fair or beautiful." Cornish.
**Alignment:** Middle
**Astrology Affinity:** Capricorn

## TREMAYNE
**Meaning(s) and origin:** "House by the rocks." Cornish.
**Alignment:** Dark
**Astrology Affinity:** Aries

## WAYFARER
**Meaning(s) and origin:** "Traveler." Unknown origins.
**Alignment:** Middle, with strong dark leaning
**Astrology Affinity:** Aquarius

# ORIGINS

The first records of the Kind families go back long before the first Roman invaders. They were the families that lived on the borderlands of the fae. The humans and fae mixed for several millennia, until the time of the Retreat. When the fae destroyed the gates between Earth and their world, thirteen families remained here.

Sometime after the closing of the gates strict laws were created, which became known as Covenant Law. Marriages were arranged to keep magic in the bloodlines. For more than fifteen hundred years the laws worked and protected the Kind, with only the occasional death at the hands of humans. All this started to change around the time of the Spanish Inquisition. Some loss in the Kind's magic had been seen when Christians arrived in Cornwall, England, but it was the witch-hunts and religious conservatism which led to the May 1645 Binding.

Too many times Covenant Laws were ignored, and many from the great houses were lost. One house suffered an almost complete loss due to this, the Wayfarers. Before 1645 many within the Kind didn't believe the Binding the Christians placed upon the old Gods and rites would work, for they were still part human. But throughout the Inquisition they continued to see a diminishing in their powers, fertility, and longevity. While they weren't immortal like the fae, most had experienced lifespans more than ten times longer than humans.

Around four hundred years ago, a female from the Carn family foretold of the Church's Binding to come. She predicted that a family who had only begotten sons for generations would be given a female, who would join with a first-born son from the light to break the Binding.

Shortly after the seer foretold their doom, a contingent of the Church appeared. Seven priests, all dressed in white and whom no hex or curse would touch, arrived. They marched into the center of Little Cornwall, Connecticut and began their binding chant. Within minutes the burden of their Binding could be felt. As quickly as they came they left, but their Binding curse imprisoned all of those with Kind blood around the world.

No one knew which family the female would come from. Three families were the most likely: the Blyghs, the Wayfarers, and the Marraks. These families had gone generations without female children. At one-point, years ago, a daughter was born to the Blyghs and the Council promised her to a Tremayne first-born male. The binding wasn't weakened and the war between families grew. The Blygh female died during the fighting.

The prophecy gave clues to the male's family: A family aligned to the light would bring forth the Guide. After four hundred years the binding has taken a toll, few children are born, lifespans are the shortest in history, and the magic continues to weaken.

# KIC OR KIND INQUISITION AND COUNCIL

The KIC is the governing body, educational body, police, and military force for the Kind.

**Administrative/Educational Branch** (Gray): When a Kind male reaches the age of 18 they're required to join the KIC. Females are also encouraged to join, but it isn't mandatory. The two- or four-year programs are a form of college, meant to help participants to develop their magic.

**Governing Branch** (Green): To be a part of local governing bodies of the KIC, a Kind may opt for this three-year program, which usually leads to a full-time position. This is in addition to, or done congruently with, the required two-year program.

**Judicial Branch** (Blue): Anyone wanting to become a lawyer or sit on the Elder Council will need to complete the two-year internship in the judicial branch. This is not a full-time service, so many will join the Military branch in addition to the judicial internship. This service requires interns to sit as a third member for several months on the KIC arbitration board. This is in addition to, or done congruently with, the required program. This requires the four-year program.

**Military/Policing Branch** (Brown): The military is a two-year program. Though small in number, there are lifelong positions within the military, especially the espionage unit (HAB, or Human Advisory Board). Those wishing to go into the policing branch need to complete this program. However, candidates in the policing branch are placed at the discretion of the KIC police board. This is in addition to, or done congruently with, the required two-year program.

*All males are required to enter service at the age of 18 for a minimum of two years. For females, service is optional.

**There are rare instances for which a male may seek exemption from the KIC programs. Those wishing to study health, science, or technology at human universities must seek approval from the KIC.

**Elder Council:** The Council is made up of thirteen individuals elected as needed for ten-year terms. To be eligible, candidates must be of the Kind, over one hundred years old, and proficient at magic. Members can be removed if a vote of no-confidence is put forward and passes by a majority.

Most meetings involve three members; the members are rotated every year. Full Elder Councils are reserved as a last resort. No more than two members can be from the same family and cannot serve together on a Council of three, to keep them from being a majority. Being a member of the Elder Council offers no amnesty from Covenant Law.

# THE 13 COVENANT LAWS

1. No Kind shall reveal themself to any human, even by accident.

2. It is forbidden to mate with a human; all procreation shall be confined to the Kind to assure magical progeny.

3. All marriages of the original 13 Covens must be approved by the Elder Council.

4. The dark arts are forbidden; practice of these will result in a stripping of powers, banishment, or death.

5. All prophecies must be recorded with the KIC offices.

6. No *true* magic can be performed for humans in exchange for money.

See CL 1. Exceptions include: fortune telling, soothsaying, gambling hustles, and professional magicians which can't be proven as "real."

7. All laws are made by the Elder Council and enforced by KIC.

8. Magical artifacts, places, or discovered spells must be reported to KIC.

9. All encounters with uncommon magical creatures (MC) or beings not Kind must be reported to the KIC. All MC are protected as per KIC laws and cannot be killed or used for magical purposes.

Exceptions include: gnomes, pixies, goblins, basilisks, and leprechauns.

Death penalty for any Kind caught hurting a dragon, hydra, unicorn, griffin, pegasus, phoenix, satyr/fawn, elf, fairy, kraken, sea monster, or deity. Full list is available at KIC offices.

a. Killing of other Kind is considered murder, carrying a sentence of death. Exceptions include self-defense, accidental, and wartime.

10. Flying is strictly forbidden.

11. No time travel or interfering with time, including stopping or slowing of.

12. Due to the relationship of sex and Kind, anyone caught fornicating with someone under 18 will be prosecuted. The virginity of a male or female is left up to the family to decide upon the best match. Any youth caught breaking these rules will be stripped of powers, their memories, and turned out to the humans.

13. Under no circumstances is magic to be used to kill or harm humans. If there is any problem with human(s) the KIC should be alerted immediately.

All serious crimes shall be investigated by KIC. If a serious crime has been committed, a trial before the Council will be held. Disputes between more than one Kind party shall first be heard by a KIC arbitration panel. If the dispute is not settled by arbitration, a full Council trial can be requested. Elder Council decisions are law and incontestable.

# MAGIC TYPES

**Blood**: Blood magic has several uses. The intent and amount determine if the magic breaks the law. Blood used to bind a person(s) to a group or family is acceptable if consensual. Exsanguination of human or Kind is forbidden. Animal blood is acceptable as long as it is not from a banned magical creature.

**Bond:** A rare form of magic, in which a child or partner is able, in times of need, to summon the magic of someone they're bonded to. Bonds are common between parents and children, or with a familiar, but are very rare among married partners.

**Charm:** A spoken magic. The caster of the charm is responsible for the results.

**Death**: Killing spells are strictly forbidden. Necromancy or reanimating the dead is not advised, but if on occasion the need may arise, then a certified necromancer should be used. Check with KIC offices to find registered certified necromancers in the area.

*Zombies are prohibited, both human and Kind. Anyone encountering a zombie must report it to KIC; zombies sometimes occur naturally.

**Defense/War:** Great power can be summoned under stress or by inflicting violence. Feats of magic have been witnessed at such times when it should not be possible. Most regret magic that occurs under such circumstances.

**Divination:** This kind of magic is one in which the individual is predisposed to having visions of the future or past. It is usually genetically inherited. But most Kind can use things like runes, cards, drugs, pendulums, Ouija boards, or divining/dowsing rods to some extent.

**Elemental**: Most Kind are born with an affinity to an element. Most often the Kind's DNA determines this. These connections help to call upon the elements to perform magic.

**Familiar**: About a third of the Kind have a familiar, and anyone desiring to have one may undertake to achieve a familiar. It is accomplished by sacrificing the animal desired to gain a familiar, unless it is a magical creature. Permission must be granted by the KIC, and all Kind with a familiar must register themselves and their familiar creature with KIC.

**Love:** Love is magic. When true it can overcome amazing obstacles. The most common examples of love as magic happen between a parent and a child. Parents have been known to have great powers when a child is hurt. The same does occur in romantic love situations, but is rare.

*Exception: Magical spells or charms used to make someone fall in love with another are not advised under any circumstances. The love is not real, but an illusion, and will end badly. While the goal is to create love, hate will grow when the effects wear off. As a matter of fact, these spells are most efficient at creating hate and should be called hate spells.

**Potion:** An all-purpose magic. Few potions are off limits, only some of the ingredients. Be forewarned though, it is an offense to drink a mimic potion to impersonate another Kind, or use a potion to kill or hurt. Also, using a potion to steal from another in the Kind is prohibited.

**Sacrifice**: Sacrificial magic is another gray area. If the animal is not on the prohibited list, the sacrifice is acceptable. Sacrifice of one's self is permitted. Human or Kind sacrifices are prohibited.

**Sex**: Currently one of the most powerful magics available to the Kind if sexual partners are properly matched. Loss of virginity is the single, greatest controllable magic, for it unlocks a Kind's true potential and powers. If both parties are virgins a bond can be created, made stronger if there is love. The dual loss of virginity creates an excess of magic, which can last up to a year in some cases. Due to this, virginity is protected and considered a family's asset to be used as the family head deems appropriate or necessary.

*Orgies: If everyone involved is consensual, then group sex for magic is acceptable, but no one under 18 and no virgins are permitted. No children are permitted to come from sex magic. Birth control must be used! Beltane Brides are excluded.

**Same sex couples do experience the same benefits with sex as straight couples and it is possible to bond, but still rare. Same sex couples are accepted and granted full rights in the Kind, though there is great pressure for them to procreate, both partners, even if it is medically induced. Bisexuality is strongly encouraged.

***Polygamy/Polyandry: The practice of taking more than one husband/wife is permitted within the Kind society, though its occurrence is rare and usually only within the Bleujan family. All spouses of such a union must be approved by the Council. All spouses are expected to procreate.

**Spirit:** Necromancers are a necessity, especially to perform death rites upon members of the Kind. There are also times when contacting or summoning spirits is needed. Using spirit magic to trap or enslave spirits is strictly forbidden.

# THE NATURE OF THE KIND

　　Through the studies and advancements of the Nancarrow family, some information is known about Kind biology. At present, the Nancarrows are nearly done mapping the Kind's genome. What is known now is that the Kind have the same double helix as humans and the same four nucleotide bases (G, A, T and C), but Kind DNA strands are longer, and there seem to be slight differences in the four nucleotides. Some Kind DNA has made it into the general human population. Human researchers have interpreted this as a deformity or mutation, writing off the information about the Kind as a predisposition to disease or deformity. The Elder Council approved experiments with Kind stem cells and DNA to be conducted by the Nancarrows with oversight by the KIC.

　　Males carry the magic chromosomes, much as they do the determination of the sex of the child. What is not known at this point is why females tend to be more powerful.

# A NOTE FROM THE AUTHOR

This story came into being in a rather unusual way. In mid-of 2015 I was preparing for National Novel Writing Month (NaNoWriMo). I'd been planning to write the second book in another series; I outlined the book and went to bed.

That night, as I slept, I had the most vivid dream of this boy who could walk through mirrors and anything he drew would come to life. But he was troubled, he hated his life and had lost the only person he'd cared about. I woke up remembering the whole dream and all through the next week I thought about him. Then I dreamed of him again; this time he told me more of his story. Intrigued, I outlined the rough draft of his tale and over the next week he showed me his world.

At this point I told old friends they would have to wait a little longer, because Gray needed help.

A note about whisky versus whiskey. The spelling of whisky was chosen in this book because it is usually referring to Scottish whisky, not American, Irish or Canadian.

*Michelle Cori*

# ABOUT THE AUTHOR

Michelle Cori lives in the Rocky Mountains, when she isn't traveling to the next Comic Con. Currently she spends her time running a bar and telling tales over drinks or in the form of novels and comics. She shares her life and home with her teenaged son, and two crazy min-pins named Harvey Wallbanger and Honey Bunny.

Traveling, bourbon, hard ciders, record shops, tea, old book stores and good ales are some of her other pastimes. She has a love for *Flash Gordon, Highlander, Star Wars, Dune, Star Trek, Planet of the Apes*, comic books, and all things 80s, as if you couldn't tell from her writing. Often, she can be found writing at various coffee shops around the country.

Facebook: facebook.com/michecori
Twitter: @MichelleBCori
Website: mbcori.com

Made in the USA
San Bernardino, CA
22 April 2019